I0737732

Books by J.T. Cooper

VIRAL
RUNNING

PLUS: A FANTASY

J.T. Cooper

Let's pretend . . .

For all my wise women

PLUS: A FANTASY

J. T. Cooper

Rachel Bowman snapped yet another photo of a sidewalk café: gaudy umbrellas, bored waiters, bobbing pigeons. Every picture was proof that she'd actually been to Paris. She'd dreamed about the trip for years, but there'd never been enough money. At one point she'd even considered the dozens of brochures that promoted sponsoring high school foreign language trips as a means of getting there, although she couldn't imagine exploring Paris as a chaperone with her French students. Instead, she'd squeezed every penny she could from her teacher's salary and finally made it happen.

All week she'd immersed herself in the city, loving its beauty and energy, absorbing the sights and culture. She'd bought trinkets to take back to her classroom. She'd practiced her French with native speakers. She'd loved every moment, but she couldn't help thinking how much better the week would've been if she hadn't come alone. She wasn't the only twenty-six-year-old woman in the world without a boyfriend or husband, but it felt that way. What was Romantic Paris without romance? Still, the week had been too short, and she wasn't one bit ready to go home to Ohio.

As the sun set, she walked toward the Pont Neuf. She'd visit it once more and then find a small restaurant, one where she didn't feel self-conscious about eating alone, and then she'd go back to the hotel. Maybe she'd buy a bottle of wine to drink while she packed. It seemed like a very French thing to do.

She strolled onto the bridge, her favorite one, with its stone faces and little niches. It was late enough for most Parisians to have gone home for the day but too early for them to be out for the evening. Maybe she'd have Pont Neuf to herself so she could gaze at the city and river and bid *adieu* to Paris.

But it was difficult to find any place in Paris that was deserted even in August when so many Parisians were out of town. A couple passed her, the woman chic in dark slacks and white blouse, the man handsome and attentive. Rachel sighed. The entire world traveled in couples, except for fat girls. And she wondered for the hundredth time whether she should've married John Shumate, the nice, ordinary boy she'd dated in college, the one she'd rejected because she'd thought there had to be more to life than three kids and an SUV. *If you'd married him, you would've missed Paris*, said a voice inside her head. John Shumate would've wanted his vacations at Myrtle Beach.

Rachel clicked another picture. Maybe the trip hadn't lived up to every expectation, but she'd always have Paris, wouldn't she? She laughed at herself.

Chapter One

The cabbie said, "*Merci, monsieur,*" and I exited the taxi. All of it came back to me: the bitter, the sweet, the intoxicating. Paris was still as heady as it'd been twenty years ago. Ahead of me stood the grand, haughty edifice that was home to Sylvestri, the ultimate in Parisian haute couture. It also housed the ultimate couturier, Sébastien Fel. I squared my shoulders, took a long breath, and entered the building.

"Oh, I am glad to see you, Edgar." Madame Pauline's English, usually as impeccable as her inevitable black suits, had slipped through her emotional cracks. She sounded like a Brit mimicking a bad French accent, similar to that inspector in the old *Pink Panther* films. I'd rather liked those flicks.

I sat in a chair by her desk, but she remained standing. "Now, Polly," I said. "Don't take on so. What's wrong with Sébastien? I could hardly understand you on the phone." Actually, she'd mumbled and ranted so incomprehensibly that I'd given up and said I'd jump on the first Eurostar leaving London. And here I was, in Paris, dressed in clothes I'd reckoned appropriate for an asylum, a funeral, or a visit to a Parisian jail. It was always about clothes with Sébastien.

"He won't come out of his studio," she said. "And there are no sketches, nothing. The workshop has nothing to do; the *vendeuses* complain. He has appointments; he does not keep them. Dumont keeps asking about him. What can I say?" Madame Pauline looked heavenward, perhaps an indicator of spiritual disturbance, but more likely a nod to Dumont, CEO of the House of Sylvestri, rather than God, even if it was easy to confuse the two.

I shrugged like a Frenchman, a mannerism I picked up during the years I'd lived in Paris. With Sébastien. "He'll sketch eventually, Polly. You know Sébastien. He procrastinates, but inspiration always strikes." She glared at me, her crow-feather brows raised nearly to her hairline. It was the look that sent seasoned seamstresses and pattern makers scattering like startled chickens.

"My dear Edgar," she started, her words now so measured and her accent so controlled that she could've been an Oxford don. "It is September. After Fashion Week he took two weeks and went to Martinique." She waved an elegant hand. "Understandable after all the excitement, after all the publicity saying this was his most incredible collection ever." Fussed as she was, Polly couldn't say those words without a swift chin-lift. "And then he comes back. It usually takes him a few days; as you say, Sébastien does procrastinate." She gave a shrug similar to mine. Maybe I'd learned the art of shrugging from Polly. We'd all been thick as thieves back then. "And now it has been weeks. Nothing. *Rien.*"

I didn't know what I was supposed to do about it. Sébastien and I had met twenty years ago, back when he'd been the Boy Wonder at Valenciana. We'd shared a flat and had a happy time of it for ten years, an unprecedented feat of monogamy for Sébastien Fel. Then it had ended. We'd emailed a few times, called occasionally, and shared a meal or two when I happened to be in Paris. We were amicable, but I was no longer an influence. I doubt I ever was. I looked at Polly. She'd witnessed those halcyon years as the genius of Valenciana's workshop, rising from a teen-aged seamstress to the top. Sébastien had spirited her away from Valenciana when he left. She was his *Première d'atelier*, his right hand, and maybe his left. If Madame Pauline couldn't do anything with Sébastien, I certainly couldn't. "I don't know what I can do," I said.

She pointed in the direction of Sébastien's studio. "He's been locked in there for three days," she said. She was actually wringing her hands. I'd read that expression, even used it in a couple of my books, but I'd never actually seen it. "He hasn't gone home, eaten, anything." A massive shrug. "I wonder if he's ill," she said. "I knock and knock. Sometimes he tells me to go away. Sometimes, nothing." I noticed a bit of gray in Polly's black hair. I would've thought she'd dye it away, but it was there: a tribute to years of Sébastien. "Sometimes," she whispered, "I hear him moan." At the last word, she placed her hand on her heart, more like an overwrought peasant than chief assistant to a top-drawer couturier.

"So you want me to roust him from his lair," I said, thinking how much I'd prefer to be back in London, dozing through a warm afternoon. "All right, Polly. I'll try." She nodded and kept twisting her hands.

I walked across the hall to the office outside Sébastien's studio. A massive door guarded the anteroom of the master of fashion. His current guardian, or clerk, was nowhere in sight. Another door, equally ornate and impressive, protected Genius from mere humans. I knocked. "Sébastien," I called out. "Let me in."

No response. Perhaps he'd sneaked out in the dead of night and gone home to wallow in creative dyspepsia. How would Polly know? Even if he'd been locked up for as long as Polly said, I wasn't particularly worried. As I recalled, Sébastien's studio had a refrigerator, microwave, and full bar. He even had a fully-equipped bathroom and a closet full of black clothes. I was more annoyed than anxious. "Sébastien, you're worrying Polly. Unlock the door."

Not a peep. When we'd lived together, I'd called him a diva at least once a week, and he obviously hadn't changed. I sighed. What would convince Sébastien to open his bloody door? I looked over my shoulder, expecting Polly to be hovering in the hall, but she wasn't. And at this point I was too exasperated to care if she heard. "Come on, Gumby," I said, using the pet name I'd called him when we were in love. "I've come all the way to Paris on that damnable train for you. The least you can do is open the door."

I waited. There was a soft noise, and then I heard the lock click. I pushed the door open to gloom, heavy drapes blocking the bright afternoon. All I could make out was Sébastien's back. He moved away from me, knelt, and, at precisely the center of his fabulously expensive Aubusson, reclined on his stomach, arms outstretched like he was rehearsing crucifixion.

I nudged the bottom of his slipper with my shoe. "Are we doing a monk's penance, a squire's knighting, or Christ Himself?"

He groaned.

I stepped over him. He was still as skinny as a whip and probably flexible as one too, thus the nickname I'd given him years ago. He wore silk pajamas, more than likely vintage Chinese. Frustrated by the dim light, I strode over and threw open the drapes as well as a window or two. The breeze outside was hot and full of Parisian fumes but smelled better than the fusty air in Sébastien's studio. He neither moved nor spoke.

I settled into a chair and looked at his right hand, an elegant, long-fingered masterpiece of sinews and bones. I remembered how beautiful I'd always thought his hands, once he'd quit biting his nails. I peered at his fingertips: bitten to the quick, nearly every one of them. "What's the problem, Sébastien? A bit blocked, are we? Or is this a love tantrum?" His head moved, disturbing his unruly dark hair, still all but black, even though he'd just turned forty-five. I always remembered his birthdate. "Gumby," I tried again. "Polly is twisted up in knots, and I came all this way to see you. Talk to me."

In a sudden and, as was usual with Sébastien, graceful move, he swiveled his body until he sat, still posed at the center of the carpet with his bony legs bent, tailor-style. He shook his head. "I can't design," he said. "I have no ideas."

His hair might still be dark, but the stubble glistening on his bony, ascetic face was silver. Dark circles ringed his eyes, but they were still magnificent. Dark, liquid.

"Everyone gets blocked now and then," I said.

"Even you?" He looked down his aristocratic, and beaky, nose.

"Even I." I knew what he thought of my books, my nice little murder mysteries that pleased people enough for me to earn a living and a rather good one at that. Trivial, he'd once called them when we were having an exuberant row that ended with thrown drinks and slammed doors. "I usually write through them. It comes. Eventually."

He raised a hand and pointed to his desk. Surrounding it like a fall of giant hail were dozens of wadded paper balls. "I tried that." He looked down. "I remembered that you did that." It was as close to a compliment as he'd ever given my work.

"Sometimes music or paintings. . ." I started.

He cut me off with a flourish of his hand. "It was Fashion Week. I cannot get past it," he said.

"But the reviews were fabulous," I said. If I'd been a snide person, which I generally am not, I wouldn't have admitted to reading his reviews. But I always have. I search for print that speaks of Sébastien. "They loved those odd, high-tech clothes," I said. "I thought they looked like rejects from a *Star Wars* movie, but you've never had such a glowing response, even back in the day." An expression my nephew uses that I'll never understand. Back in *what* day?

Luckily he chose to ignore my comment about alien fashion. Lifting himself from the floor like a cat, he went to an elegant armoire on the other side of the room. "Drink?"

"Yes, please."

"Still bourbon?" He pronounced it the French way even though we'd been speaking in English. He always insisted upon English, complaining that my French sounded like sucking sewers.

"Yes."

Holding two glasses, my bourbon and gin and lime for him, he shuffled back and collapsed into the chair opposite me. "That's the problem, Eddie: the old cliché. What have you done for me lately?" He took a long drink. "If the Fall/Winter collection had been mediocre or just passable, or even, God forbid, bad, then I would be fine. But it was magnificent. How do I follow that?"

I sipped. It was a familiar feeling. Recently the reviewers had been saying things like "formulaic" and "passé" about my books. One had even gone so far as to accuse me of being in my dotage. For God's sake, I was only fifty-six. I too needed something spectacular but doubted I could summon the imagination or the energy to write it. "So you're competing with yourself."

He nodded. "Of course. The Galaxy Collection was genius. The next one must be spectacular as well." He looked across the room. "Some compared me to Pauli."

If Sébastien had a hero other than himself, it was Kristof Pauli, God of Fashion, who'd held that post for decades. Arbiter of taste, genius of design, Pauli sat atop a mountain of successful collections and was revered by everyone, even if he was Italian. "Quite a compliment." I lifted my glass.

"I need another twenty years of perfection before I come close to Pauli," he said. "But," he shook his head, "it will not happen if I lose my inspiration."

There was nothing wrong with Sébastien's self-image. I thought a moment. "You could do something retro like Jackie O. You know, outlandish pillbox hats and a new take on sheaths. Or," and I had to snicker at my wit, "you could channel Chanel."

He blinked at me.

"I suppose not." I thought for a moment. "Country gardens? Africa? Recycled hippie chic?"

He continued blinking. I was running out of steam. "Retro Princess Di ruffles?"

"You're embarrassing yourself," Sébastien said in a voice that could've sent snow to the Sahara.

He gulped the rest of his gin, and I took secret pleasure in watching his throat as he swallowed. I truly had loved him. Back in the damned day. I finished my drink as well and stood. "I doubt that inspiration is going to hit when you're hiding in a cave. Get cleaned up, take a walk. Later on, we'll have a nice dinner." He'd said nothing about me staying with him, nor had I expected it. "I need to get a room. I came here straight away."

He mumbled, "Nine? At the Royale? You really think it will come?"

I nodded. "Some food, some wine. Genius will prevail." I paused at the door. In a painful fit of generosity I said, "Perhaps you need a new person in your life. An inspiring lover?"

He quirked an ironic eyebrow. "I think not."

Rachel had walked dozens of miles the last week; enough, she hoped, to counteract the dozens of pastries and croissants she'd eaten. She grinned to herself. All those glorious, creamy desserts. All those yummy *pommes frites*. Eating was part of the Parisian experience too, wasn't it? Her hand went to the button on her jeans. Yep, they were tight. She supposed that five pounds could count as a souvenir of Paris.

She lingered on the bridge, sitting in a niche, watching people pass by. Finally she stood and leaned over the bridge's lip to peer down at the river, green and lazy. Down the way, she saw one of the cruise boats, similar to the one she'd ridden as an introduction to Paris. She sniffed, smelling river and heat and Paris. When would she ever accumulate enough money to come again? Her mother, who'd given up on Rachel ever marrying, said that she ought to be saving for a little house or a condo. Settling down, her mother said. Settling, was what Rachel heard. She switched her gaze to the bridge itself and immediately started trotting. Near the other end, a man, a very tall man, had climbed upon the ledge and was perched there, holding onto a lamppost with one arm. His gaze was concentrated upon the Seine below. Dear Lord, was he going to jump?

Her mind skittered through her verbs. "Sir," she exclaimed in French as she ran. "Don't swim!" That wasn't right, but she couldn't remember the French for "jump."

She raced to him, ready to grab his leg or something, although she doubted she could save him. He paid no attention to her repeated babbling about life being good, suicide a foolish solution, and all sorts of platitudes in an incoherent mix of French and English.

He didn't jump, but he didn't climb down to the sidewalk either. Rachel turned to see if any passersby might help, but, wouldn't you know it, there wasn't another soul on the bridge. "Please, sir. Come down." She was pretty sure her French was correct on those phrases. She held her hands up to him.

Slowly, slowly he turned his head to look over his shoulder at her. He was an older man, maybe forty or fifty, with dark, wavy hair falling nearly to his shoulders. "For God's sake, speak English," he said in a level voice. "You're murdering my language."

In a flash, Rachel switched from concern to anger. How dare he? Last year she'd won the award for foreign language teacher of the year in Hollister County, Ohio. Of course there were only three foreign language teachers in the entire county. She frowned at him. His English wasn't exactly pure either, and it sounded more British than American. She started to move away. Anybody that insulting could off himself and be welcome to it.

He moved to a crouch and jumped off the ledge onto the sidewalk, catching up to Rachel and touching her arm. "A moment," he said, staring at her when she turned her head.

She gave him her teacher's look, a long, steady stare that intimidated all but her most incorrigible freshmen. The man's eyes raked her face, traveled down her body, and came back to her eyes. She was perturbed. "What?" The guy was probably some wacked out sex maniac who'd escaped from an asylum. He was dressed nicely, though, in skinny black jeans and a black shirt. Silk, she guessed. "What?" she repeated.

"The skin," he murmured. "And the hair." His brows drew together. "Titian. Raphael." He made a little humming noise. "Renaissance, yes. Of course."

Rachel backed away.

"Shirred silk. Draping. Jewels and tapestries." He lifted his chin and peered down his long nose at her. "Rubens. Ah, yes. Leda. Don't go."

"I believe I will." She took another backward step. "My friends are waiting for me," she lied.

"No, no." He shook his head. "I'm Sébastien Fel."

So? It meant nothing to her, and she wasn't about to tell him her name.

"The designer," he said. "Sylvestri."

She had heard of Sylvestri. Maybe she'd sniffed a sample of their perfume from a department store catalog. "Okay."

He took a step toward her. "Your coloring. Stunning." A puff of hot wind stirred his hair. "I must know your name." He held up his hands like he was showing her that he could be trusted. "Please."

She felt her cheeks turn pink. "Rachel," she mumbled.

"Rachel? Raquel. Lovely." He smiled, and it was one damned charming smile, but Rachel didn't return it."I have startled you. I'm sorry." He gestured toward the river. "I was not going to jump, although I was very sad." He put a hand on his chest. "I was in despair. Have you ever despaired?"

Nutcase. Complete and total, but he seemed harmless, and it was a good story for the teacher's lounge. She shook her head.

"Good. It puts wrinkles on the face, and your skin is so fine."

Rachel's insides started twisting up. She'd never been good with compliments.

"You see, I had no inspiration." He hung his head. "But now," he brightened, "I have Raquel. I have my muse."

He grabbed her hand, raised it to his lips. That felt pretty damned strange. "You must dine with me and my old friend Edgar. I must look at you." He tried to smile again, a little twitch of his lips that wasn't very reassuring. "I frighten you."

You've got that right, Rachel thought. "No, I don't think so."

"Forgive me, Raquel. I apologize. Edgar will explain. I want only to see you, nothing. . . ." He searched for a word.

So used to helping her students, Rachel said without thinking, "Sinister?"

His lips twitched again, and he squeezed her left hand. "Yes, but of course, sinister. I'll get a taxi and we'll go to your hotel." He added quickly, "I'll stay in the lobby while you change, and then we'll meet Edgar." He looked at his watch. "If we are early then we'll have an a*péritif*, and I will sketch. I must sketch. Please say yes."

Somehow or the other Rachel found herself in a cab with him. Sébastien, for that's what he said she must call him, commented that he'd never heard of her hotel, which was no surprise. "It's cheap," she admitted. "The room's tiny, and the elevator wheezes. But I'm a teacher. No money."

He nodded, but she wasn't sure he'd paid attention to a word she'd said. He kept searching her face like she had spinach between her teeth.

At street level, her hotel was no bigger than a bathroom at McDonald's. Most people wouldn't realize it existed. Sébastien frowned and told the cabbie to wait. As they entered the tiny lobby, Sébastien nodded at the female desk clerk and said to Rachel, "Nothing too grand. We eat simply tonight."

As if she'd brought anything grand, Rachel thought. She'd planned to eat dinner in her jeans. But the desk clerk's eyes widened at the sight of Sébastien, and the fact that she recognized him made

Rachel realize that maybe he really was someone famous, at least in Paris. It also made her feel more secure. Maybe he truly was a Great Designer rather than one of those sex traffickers they wrote about in the tabloids. She wouldn't know; she paid no attention to fashion. But what would he want with her? She was overweight and bought most of her clothes off the clearance racks at Penney's. He was crazy, but it was a fun sort of crazy. And she liked hearing that she was an inspiration.

After a slow trip on the asthmatic hotel elevator, she whipped off her jeans and changed into her utility black skirt, which was buried under stacks of maps, brochures, and postcards littering the twin bed she didn't use. She'd have to pack all this clutter tonight, she thought, but in the meantime, she tried to shake the creases out of the skirt. She hadn't worn it all week but had packed it, just in case. Yeah, well, this was the case. The only clean top she had left was an aqua blouse, fake silk and as wrinkled as the skirt. She'd planned to wear the blouse on the plane tomorrow because it was loose and comfortable. At least it hid the muffin top around her waist. The Great Designer was going to be thinking makeover rather than inspiration when he saw her in this. She jammed her feet into black sandals and spent two minutes fluffing her impossible hair and dabbing on a little makeup. He had remarked that her skin was fine. Grimacing at herself in the mirror, she saw plain old Rachel Bowman: plump, dowdy, and friendly.

Downstairs, Sébastien was pacing the lobby like a jail cell and ignoring the flushed desk clerk who was also dowdy but not plump. No one in Paris was plump. The clerk pointed a dubious look at Rachel as if to say, what are you doing with this icon of French creativity? Rachel gave her an insincere smile. "Where are we going now?" she asked Sébastien.

"The Royale," he replied. "A nostalgic place for Edgar and me." They got into the cab. "We ate there often when we were together."

Okay, Rachel told herself, he's gay. It didn't bother her; as a matter of fact, this made her feel better. She'd been friends with several gay guys back in college. One or two, not quite ready for full disclosure, had even used her as a decoy when their parents wanted to meet a girlfriend. Good old Rachel.

Edgar, the ex-lover, was nothing like she expected. For one thing, he was older, much older than Sébastien, and he was British with a ruddy complexion that screamed that he'd spent too many hours out on the misty moors or inside a pub. But he had old-fashioned manners and a friendly smile. She liked him immediately. After the encounter on the bridge when he was trying to ingratiate himself, Sébastien hadn't smiled once.

"Champagne," he barked at the waiter.

Oh, Lord, Rachel thought. She'd already had two drinks while they waited for Edgar, Sébastien sketching like a madman the entire time. She'd get sloshed if she wasn't careful. Turning to Edgar, she asked what he did for a living or if he just tooled around in his castle. Her face went pink when she realized what she'd said. Maybe she was already sloshed.

He smiled. "No castle, I fear. Just a flat in London and a little holiday shack in Cornwall where I'm from."

Sébastien snorted. "The shack has six bedrooms, Raquel. And stables and a glorious garden."

Edgar lifted a hand. "But not a castle."

Rich, then. It was too, too Tacky American to ask whether he'd made his money making PBS specials or managing Harrod's or whether he was an obscure relation to the royal family. She didn't think he was an aging rock star.

Edgar rescued her. "I write. Mysteries."

Suddenly she realized who he was. She felt her pulse quicken. "Edgar Tremaine! Of course. I've read nearly all of your books. Inspector Hannaford from Truro. I love them."

Edgar patted her hand. "You've made my day, child."

The waiter arrived with champagne, and Sébastien looked a little sour when he tasted his. "She's mine, Eddie," he said.

Even before she tasted her wine, Rachel's head was spinning. This was one amazing adventure. She smiled at Sébastien. "I'm not anybody's," she murmured, feeling brave. Or drunk.

After a glass of champagne, she held up one of the purple napkins and asked Sébastien if the color suited her. After another, she gobbled down steak drowning in a luscious béarnaise along with *frites* and bread, somehow thinking tons of food would soak up the alcohol. But then, remembering it as the favorite drink of some character in a book she'd read, she asked for a glass of calvadós after dinner. Sébastien looked impatient but indulgent, and Edgar, who'd said she should call him that, treated her like his favorite niece. After dinner, they went to Sébastien's studio at the House of Sylvestri, a magnificent place, and it still seemed like a light-hearted, if boozy, dream. It was when Sébastien asked her to take off all her clothes that reality came crashing down, and she sobered up.

"No," she said. He'd posed her against the heavy draperies in his studio, a few feet from the massive desk where he sat.

"I say," Edgar protested.

Sébastien twiddled a pencil. "Oh, all right. Just strip down to your lingerie," he said. "And turn on that lamp beside you."

Rachel didn't really think they were going to ravish her and send her to a sultan's harem. Edgar looked as though he'd like to stretch out on the long leather sofa and take a nap. Sébastien was glaring at her with nothing resembling lust. But she didn't show her body, her lumpy, pudgy body, to anyone. She asked, "Why?"

A dramatic sigh. "Because I have to get a sense of your proportions. I want to see your skin. And even shabby underwear would look better than that dreadful skirt and blouse. Anyone would think you were a nun."

She scowled at him. "I won't."

Sébastien rolled his eyes. "Edgar," he said.

Edgar opened his eyes but didn't move. "We're quite harmless, my dear."

Rachel felt like she was having a panic attack.

"This is simply a necessary part of the creative process," Sébastien said.

He sounded like he was instructing a child. "If I create clothes for your body, it follows that I must see your body." He shrugged. He had bought her a wonderful dinner. And champagne. She'd be home tomorrow and never see either of them again. "All right, but in ten minutes you're calling me a cab." Slipping out of her clothes, she faced him, hands on her hips.

"Good Lord, her lingerie looks like a nun's too. Edgar, are you watching?"

"Not really, old boy," was the sleepy reply.

Rachel shivered from anxiety rather than cold, but Sébastien paid no attention. His focus was entirely on the paper in front of him. He mumbled for her to turn, to turn again, but after a few long gazes, he hardly glanced at her. She looked down at her bra: plain, white, serviceable. Her underpants were the same. Sébastien was right about her underwear, but at least they didn't have holes in them. Her mother had always warned her about that. What if she were in a car wreck? Or posing for a designer? A wave of champagne giggles swept over her, but nobody noticed.

Way more than ten minutes passed, but Rachel didn't ask for a cab. She looked around at the gleaming furniture, the deep carpet. Standing still was tedious. When Sébastien wasn't looking, she leaned against a chair, then sat in it, crossing her arms across her belly. Edgar snored. Rachel yawned. The only sound was Sébastien's pencil scratching against paper. Suddenly, he stood, waving the paper around, and shouted, "My God, this is genius!"

Edgar nearly fell off the sofa. Throwing her skirt and blouse back on, Rachel went to the desk and looked down at two large sheets of paper covered with drawings of faceless women dressed in slacks, suits, evening gowns. Edgar peered down at the sketches. "Well, they're certainly original," he commented.

Rachel squinted at them. She'd seen designers' drawings in magazines, and even though she'd never paid much attention to them, they didn't look like these. Most sketches she'd seen looked like stick women with impossibly long necks, sort of like that Audrey Hepburn her mother liked so much. These figures were plump. "They're fat," she said. "Like me."

"No, no, no," Sébastien exclaimed, waving his hands over the drawings. "Fresh. Natural. Woman as she was meant to be."

Edgar shook his head. "I'm not sure even you can pull this off."

Rachel pointed at one of the thick-waisted suits. "Chubby, plump, big-boned." She counted off the words on her fingers; she'd certainly heard them all before. "Full-figured, mature, overweight, or, as my granny used to say: *obeast*." She walked away and sat on the sofa Edgar had left. The adventure didn't seem fun anymore. If it hadn't been for the effort Sébastien had put into his drawings, she would've thought he was mocking her. "Not funny," she said.

Sébastien was perplexed. "No, not funny at all. I never joke about fashion. This is as new as Coco banishing the corset. A Renaissance." He moved his eyes from Rachel to Edgar. "That's it," he shouted. "The Renaissance Collection. I have to go to the Louvre."

"Closed now, my boy." Edgar pointed at the paper. "There is an allure here, though." Sébastien beamed. "A sense of femininity."

"And wait until you see the silks, the draping," Sébastien said. "I must call Pauline and look at swatches." He picked up his phone.

"It's midnight. You can't call Polly now."

Sébastien drooped into his chair. "What is time to creativity, I ask." But he set down the phone.

"I need to go back to the hotel and pack," said Rachel. "My flight's tomorrow."

Edgar smiled. "Of course, my dear."

But Sébastien stood again. "No. Never. You cannot leave me now."

"But," Rachel started.

"Absolutely not." He grabbed both her hands. "I cannot let you go." He nodded at the sketches. "This is just the beginning. You, Raquel, are the centerpiece of the collection. You are my muse."

"School starts on Tuesday," she said, shaking her head. "I have to get home. My job. . . ."

He interrupted her. "Call them. Resign. I need you here until February," he declared.

"Now, Sébastien," Edgar started.

Sébastien whipped his head around to look at his old lover. "I must have her," he insisted. Then he focused on Rachel. "I'll pay you. Very well. You can live in a hotel or in my apartment, whichever you prefer, but you must be where I can see you." He paused. "I would prefer that you stay at my apartment, assuming you can behave quietly and courteously."

Rachel was too flabbergasted to be either insulted or coherent. "I can't," she said. "My contract."

"You can and you will." Sébastien squeezed her hands. "Maybe we can persuade Eddie to visit again. He'll show you Paris like nobody else." Once again he gave her his rare, and devastating, smile, humoring her like she was a stubborn child. "You said you regretted having only a week in Paris. I'll give you months and money and the most glorious collection of clothes in the world designed for you. You'll be a star."

Images of her principal, her students, and her tiny apartment back in Morton flashed through Rachel's head. But even more than her obligations, she saw her mother. Her mother, who years ago had ushered her into the only dress shop in Morton with the words, "she's bigger than she looks." Her mother, who made a strawberry Jello mold instead of a cake for Rachel's thirteenth birthday. With reduced fat Cool Whip for frosting. Her mother, who'd suggested they try the maternity department when Rachel needed clothes for teaching. Jean Bowman would never believe this, and Rachel couldn't help but smile at the thought of her mother's shock. It might be worth all the hassles. "Okay," said Rachel with an evil grin. "Why not?"

Chapter Two

At first Rachel didn't know where she was. The bed was huge, nothing like the narrow one in her hotel room. Then she remembered the craziness of the night before, how Sébastien had bundled her and Edgar into a cab, dropping Edgar at his hotel and making her pack up all her belongings at hers. It had been one o'clock when he'd opened the door to his apartment and ushered her down a hall to this room. She'd fallen into bed and sunk into an instant coma.

Oh, God. What had she done? On the bedside table, a creepy clock that looked like a modernistic spider web said it was seven-thirty. Morning light brightened the shades at the double window. She looked up at the incredibly tall ceiling and saw ornate plaster rosettes clustered around a stark chrome and glass chandelier. This entire experience freaked her out. Yawning, she stumbled over to a chair shaped like the letter U and put on the robe Sébastien had tossed over it last night. Alice is in Wonderland, she thought. And it's scary.

About that time, there was a knock on her door. "Good morning, Raquel," Sébastien said in French. "Breakfast in ten minutes."

"*Oui, merci*," she replied, then remembered that he didn't like her speaking French. "Okay," she said. "Thanks."

After washing her face and running a comb through her tangled curls, Rachel followed her nose to the kitchen, a bright, sunny room with a small table at its center. Copper pots gleamed from a ceiling rack, and the white tiles on the counters and walls were bright as mirrors. Sébastien motioned for her to sit and set a huge plate of scrambled eggs, ham, and a croissant in front of her. "Butter? Jam?" he asked.

Rachel shook her head. She rarely ate breakfast. "Coffee?" she asked.

"*Mais oui*," he chirped, way too cheerful for this hour.

After he poured coffee and settled in with his own plate of food, considerably less filled than hers, she asked, "How come you sometimes speak French to me, but I'm not ever supposed to speak it to you?"

He had a forkful of eggs nearly to his mouth. "It's simple," he replied, in English this time. "The more you hear correct French, the better you'll learn."

She nibbled on her croissant. Delicious. Maybe she'd been missing something by ignoring breakfast, but it did cut a few calories. "Then how will you or I ever know if I'm improving?"

He shrugged, clearly uninterested. "It will happen." He swallowed. "First we're going to the Louvre to look at pictures. Then we're meeting Madame Pauline at the *atelier*. After that we'll discuss some adequate clothes for you to wear the next few months." He waved his croissant. "Nothing special."

Rachel looked down at her plate. A tiny stream of butter oozed from the eggs. Fat. She mumbled, "Good luck. I tried a couple of places, but they didn't have anything big enough for me."

He frowned. "What size do you wear?"

"Sixteen," she whispered. Actually, a lot of the time it was eighteen, but some stores even in the fat, old USA didn't go up that high.

"What is that in France?"

She hadn't known but learned the hard way by sifting through ridiculously small garments and watching the numbers on racks ratcheting upward. "Forty-eight." It seemed like an appallingly huge number. "Or so." Rachel figured that this, more than anything else, would discourage his crazy idea of designing clothes with her as a model. She knew what kinds of horrific styles graced the fat girl departments. Garish, matronly, dreadful. Nothing Fel would do.

Undeterred, he nodded. "We'll have the seamstresses throw a few pieces together. Your jeans are all right." But he wrinkled his prominent nose. "Set what needs laundering outside your room and Yvonne will take care of it."

Rachel raised her eyebrows.

"Yvonne's my housekeeper. I've called her to come in today. Eat. I don't cook breakfast for just anybody." He bit into a sliver of ham. "Besides, you must maintain your weight."

She couldn't remember anybody ever urging her to eat. This should've felt liberating, she thought, but it wasn't. She shoveled in some eggs. They were yummy. But then she thought about her principal, about the flight she should be catching in, she glanced at the clock, six hours. She needed to call people and tell them she wasn't coming home, but it was too early, the middle of the night in Ohio. What had she done? What would she say? Suddenly the eggs tasted terrible, and she felt sick.

A

As they crossed the plaza in front of the Louvre, Rachel had to all but run to keep up with Sébastien's flying Nikes. Even after they entered the museum, he knew exactly where he was going and wasted no time getting there. "Here," he mumbled, pointing to a bench in front of a painting of a naked woman with alarming cellulite. "Be still," he said.

So Rachel tried to be still. He sketched, looking back and forth from the painting to his pad of paper. From what she could see, he was good at it. She'd never been able to draw anything. She yawned and twitched. She'd never been good at museums either. They always made her feel like she needed ritalin. But she trailed after Sébastien as he went from one dim gallery to another. Sometimes he'd draw bodies, other times draperies or clothing. He scrutinized naked goddesses, Madonnas, angels. The artists' names would've made her students think of Teenage Mutant Ninja Turtles. She fidgeted.

Twice he made her stand and squinted at her from under thick, dark brows. Sometimes he made little noises like he'd done last night while he was drawing. Rachel sneaked a look at her watch. It was still too early to make her phone calls, but not too late to catch her flight. Maybe he had enough. Maybe he didn't need her any more.

Sébastien sighed a sigh of the long-suffering. "Yes, I'm done," he said. "You can stop looking at your watch."

"I wasn't," she started but gave it up and mumbled something about time zones and phone calls. He wasn't interested; besides, it took most of her energy to keep up with his long strides as he said something about just one more gallery. And then another.

He looked at his watch this time. "Pauline should be at the *atelier* by now." He patted his portfolio. "She'll be delighted with these."

Rachel wasn't so sure, and she was even less convinced once she met Madame Pauline Robert. "My *Première d'atelier*," Sébastien said as he presented Rachel to a compact middle-aged woman whose smile looked more like a sneer. Until Sébastien said that he'd drawn six costumes so far and others were merely hours away. Then the haughty woman grinned, clapped her hands, and demanded to see the sketches.

The two of them spoke French, of course, but Rachel got most of what they were saying. She'd always been better at understanding French than speaking it. When Sébastien laid his sketches on the long, dark table in Pauline's office, the woman's hand went to her mouth. "My God," she exclaimed, "these are absurd. Preposterous. What are you thinking, Sébastien?"

He jabbered on about the Renaissance of Beauty and the freshness of the designs. Over by the window, Rachel stared out at the darkening Parisian sky. Thunderstorms, she thought. Flights might be delayed. Maybe she could still go home. Madame Pauline obviously thought Sébastien's ideas were crazy. Maybe his grand scheme would end right now. Growing louder by the minute, Sébastien and Pauline were all but shouting, both at the same time, and the words came so quickly that Rachel missed many of them. The woman pointed at Rachel and said something about pigs and peasants. It should've hurt, and it probably would upon reflection, but at that moment Rachel was as angry as the skies above the Eiffel Tower. She hated it when people talked about her as if she weren't there. Turning to the pair, she sputtered in instant, and what she thought was perfect French. *"Ne parlez pas de moi comme si je n'étais pas,"* she said, summoning up her most acrid teacher voice. "I didn't ask to do this." With this she turned and went out into the hallway. Once again, she looked at her watch. There was still time, especially if Sébastien shipped her clothes and souvenirs to her. If he wouldn't do it, she bet nice old Edgar would. And he'd given her his cell number. She ducked into a room full of bolts and stacks of fabrics, beautiful things that shimmered even in the dim light. She shut the door and pulled out her phone, punching in Edgar's numbers from her ticket envelope where she'd written them last night.

He answered right away. "Tremaine."

"Edgar. It's Rachel." She took a deep breath to rid her voice of its annoying wavers. "I don't want to do this. Madame Pauline hates Sébastien's designs, and she just called me a pig. I want to go home. I can get a taxi to DeGaulle. Would you send my things to me?"

"Steady on, Rachel." His voice was gruff and warm. "Polly's all right. Sébastien's just shocked her after all those weeks of procrastination. And she probably doesn't realize that you understand French. Most Americans don't."

"Does that make it any better?" Damn, tears were starting and she had to sniff.

"Well, no. Poor girl. As usual, Sébastien is thinking only of himself. Are you at the workshop?"

"Yes. He wants her to start choosing fabrics for the designs, but all they're doing is arguing. I could still catch my plane if I hurry."

"No, no. Don't do that. I can be there in ten minutes. Be brave, Rachel. I'll have a word with Polly and Sébastien. We'll get this sorted."

She wiped away the tears on her cheek. "I don't want it sorted," she said, but he'd already clicked off.

Against one wall there was a three-way mirror, a three-headed monster for the overweight, she thought. Rubbing away at her smeared mascara, Rachel looked at her reflection for a long time, long enough for the tears to stop and her brain to calm down. Another week or so was probably all Sébastien needed even if he'd said January last night. The school could get a substitute teacher for a week. Her principal wouldn't be happy about it, but he probably wouldn't fire her. She'd never been fired from any job, even the horrible summer ones she'd had during college. Edgar had said that it would all work out. Maybe he was right. But he couldn't erase the ridicule and shame she expected from the skinny, skinny world of fashion.

She remembered one particular gym class when she was thirteen. After her shower she'd been coming into the locker room wrapped in a towel that wasn't quite big enough when stick-thin Jennifer Howell and her bitch buddies were pawing around in Rachel's bookbag. They'd found her stash of Butterfinger candy bars, ones she sometimes ate on the long bus trip home. "No wonder she's huge," Jennifer had said. The others had tittered and giggled, not even bothering to stop when Rachel caught them. All through high school she'd heard people call her "Butterfingers" or "Butter Butt" almost behind her back. She'd never said a word.

She narrowed her eyebrows at her reflection. She was not going to take crap from anybody any more. Pig? She didn't think so. She nodded at herself in three versions, straightened her spine, and was ready to go back to the fray when Sébastien and Madame Pauline entered the room, switching on enough lights to illuminate the city.

"There you are." Sébastien beamed at her. Another of his rare, heart-melting smiles. Evidently he'd won a battle. "Look, Polly." He unwound a bolt of rich blue crepe on the huge table in the middle of the room. Then he grabbed another, this time of coppery, shimmering satin, and threw the glowing stuff across the blue. "Madonna blues, royal purples, rich golds. All the colors of the Renaissance."

Madame Pauline refused to unbend. "Too dark." Her pointed little chin was as sharp as a weapon.

Sébastien lifted a languid hand. "So? Come here, Raquel." He motioned her to the table and draped the copper fabric over her shoulder. "Exquisite, no? See how stunning this is on her? And new, Polly, new. Look at this." He unwrapped bolt after bolt and swathed Rachel with it.

Madame Pauline stood as rigid as a soldier on review. "But surely you do not mean to use her to model your creations?"

"I most certainly do." Sébastien whisked the fabric off Rachel's body and raised his own chin. "She will be my *premier mannequin*."

Madame Pauline started squawking again, and Rachel felt her face get hot. What composure she'd mustered evaporated. She spurted, "What? No way, Jack. I'm not a model, and I'm not about to get out there and make a fool of myself. Forget it." She gulped and took a breath. "You can find another fat girl."

As she turned to storm out of the room, Edgar appeared in the doorway. "Such a fuss," he commented. "I could hear you all the way downstairs." Cool and calm, he wore an old-fashioned white suit like he was ready to play cricket or croquet or whatever Brits did on their vast, green lawns. Rachel couldn't think clearly enough to remember what movie she'd seen with men dressed like that.

She pointed at Sébastien. "He thinks I'm going to model his clothes, and I won't." She folded her arms across her chest. "High-fashion models are skinny to the point of anorexia. The world will laugh its ass off at Rachel Bowman walking down a . . . what do they call it?"

"Catwalk," Sébastien said. He, too, seemed unruffled by the ruckus. "But all the models will look like you." He grabbed her hand. She jerked it away. "This will be a revolution, a renewal. A celebration of the feminine woman who has curves and soft, delicious flesh, the way a woman is meant to look."

Madame Pauline let out a flood of furious French. "The girl is right. They will laugh at us, ridicule us; they will scorn us. It will be a disaster!" She put her head in her hands. Madame Pauline was pretty good at being dramatic herself. "Please, Sébastien," she begged. "Do not subject us to such mockery. The House of Sylvestri!" She looked like she was going to faint. "Dumont! What will Dumont say?"

Rachel had no clue who Dumont was. She glanced at Edgar who mouthed, "Head of Sylvestri."

Sébastien was still composed. "He will love it. Calm yourself, Polly."

Rachel felt as if she'd grown three feet in every direction. Her mother always said she puffed up like a bullfrog when she got angry. "Polly's not the only one who needs calming down. Okay, I let you draw clothes for me. In my underwear, for God's sake. But I'm not about to embarrass myself like that. I'll, I'll just go home!" she sputtered.

"Come along, my dear. We'll let Sébastien and Madame Pauline discuss this," said Edgar, holding out his hand. "We'll get an ice cream or something."

Clenching her teeth, Rachel said, "I'm not a child, and I don't want to eat."

"A coffee then," said Edgar.

"Have her back in an hour," said Sébastien. "We need measurements."

"Arggh!" screamed Rachel, but Edgar had a tight hold on her hand and was pulling her out the door.

Chapter Three

I watched Rachel stomp down the pavement as if she were crunching Sébastien's skull with every step. Neither of us said much, but I managed to take her elbow, lead her to the nearest café, and get inside before the rain started. There was a flash of lightning. Pathetic fallacy, I thought.

"What would you like?" I asked. "Coffee? Whisky? My old nanny would prescribe a cup of tea with mountains of sugar." She glowered at me as if I'd been the one to cause all this turmoil. Terribly unsporting of the girl, but I did admire her spirit.

"Whatever," she muttered. "Not whisky."

I ordered two coffees and didn't say a word until the waiter brought them and she'd had a sip. "Now, what are we going to do about this?" I asked.

She looked at her watch, a hideous, wide-banded thing with sparkles. "It's too late to make the flight now." She sounded like a pitiful child, although she'd told us the night before that she was twenty-six.

"If you insist upon leaving, there are other flights, you know."

She shook her head. "I don't have money for another ticket."

"Sébastien would pay for it. Or I."

She ignored this, and I couldn't tell whether she truly wanted to leave or stay. Something about Sébastien's plan did intrigue her, I thought. But she was also very frightened. The café was humid, full of rainy air and some variety of soup simmering somewhere. Chicken and vegetables, perhaps a hint of lemon; it smelled heavenly. The damp was making Rachel's hair curl up into charming waves. She truly was a pretty girl, even with smeared makeup and a disreputable black tee shirt that was wrinkled and looked none too clean. Staring at her coffee, she murmured, "I can't model. I'd fall on my ass."

"I'm sure Sébastien intends to get lessons for you. It's not physics, you know."

"But Edgar," she looked up, her eyes swimming with tears, "I'm too fat. I know it. You and Madame Pauline know it. Why won't Sébastien see it?"

Until then, I hadn't noticed how very green her eyes were. But Sébastien had, I warrant. "Because what he sees in you is beauty."

She waved her hands about, knocking over the cream pitcher. I mopped up most of it while she went into frantic apologies.

I shook them off. "Shall we have a little philosophical discussion upon the subjectivity of beauty?" I asked. "How very different Rubens and Picasso are, but yet they both paint beauty?"

I was prepared to deliver quite a persuasive treatise, but she waved her hand at me. More cautiously this time. "No Rubens please. Fat women."

"All right. Handel and Stravinsky, Shakespeare and Joyce: artists all, creators of beauty. But very different kinds of beauty, Rachel."

She played with an empty sugar packet. Three of them lay by her saucer. "I'll lose my job," she said.

"Now that is a problem," I conceded, "if you love your position. But Sébastien will pay you. Well, too, I suspect. And who knows what might happen after Fashion Week? More modeling, movies. . ."

She gave me a tart smile. "Now I know why you write fiction, Mr. Tremaine."

I smiled back at her. "Let things happen, my dear. This must be quite exciting compared to teaching French verbs."

She took a deep breath. "Exciting is an understatement. It's like jumping off a cliff," she said.

"Ah, the fall is so exhilarating."

"But the landing's a bitch."

I laughed. "I'm ordering some of the soup that smells so enticing. Won't you join me?"

"Does the whole world want me even fatter than I am?" But her eyes had a little life back in them.

I gave her a French shrug. "It's just soup. Of course I spied some lovely cream cakes and napoleons in the pastry case as we walked in."

She kicked me. Gently, of course.

After luncheon, we huddled under my umbrella on our walk back to the House of Sylvestri. Rachel was definitely calmer, and I resolved to tell Sébastien that he owed me. Just once I'd like to hear him admit this. We found him still rooting around in the fabric samples along with Polly, who seemed, if not calm, resigned to following her questionable commander into battle. Sébastien pointed to a bolt of deep purple silk, spread on the table. "Won't this be fabulous on her?"

Rachel didn't allow me to reply. She marched up to Sébastien, put her hands on her ample hips and started in. "I have something to say." I felt nothing but pity for any students of hers that had ever dared to misbehave. "I will not be talked about as if I'm a thing. I do understand French." She directed this at Polly whose eyes widened at the direct assault. "If I must model, then you," she pointed at Sébastien, "must make sure I'm taught how to do it and do it well." He looked like he did when something amused him but wasn't about to let anyone know it. "I must receive a salary and a few pieces of clothing to get me through February. And haircuts, make-up, all that."

Sébastien said, "But of course. I was just talking to Polly about running you up a few pieces, and . . ."

Rachel interrupted. "And I want a bottle of Sylvestri perfume and a pair of their incredibly expensive sunglasses. Okay?"

I smothered a laugh at her spirit. Obviously she'd been thinking the entire time she ate her soup. And her napoleon.

"Deal," Sébastien said, holding out his hand.

She lifted her chin. I hadn't noticed the coy little dimple before either. "Deal." She raised her eyebrows at Polly who quickly nodded.

"Now we must measure you for the patterns," Sébastien said. He looked at Polly who had a tape measure around her neck. "Normally the head seamstress does this, but Polly is coming in tomorrow to start things for you."

This seemed to surprise Rachel. For heaven's sake, it surprised me. Madame Pauline, the *Première d'atelier*, hadn't done any sewing since those early days at Valenciana. And on a Sunday, to boot. Rachel seemed to sense the honor and nodded at Polly, who said, in English, "How tall are you?"

"Five feet, seven," replied Rachel.

Polly rolled her eyes. "Americans. They absolutely refuse to give up their antiquated measuring system."

I gritted my teeth for another tantrum, but Rachel grinned and gave Polly an exaggerated French shrug.

A

It was late afternoon by the time Rachel dragged herself back to Sébastien's apartment. She'd left him working in his office with Edgar once again snoozing on the sofa. Sébastien had mumbled something about dinner, but she hadn't paid much attention. Before she left, he'd called his concierge and told her to give Rachel a key.

She kicked her shoes off in the living room, the "lounge" in Sébastienese. Like the guestroom, it was too-too contemporary and decorated mostly in black and white. It had a kick-ass view, though. Through the tall, narrow windows she could see Sacre-Coeur in the distance against a sultry, gray sky. Four stories below her, she watched people walking on damp sidewalks, peering into the cookery shop across the wide street. Even from here, she could see a display of shiny pans in the window of the store. Maybe she'd spend some of Sébastien's money on those and take them home. They'd look real fine in her dingy apartment. Then she sighed. Unless she paid rent for the next six months, she wouldn't have an apartment to go home to, and she had no idea how much Sébastien was going to give her.

She took her shoes down the hall to her bedroom. There, neatly folded on her bed, were her clothes, clean and fresh. And sad-looking compared to the fabulous garments Sébastien and Madame Pauline were making for her. They'd mostly let her decide what she wanted except that Sébastien had decreed, "No black." She had to admit that the fabrics were beautiful, nothing like she'd ever seen before. Of course she'd never really paid much attention to clothes at all. Nothing looked particularly good on her, in her opinion. Madame Pauline had sworn that these would flatter her, but Rachel would have to see it to believe it.

Opening the drawers of a stark, ebony chest, she put away her pitiful underwear and pajamas. Yvonne must've thought Sébastien had brought in a stray from the homeless shelter. Rachel peeked in the huge closet that smelled of lavender and found her other pair of jeans and shirts, ironed and on cushioned hangers like they were something special. Crazy.

It felt odd to have a stranger do her wash, and she'd just as soon do it herself. Despite modeling lessons and fittings, activities as foreign to her as spelunking and cattle roping, she'd still have a lot of time on her hands. After tomorrow. Sébastien had asked Edgar to amuse her on Sunday, which sounded like babysitting to Rachel. Still, since she hadn't been able to fit a trip to Versailles into her week, she was glad when Edgar said they'd go. But he was leaving for London the next day. Even if she, by herself of course, explored every nook and cranny in Paris over the next few months, it still sounded very lonesome.

Rachel went into the hallway, and, aware that her mother would call it snooping, hesitated for five seconds before pushing open the door to Sébastien's bedroom. Holy shit. The room looked like a movie set for sultans and harems and the Arabian Nights. His gargantuan bed resembled what Granny had called a *campony* bed and was swathed in sheer curtains with huge, ornate cushions piled all over the deep red comforter. The carpet was thick and shaggy, and Rachel didn't envy Yvonne the job of vacuuming it. All the lamps looked as if they'd summon genies if you rubbed them just right. Rachel grinned. She could just imagine Sébastien setting up an exotic movie set for his overnight guests. But she couldn't picture good old Edgar getting into the fantasy. Actually she couldn't imagine the two of them in any kind of romantic setting and whispered to herself, "Don't go there, girl."

There was another door, but Sébastien had said this morning that it was his office. And off-limits. Okay, she'd curb her curiosity. She wandered back down the hall through a dark, starkly modern dining room, and into the kitchen, the room she liked best. The dirty dishes from breakfast were gone, and a baguette of bread as well as a basket of fruit sat on the tile counter. The indispensable Yvonne had cleaned, laundered, *and* shopped. It was like magic. Rachel shook her head. She guessed if people made enough money, they could buy magic. Opening the refrigerator, Rachel caught sight of several cans of Coca-Cola, the real kind with sugar and one of her many weaknesses. Hurray, she thought, reaching for one. Either Sébastien liked Coke or Yvonne truly did have special powers.

Rachel went to the sink to rinse her hands. Four deep blue pots containing African violets sat on the wide windowsill behind the faucet. They looked puny, and their soil was bone dry. Under the sink, she found a fancy copper watering can that nobody seemed to use. A demerit, Yvonne. But the plants looked so needy that Rachel put back the can, turned on the faucet, and let a dribble of water run over one. She remembered her grandmother preaching that you were never supposed to get African violet leaves wet. Rachel's dad had shaken his head at that. Out in nature, he'd said, they'd get rained on. The leaves probably would welcome some moisture. She gave all four plants a bath and dried her hands, looking at the big clock next to the refrigerator. Quit putting it off, she told herself. You've got people to call.

She opened her Coke and sat at the kitchen table. Shelley first. She was Rachel's best friend; they'd known each other since junior high and both ended up working at Hollister County High School. Shelley taught biology and sponsored the Science Club, full of kids as geeky as Rachel and Shelley had been when they walked the same halls where they now taught. They were still buddies even though Shelley was very much the adult now, married with two kids and hardly recognizable as the brainy girl with braces who used to get the giggles every five minutes, especially in handsome Mr. Mahan's history class. She clicked Shelley's name.

She answered on the third ring. Underneath her voice, Rachel could hear Shelley's two pre-school boys squabbling in the background. "Hey, Shelley."

"Hi! Are you home?" Shelley hesitated. "No, it's too early. What's wrong?"

"Nothing's wrong. I'm still in Paris."

"Still in Paris? Did you miss your plane?" Shelley's voice changed. "Put that down right now. I mean it. Do you want a time-out?"

"Well." This was the easy call, but Rachel took a deep breath anyway. "I'm staying until February. The end of February."

Shelley's voice was greedy. "You met a man, didn't you?"

Yeah, she'd met a man, but it was too complicated, too crazy to explain. Besides, she still felt foolish about being an "inspiration," let alone a model. "No, I didn't meet a man, but I have a new job here."

Shelley yelled for her husband. "Tyler's stuck a Lego up his nose. Haven't I told you never to do that? We'll probably have to go to the Emergency Room, and you won't like that one bit."

Rachel waited while Shelley fussed at three-year-old Tyler, he whined, and his dad said he'd get the tweezers. Evidently it had happened before.

"Sorry," Shelley said. Tyler was screeching from playing real-life Operation. "What kind of a job? What about your classes?"

"It's in motivation and sales," Rachel said, hoping her nose wasn't growing. It wasn't exactly a lie. Besides, Sébastien had already told her three times today that everything about her new job must stay secret. "Too good to pass up, but I do need to talk to Mr. Jones."

"He's going to have a fit," Shelley said. "A you-know-what fit. You'd better call soon. It is Labor Day Weekend, you know. He'll have trouble getting a sub. Might not even answer if he's out with his family."

"At least I could leave him a message."

"Oh, he'll like that." Shelley made her voice go funny. "Oh hi, Mr. Jones. I'm staying in Paris so you'll have to find someone else to take my classes. With no notice, no warning. Girl, you're going to be in deep shit." She whispered the last word.

"I know. He'll fire me."

"You can't even get a leave of absence now. You have to request those in advance through the Board Office. All kinds of paperwork."

Rachel knew this too. She might as well say good-bye to Hollister County High School. "I'm not asking for anything. Just telling."

"This job better be worth it. Where else are you going to get a teaching job except Hollister? Unless you want to move away." Shelley paused. "Are you sure there's not a man involved? It's not like you to do something so crazy."

"No man. But maybe it's time for me to cut loose. What the hell," she said, trying for insouciance. "I love Paris. The job's intriguing." Or absolutely nuts.

"Well." Shelley turned the word into three syllables. "I'm worried about you."

"I'm fine." Right. Living with a mad artist and modeling. Oh, hell.

"Call me. Really. I'll worry."

"Don't worry. I'll call." Rachel thought for a second. "Could you get the stuff out of the bottom desk drawer in my classroom? It's personal."

"Sure. What's in there? Your flask of booze to get you through fifth period?"

"Right. No, my mug, French cd's, and the stuff from our trip to Maine and Nova Scotia. It's hard to tell who'll be using my classroom, and I don't want to lose those."

"Jones is going to kill you," Shelley repeated.

Rachel listened to Shelley's dire warnings for another minute and then managed to end the call. She stared at her phone. Maybe Mr. Jones wouldn't pick up. Leaving a message seemed cowardly, but she couldn't help but hope for it. She pressed his number slowly, imagining the bald-headed principal teeing off. Please be busy, she whispered as the phone began to ring. Luck was with her. Expressing what she hoped sounded like sincere regret, Rachel left a message and, in a fit of guilt, asked him to call her. Maybe she'd accidentally on purpose lose her phone. Sébastien would get her a new one. Right now, he'd do anything for her.

She swallowed the last of her Coke and went to the sink to rinse the can. She'd feared talking to her principal, but that was nothing compared to her mother. God. She could only hope that her father would answer. He was easier about things, always telling her to enjoy life while she was still young, never asking when she was finally going to get married. Dad had never cared about her weight either. Just like her, he'd always carried a little around the middle, but her mother, a whopping size four, had never seemed to understand that Rachel had taken a full plunge into the Bowman gene pool rather than her mother's. According to svelte little Jean who could consume an entire chocolate cream pie without gaining an ounce, a girl was supposed to resemble her mother.

Sitting back down at the kitchen table, Rachel remembered when her father and she had spent a summer concocting special ice cream sundaes for each other every Sunday night. "Sundaes on Sunday," her dad had called it as he created treats like peach ice cream topped with mandarin oranges, shaved chocolate, and shredded coconut. He'd declared one of Rachel's the absolute winner: chocolate ice cream hidden under mounds of marshmallow crème and melted peanut butter. Rachel smiled at the memory. She'd been maybe eleven or twelve, wearing special "chubby" sizes at the time, and her mother had given Wayne hell for encouraging Rachel's sweet tooth. "She's a kid," Dad had said. "She'll grow out of her baby fat."

He'd been kind but wrong, she thought, giving the roll around her middle a quick squeeze. Answer the phone, Dad, she begged as she punched in her parents' number.

So much for luck. "Hi Mom," she said.

"Rachel? Aren't you in the air? What's wrong?"

Everyone assumed something was wrong. "Nothing. I'm still in Paris."

"Are you sick? What happened? Did you lose your ticket?" Her mother's voice rose higher and higher.

"No. I'm staying in Paris. I got a job here. I'm fine."

"A job? Have you been kidnapped? What's going on?"

So, her mother had seen the articles about human traffickers too. "I'm fine, Mom. Really. I got an opportunity to work in sales and motivation here, and I'm going to stay." Rachel could imagine her mother's face, white and stretched, thin and nervous.

"But you have a job," Mrs. Bowman said. "You can't just leave it." There was a second's pause and then a flood of hysteria. "You've met a man, and we know nothing about him, nothing at all. He's European, isn't he? Or worse. Dear Lord. Have you eloped?"

Rachel rolled her eyes and plucked a grape out of the basket on the table. She popped it in her mouth and talked while she chewed. "It's nothing like that at all, Mom. I'm working. I was tired of teaching anyway. I've called Mr. Jones. It'll be fine."

Mom must've heard her chewing. "Are you eating? How could you eat at a time like this? If your grandmother had known you were going to run off, she'd never have left you her sewing machine. She expected you to marry and have a home."

Rachel doubted it. From what she could read between the lines of family stories, Granny had been a wildass. She'd probably have cheered Rachel on. "Calm down, Mom. Really. Everything's good. But I do need you and Dad to do a few things for me."

Mrs. Bowman interrupted her with a voice like broken glass. "I don't know why we should. You just traipse off leaving your family and job behind to do whatever you want. Are you using drugs?"

"No." Although about then Rachel wished for a stiff drink. "I know this is sudden, but it's a good opportunity." She waited a second, thinking her mother would start in again, but all she heard was cold silence. Rachel figured the usual chill was coming. She remembered the time her mother hadn't spoken to her for two full weeks. Not a word. "I'll email the landlord, but I need you to get into my bank account and send him the last month's rent and then get my stuff out. There's room in Rob's garage, isn't there? I don't have much. I know this is a pain, but maybe Rob can help." Her saintly brother Rob was slim, responsible, married, and everything Jean Bowman wished Rachel would be. "He could store my car too, if he would. And I'd love it if you could take care of my plants; I'd hate for them to die."

There was a significant snort, and Rachel heard her mother lay down the phone and say, "Talk to your daughter."

Thank God. "What's up, Punkin? Your mama's pitching a hissy fit."

She went through it all again, and he didn't interrupt once. "Sure," he said when she asked him to clear out her apartment. "Are you having a good time, little girl?" he asked.

"I am." She bit her lip. "It's just six months, Dad."

"That's fine. And I'll take care of your plants, the car, everything. No problem. You got somewhere decent to live?"

"Yes. Really, I appreciate this, Dad. I really do."

"Happy to do it, Punkin. But you call or email real often, okay?"

She promised and laid down her phone, letting out a sigh like a balloon losing air. Dad would enjoy handling the plants. They'd always kidded each other about their green thumbs, holding their digits up and pretending to look for color. When she was just a kid, he'd taught her how to plant flower seeds outside and given her a spider plant and a cactus for her room. He'd take care of them. And everything else. She already missed him.

Chapter Four

I'd intended to take an early train back to London on Monday, but while spending Sunday with Rachel at Versailles, I decided upon a later departure. She'd been droopy as a thirsty flower when I first picked her up, but with every minute of our pilgrimage to the eighteenth century version of conspicuous consumption, she perked up. She pretended to do a minuet in the Hall of Mirrors and giggled at the naked statuary. I'd like to say that the metamorphosis was due to my charm, but I knew better. After a week in Paris by herself and then the dizzying heights and subsequent lows of Sébastien's inspiration, attention, whatever you bloody well wanted to call it, the girl was lonesome. And, she told me, her mother was being a beast about her staying and her headmaster had called and dismissed her, both of which she expected, she said. Brave child. Truly, it was amazing how well she recovered in the company of an old poofter such as I. She needed a handsome lad to woo her, but then, don't we all?

Rachel and I had our luncheon, just sandwiches, in the gardens of Versailles. I watched her absorb the colors, the geometric designs, the parterres. She loved the flowers. The sun caught in her auburn hair making fire of her curls, and when she looked at me, the light turned her eyes as green as moss. Fascinating coloring. I'd already fashioned her into a character and was well on my way to writing her description. "Do you know where the stables are?" she asked.

I shook my head. "But we can certainly ask. Why?"

She had a faraway smile. "My grandfather lived here when he was in the Army during the war. What's the correct word for that, Mr. Writer?"

"He was billeted here, I suppose. Fascinating. Are you close to your grandfather?" Yes, I confess I was building back story.

"No. I don't think anyone got very close to Grandad." She scrunched her nose and smiled at a bed of geraniums beside us. "I was much closer to my grandmother. She was a real character." Rachel sipped her lemonade. "They're both dead now."

"I'm sorry," I murmured. "Family is so dear." Bless her, the girl was homesick.

She twitched a shoulder. "Even when they drive you crazy."

I had personal knowledge of that. Anyway, I sat up a bit straighter and declaimed, "'Home is the place where, when you have to go there, . . . '"

She grinned and interrupted, "'They have to take you in.' Robert Frost. I remember that poem."

All right, along with her courage, her beauty, and her awkward, youthful charm, I was completely and thoroughly disarmed by her literacy. What should I name her?

We continued our picnic, chatting about this and that, and it came out that despite his promises, Sébastien had not shared dinner with Rachel on Saturday night, nor had he come home at all, to her knowledge. I tried to explain that this was normal behavior whilst Sébastien was in a creative frenzy, but she didn't seem to believe me. If I'd known, I would've canceled the dinner with my writing friends, or included her.

So, on Monday morning, instead of proceeding to Gare du Nord, I went to the House of Sylvestri and brushed off the magenta-haired young woman meant to guard Sébastien's lair by telling her that of course Sébastien would welcome my presence. He was at his desk, sketching like a madman. Without looking up, he barked in French, "I said, no interruptions."

"And I'm ignoring you," I replied, going over to the counter by the armoire and pouring myself a cup of coffee. "*Un café?*"

He rubbed at his face. "Yes, why not. I could use a break." He stretched, a rather impressive performance, and joined me on the sofa. He sipped from the cup I'd handed him: cream, no sugar. I remembered. "I thought you were leaving early today," he said, a gigantic yawn giving his facial muscles a bit of a stretch as well.

"Changed my mind. I'm leaving this afternoon." I could tell he was paying more heed to the pictures in his mind than to my words. "Is it going well?"

He nodded. "Fantastic. Stunning. The colors, the shapes." He threw his hands up in the air, without spilling his coffee. "She's inspired me to create beyond anything I've ever done."

I raised an eyebrow. "More than the Oceania collection that final season at Valenciana?"

"Yes, much more. Look." He stood and brought me pages of drawings: rich, flowing clothes perfect for, shall we say, a womanly woman.

"People will accuse you of designing for, what do the Americans call them? Plus Sized Ladies," I said. "Overweight cows."

"Is that how you see Rachel?" His voice was icy.

"Of course not. I'm not saying it, but the Press will. And all the fashion wizards."

He started with his condescending act, voice and facial expressions appropriate for explaining simple concepts to a particularly annoying, and stupid, five-year-old. I'd left him once over condescension, but I'd come back that time. "These can be worn by women of any size, but the inspiration, the freshness comes from a new ideal of beauty," he explained. His enthusiasm won over his more usual sarcasm. "We've idolized the androgynous female for ninety years now. It's time for a change."

"And you think you can effect this change?"

"Of course."

"Fine, but I've come to talk with you about Rachel," I said, setting my cup on the table at my knees.

"What about her?"

"I will not for one minute allow you to turn into Henry Higgins. Nor am I that bloody oaf, Colonel Pickering." I spoke with some asperity.

"I haven't a clue what you're talking about." No one could do vapid blinking as well as Sébastien.

"*My Fair Lady*," I spat. "You know precisely what I'm talking about." I truly was rather put out with him. "Or *Pygmalion*, if you choose to be intellectual." My tone indicated that this was unlikely.

He shook his head. "What does Audrey Hepburn have to do with our Raquel? Total opposites, I'd say."

Ha, I knew he'd devoured every musical ever produced. We both had. Together. "I will not allow you to turn her into nothing more than a project. She's a human being and a lonely one, whiling away the hours alone in your flat." I glared at him; I'd always been good at glaring. "What is she supposed to do with herself from now until Fashion Week?"

"Oh, she'll be busy once we get started. Fittings, lessons, hair, makeup. Photos. I do want to schedule a secret photo shoot to see how the camera takes to her." He shouted toward the door. "Alexis? Get me Kurt Mann."

"Why secret?" I asked. "And for God's sake, why Kurt Mann? That bloke devours women."

Sébastien hunched his shoulders. "So? It's whispered that he's rather fond of high stakes wagers too. How does that affect Raquel unless she gives him money or decides to sleep with him?"

Well, all right. Rachel was a grown woman, and I'd rapidly become overprotective. Mann's gambling would have no bearing on a photo shoot, and it was doubtful that he'd fancy her, considering all the other bodies available to him.

"And as to the secret," Sébastien went on, "no one must know anything about Raquel or the collection. The show must be a beautiful surprise."

Secrets were nothing new in the rag trade; collections were always swathed in mystery, but I feared for Rachel. "Do you plan to keep her locked away?"

Sébastien frowned and bit at his nail. "Not entirely. But I've told her to keep her mouth shut," he mumbled. "No parties or paparazzi catching us together, that's for sure." He thought a bit more. "It's unlikely that anyone would suspect her of anything unless they connected us."

Arrogant bastard. I played my trump. "Perhaps I should just keep her in London with me. I'm plotting a new novel. A fresh idea with a young American girl tempting Hannaford."

He stood and towered over me. "You cannot have her," he declared. "She must stay here where I can see her." He gave me a narrow look. "Are you really going to write about her?"

"Perhaps."

Alexis called through the door. "I have Kurt Mann on the phone for you, Monsieur Fel."

Sébastien didn't move. Neither did I.

Finally he emitted a great gust of a sigh. "All right. I'll go home occasionally. I'll eat a meal with her now and then." He moved toward his phone. "She's my inspiration, not my best friend." His voice was petulant.

"She's quite charming actually. And intelligent, if naïve." I rose to take my leave. "I'll be checking on Rachel," I said as I opened the door. "And you."

Rachel had thought it very sweet that Mr. Tremaine had delayed his trip back to London to take her to a bistro for lunch and had even kissed her on the cheek when he left. He'd given her a book on Paris, one that explored it by inches, he said, and had urged her to get to know the city like a Parisian. And he'd added a couple of books by Hemingway. "He loved Paris as you do," Edgar had said. "See it through his eyes."

So that very afternoon she started reading and taking notes, determined to do as the guide suggested: divide the city into its *arondissements* and explore them one at a time. While Rachel was in the kitchen reading, Yvonne showed up to clean and start a pot of soup. Rachel was happy for the company as well as the opportunity to practice her French with someone less picky than Sébastien, but Yvonne was all business. After giving Rachel about ten moderately polite responses, she finished chopping onions and turned her tight, little jeans-clad butt toward the living room and the vacuum cleaner. Even the cleaning ladies in Paris were chic and slim.

Late in the afternoon, Madame Pauline called and told Rachel to come to the *atelier* for a fitting for her get-through-February clothes. Immediately. Rachel couldn't claim any kind of previous engagement, so she threw a hoodie on over her tee shirt and headed for the closest Metro station. She refused to travel everywhere by taxi like Sébastien and Edgar. They were old. Plus she still had no idea how much Sébastien was paying her. The money she'd brought from home was nearly gone.

When Rachel arrived at Sylvestri, a tall, gorgeous stick of a girl was standing by Madame Pauline's desk, arguing and slinging her hands around. Although the weather was warm, she wore yoga pants under a black skirt with a tee shirt, sweater, and jacket peeking out from under a flashy orange anorak. Rachel was reminded of homeless people who wore their entire wardrobes all at once. Even with all those clothes, the young woman looked like a starving refugee. She was babbling, in French of course, and Rachel had a hard time following her tirade. "What do you mean? Are you saying he will not be using me? His *prémier mannequin* for three shows now?" Of course she was a model.

Rachel stood in the doorway and watched. Madame Pauline, in a little black suit, stood impassively as the model ranted. Rachel wondered if Madame Pauline's closet contained anything but little black suits. The model lit a cigarette, gesticulating the whole time, and tossed her thick, black hair around like she was posing for a shoot. Rachel caught something to the effect that Sébastien was a bastard if he thought he could ignore her, that she would avenge this slight, that he could . . . . Madame Pauline broke in, speaking slowly enough for

Rachel to get every dignified word. "Lucy, you know I have no control over the models Sébastien chooses. Nothing to do with it at all. Go see Jean-Pierre or Suzanne if you want to protest," she said in a quiet voice. "Besides, it's early for modeling decisions."

Rachel stepped down the hallway a few paces. She could still hear everything.

"It isn't that early," the model screeched. "He always contacts me by now. I will talk to Dumont. I will track Sébastien down. No one treats me like this."

Madame Pauline said, "That would be unwise."

A tall, bony man with a boyish lock of black hair falling onto his forehead, loped into the hall. Stopping suddenly at the doorway, he grinned and winked at Rachel. "That's trouble," he whispered and turned. "I'll come back later." He spoke English. American English.

Lucy kept ranting until she ran out of steam. With a clatter of stilettos, she stalked toward the door. Rachel slipped farther down the hall to avoid her and hid in the fabric room until the steps died away. Then she went back to Madame Pauline's office. The woman was pulling on the hem of her suit jacket. "A little upset?" Rachel asked.

"Hmm." Madame Pauline straightened her shoulders. "Only the beginning, I fear." Rachel noticed a twitch to the woman's lips and realized that the venerable *Prémiere d'atelier* was treating her with sympathy, or amusement, rather than irritation. Rachel figured that somewhere along the line, old Polly had decided to support Sébastien's crazy ideas and Rachel along with them. Formal again, Madame Pauline said, "Thank you for being so prompt."

She guided Rachel downstairs where a fitter put her through the embarrassing process of tailoring clothing to her body. With chalk, pins, and a continual stream of disapproving grunts, an older woman marked a skirt, jacket, blouse, and two pairs of slacks. Rachel couldn't move, was afraid to breathe. Madame Pauline looked on, so the fitter never said anything outwardly insulting, but Rachel knew the old woman thought she was too fat for such fine clothes. And they were very fine: luscious silk, feathery crepe. Rachel had never seen such garments. But the fitter had seen fancier clothes than these and certainly better bodies. Exasperated, she tugged on Rachel's bra straps to lift her breasts and finally could keep her mouth shut no longer. "She needs foundation garments," the woman complained to Madame Pauline. "These are useless." Rachel's face burned. They must all figure she knew no French. The fitter gave Rachel a curt nod that she interpreted as an order to put her clothes back on.

"We can fix that," murmured Madame Pauline, and she jotted something on a slip of paper and stuffed it into the pocket of Rachel's hoodie. "Go to this shop tomorrow," she said. "And then come back for another fitting." She'd nearly turned away when she said as an afterthought, "Sébastien has told you to keep our work secret?"

Rachel nodded.

Madame Pauline pointed to Rachel's pocket. "You can trust this woman."

A

The next morning, Rachel walked to the address Madame Pauline had given her and considered the topic of breasts. She had a real love/hate thing going for boobs. Back when they'd sprouted, she'd felt as though her body had betrayed her, but guys seemed to like them. The attention had started early, just like her bosoms. She remembered how the boy who'd sat in front of her in sixth grade math had nearly swallowed his tongue every time Rachel stretched. Personally, she'd just as soon they were smaller. They sat like heavy, hot lumps on her chest; besides, nobody made pretty, lacy bras for large cup sizes.

Her mother hadn't helped. Rachel had used her mother's bust to help her memorize the definition of the word 'concave' for vocabulary tests. Jean Bowman had been appalled when Rachel started budding breasts at age ten. Her "Littlest Angel" bra had lasted about three months before she was a B cup, a size bigger than her mother ever achieved. That's when Mrs. Bowman had threatened to take Rachel to the doctor for testosterone shots.

And the twins had continued to blossom. When everybody else was buying wispy little bras at Victoria's Secret, Rachel searched out sturdy underwires that looked as though they'd been designed by mechanical engineers. Yeah, embarrassing as it was, the fitter had been right. She'd challenged and exhausted the elastic in all her bras until they had given up the fight, but she hated to shop for them. She hoped Madame Pauline knew what she was doing. Little bits of Parisian lace were no match for a 38 DDD.

The lingerie shop had a bright pink door and was tucked between a café and an intriguing junk shop. For a moment she wished she had an apartment in Paris so she could buy interesting things and feather a little nest. But this gig was only going to last six months, she told herself. She couldn't decide whether she was happy or sad about that. And then? Unemployment.

Rachel ducked her head as she went into the tiny shop. A half-mannequin wearing a gorgeous, pale blue bra sat on a round table, surrounded by a color wheel of bikini underpants. She imagined the tiny garments struggling to cover her rear end. Rachel always chose stretchy, full-fit panties, usually in beige, to rein in her belly and butt. Back in college, she'd bought a thong, but stuffed it in the back of her underwear drawer after wearing it once. She grinned at the memory. The best thing about it was her roommate's hysterical laughter when Rachel called the thong 'anal floss. '

The proprietress, a very large woman herself, with frizzy, fake red hair, greeted Rachel and started smiling and fluttering her eyes as soon as Rachel told her that she'd been recommended by Madame Pauline Robert. Madame Nolin, who said Rachel must call her Gisèle, seemed to have no problem with Rachel's French or her figure. "But of course," she said, guiding Rachel to a fitting room. "We can fit you."

Gisèle was the only fat woman Rachel'd seen in Paris, or at least it seemed that way. And maybe that's why she had lingerie in super sizes, lots of it. Whatever the reason, Rachel relaxed and didn't mind a bit when the woman pushed and tugged at her breasts to fit them securely into lovely silken things the colors of wedding mints. She clucked over Rachel and brought out piece after beautiful piece. Rachel had no idea if she could afford them, but she chose a half-dozen pairs of panties, a few camisoles, and bras suitable for honeymoons and trysts. It was so intoxicating and Madame Gisèle was so kind and enthusiastic that Rachel was tempted to tell her that she would be modeling for Sébastien. But despite what Madame Pauline had said about Gisèle, the thought of betraying the Big Man was more than a little scary. Rachel kept her mouth shut.

After the woman wrapped each precious item in tissue paper and filled a shopping bag, she said, "You are a beautiful girl, Mademoiselle Bowman. Worthy of Sylvestri's attentions. Come back and see me soon, just to visit, yes?" Rachel blinked at what the woman had figured out, then grinned at her. She was pretty sure Gisèle had meant what she said.

The next evening, Sébastien asked, "Did the fittings go well?"

He'd actually come home for dinner that night, and the two of them sat in the kitchen finishing the soup Yvonne had made the day before. Rachel liked the soup very much, but she wished she could cook for them on Yvonne's days off. She'd already figured out that she couldn't walk and sightsee all day every day.

"Yesterday the fitter complained about my, um, underwear," she said, feeling a blush heat her face. "But Madame Pauline sent me to the most wonderful lingerie shop, and today things went well." Even though she'd still felt as trapped as a lightning bug in a jar.

He pushed his half-full bowl away. The man didn't eat much. "Let me see," he said. When she didn't move, he gestured at her chest.

Rachel set down her spoon. What? In the kitchen? With bright kitchen lights shining down on her head and everything else? "Umm."

"Don't be absurd. I've seen you in your underwear before, and a sad little sight it was, Raquel." He raised a sardonic eyebrow; she'd decided this was a facial version of the Parisian shrug.

Rachel rubbed at her nose, glared at him, and then acquiesced. She knew he wouldn't give up. So, she pulled her tee shirt over her head and said, "Ta da." It was the pale green bra, lacy yet supportive. The grumpy fitter had even nodded approval at it.

"Remarkable," murmured Sébastien, which made her blush. "Gisèle did well."

"Oh," said Rachel. "You know her?"

"Certainly. From years ago. Gisèle was a fitter with us many, many years ago, and she and Polly are great friends."

Rachel felt stupid sitting at the table in her bra, but when she reached for her shirt, Sébastien shook his head. "Take off your jeans. I'll be back," he ordered.

They were on the top floor, four storeys up. The shutters on the kitchen windows were closed, but she still felt exposed. She took another spoonful of soup and some dribbled on her boob. Sexy, she thought. On anybody else it would be champagne or whipped cream, she thought, but on Rachel Bowman a fantasy lover would lick chicken and white bean soup off her *volumptuous* bosoms, she thought, using her grandmother's pronunciation.

"Here." Sébastien came back with a man's long-sleeved, white dress shirt. "Put this on, but don't button it."

It was far too big to be one of his. He wore his shirts so tight you could count his ribs. The shirt floated around her body down to her knees, threatening to slide off her shoulders. It had French cuffs, elongating the sleeves far beyond her fingertips. "Come here," he said and rolled those up above her wrists.

"Now what?" She felt way beyond stupid.

"Play," he said, sipping his wine. "Pretend you're at the beach or with a lover or acting in a movie."

She felt her nose twitch.

He sighed and filled her wineglass, motioning that she should drink. "All of it."

Feeling like she was at a fraternity party, Rachel chugged her wine, which was far too good to gulp, but in for a penny, in for a pound. She'd heard Edgar say that, and it made her giggle. Sébastien nodded his approval, but she still didn't know what to do.

He sighed again. "All right. Pretend you are Audrey Hepburn."

Her mother's ideal. Rachel pulled the shirt close around her, stretched her neck as far as it would go, and glided around the room trying to look serene in her bare feet.

Sébastien gave her a stingy smile. She must've done okay. "The Queen of England."

This was harder. She let the shirt flap open just a little and tried to look royal as she smiled and waved. He didn't seem to like that one much. He said, "Scarlett O'Hara."

Her mother's favorite movie. God, was Sébastien channeling Jean Bowman? Rachel primmed up her mouth, lifted her chin, and said, "Fiddle-dee-dee."

It made Rachel feel good when Sébastien laughed. "Okay, move a little; use the shirt. Walking on the beach, looking at the surf and searching for shells."

She tried. And even though the wine was making her a little dizzy, she kept trying hard to act out his prompts: standing on a windy hill, stretching after a nap, and ignoring a rude comment. Then he said, "Invite your lover to bed."

And without thinking, she gripped a button on the shirt, holding it away from her body as she tilted her head and gave him almost a smile. But then she realized what she'd done and got the giggles.

He motioned for her to sit down. "Not bad," he said, pouring her more wine. "Those are the kinds of things the photographer will ask you to do."

"What photographer?" She took a healthy swig.

"Kurt Mann. He's the best fashion photographer in the business. I have an appointment for you to do a session with him in a couple of weeks." Sébastien frowned. "His schedule is impossible. Even I had to beg to get it."

Rachel sobered instantly. "But I don't know how to model yet."

Sébastien toyed with his napkin. "It doesn't matter. This is just to see if the camera likes you or not. I suspect it will." He gave her a long look. "But we do need to settle on your hair and makeup before then." He seemed to add this to a mental list. "Mann has no idea you're modeling in my show, and you will not tell him." He sounded as stern as Mr. Jones disciplining the freshmen.

Same old, same old. Rachel nodded but shrugged at the same time. She was getting a little tired of him treating her like a child. She changed the subject. "The other day I saw one of your models, Lucy? She was giving Madame Pauline hell because you're leaving her out of the lineup this time."

"Alexis says she calls every day." He didn't seem concerned about it.

"Well, I can't wear thirty-five outfits," Rachel said. He'd told her the number. "Who else are you going to get?"

"Costumes," he corrected and then frowned. "I don't want conventional models."

"You mean the skinny ones, right?"

He nodded. "You must all be about the same size."

Rachel shook her head. "But where are you going to get all those fat girls, Sébastien? I don't think there are that many in the whole of France."

Chapter Five

September crept by. Early on, Suzanne, whose job entailed dealing with models and contracts and an awful lot of other tasks, accompanied Rachel to Brussels to get her work visa. Rachel had looked forward to seeing another European city, but Suzanne marched her from the train to the consulate and back to the train without stopping for so much as a quick touristy photo. On the train, Suzanne avoided talking to Rachel by keeping her phone engaged nearly the entire time. Rachel was fairly sure Suzanne considered an overweight model, and collection, a very bad idea.

Otherwise than that hasty trip, the days were all the same. Each morning before she started her exploring, Rachel went to an Internet café not too far from Sébastien's apartment. She figured he probably had a computer in his home office, but she'd obeyed his orders about staying out of the holy sanctum. It was probably a gigantic mess. Sébastien dropped papers, jackets, wineglasses, and sketchpads everywhere he went. Sort of like a big, fuzzy cat shedding hair. No wonder he needed Yvonne nearly every day. Rachel had even started picking up after him.

Rachel liked the Internet café. She'd get a coffee and smile at the regulars, even chat with them a bit sometimes. One sort of cute young man often looked up from his cyber war game and smiled at her, then blushed so badly she felt sorry for him. After a few days of this she almost had enough nerve to ask him to go to the movies or have lunch or something, but then he showed up with a girl with long dark hair and the waist of a ten-year-old.

On Wednesday, her mailbox had three messages: one from her brother, one from her father, and one from Edgar. Good old Edgar; she'd save him for last. A week ago she'd sent a long, detailed email to her parents, brother, and Shelley, revealing a little about what she was doing but warning them that they couldn't tell anyone. She just said that she was working as an assistant with Sylvestri and would be tied up until after Fashion Week, but she hated to think what Sébastien would do if he knew she'd told them even that much. Shelley had written back, in all capital letters, saying she thought it was beyond awesome that a designer had chosen her as his assistant. It was a dream come true. Maybe he'd even design some clothes for her. Rachel shook her head. Oh, he was, Shelley. He was.

Her parents and Rob weren't as enthusiastic, but then Rachel doubted if they understood what little she'd told them. Couture was not a big thing in Morton, Ohio. Her grandmother continued to wear the ancient velour jogging suits she called "designer."The labels had said "Bill Blass," so Rachel supposed they qualified as such, but the funny thing was that Granny always called the guy "Bill Blast."

She read the email from Rob first. He was fine, but the garage certainly was crowded with her stuff. He didn't see why she couldn't have rented a storage unit, but could they use her crock pot? They didn't have one. And Heather's car was acting up; could she borrow Rachel's for a few days? It was just sitting there. Probably needed to be driven anyway. And didn't Rachel think it was irresponsible to stay in Paris so long, especially since it was just about clothes?

She shook her head at the screen but wrote yes and yes again and maybe. She wished she were closer to Rob, but it wasn't going to happen. He'd married Heather, who was about as exciting as a bowl of cream of wheat, right after getting his business degree and sliding into a job at an insurance agency. Rob was only two years older than Rachel but had always seemed middle-aged. As a kid, she'd even wondered if she'd been adopted, but then there was her dad. They were two of a kind. "Two twigs off the same tree," he'd often remarked.

Her dad's email made her smile. The plants were doing well, the landlord had returned her deposit, and Dad had put the money into her account. Her mother was helping with the Fall Festival at church. Probably supervising the placement of every pumpkin, Rachel thought. Mom hadn't written yet, but that didn't surprise her. Jean Bowman could hold a grudge so long she sometimes forgot what had irritated her in the first place. But Dad did say that her mother wanted to know if Rachel had a warm coat. It wouldn't be long before the evenings would turn chilly, and she'd mail her jackets and sweaters if Rachel needed them. This was practically an olive branch.

Edgar's was, as always, witty and cheerful. He invited her to London. He urged her to scratch back if Sébastien was being a bully. Instead of typing a reply, Rachel went outside, leaned against the wall of the cafe, and called him. She wanted instant gratification. He picked up on the third ring. After she said hello, he exclaimed "Rachel!" in his plummy accent. "Are you quite all right?"

"I'm quite all right, Edgar. How's the writing going?"

"Swimmingly, my child. I have this luscious American girl getting into all kinds of trouble with terrorists and art smugglers."

Her head jerked. "Sort of me?"

"Very much you. I hope you don't mind."

"I don't guess so." When she was back in Ohio, hunting for a job, she could write "muse" on the experience line of her résumés. Weird. "I've read both the Hemingway books you gave me, and then I went to Shakespeare and Company to buy some Fitzgerald and Gertrude Stein. I like Fitzgerald a lot."

"Marvelous. Of course the store's not in the same location as it was in the twenties."

Such a lovable, pompous man. "I know. The people there told me the complete history. And I explore a little bit of Paris every day. The antique stores are amazing. And I love the sidewalk artists."

"Good, good. Is Sébastien being a beast?"

"Not really. He's nearly done with the designs." She giggled. "Last night he made me stand on a stool with a purple sheet draped around me. I felt like I was at a toga party."

"Oh, my." He obviously didn't get that one.

"He's sending me to a hairdresser tomorrow and next week I have a session with a photographer named Kurt."

Edgar's voice dropped an octave. "Kurt Mann."

"I think that's his name. What about him?" She grinned into the phone. "One of your old flames?"

"Hardly," said Edgar. He was not amused. "He's a gambler as well as a Don Juan, a Casanova." She could hear him ask someone in the room, "What do you young people call a womanizer these days?" She heard a murmur, and then Edgar spoke into his phone again. "My nephew Jeremy says Kurt would be called a 'player' in modern parlance. Be very careful, Rachel."

She laughed. "He won't want to play me, Edgar. Remember, I'm the fat girl." She'd called herself that for years to head off someone else saying it, but with Edgar it didn't seem like anything but a fact.

"You're a charming girl." The words were as solemn as church.

She changed the subject. "So your nephew is visiting?"

"Yes. Jeremy's in town to go to a symposium on Dutch bulbs or creeping yews or something botanical." She could hear laughter in the background. "He runs a greenhouse and nursery in Cornwall."

"Sounds wonderful," she said. "I love plants."

"As does he," Edgar said. "Although my mother Margo, Jeremy's grandmother, swears that this is simply a sign of stunted development, that he's never grown out of playing in the dirt." There was a pause. "It's turned chilly here the last day or so. Do you have warm clothes?"

Rachel smiled again. She had the strongest urge to call him 'Uncle Edgar.' "I'm okay. I went back to Madame Pauline's friend Gisèle. The one with the lingerie shop? And she told me about a store out in the suburbs that has larger sizes. I bought a couple of sweaters. I might order some things off the Internet too."

"Good. I know Gisèle. And what did our Sébastien think of those sweaters?"

"He said they looked like garments for people who sleep under bridges."

Edgar snorted. "That bad?"

"No, they're perfectly okay. I had to have something to wear with jeans."

"Of course. Your Sylvestri clothes are a bit posh for that."

She liked that word. "Posh. Maybe I'll wake up one morning and be totally posh. Sébastien would like that, wouldn't he?"

Edgar laughed and went on to invite her to London once again, and she, once again, said that she didn't think Sébastien would be allowing her out of Paris any time soon. And Edgar repeated his warnings about Kurt Mann. Rachel shook her head. Uncle Edgar for sure. "I'm a big girl," she said. "Call you again soon." And she tucked the phone into her jeans. Although Sébastien persisted in trying to keep her and everything about her a secret, maybe she'd sneak into the *atelier* and talk to him or Madame Pauline about a winter coat. The sweaters, ugly or not, weren't all that warm, and maybe a designer coat would be fun.

🗼

A week later, though, she did remember what Edgar had said about Kurt Mann and developed a huge case of jitters the evening she went to his studio. Sébastien had told the photographer that Rachel was the daughter of a friend who wanted a portfolio of pictures for publicity. Publicity for what, Rachel didn't know. In her opinion, lies were better when they were more specific, but Sébastien thrived on mystery. The night before, he'd brought her a dress to wear for the photo session:

47

drapey, purple, and sewn from whispery silk. It was nothing like the purple sheet he'd made her model. The dress was what Edgar would've called a "posh frock," and it was the most beautiful garment she'd ever seen. When she tried it on for Sébastien, she remembered Shelley's comments about a "dream come true" and forgot to be self-conscious. She felt like a princess. She'd asked about shoes, but Sébastien'd said she should be barefoot. "No jewelry, minimal makeup. I've given the hairdresser and makeup artist very precise instructions."

She'd thrown on a pair of jeans and the cute, warm jacket Madame Pauline had unearthed from a previous Sylvestri ready to wear collection. It was plenty big enough; oversized must have been the style that season. She'd zipped up the stunning purple dress in a garment bag Sébastien had provided. Holding this above the streaming gutters, Rachel stepped out of a taxi into pouring rain and eyed the dingy building where Mann had his studio and went into a mild panic. These people were accustomed to models so thin they hardly made shadows. She took a deep breath. Little by little, she was getting used to the fashion world gasping at her size, but she still didn't like it.

The studio was three floors up, so she trudged past two landings with doors on either side until she reached the top of the building. There was only one door, and it stood open to a cavernous space that not only looked but smelled like an old attic. Heart still racing from the climb, and fear, she took two steps into the room. A very young man rushed out from a walled off, brightly lit corner of the room and started jabbering in what she thought was Arabic with an occasional French word thrown in. He made a funny little clicking noise between sentences. Pointing to a Japanese screen, he gestured that she should change into her dress. Rachel nodded and unzipped the garment bag, admiring the dress once again. It had a square neckline with seams that looked like sunbeams coming from the bodice, and the hem reached nearly to the floor on one side and angled way up her thigh on the other. She was careful not to let the dress touch the filthy floor, littered with snippets of hair, cotton balls, and dust bunnies, but she wasn't crazy about walking on all the dirt either, regardless of Sébastien's barefoot edict. So she left on her socks, the ones she'd bought when she, Shelley, and another friend had gone to Maine when they were in college. The three of them had been tooling down a narrow road in Shelley's car when they'd run upon, and nearly run into, a moose. All three of them had snapped bunches of photos and later couldn't resist buying socks decorated with a black moose on each ankle.

The hairdresser pointed to a chair and flung a cape around her. The entire time he was wielding a curling iron and plastering her hair with goop and spray, he talked and clicked. Rachel got barely two words out of twenty, but his work was remarkable. She'd visited another hairdresser a week before, and he'd enhanced the red in her auburn hair. But this guy had somehow or the other turned her hair into a Medusa's mop of snaky curls and waves. "I look like an Irish dancer," Rachel murmured in English.

Taking this as a compliment, the hairdresser smiled and bowed and then barked a command. In came the makeup girl, or, in this case, woman. She was tiny, of course; she was French. But she was also wrinkled and looked as though she smelled something foul. Instead of clicking her tongue while she worked, she mumbled, most of it unpleasant and directed at the hairdresser. In a smeary mirror Rachel watched as the woman applied eye shadow, liner, and about thirty-two coats of mascara. Then she rubbed a tiny bit of nearly white foundation into Rachel's face and made her sneeze with a flurry of powder. "Mann," she bellowed. As she removed Rachel's cape, she hissed, "Good skin."

Rachel stared at her reflection, which looked like a cross between one of Henry the VIII's wives and a Celtic witch. She was pale, exotic, and sort of spooky. But this was evidently what Sébastien wanted. She padded into the main room. It was dim. Several skylights topped the incredibly high ceiling, but it was too late and too rainy for any light to pass through them. She didn't see the photographer. In the center of the room were lights, all dark at the moment, on poles or stands alongside odd-looking black boxes, lighting umbrellas, and fans. She saw a single chair and an old-fashioned sofa upholstered in dark red, and it made her remember Edgar's warnings. She stood in the vast, shadowy room and waited in front of curtains and curtains of backdrops. And waited.

Finally, with a loud clomping of boots, a man came from the stairwell, calling out to someone named Bret. He stopped about two feet from Rachel and exclaimed something in German. Damn. She knew English, of course, and was getting better every day with French. She even knew a little Spanish, but a girl needed a UN translator to get through this ordeal. His comment had probably been something like, "Holy shit, what a pig!" She narrowed her eyes and said, "Rachel Bowman."

He was still sizing her up, and that verb had never been so apt. He looked up, down, shifted to see her side, her back. "Would you like me to pirouette?" she asked, punching a bit of nasty in her voice.

He shook his head. Okay, so he did understand English. That helped. Then he saw her feet and started laughing, one of those silent laughs that jiggle the belly, not that he had one, and make the laugher breathless. He pointed at her socks.

Rachel had to concede that they were comical. She gave him a tart smile. "The floor's dirty."

He'd just about quit laughing but was still smiling. Oh Mama, he was hot-looking. "Where are the shoes?"

Shiny, white teeth. Dimples, for God's sake. And thick, dark blond hair gathered into a tight ponytail at his neck. She could see how he attracted women. "I'm not supposed to wear any," she said.

He frowned, walked over to a corner of the studio, and scrounged around in a big box, bringing back a pair of ballet slippers nearly as dirty as the floor. Rachel couldn't help but think about athlete's foot or some other dire fungal disease. He said, "Better than reindeers." He grinned at her, the corners of his eyes crinkling up into smile wrinkles, and her heart about stopped.

She pulled off her socks and pointed to the pictures. "Moose," she said.

"Whatever."

Rachel stood in the slippers while Mann hollered again for Bret, a skinny young man who stared at Rachel and shook his head. She gave him the nastiest look she could muster, but he kept staring. The photographer barked out orders, Bret switched on lights and found the backdrop Mann wanted, and then they focused on her. She felt her cheeks go hot.

"Have you done photos?" Mann asked. His accent was thick, but she understood him.

"No."

This didn't seem to bother him. "No smiles now. Keep moving. Touch hair, body. Turn to the side." He pointed at his camera. "Move with each click."

All Rachel could remember about photography was posing by the Christmas tree for her dad or linking arms with Rob in front of a scenic overlook. She felt stiff and clumsy. He clicked. She turned her head toward a desk at the end of the room and saw a laptop with her face on the screen. She froze.

"Move," he ordered.

She scratched her nose, put a finger to her hair, looked down. The lights were as hot as Mississippi in August, but her hands were freezing.

"Damn, we've got us a robot," breathed Bret, who had a British accent.

Mann set down his camera. "Okay, umm." He'd forgotten her name. "How will you relax? Vodka? Wine? Weed? Coke?"

Fairly sure he didn't mean the cola drink in a red can, Rachel shook her head. They'd take away her teaching certificate if she got busted for dope. It wasn't legal in France, was it? "Maybe a glass of wine," she said in a tiny voice. "And I'm Rachel."

Bret didn't look happy about it, but he went to a door at the end of the room and disappeared. He came back a minute later with a plastic McDonald's cup half-full of red wine. "Drink," ordered Mann.

He said nothing about her sitting down, so she stood in the middle of the white-hot loft and gulped down a few swallows. Everyone seemed to think they had to get her liquored up to do what they wanted. "Enough," she said. The last thing she wanted was to get tipsy and stupid.

"We see," the photographer said.

She remembered the little charade in Sébastien's kitchen and pretended she was Audrey, Scarlett, the Queen. She went from one to another and then mimicked her mother, Shelley, Sébastien. Mann moved with her. "More to the right, sweetheart," he mumbled. "That's good. Now you may smile, like you see your lover for the first time in a year. Good."

And so it went for several minutes until she ran dry. Bret put down a light reflector and handed her the cup. Ronald McDonald grinned at her from its side. "Asshole," she muttered and shook her head. The lights were making her sweat.

Mann laughed. "Take the cup," he urged Brett. "Like that. Give me the dirty look. Nice." He circled around her. "Now I am Kurt, your friend. You've known me since kindergarten. I wet my pants the first day of school." Rachel laughed. "That's it." He turned toward Bret. "Use the umbrella now. No shadows."

Kurt continued his patter. "I took away your chocolate. You like candy, yes? Pout for me, little girl. Ah."

Then they posed her on the sofa, an arm lying along its top. He grinned again. "Now Madame Recamier, yes? You are waiting for your lover. You hunger for him." This embarrassed her, and she shook her head.

Mann sighed. "We take break now. Jeanne!" he shouted. "More powder."

Rachel stood, and the wizened little makeup Munchkin came out and threw a cape over Rachel's shoulders. Then she fluffed a giant brush all over Rachel's face and scurried away, trailing the cape behind her.

Mann pointed at the cup, still half-full of wine. Rachel shook her head and murmured, "Music?"

He nodded so sharply she expected him to click his heels, like the Germans always did in WWII movies, and this made her smile. Too bad he wasn't taking a picture just then. Her stomach growled. She hadn't wanted to eat before the session, too nervous and afraid even a cracker would make her look fatter, but it was late now and she was starving. Then the music started, and she forgot about hunger. Deep bass notes throbbed from the speakers over by the laptop, and then an eerie melody line came in. The two played together until a thin, sinister tune was laid on top of those. Rachel closed her eyes.

"Ready?"

Mann's voice surprised her. She nodded.

"Let it take you," he murmured.

Rachel remembered how she'd felt in Sébastien's kitchen, when he'd ordered her to invite her lover to bed. The music sounded like bed, like slow, dark lovemaking. She swayed, turned her head, moved her hips. She barely heard Mann's approving noises, but she didn't take her eyes off him. With the camera held to his eyes, he was a faceless creature stalking her. The light caught his hair, shadowed his jaw. She smiled and encouraged him. The beats mimicked her heart and made her breathless. He clicked and crooned, moving to catch her on every side. She didn't want it to end.

"Good, very good," he said. "We finish, Bret."

She squinted against the harsh light to see the photographer, but suddenly the lights went out and she could see nothing at all. The music stopped. She could hear Mann telling the others to go home. His steps came closer. "Rachel?"

At least he'd remembered her name. She nodded. Her eyes still hadn't adjusted to the dimness.

"You change now," he said.

Again, she nodded and searched until she found her moose socks. She heard him chuckle as she walked back to the hair and makeup cubicle. It smelled of hair spray and cigarettes. Behind the screen, she took off the purple dress, feeling almost like she'd used some of the dope he'd offered. She slipped into her jeans and sweater and then sat in the hairdresser's chair to put on her socks and shoes. In the mirror, she saw Mann's reflection from the doorway. He was watching her.

"Incredible dress," he said.

"Thanks." She bent over to tie her shoe.

"Not yours, I think." She didn't reply. "Probably Sébastien's design." She stayed silent. "I do not think Fel has female lovers. Nor do I think you buy from him. So, why do you have such a dress?"

Rachel raised up. Her face was still hot from the lights. Or something. He was smiling at her, looking both sly and uncommonly handsome. "Just lucky, I guess," she said.

He reached forward to touch one of her curls. "Lucky is good." His fingers dug through her hair to reach her scalp and caress it. He said, "Let's have dinner."

Rachel stood, but she wasn't sure her feet were touching the nasty floor. "Is dinner part of the photo package? You know, like the frame and the matting?"

He pursed his lips. Nice ones, she thought. Very kissable. "Yes, I think it is the whole package for you, Rachel. Special deal."

Chapter Six

My mother, whom I'd called Margo since I was ten, always disparaged our family home, calling it a "haunted old heap." She usually went on to say that it was dark, impossible to heat, given to damp, and far too troublesome to bother with. Decades ago, not long after I'd left university, she bought a roomy semi-detached with all the mod cons in Truro and told my sister Vivian and me that we could sort out ownership of "Bleak House." Actually, its name was Penmore. As long as I could remember, I'd loved the house despite its gloomy corners and problematic drafts and drains. Three storeys tall with dreary hemlocks brushing its old quarry stone walls, it was deliciously Gothic. Despite its distance from Heathcliff country, I expected a Brontë ghost to come swirling around a corner any moment.

I'd come down from London at mid-week to check on the old place, although there was no need. My nephew Jeremy lived there year around. He seemed to love the house as much as I, but then he'd never truly had a home until he was an adult. Vivian's husband had worked for a petroleum company, and they'd lived overseas most of their marriage. Jeremy had attended schools in Kuwait, Texas, and Venezuela. When he was eighteen and at university here in Cornwall, my sister and her husband died in a plane crash in the Middle East. That's when he'd come to live at Penmore. After the tragedy, Margo and I tried to do our best by Jeremy, and I thought the lad had turned out reasonably well. Margo did not agree, but Margo rarely agreed with anything, especially when someone opposed her wishes. I remember the monstrous rows she and Vivian had carried on when we were young. Jeremy didn't fight with his grandmother; he simply did what he wished very quietly. I glanced at his door and saw light peeping out and started to knock. But I tried to respect Jeremy's privacy when I came to Cornwall and chose to pace about the house instead.

I walked back to the study, my father had called it the library, and checked my email once again. Nothing. And the cell phone in my pocket stayed ominously quiet. Rachel had promised that she'd call after her photo shoot with Kurt Mann, which, she'd said, was to begin at six-thirty in the evening. It was past eleven now; surely the photography had ended.

There was absolutely no logical reason why I should feel such protectiveness for Rachel, except that, as a model for the protagonist in my current novel, she felt like my daughter, or niece. I frowned at my laptop. I could, of course, make use of this time; I'd planned to get several chapters done while in Cornwall. But I'd already done several pages that afternoon and felt as though I'd used up my allotment of words for the day. I once used that phrase with Sébastien and received a sneering reply: "As if you would ever run out of words."

I heard steps. "Still up, Uncle Edgar? Are you working?" Jeremy was wrapped up in a heavy sweater. His room's proximity to the kitchen didn't completely alleviate the house's usual chilly temperatures.

"Yes. No." I was a bit testy. I abhor being caught at idleness, even if I do spend far too many hours in that state. My editor had been hounding me about a deadline for weeks.

"Well, I'm for bed," he said. "I'll start on those bulbs you wanted for the south end of the house in the morning."

I had to soften at this. Jeremy had been running his own greenhouse and nursery for years now and was doing well. And with all that, he still took care of the grounds around the house and cheerfully suffered through my visits and infrequent but passionate bouts of home and garden domesticity. Margo wasn't so charitable about Jeremy: "University education, a bit of money, and what does he do with it? Digs in the dirt."

"Excellent. I'll look forward to seeing tulips and daffodils next spring."

"Right," the boy said. "Good-night."

I wished him a good night as well and realized I shouldn't be thinking of him as a boy. Jeremy had turned thirty a month ago. Once again I checked my email. Nothing. I wandered around the house, listening to its creaks and moans and stopped off in the lounge to pour myself a tot of whisky. I could call Rachel, I suppose, but that seemed horribly presumptuous. It was just that I'd heard so many tales about Kurt Mann. He'd bedded nearly every model in the business and was as faithful as a tomcat. I didn't think Rachel was prepared for that. Making up my mind in an instant, I dialed Sébastien's number instead, figuring he'd never answer. But he did.

"Have you seen Rachel since her session with Mann?" I asked.

"And hello, how are you, Sébastien?" he drawled. "Manners, Mr. Tremaine."

I ignored this. "I'm worried about her."

Sébastien's reply was a yawn. There was noise in the background, music and conversation. He was at a party or bar.

"You're not even home," I said. "You're drinking and playing while something terrible could be happening to that girl. You know Mann's reputation."

"She is an adult, Edgar. Quit being a mother duck."

I supposed he meant 'hen,' but I'd taught him English, so I took the blame for his idiomatic lapses. "She's a French teacher. From a small town in Ohio, wherever that is. And now she's in a foreign country with the biggest playboy in Europe."

Sébastien didn't speak for a moment. Someone near the phone laughed. A masculine laugh. "I'm not ready to go home." He sounded as annoyed as I felt. "I'll check on your precious girl in the morning."

"My girl? You're the one who made her stay." He was with someone; that was obvious. After our break-up I'd never found anyone who'd come close to replacing Sébastien, even short term. He'd found dozens of substitutes for me. "Should one of us call her? You could leave your new boyfriend for a moment, couldn't you?"

"How very prissy, Eddie. She'll call if she needs us."

"Will you at least go home, then?"

He muttered something to someone else. "As you will have noticed," he said, ice in his words, "I do have my phone turned on in case she calls, but I have no intention whatsoever of returning home." And he hung up.

There was nothing more I could do. I sipped my drink, checked my email again, and went to bed, sure our little Rachel had been ravished.

The next day I awoke early with the firm resolution of returning to London immediately. I'd planned to stay longer, and it made no sense to leave except that it was much easier to get to Paris from London than Cornwall. And my London flat was far warmer than Penmore. Perhaps I'd write more easily there too, I thought, but I knew this was a pale excuse. Discipline doesn't require a locale. When I wandered down to the kitchen to make tea, I caught a glimpse of Jeremy trekking across the back garden carrying a muddy, bulky parcel and a trowel. "Hello," I called out the back door.

"Morning," he replied. It was cold, gray, and windy. Although we had no view of the sea from Penmore, I could smell it.

"As soon as I gather up my things, I'm going back to London," I said. "Could you take me to the train or should I call Tony?" Tony worked for Jeremy but enjoyed the extra money he earned by carting me around and doing errands. He also enjoyed driving my auto, a rather nice BMW that I kept in the country.

"Of course I can. The usual train?" He struggled to see his wristwatch, but he knew, as did I, that we had plenty of time to get to Truro.

"Yes, the usual." I thought for a moment. "Also, would you ring your grandmother and tell her I won't be joining her for dinner tomorrow evening? It's too early to call her now."

He shifted the bulky bag. "Sure, but she won't like it." The wind whipped at his brown hair, worn a little long, according to Margo. "What shall I tell her? It usually helps to have some kind of excuse." This was accompanied by a charming grin. I couldn't understand why the local girls weren't vying for him, but then maybe they were. As I recall there'd been a girl when he was at university. He'd even brought her home to meet Margo, which had probably ended the romance right then and there. He'd never spoken of her again, as I'd never mentioned my break-up with Sébastien. We didn't pry, but often I wondered if he ever brought a girl home from the pub. I hoped so, but I doubted that I'd ever know. Jeremy had made inscrutability into an art form.

I shrugged and waved my hand capriciously. "An excuse? For Margo? Hmm. Just tell her it has to do with a woman."

His mouth dropped open, and a wayward wisp of hair caught on his eyebrow. He still hadn't shut his mouth when I closed the door against the chill.

Chapter Seven

It had been the special package all right, Rachel thought as she stared at the ceiling above Kurt's bed. A special delivery special package. Twisting one of her curls around a finger, she grinned. Last night, after they left the studio, they'd walked in the rain two or three blocks to a tiny restaurant near one of the bridges. She didn't know which one. They'd eaten plain food, stew of some sort, and hard, crunchy rolls that he'd broken into bits and fed to her. He'd focused his eyes on her as meticulously as he'd done his camera. And she'd performed. Oh, yeah.

She heard him splashing around in the shower and sat up to move the window blind. It was full morning; the rain had stopped, and the gray sky was light, like Kurt's eyes. Flopping back down on the bed, she recalled how back in college she'd thought lovemaking with John Shumate had been nice. Maybe it had been, but *nice* had nothing whatsoever to do with Kurt Mann. She sighed. He'd run his hands over her belly, her thighs, all the plumpest parts, and whispered that she was a ripe peach, she was sweet cream. And then he'd kissed, licked, kneaded, and thoroughly enjoyed every bit of her. Nice didn't even begin to cover it.

The water stopped. Rachel scanned the room for a robe or something she could cover herself with. Last night they'd drunk a lot of wine. And it had been dark. She settled for a fuzzy afghan and wrapped it carefully around her body. In the daylight he might think she was a watermelon rather than a peach.

After the restaurant but before they'd come back last night, they'd stopped at a smoky bar and drunk cognac. He'd swirled the amber liquid in his glass, lifted it, and said, "Up the bottom, Pancake," which had made her laugh so hard she'd spilled liquor on her jeans, now lying crumpled on the bedroom floor. She hated the idea of putting on yesterday's clothes.

"Bottoms up," she'd corrected him when she'd finally been able to speak. She'd wondered at the "Pancake" too. There was nothing flat about her, but he seemed to use food terms as endearments. Last night when he'd been kissing her, she was pretty sure he'd called her "Strudel." She wrinkled her nose.

Rachel showered, and they dried each other's hair, his was longer than hers, and then he suggested breakfast. His vast, modern apartment, one floor down from the studio, did have a kitchen. She'd caught a glimpse of it the night before, but it didn't look as if anybody used it.

As they walked to a café, they held hands and kissed at stoplights. She loved the feel of his lips, and when his hip brushed hers, she felt little shivers spark her body. Oh, Mama, she thought. She was falling hard for this guy. Over croissants and coffee, he asked her about Ohio but mostly wanted to know why she was in Paris.

"Just touring around," she said. Damn Sébastien and his infernal need for secrecy.

And who was her father? How did he know Sébastien? Why did she need the portfolio of photos? Publicity for what?

"My father's in communications," she replied. Wayne Bowman had been the postmaster in Morton, Ohio for sixteen years. "But no one you would know," she added.

Kurt took a huge bite out of his croissant. "So why do you need publicity photos?" His eyes had her as fixed as a butterfly on a pin.

Rachel shrugged. "I'm opening up another aspect of his business." She certainly hoped not. Being a postal worker didn't thrill her at all, but after losing her teaching job, she might be lugging mail all over the county. On one of the awful rural routes. Then again, when she looked at Kurt's dimples, she thought she might be staying in Paris the rest of her life.

Kurt repeated his earlier question. "How does he know Sébastien?"

He was a persistent little thing. Not so little, she corrected herself, remembering his shoulders and muscular thighs. But he wasn't much taller than she was.

She waved an airy hand. "Oh, my father knows lots of people." And all of their addresses. She touched Kurt's hand. "Tell me about you," she crooned. "Where are you from and how did you end up in Paris? I want to know all about you." She gave him a look that made her blush at herself, and he chuckled and went off into a long verbal résumé.

Finally, though, he looked at his watch and threw some euros on the table. "I have a meeting," he said. "And then I shoot pictures at 2:00. We have dinner tonight?" He smiled. Those dimples. Last night she'd kissed them and dipped her fingers into their crevices. "And maybe dance?"

Rachel grinned and nodded although she didn't feel too good about her dance moves. "When?"

"Maybe nine," he said. "I pick you up where?"

Back to the secrecy again, Rachel thought. "I'll meet you," she said. "Or come to your place."

Kurt frowned. "Are you staying at a bad hotel? What?"

She was about to make up some story about a prudish traveling companion but decided to use the all-purpose Parisian shrug. "Where and when?"

"Okay. *Le Club Clic* at around nine. In the bar." With an open-mouthed, enthusiastic kiss that tasted of butter and coffee, he left Rachel sitting at the table, staring at her half-eaten croissant and wondering if she'd landed in Fairyland.

But the cool morning air and a trip on the Metro brought her back to earth, at least a little. She got off the train near the Luxembourg Gardens, which over the past few weeks had become one of her favorite places to wander. The geraniums and sturdy old zinnias were looking puny now, but the fallen leaves were nearly as brilliant as the blossoms she bought every few days and displayed in her room or the kitchen. Exotic lilies, a nosegay of violets, honest carnations—she loved the flowersellers of Paris. She strolled for a while and then sat on one of the chairs strewn about the park. The leaves reminded her of barbecue potato chips, one of her favorites. She wondered if she could buy them anywhere in Paris.

Paris, she thought. I'm in Paris and I have a lover. Her body produced a faint facsimile of last night's sensations. And I'm meeting him tonight, she thought. Dancing! Lord, it'd been years since she'd gone clubbing, college actually, and even then it'd been rare since they'd had to drive all the way to Columbus to find a club. She had a *boyfriend*, she thought, putting the title into italics in her head. This made her smile so broadly that an elderly woman walking a tiny dog stared at her. Kurt was a man of the world, Rachel thought. He tossed off cities where he'd lived and worked like they were nothing: Munich, Berlin, Barcelona. Geez, it sounded like one of those whirlwind European tours. Speaking of whirlwind, she thought, and felt a tiny clutch of guilt. Too fast, too crazy, and for one second, she remembered dear old Edgar's warnings about Kurt. But this was Paris, sophisticated

Paris, and he liked her. He really did. So what if she'd fallen into bed with him on the first date?

She probably should go home, maybe take a nap since she hadn't slept much last night. This made her grin again, and she looked up and down the leaf-covered sidewalk to see if anybody was watching. And she'd have to find out where this club was. Maybe she'd give herself a facial; her hairdresser, Sébastien's choice of course, had given her some creams and lotions. She needed some new make-up and some lipstick, although she'd never been too fond of it. Red, she thought, bright red so she could leave her mark on Kurt. This brought yet another smile. And she'd have to decide what to wear. Clubbing could be designer jeans or skin and sparkles; she knew that much, but she didn't have clothes for either one. Although it seemed as though her entire reason for being these days was clothes, her wardrobe was limited. Too bad Sébastien wouldn't let her wear the purple dress. He'd said it was hers to keep, but, other than the photography session, she wasn't supposed to wear it until Fashion Week. She felt like she looked pretty hot in that dress. Hadn't she attracted Kurt in it?

And then she stood up, panic screeching through her brain. She'd left the purple dress at the studio. They'd gone for dinner and then drinks and then Kurt's apartment, and she'd never thought once about getting the dress. Sébastien would kill her. Retracing her steps at a run, she jumped on the subway and kept tapping her foot until the train reached the stop near Kurt's. The dress was fine, she thought. She was positive that Kurt had locked up his studio before they went to dinner, but she still felt anxious.

She bolted to the top floor and jiggled the studio doorknob. Locked. Of course it was. He'd said that he didn't have another shoot until 2:00. She went down a floor and knocked on Kurt's door. No answer. Leaning against the wall, she fumbled in her purse for her phone. Last night when he was nuzzling her neck, she'd made him give her his number. She punched it in, but it went straight to voice mail. Then she texted him and told him about the dress and asked him to put it in his apartment. And then she wrote a note saying the same thing, made a copy of it, and stuck one under both the studio and apartment doors. There. That was the best she could do, and she wasn't about to let a little forgetfulness ruin this momentous day.

She'd shop. Sébastien had taken forever to pay her, but it had been worth the wait. She had her own French bank account now, bulging with euros. She could afford something new. If she could find anything that fit. Maybe she'd buy some kick-ass shoes. Waist measurements didn't matter when you bought shoes. But she wasn't quite sure what else she'd wear. Maybe she could find something somewhere.

A

It was after seven when Rachel heard Sébastien come home. She was in her room, staring at the clothes on her bed. She'd found an incredibly expensive black swing jacket that gave her enough room to breathe, and she'd visited Gisèle's shop and bought a dark red camisole that was really underwear but would do as a tank. And then there were the shoes. Gorgeous black things with pointed toes and stiletto heels that made her feel like a tramp. She giggled. She'd rather be a tramp than a pancake. "Hello," she called out to Sébastien. "Come see what I've bought."

He leaned against the door frame. "What do you think?" she asked.

Touching the beautifully tailored gray pants, he nodded. Of course he did; they were from his *atelier*. He examined the shoes. He'd better approve, Rachel thought. They'd cost a fortune. He gave them a tiny nod. But he frowned at the jacket and ignored the camisole. "You're going out," he said.

Pretty obvious. "Yes."

"With Kurt?"

Rachel nodded.

Sébastien lifted one of his eyebrows. "Edgar fears for your virtue."

"I know," Rachel said. "He left six voice mails on my phone. I finally called the old dear and told him I'm fine." She looked up at Sébastien. "Are you going to fuss too?"

"No. Enjoy yourself. But Monsieur Mann is for enjoyment, not, shall we say, permanence."

"I figured." She could hope, though, couldn't she?

Sébastien looked at her closet. "Where's the dress?"

She waved her hand at the few garments hanging there. "Oh, I forgot and left it at Kurt's studio. I haven't been able to get in touch with him, but I'm sure it's safe."

Sébastien swelled up until he seemed seven feet tall. "You imbecile! You just left the dress where anybody could see it? A work of art from the new collection?" He smacked the wall, which, Rachel thought, was probably a substitute for her face.

"I'll get it tonight," she said. He was such a drama king. What did it matter?

But his anger went way beyond dramatizing. "You idiot," he spat. "If that dress ends up in the hands of the press, everyone will know what I'm doing. They'll look at the size. They'll see the style." He flew off into a flurry of French that Rachel couldn't translate, nor did she want to. "The surprise," he shouted, back to English. "The originality. Gone, all gone, because a silly girl can't think of anything but sex."

"Now, wait a minute," Rachel cautioned.

But he didn't stick around to get her reaction. Spinning, he left the room, slamming the door like an overwrought teenager. She could hear him shouting as he went down the hall. Her temper was rising too. What was she? A well-paid slave? He didn't have to suffer insults about size and weight. He didn't have to spend hours by himself without friends or family. Until she met Kurt, the nearest thing to a friend she'd had was Gisèle. All over a stupid dress, she raged inside her head. She'd told Kurt a gazillion lies about where she was living and why she needed the photos. Wasn't that enough? It wasn't like a purple dress was a state secret. She kicked off her athletic shoes and stormed into the bathroom.

By the time a taxi dropped her at *Le Club Clic*, Rachel had calmed down. She touched her wrist to her nose: Sylvestri Silver. She smelled wonderful and looked pretty good too, she thought. The bar wasn't particularly crowded, but it was early by club standards. She smiled at the barman and ordered wine. To sip, she told herself. Alcohol had blurred last night's bliss a little. She wanted to remember every minute tonight. It was another thirty minutes before Kurt showed up wearing what he'd thrown on that morning. Right after they'd made love, Rachel thought with a lovely twinge that tickled her belly. She leaned into his hug. "Busy day?"

He nodded at her and at the barman who'd asked if he wanted his usual. "Meetings and pictures," Kurt said. He took a swig from what looked like gin or vodka. "Another day in Paris." He smiled and kissed her neck. "Umm, delicious. Oranges, yes?"

There was a hint of citrus in her Sylvestri perfume, and maybe she didn't care if he talked like she was something on a menu as long as he kept sampling the dishes. God, she loved his lips.

"I want to see you in brown," he said, looking at the cleavage peeking over Gisèle's camisole. "Chocolate, like mousse."

Thinking of her moose socks, Rachel giggled. "I'll keep that in mind," she murmured, thinking she didn't need wine to be giddy.

"Oh, and the dress," he said. Damn, she was about to forget it again. "I took it to my apartment. It is safe." His hand slipped under her jacket and slid over the silk to her breast. "We'll go there later, yes?"

To hell with dinner, Rachel thought, probably for the first time in her life. She was ready to go right now, and it had nothing to do with the damned dress. "Mm, hmm," she murmured in what she hoped was a sexy purr.

But they didn't leave. *Le Club Clic* was a bar, restaurant, and club. They ate, sitting hip to hip, and between courses, Kurt dipped his hand under the table and skated it up and down her leg. Rachel wished she'd worn a skirt, but they probably would've been arrested if she had. Well. Maybe not in Paris where people seemed to do all kinds of sexy things in public. Around ten, when they were finishing a meal she'd paid no attention to, she heard a deep thud of electronic percussion coming from the club area. Kurt was feeding her cheesecake. "We dance?" he asked. His eyes were no more than six inches from her face.

"Yes. We dance."

For the most part, the club area was black as midnight in the jungle. Bright pink neon stripes flashed from corners and onto the ceiling, but they didn't do much to illuminate the place. Rachel would've stumbled if Kurt hadn't been holding her tight against his body. The music was loud, percussive, and continuous. Although some people danced, many stood around the edge of the room. It was too dark to see gender. She could see shadowy arms raised and hear occasional shouts. For joy, she supposed. Kurt was moving, shuffling in rhythm to the music, so she tried to imitate him. She couldn't see, but that was okay by her. Other people couldn't see her either.

The room reminded her of a grown-up version of the rave she'd let her roommate drag her to their freshman year at college. Like the warehouse where the rave had been, this room was scented with cigarettes and stale liquor. And Kurt, who smelled like a healthy animal. He was rubbing against her, and there was no way to ignore his umm, interest. She wasn't sure whether to be embarrassed or proud. At the other end of the room people clustered around a dimly lit, glassed-in booth. A long-haired girl was working the turntables, flicking knobs, and swaying to the beats she created.

"She is Emma," Kurt shouted in her ear. "The best mixes in Paris, and she's adorable."

The music was good; Rachel knew that much. Life was good. Dancing was good. She gave over her mind and body to Emma's music. And Kurt. When they'd shuffled for quite a while, he grabbed her hand and pulled her toward the door. She figured they were leaving, but he stopped at the bar, pulled out a handkerchief, and wiped the sweat from his face. "Very hot," he said, grinning at her.

"Very." It was much lighter in the bar, and she wondered if her hair and make-up had melted.

"Drink for you?" he asked. "Maybe champagne?"

It was tempting. "Just a soda. A Coke," she said. He shrugged and ordered.

Rachel heard a high squeal, and a tall, thin woman flew across the room to envelop Kurt in a hug. She started babbling in French and kissed him. Right on the mouth. He didn't seem to mind. Rachel pasted a smile on her face. When the woman turned her face toward Rachel, she recognized her. Lucy, Sébastien's ex-model, the one who'd had such a fit with Madame Pauline. Kurt waved a hand at Rachel and said, "Lucy, Rachel, American." He kept an arm around both Lucy's and Rachel's waists.

Lucy gave Rachel a blatant once-over, but then her focus went back to Kurt, whispering in his ear and laughing as she took tiny sips from a glass full of red liquid. Rachel was glad she'd run from the room that day in Madame Pauline's office. She felt sure that Lucy didn't recognize her, but she did seem to be talking about her. Between the whispers, the giggles, and the rapid speech, Rachel got only about one word in five, but her French had improved dramatically over the past few weeks, and she was fairly certain Lucy was teasing Kurt about his taste in women.

Watching Lucy twine her skinny arm around Kurt's back, Rachel sucked on her Coke and thought about making an exit for the bathroom. Instead, she moved a couple of inches closer to Kurt, pressing against his hip. Ownership, bitch, she thought, but kept her smile. Kurt spent a long minute whispering in Lucy's ear.

Lucy let out a loud trill of laughter and then kissed Kurt again. Looking straight into his eyes, she asked, "We both get what we want, yes?"

Kurt said, "Okay. Yes. We will work on it. I'll call you." Lucy waved and threaded her way through the crowd. Kurt turned to Rachel like nothing had happened. "Old friend," he said. "I have taken her picture many times. A model, yes?"

"Oh, yes," replied Rachel. She watched Lucy's impossibly high-heeled boots disappear. "Maybe old lover?"

"No, no," he protested. "Business, only business."

Right, thought Rachel. But Lucy had left, and Kurt was still there with her. She grinned at him. "Do we have business?"

A

The next afternoon Rachel went again to see Gisèle. It would have to be brown lingerie, she thought, because yesterday's shopping had again confirmed that she couldn't fit into clothes the nice shops carried. Finding the black swing jacket with its generous cut had been a fluke. And even though the place Gisèle had sent her for sweaters did have larger sizes, they had only casual, cheap clothes, nothing cool enough for Kurt. Kurt, who wanted to see her in brown.

"My little American again!" Gisèle gushed, pushing Rachel to the back of the shop where there was a small kitchen. "You wore the red camisole last night? He liked it? She pointed at a table. "Sit. I'll make tea."

Rachel assured Gisèle that Kurt had liked it very much, except that she never called him Kurt. She didn't know if he was famous or not and didn't want to deal with it if he was, so she just called him "my photographer" or "my lover," which made Gisèle twinkle. "He says he wants to see me in brown," she said. "You know I can't find anything in the shops, and there's no time to order anything online."

Gisèle was busy at the stove. "As I told you, there are places; otherwise I would go naked, yes?" She winked one very blue eye at Rachel. "But you need this for tonight?"

Rachel nodded.

Gisèle dipped teabags up and down in two large mugs. Rachel smelled apples and spice. "I thought maybe you'd have a brown camisole. I'd rather have a jacket or a dress, but there's not time." She'd rather have one of Sébastien's incredible creations, but that was impossible. Besides, he'd never let it out of his sight after the fiasco with the purple dress, which was, once again, safe and sound in her closet. She'd brought it home that morning.

Gisèle set the two mugs and a plate of little butter cookies on the table. She raised a penciled eyebrow. "Is this man worth all the trouble?"

"Oh yes," Rachel chirped. "He takes me lovely places, and he compliments me." She could feel her cheeks redden about the other things Kurt did. "He's good to me."

Gisèle crunched her way through three cookies and washed them down with a great gulp of tea. "So, you do whatever he asks?"

Rachel saw nothing wrong with that and nodded again. For a man like Kurt Mann to find her attractive was a miracle. She wanted to clean his apartment and make his meals. She wanted to iron his shirts.

Gisèle frowned but said, "Never mind. I worry too much. We must find you something brown for your lover." She shouted at her clerk and told her she'd be back in a moment. Lifting her huge body from the chair, she patted Rachel's shoulder and went out the back door. Rachel could hear her outside lumbering up metal stairs. Maybe like Kurt, Gisèle lived where she worked.

In no time, Gisèle returned, holding a brown jacket. "Silk velvet," the woman said. "I wore it twenty years and twenty kilos ago. I think it will fit you."

She held it out to Rachel, who shook her head. "I don't feel right about borrowing it."

"I insist," Gisèle said. "Try it on."

Rachel shed her sweater and slipped into the jacket, loving the softness of the fabric and the way it skimmed her body. It was a riding jacket, Rachel thought, fitted and long. It took her a while to fasten all the little buttons. Gisèle smiled and held up her hands as if to say I told you so, and Rachel hurried into the shop for a mirror. It was lovely, a perfect fit, and Kurt had been right. The brown complimented her hair and brought a glow to her skin. "I'll be very careful with it," she promised Gisèle.

"Wait," the woman said. She disappeared again and came back with a frothy lace bra. "Put this on."

Rachel took off the jacket and her bra right in front of Gisèle and thought how worldly and sophisticated she'd become. Cut very low, the bra was deep beige and pushed her breasts up to mind-boggling heights. The valley between them wasn't cleavage; it was a crevasse. "Now, the jacket," Gisèle ordered.

Rachel obeyed.

When she'd buttoned all those little boogers again, Gisèle smiled. "That is fine for when you see your grandmother. For your lover—" She unbuttoned several of the top buttons, revealing creamy breasts threatening to break out of their cage. "*Voilà.*"

Damn. This was chocolate mousse with whipped cream on top. "*Voilà,*" agreed Rachel.

"What will you wear with it?"

Rachel thought. "Jeans. My other pair."

Gisèle nodded. "Good. But not the gym shoes I hope?"

Giggling, Rachel said no, maybe some brown heels.

"No, no, no. Flats. Maybe bronze or with a jewel. Flats. And some very long, dangling earrings." She gestured so Rachel would be sure to understand.

Gisèle had a good eye, probably developed by the Great Man himself. Yesterday, Gisèle had said that she knew all the secrets. She'd talked to her friend, Madame Pauline. Lifting her finger to her lips, she'd asked Rachel to tell her about Sébastien's current designs and nodded knowingly when Rachel described them. Very Fel, Gisèle had said: artistic and beautiful. She'd said that she'd helped him with his very first collection, even before Valenciana.

Rachel said, "Okay, flats. And I'll return the jacket to you tomorrow."

"It's yours," the woman said. "The only way I could fit into it again was if I was dying of cancer. And then I wouldn't care."

Horrified, Rachel started to protest but, seeing the mischief in Gisèle's eyes, laughed along with her. She hugged the woman, paid for the bra, flew out of the shop, and made a beeline for a bench where she texted Shelley: *I'm in love!!! He's German and a photographer and has long, blond hair in a ponytail. OMG!!! I just got the most gorgeous brown velvet riding jacket to wear for him tonight, and I think I'm in heaven. I'll write you more soon—I have to get SHOES! Again! I bought stilettos yesterday, and I'm buying flats today. Will send pic tonight. I'm delirious!*

She didn't text her mother. Or Edgar.

For a glorious two weeks the pattern was the same. Kurt and Rachel ate dinner together, drank or went to a club--another smoky, sexy one the night of the brown jacket-- and ended up at his apartment for lovemaking that felt like an Olympic event. He never tired. Rachel, however, crept back to Sébastien's each morning for a long soak and a nap. She ignored her "Paris by Inches" plan. She quit stopping at *pâtisseries* to get eclairs or chocolate croissants. She was in love. Sure, it bothered her that women kissed and fondled Kurt everywhere they went. Edgar's warnings flashed through her mind with aggravating regularity. But this was a different world, and Kurt spent every night with her. That was fidelity, wasn't it? The lying, which she was doing only because Sébastien demanded it, annoyed her more than the other women. Kurt made no secret of the fact that he flatly disbelieved most everything she told him, although he persisted in asking her questions about Sylvestri. It was frustrating. She might not be the most experienced woman in the world, but she knew a healthy relationship was built upon honesty, not lies, and she dreamed of a long future with Kurt. Sébastien was barely speaking to her, even after the quick return of the purple dress, and she knew he'd never allow her to tell Kurt the truth.

On Saturday morning while they were eating breakfast in their usual steamy café, Rachel asked Kurt if they could go to a movie that night or just have a long, leisurely dinner at home. She was tired of clubs, and she was especially tired of watching Kurt make no effort whatsoever to fend off the hordes of women who mobbed him every night. "I know," she said. "Let's stay in tonight. I could make dinner at your apartment. It would be fun. I could shop this morning and find some good wine, some nice vegetables, maybe steaks or some fish. I'd love to cook for you. And we could rent a movie. You have a DVD player, don't you?"

He was shoveling omelet into his mouth. He loved to eat, and she loved watching him do it. When he finally swallowed he said, "No."

"Oh," she said. Hell, she had money. "I'll buy you one."

"No," he said again. "I have a machine. I do not want to stay in."

"Why not?"

"Boring." He attacked the eggs again but slipped his other hand between her knees. "We go out; then we go back to the apartment."

She was disappointed. The only time she had him to herself was in bed, and although that was beyond wonderful, she wanted conversation and cuddling. All they ever did was eat, drink, dance, and make love. But she tried to hide her discontent. "Okay, so where will it be tonight?"

He slid his hand a little higher. "A party. With all kinds of beautiful people. We will have a good time, yes? Here, I will write down the address since you must be so mysterious. I would pick you up, you know."

Rachel had been thinking about this. If she moved in with Kurt there wouldn't be any question of her address any more. Maybe she would bring it up tonight or tomorrow. It seemed awfully soon to be considering this, but everything else had moved fast. She grinned at the thought. Maybe fast was good. Fashion Week would be here soon.

He was in the process of slugging down the rest of his coffee when his phone rang. Frowning at the number, Kurt growled, "*Oui*" into the phone and listened with a scowl on his face. Rachel could hear a faint voice, decidedly male.

"I said it would be soon." Kurt turned his head away from Rachel. His French was guttural, accented, and sounded menacing. After another pause, he said, "Some now. Some later. As I said. Soon." He listened another few seconds and clicked the phone shut without saying anything more.

"Problems?" asked Rachel.

He shook his head and said something in German that she would've bet was an obscenity, but he wouldn't tell her anything more. She guessed she wasn't the only one with secrets.

A

He'd said that she shouldn't arrive until ten o'clock, late enough that she took a cab rather than the Metro. Since she'd met Kurt, she'd all but given over to taxis. The address was in an arty section of Paris, according to the book Edgar had given her. Great, she thought, beautiful, talented people. And dumpy old Rachel Bowman. She was still ticked off that Kurt thought an evening alone with her would be boring, and she didn't feel good about what she was wearing: her ancient, all-purpose black skirt and once again the black jacket and red camisole. Back home she hardly ever paid attention to her clothes, but in Paris they seemed to matter way too much.

She paid the cabbie and went upstairs. The door to the apartment was open and people oozed into the hallway and landing. A languid blonde near the doorway smiled. It took a few seconds before

Rachel realized the woman was an actress, and she'd seen at least two of her movies. The apartment was huge and absolutely jammed with people. She wondered how she'd ever find Kurt. Music thudded in competition with loud conversation and occasional bursts of laughter. It might as well be a club, except there was a bit more light. Rachel scanned the room as best she could and tried not to step on all the well-shod feet. Edging over to one wall, she managed to make her way through silk, cashmere, and perfume until she came up against an immovable mass of bodies at the bar. She tried to get around them, but as she was inching her way, she bumped into a tall man in black. Nearly all the men wore black. Head down, she muttered, "*Excusez-moi.*"

She'd stepped on his shoe when she lurched into him, and she sensed his irritation. "*Pardon?*" he sneered. It was Sébastien.

Rachel raised her head and smiled. "I didn't expect to see you." She had, of course, switched back to English.

He frowned. "You do not know me," he ordered. "Go away."

Her smile faded. "Okay. You're just a bad-tempered stranger."

"What are you doing here? Do you know these people?"

She shook her head. "I'm meeting Kurt, but I haven't found him yet."

Sébastien looked from side to side, but no one was paying the least attention to them. Then he surveyed the room. It must be nice to be that tall, Rachel thought. "He's over there." Sébastien pointed. "With a woman."

She mumbled her thanks and ducked her head again, trying to move through the throng to where Sébastien had pointed. It took a while before she spotted Kurt. A gorgeous red-head in a very short skirt was standing next to him, but Kurt was talking to a bald guy with a pronounced paunch. Wow, another fat person in Paris. Baldy was chatting up a storm and glancing over his shoulder to aim his eyes at the bar. She could still see Sébastien there, nearly a head taller than everybody else. As Rachel came closer she noticed that Kurt wore an odd half-smile, an expression Rachel recognized from their hours in bed. Something or someone was pleasing him. She took a deep breath, stuck a smile on her face, and broke through the crowd. "Hello, Kurt."

He didn't look remotely guilty. "My strudel. Come here." He kissed her, one hand gliding over the cheap polyester covering her rear end. "It's a fine party, yes? Your friend Sébastien is here. I think he is doing the Academy Awards gown for Melia." Okay, that was the actress's name. "She's here too."

"I didn't see him," Rachel lied. "But I noticed Melia when I came in." The fat man stared at her for a long minute, probably appalled at her weight although he was far from a gym rat. Finally he and the red-head drifted away. Kurt introduced her to their host, a painter, and then eased her around the room to show her one of the man's works. She asked for wine.

As usual, Kurt pumped her about Sébastien, but he was more specific this time. "Does he say things about the collection? What is the theme this year? Tell me." His intent stare made her uncomfortable.

She looked away. "I don't know anything about it. I don't see him."

Kurt made a disgusted little noise. "I think you lie to me." But he smiled.

Rachel smiled back and brushed her hand against his jeans. "Never."

Two glasses of wine later, Rachel wanted a bathroom, and Kurt was helping her find one when they entered a dim bedroom with wide windows offering a spectacular view of Paris. A short man stood alone at the window and turned when he heard them. His face was corrugated with wrinkles, but he stood as erect as a soldier. A thick wave of white hair dipped over his forehead. Immediately Kurt started sputtering apologies in what she thought might be bad Italian. He was all but bowing and scraping as he grabbed Rachel's hand and pulled her from the room. "What's that all about?" she asked, annoyed because she really did need to go. "Who was that man?"

"You do not know him?" Kurt was incredulous. "That was Kristof Pauli, the most important designer in the world. The top, the very top. I would give anything to have work from him. Anything."

Rachel knocked back the rest of her wine. "He looked like a very old horse jockey to me. Do you think there's another bathroom down this way?"

Å

Hours later, Rachel awoke for the sixteenth morning in a row in Kurt's bed. She'd counted. Stretching, she noticed that, as usual, his side of the bed was empty even though it was very early. He always woke before her, and the thought of knowing this little quirk, this little pattern of his, made her smile. Pressing her forearm to her nose, she smelled his skin, not hers, and she liked that too. She also smelled coffee. They'd always gone out for breakfast, but it would be fun to lay around together on a Sunday morning. She slipped into the robe Sébastien had loaned her, one of several little things she'd brought over to Kurt's apartment and kept there. She was still thinking about how much she'd love it if he agreed that she should move in. And she wasn't about to let Sébastien get in her way if he did.

It was the first time she'd seen Kurt in the kitchen. He was fully dressed, even to his leather jacket, and was folding papers into his messenger bag. "Good morning," she said, walking over to him and kissing a dimple. "You're up early for a Sunday."

He gave her a faint smile and grabbed a mug out of the cabinet. "Coffee?"

When she turned to fill her cup, she saw a duffel bag by the front door. Another bag, probably full of cameras and equipment, leaned against it. "Are you going somewhere?"

"Yes. I've just called a taxi." He upended his mug and set it in the sink. "I'm doing a shoot in Egypt, and then I go to another in Greece. I am gone a long time."

Rachel wondered if she was still dreaming. A really bad dream. "You're leaving?" Without her. Without saying a word about it. "When were you going to tell me?" She spied an open pen and pad of paper on the counter. "Or were you just going to leave a note?" He blinked. That's what he'd intended, the jerk.

"No, no," he said. "I was waking you soon. You must take your things when you go this morning. He looked away. "I am gone a long time," he repeated.

Her heart was beating way too fast. Had she annoyed him in some way? They'd left the party early, stopped at a bar for a drink, and come home. She'd started thinking of his apartment, not Sébastien's, as home. They'd made love twice, once only a couple of hours ago. "I could go with you," she said.

Kurt shook his head. "I'll be shooting. Busy."

"Not all the time." It sounded lame and needy. She should just shut up, but she couldn't help herself. "When will you be back? Will I see you then?"

He shrugged. "I call you."

Right. She'd been warned. Her use-by date was today. He fished a key out of his pocket. "Lock up when you go. Then push key under the studio door. Bret will get it later today." Kurt's eyes and voice were all business. He was telling her she'd better not keep the key. "I have a travel phone. Different," he said. And he was telling her not to call.

She held out her hand for the key. It was warm from his body. "How long have you known you'd be leaving?"

"Oh, a while. Business." He shrugged again and leaned to kiss her cheek. "Lots of fun, Rachel. You are a fine girl." Then he turned, grabbed his bags, and left, giving her a big, dimpled smile and a wink as he left.

Her first instinct was to throw the mug at his front door or find scissors and cut up his clothes. Or maybe flood his bathroom or burn his furniture. Something a psycho lover would do. But she wasn't psycho, or at least she didn't think so. Stupid, maybe. She set her full mug next to his empty one in the sink. He'd never said anything about love, nor had she. And he'd certainly never hinted at the future. It had just been for fun, as he'd said. Except it hadn't.

She gathered up her makeup and toothbrush and stuffed everything she'd been keeping at his apartment into a bag. Crying wouldn't do any good, but she did it anyway, sobbing for a minute or two. She put on her jacket, closed and locked the door, and left, just as she'd done the past few mornings. It might've been easier if it had only been one night. She might not have fallen for him. Maybe, like him, she might've just considered it fun, except she couldn't do that. She was a small-town ignorant fool. After sliding the key under the studio door, she trudged down the steps and went out into the gray, chilly morning. She dreaded facing Sébastien who would probably be home since it was Sunday morning, but she didn't have anywhere else to go.

Chapter Eight

Sébastien was sitting on the living room sofa, wearing glasses he didn't like to admit to needing, and reading a newspaper. He had on his green Chinese pajamas that Rachel teased him about but really thought were sort of cool. He gave her a long look over the top of his glasses. "He dumped you," he said. It wasn't a question. "Is that the correct verb?"

Rachel set down her tote and shrugged out of her jacket. "It's the correct verb all right." She hardly expected sympathy from Sébastien, but she didn't want to hole up alone in her room. She sat on the chair across from him and sighed.

His eyebrows bunched together. "Do you want to get drunk?"

She almost laughed. "Not at eight-thirty in the morning."

"Oh." He kept looking at her. "Do you want to call Eddie? He's good at comforting."

She shook her head.

"When Eddie dumped me . . ."

Rachel interrupted. "I thought you kicked him out."

Sébastien shrugged. "Every other time he came back."

Once again, miserable as she was, she had to chuckle. "I'll be all right."

He made a doubtful noise. "I know. We'll have breakfast." He folded up the paper. "Or would you rather eat chocolate? I have a whole box of creams and caramels just for you."

"Breakfast," she said, although she didn't feel a bit hungry. "It's a little early for chocolates too."

He strode into the kitchen, beckoning her to follow. Slamming refrigerator and cabinet doors, he pulled out pans and plates. Rachel went to the window to look at the African violets. She'd not touched them in over a week, but they were thriving. "Drink some coffee," Sébastien barked, pointing to the coffeemaker.

"What are you making?" She hadn't been surprised when he broke eggs into a bowl. Sébastien seemed to live on omelets and scrambled eggs. But then he added flour and salt.

"Crepes. Pancakes to Americans. Hand me the butter."

She did and then poured herself a cup of coffee. It seemed as though she'd just done that, but she hadn't drunk Kurt's coffee, had she? He'd called her "pancake." What a silly man he was. But she'd wanted him really bad. "Kurt said he had to go to Egypt for a shoot," she said.

"He probably did, unless the loan sharks are chasing him." Sébastien beat the mixture with a whisk and gave her a long look. "He gambles, you know."

She didn't know.

Sebastien went on. "Of course he's also probably known about the shoot for weeks, if not months. He's always booked far in advance. We have to wait forever to get sessions."

She wrapped her fingers around the warm cup. It was what she'd figured too, and Sébastien wasn't one to sugarcoat anything. After all the lying, she preferred the truth. "He didn't want me to go with him."

"No. But I need you here. You couldn't have gone anyway."

Maybe Sébastien meant this kindly. Maybe he'd missed her the last week. How would anyone know?

He poured batter into a copper skillet. "He sent your photos. They're magnificent."

She didn't care. "That's nice. I guess he's good."

"The best." The batter sizzled. "A bastard, but good at what he does."

Unbelievable as it was, Sébastien was trying to be kind. It made her want to cry again. She gulped down some coffee. "So what do the photos tell you?"

He didn't respond for a while, too busy cooking the paper-thin pancakes one at a time and stacking several on a plate. Finally one shoulder lifted. "That you could do print modeling. That the camera loves you. That you will look beautiful in the clothes I create."

Rachel made a doubtful noise. Sébastien turned to glare at her. "You are beautiful. I saw it on the bridge that day. I still see it. Just because that . . ." He mumbled several obscene French words at the skillet. "Do not allow such a man to make you feel bad." Sébastien stopped, spatula raised like a torch and then lowered it, raised it, lowered it. "He is nothing more than his zipper. Up, down, up, down. Tedious." He turned back to the stove. "Unless, of course, he is taking pictures. Then he is a genius."

He spread each crepe with raspberry jam, rolled it into a tight cylinder, and sprinkled all of them with powdered sugar. "We will eat," he said. "Then you should take a long bath with bubbles. Then you call Eddie or your mother."

"Not my mother," declared Rachel.

"Whoever makes you feel good." Sébastien brushed sugar off his pajamas. "And then you must get ready for next week. You have fittings tomorrow, and the modeling class starts Wednesday. Every day for four weeks. Being busy will make you feel better."

Rachel swallowed. The crepes were heaven. "Actually, you're doing a pretty good job of that yourself."

He concentrated on his plate.

A

The next morning Rachel rode to the *atelier* with Sébastien who dropped her with Madame Pauline and then barricaded himself in his office. He was not to be disturbed, he said. "Aren't the designs all done?" Rachel asked Polly. She couldn't quite bring herself to call the woman anything but Madame Pauline to her face.

Madame Pauline sighed. "Nearly, but there are problems with finding models. We must choose the music, the décor. And he has regular clients, appointments." She lifted her hands in frustration as the two of them walked to the fitting rooms. "Many, many things to do."

"How many models do you need?"

Madame Pauline opened the door, and two women armed with pins and chalk came toward them. "Most times the girls do one or two costumes each, so thirty or so at best, seventeen or eighteen at the least, but he wants you to do more." She shrugged. "I do not know how you will make the changes, but Monsieur Fel requires that you do five."

"Five! How the hell am I going to do that? Don't the models prance down the runway one right after another?" When they arrived at the fitting room, Rachel pulled off her sweater and sneakers. She knew the routine, and it didn't allow for modesty.

Madame Pauline nodded, looking worried. "I do not know. He must decide."

"So you need seventeen fat models, right?" Off came her jeans. She peeled out of her shoes and socks and slipped on the heels she'd bought to dance with Kurt. A wave of hurt rolled over her when she thought of that.

Wincing at the word, Madame Pauline pulled the linen mock-up of one of Rachel's costumes over her head. "Yes."

"And how many has he found? Rachel settled the dress. It was short, odd.

"Seven. Five American, two German."

"Damn." No wonder Sébastien was biting his nails until they bled these days. Her grandmother would've said he was as nervous as a hen on a hot rock. Granny'd had a way with words. For about five minutes, she forgot about Kurt.

A

When the phone rang yet again, I stopped typing and muttered a curse. Most times I'm happy to be interrupted while I'm working. I am a lazy man. But the words were flowing, literally pouring from my fingertips, and I didn't want to stop. "Tremaine," I bellowed.

"Hi Edgar. It's Rachel."

Unlike charities begging for money or my editor fussing about the deadline I'd missed, both of which I'd dealt with that morning, I didn't mind this call at all. "Darling. Are you better today?"

"A little, maybe. I had fittings this morning, and as long as I'm busy it's not too bad."

She still sounded forlorn, if not quite as heart-broken as when she'd called yesterday. Even if the girl had ignored my warnings, I could gladly have throttled that photographer. "Then you must stay busy," I said. "What are you doing now?" I looked at my watch. Good heavens, I'd worked straight through luncheon. Unheard of.

"Nothing. Well, I'm sitting at a café near *L'Opéra*. I thought I'd go see the Chagall ceiling again. It makes me smile." She made a feeble attempt at a laugh. "Maybe the Phantom will grab me. Then I'd have a boyfriend, wouldn't I?"

"I fear he has a preference for singers." Poor child. I was imagining how my lovely American protagonist would've dealt with such a blow. Hannaford probably would've punched the photographer's lights out, in American parlance, which I was struggling to imitate in the girl's dialogue.

"Have you ever ordered a lemonade in Paris?" She obviously wanted to change the subject.

"Yes, a few times."

She paused. "I knew you were supposed to make it yourself." If a voice could be called *wan*, hers was.

'Yes."

"Annoying, isn't it?" Rachel was hesitating over something, but I wasn't sure what.

"My hands are all sticky, and the lemonade tastes terrible." She paused. "You know how you keep asking me to come to London?"

"I'd adore having you here."

"Well, Sébastien has changed his mind and thinks it might be a good idea. Just for a weekend. I guess he feels sorry for me."

"Marvelous! At the end of this week then?"

"Yeah. I'll take the Chunnel train on Friday, if that's okay."

I could hardly speak for smiling. "It's much more than okay, dear girl. Give me your arrival time, and I'll be at St. Pancras to meet you."

"Okay. I wish the train went to Paddington. You know, like the bear."

It took me a second. "Oh, yes. The children's story. We can certainly visit Paddington if you wish."

"No. I'm being stupid."

"Not at all. Think about where you want to go. We won't be able to see much in a weekend however." I was already contemplating museums, restaurants, and theater. I had no idea whether Rachel liked musicals as much as Sébastien and I.

"Thanks, Edgar. Hope I won't be a pain. I've been as gloomy as Eeyore." She paused. "You know who he is, don't you? Another bear story?"

"Oh, yes. I resemble him myself at times."

She rang off, and I saved my work and closed down the computer. It was Monday, and I had plenty of time to prepare, but I immediately wanted to go to the shops and buy lovely foods and wines and flowers. Considering her references to stuffed animals, I thought, silly old bear, and grinned at myself. Then I called my editor, whom I'd promised to meet this week. Get it done, I told myself. Rachel's coming. I asked, and the Dragon of Publishing had a spare minute that afternoon, if I could get there in an hour. I started up the printer, rolled out the two hundred pages I'd finished, and headed out the door.

When I arrived, she looked miffed, as of course she had the right to be. I'd promised her a complete manuscript by the first of September. She glanced at the box of pages and peered at me over the top of her scarlet glasses. "You say this is a departure from your norm. Not always a wise move, Edgar. Do we still have Inspector Hannaford?"

"Yes, but he's less the star than usual. I have an American girl who quite captures his attention. And everyone else's." An intelligent and lovely auburn-haired girl, fresh as the breeze off Cornwall's coast.

"A love interest? My, my. Hannaford's been the perpetual monk. Is it sad? Is she the victim?"

"Only of mistrust and doubt. Hannaford is led to believe that she's the murderer. And absolutely abhors the idea."

She read the first page. "You seem strangely excited by this one."

"Oh, I am," I agreed.

She gave me her headmistress stare. "Excited enough to merit missing your deadline?"

I refused to feel guilty about all those weeks when I'd written nothing. All those weeks before Rachel had kindled my imagination. "Absolutely. I'll have a complete draft in another month."

"Astonishing," she murmured and went on to the second page.

By Friday I'd filled the larder with treats, the liquor cabinet with bourbon, smiling at the fact that Rachel and I shared the same taste in liquor. And I'd filled the bathroom with special soaps and lotions. My occasional housekeeper had come the day before and changed the sheets in the guest room. I'd put flowers in there as well as on the dining room table. By mid-afternoon I'd prepared a steak and potato pie and polished wineglasses. I was as excited as a child at Christmas.

She rested her head against the seat and felt the train's steady vibration. She would've preferred to have scenery to distract her, but it was nearly dark and even before the train reached the Channel, it traveled too low to see anything but the ditch carved for it. Shutting her eyes, Rachel saw what she did every night when she tried to sleep: a picture of Kurt, smiling at her, leaning in close for a kiss. She immediately lifted her lids and stared at the book in her lap, one of Edgar's, the first Inspector Hannaford mystery. This entire experience had been a colossal mistake, she thought. Some girls might love the glamour, the fabulous clothes and the possibility of fame and romance. No romance for Rachel. Her mouth turned bitter at the thought. Sure, her time with Kurt had been fun for a while, more than fun, but if she were honest with herself, she'd known all along that it was too good to be true. Just like Sébastien's crazy collection.

Sure, the clothes were fabulous. She remembered how it'd felt when she'd first tried on the purple dress. It actually looked good on her. But where was she supposed to wear it back in Morton, Ohio? A night out at Wendy's and Wal-Mart? And the clothes were hardly worth the ridicule and anxiety about her body.

And she was worried sick about the modeling classes. Before they started, Polly had taken her to the basement to view recordings of past runway shows, seating her in front of a screen and ordering her to pay attention. The tall guy Rachel had seen outside Madame Pauline's door was a couple of desks away. He had smiled and come over. "What's up?" he'd asked.

Rachel had shrugged at the screen. Pouting women in bizarre clothes stalked the catwalk and turned, one after another. "I'll never be able to do that," she'd mourned.

"Sure you will," he'd said. "I'm Jesse Kemper, and I know you're Rachel." He stuck out his hand.

She'd shaken it. "You're American, aren't you?"

"Yep. From Maine. And you?" His smile was wide. She'd had to stretch her neck to see it. Tall guy.

"Oh, I love Maine." She'd grinned at him. "Ohio."

"Never been there," he'd said. "But I'm sure it has its charms. I'm working on graphic designs for your publicity right now." He motioned back to his desk.

It was a relief to dismiss the ever-loving secrecy as well as a joy to meet someone from back home. "Lucky you," she'd said.

He'd tilted his head. "I think so. We're all pretty excited about what Himself is designing just now."

She'd chuckled. "Himself. I like that."

"Gotta get back to it, but hey, listen, why don't we grab a coffee sometime and you can tell me why you love Maine. Okay?"

"Sure." She'd lowered her head to go back to the video and figured that the coffee would never happen.

But prancing down a stage would happen and she was scared to death of it. So far, she'd failed miserably at her class, producing only snickers and rude comments from her fellow students and instructor. Glancing out the train window, she sighed. It all seemed so false and pointless. She'd given up honest, important work for fashion and a superficial fling. Stupid. At least her crazy decision had allowed her to explore Paris and get to know Edgar. She patted the paperback in her lap. He'd make her feel better. He always did.

Rachel's train was right on time. I saw her before she saw me, and it gave me a minute to observe her. Sébastien's pet hairdresser had enhanced the auburn lights in Rachel's curls, and her hair was a bit longer. Her face was still perfect, a Madonna's oval. It was obvious what Sébastien saw in her. But the perfect face was dreadfully pale, and, as she scanned the crowd to find me, I saw little light in her eyes. "Here, Rachel!" I shouted, holding up my hand. Then there was light, and I'd be lying if I didn't admit that it flattered me.

"That was a trip," she said, struggling with her ratty old duffel bag. Rachel might be a Parisian model, but she wasn't a bit elegant.

"Yes, it was," I replied, thinking this a rather obvious observation. "A good one or a bad one?"

She didn't seem to know how to greet me. A hug? A handshake? She touched the sleeve of my coat. "A freaky one. I kept thinking about all that water over my head." She blinked several times.

"Technology, my dear. It's all very frightening."

I hailed a cab, and we set off for West Kensington. It was dark, but she kept her eyes glued to the window and slowly regained the spirit I so much admired in her. "You do drive on the wrong side of the road," she murmured.

"We think it's the correct side."

She just nodded. "And look at how tiny those cars are."

When we pulled up in front of my building, she was oohing and ahhing again. "You must be as rich as Sébastien. Look at this place!"

It was a rather gauche comment, but I'd noticed Rachel's endearing tendency to say whatever popped into her head from the first time I'd met her. It was a trait I'd bestowed upon my American character as well. I ignored her lack of tact. "A bit wealthier, I daresay, counting family money and property, but, my dear, I don't own the entire building. Just a flat in it." At least she'd regained some color in her cheeks.

I introduced her to Duncan, the porter, who took her pitiful bag, greeted her solemnly, and joined us in the lift. She whispered, "Damn," and touched the gilded scrollwork of the cage.

"Edwardian," I said. "Very ornate."

Eyes wide, she nodded. My flat seemed to have the same effect on her. She wandered around the lounge, touching the furniture, eyeing the paintings, and murmuring "damn" every few seconds. I was amused but surprised. Sébastien's digs were more opulent than mine. Perhaps she'd thought all writers were poor. She'd be correct in most instances, but years ago Vivian and I had shared a generous bequest from our father, and there was more to come when Margo gave up the ghost, not that I could imagine life without her. Plus, I was a thrifty soul in most respects. The pieces Rachel was exuding over were mostly family, and ancient by her young standards.

"Would you like to take your coat off? See your room?"

She nodded. I was beginning to think she'd lost the power of speech.

I pointed down the hall. "Last door on your right. I believe Duncan left the door open."

Wordlessly she went down the hall, her trainers squeaking on the hardwood. I brought ice from the kitchen and was in the middle of mixing her a whiskey when I heard a little cry. She ran into the room and threw her arms around me. "You are the sweetest, sweetest man!" she declared, crushing the toy bear between us.

Earlier in the week I'd purchased a Paddington Bear and perched him on her bed. I thought she'd like it, but I never dreamed it would be this much of a hit. "So you found your bear?"

She grinned and kissed my cheek. It pleased me no end.

Sitting on the sofa, she nestled the bear right beside her and accepted her drink. She took a sip and made a face, which she immediately tried to hide. "I thought you liked bourbon," I said.

"I do." She ducked her head. "But I usually drink it with Coke or Pepsi. Like a kid."

"I can remedy that." I took her glass and went to the kitchen, Rachel following right behind me, holding the bear against her chest.

"Geez," she said as we passed through the dining room. "You and Sébastien have really different taste. Your stuff is colorful and comfortable, and his is modern and . . ." She stopped.

"Rather chilly. Yes, I know. But our kitchens are similar." We went into the kitchen, and she nodded as she took in the copper cookware and tiled walls. I fetched a Coke from the refrigerator. I never drank them, but I usually kept a few.

"Did it matter?" Rachel asked. "Was that the problem?"

"What?" I turned on the cooker to bake the pie.

"Did you break up because you liked different styles? Style is so important to Sébastien."

I mixed her a new drink, and we settled once again in the lounge. "Not at all. When we lived together in Paris, it was in a different flat, a larger one than he now has. And it was mine first. He simply moved in and tolerated my decorating, although his office was rather chrome and cream." I smiled. "And, of course, black."

She sipped her drink and gave me a thumbs-up. "So why did you and Sébastien break up?" She scrunched up her nose. "I don't guess that's any of my business, but the three of us almost seem like family."

Again, I was inordinately pleased. "I know that both of us like you very much, Rachel."

She gave me an embarrassed smile. "Me too. I mean, I like both of you, although sometimes Sébastien irritates the snot out of me."

Immediately her face reddened at the crude term, although I chuckled at her eloquence. "Let's see. Why did Sébastien and I part company? I suppose the simplest answer is that we were both too self-absorbed."

"Not you."

"Yes, I. Oh, my dear, Sébastien is an arrogant bastard most of the time, but I, too, can get rather cross when I feel someone is taking advantage of me. Too much bullying when I was at school, I fear. And it was that much worse coming from someone who said he cared about me." It seemed strange to be speaking of incidents that had happened so many years ago. I took a couple of gulps from the bourbon I'd poured for myself. Without Coca-Cola.

She slipped out of her shoes and curled her legs under her. "There's a line, isn't there? A line of respect that you shouldn't cross?" Her voice had become very low, and I sensed she was speaking of herself, not Sébastien and me.

"Indeed. Compromises. Consideration, but always respect." I shrugged. "It's all part of the drill."

For a moment, she said nothing, just petted her bear. "I was so thrilled that someone wanted me."

"And why shouldn't someone want you?"

Her entire body wriggled. "You know."

"I do feel our culture responds like sheep to media-induced standards of beauty." Oh dear, I was doing my Oxford don impersonation, as Jeremy called it. Rachel kept a polite silence while I went on. "Unfortunately, just now society favors an unrealistic standard of beauty for women. If you had been born in another time . . ."

"Yeah, yeah," she drawled. "My poster would've decorated boys' walls back in the Renaissance. Miss France of 1582. Sébastien feeds me this garbage all the time."

I chuckled. "And what, out of curiosity, would you have been wearing in those murals? They couldn't have been posters. And who would've painted them?" She laughed. "A bevy of sensualist fresco artists?"

"Maybe gowns that showed my ankles? Some modest cleavage?" She was trying, the dear thing. But her smile didn't last long. "You know what I mean."

"Of course I do. I just regret that you have yet to meet men who appreciate what you are and the special beauty you possess."

She became very interested in her fingernails.

"So," I said. "What do you want to do in London? I could probably get tickets for a play. We could spend some time in the British Museum or the Tate or the Victoria and Albert. What say you?"

From the expression on her face, I knew I hadn't tempted her at all. Our Rachel would be a dismal failure at either poker or espionage. "Tell me what you'd like to see," I urged.

"Well." She sat forward and Paddington dropped to the floor. She picked him up by one arm and smoothed his hat. "I'd love to see the city from the river. Do they do boat trips on the Thames like they do on the Seine? Maybe Buckingham Palace and the changing of the guard. And I want to eat fish and chips and maybe see the Tower." Her face was glowing. "You know, where they chopped off heads. Axes, armor, swords."

What a bloodthirsty child she was.

But she wasn't finished. "And Baker Street, where Sherlock Holmes lived. You know how I love to read mysteries." She must've seen dismay on my face. I fear I'll never be accused of being inscrutable either. "Oh, I know he was fictitious, but isn't there a place on Baker Street that's all about him? A museum or something?"

Ah, the amazing recuperative powers of youth. "I believe so." My voice sounded rather faint. I finished my drink, thinking it would perhaps be wise to carry a flask of whiskey to get me through all these excursions. "We might not be able to do all of that in one day, you know."

She beamed. "I'm not going back to Paris until Sunday evening."

Chapter Nine

I was exhausted by noon. We'd been in the first tour of the day at the Tower, and Rachel had nearly salivated over the gruesome details, the armaments, and the jewels. American television, I surmised. Then we'd visited Baker Street for all things Holmesian and gone to a fish and chips shop for totally indigestible food. I'd demanded a rest as we walked through Green Park toward Buckingham Palace. My stomach and feet were crying for a reprieve. Rachel, however, was radiant, just like the young woman in my book. I said as much. Truly, I wanted to pump her for details, American expressions that I could use, but I felt it would be selfish of me to interrupt her enjoyment. Perhaps this evening at dinner.

She brushed wisps of hair out of her face. There was a chilly breeze, and I wondered if we'd both catch colds. She said, "What's my name in your book?"

I thought she'd never ask. "Her name is Marcia, and she's a twenty-six year old historian." I was prepared to go on until I saw Rachel's expression. "Oh dear. What?"

"I don't know any Marcias. That name is sort of old-fashioned in the States." She looked up at the gray clouds. "There's a Marcia Brady in old reruns of *The Brady Bunch*, but I think they're from way back in the seventies."

Way back then. "Well, then. What's in vogue for a young woman your age? I can easily change her name." Even though I'd become very fond of Marcia.

"Oh, let's see. Jennifer, there are tons of them, but I don't like that name. Lauren, Emily, quite a few Rachels." She smiled. "Tiffany, Samantha, Kate."

I didn't care for those. "What about Chloe? That's a lovely name." Early in my writing process I'd seen a newspaper article about a young woman with that name and considered it.

"The only Chloe I know is a cat, but she's a great cat. Sure, why not? It sounds modern." She stuffed her hands in her pockets. Cold, probably. She should have gloves. "What is Chloe/Marcia doing over here?" she asked.

"Research into ancient Cornish artifacts and ruins. She's here in an exchange program through Oxford and attends a few classes there.

It is while doing archaeological digs in Cornwall that she meets Hannaford."

"Nice." Rachel stared at the back gardens of the houses across from us. They were, as Rachel put it, "real ritzy." She had this endearing trait of scrunching up her nose when something bothered her. I might give that bit of business to Marcia. I mean, Chloe.

"What is it?" I asked.

She looked down. "Well, it's just that you and Sébastien both are using me as an inspiration, which is really a big compliment," she said, giving me an anxious smile. "But I wonder how much his Renaissance princess and your Chloe really have to do with me. Neither of you knows me very well." This time she scrunched her nose so much that she ended up rubbing it. "Or sees me as I really am."

It truly seemed to bother her. "My dear, we may see more in you than you see in yourself, you know. But," I touched her cold cheek, "an inspiration need not be an exact copy." I'd started to say, "carbon copy," but realized that those were ancient artifacts, undoubtedly worthy of Chloe's research.

"That's for sure," she retorted. "I'm not nearly as wonderful as you guys think I am." She looked past me, absorbed in a bare-limbed oak. "Is Chloe fat?"

"Whatever difference would that make?"

She shook her head, ready to quit talking and start moving. Another bit of character for Chloe. I could add it in.

By late afternoon, I was done in, and even Rachel was flagging a bit. I suggested that we return to my flat, have nice hot baths, and go to a restaurant for dinner. She agreed. As I waited for her to bathe and dress, I swallowed a couple of stomach tablets as penance for my fish and chips. I had no appetite, but I'd booked a table at a popular restaurant that catered to a younger crowd, hoping she'd enjoy it. Rachel came into the lounge looking particularly delightful in a brown riding jacket. I said that she could be taken for a royal, maybe even a duchess; all she needed was a horse. And she told me about the jacket, Gisèle, whom I vaguely remembered, and, unfortunately, more about that cad Kurt Mann. He was a sore she couldn't quit touching.

But she pulled herself out of that particular pool of gloom and asked, "Want to see what I've learned in my modeling class?"

I nodded. We still had plenty of time. I'd mistakenly assumed that all women took as long to dress as Margo always did. Rachel stood, lifted her chin, and walked through the lounge as if it were a catwalk. "Never, never smile, mademoiselle," she chirped in imitation of her instructor. "Pelvis forward." She turned her head to me. "Sounds sort of crude, doesn't it?" She turned with a flourish and strutted toward the hall. Well. She wasn't particularly graceful, a bit absurd-looking actually, and I was laughing as hard as my cranky tummy would allow.

She strode back to the lounge, a perfectly insolent pout on her face, and then she grinned and flopped onto the sofa. "Have you ever seen anything so silly?"

"Actually I have," I admitted. "I used to go to Sébastien's shows."

Again, she mimicked a French accent, although she spoke in English. "You are not women, nor men. You are just models. The clothes, the clothes are all that matter." She rolled her lovely eyes. "It's a good thing Sébastien's paying me so well."

"Is he?" I'd wondered. He was rarely stingy, but this was an exceptional situation.

"Oh yes. Very well."

I suggested a drink, and Rachel trotted off to the kitchen to get a Coke to go with her whiskey. I looked tired, she said as she left, walking normally this time. And to be truthful, I didn't feel at all well. Although I'd blamed everything on our regrettably greasy luncheon, I feared that I was coming down with something. Nonetheless, I was enjoying Rachel's company too much to beg off and aimed to soldier on as best I could.

A

When Rachel returned from the kitchen, she saw that Edgar had left their glasses on what he called the drinks cabinet and collapsed into his armchair. His face was gray."What's wrong?" she asked, hurrying over to him.

"I have the most alarming pain," he murmured. He barely had enough breath to say the words.

"Where's the pain?" Rachel's grandmother had suffered from heart disease and died of it. She knew the symptoms.

He gestured toward his chest and then squirmed, biting his lower lip. "I can't get it to ease," he whispered, sitting up, then standing, then sitting again. He pressed his hand to his lower chest and moved it around to his side and then his back.

Rachel didn't think heart pain moved that way, but she was no nurse. Sweat popped out on Edgar's ashy forehead. Lord, if she'd overtired him to the point that he was having a heart attack, she'd never forgive herself. "We need to call for help," she said, expecting him to contradict her.

But he nodded and reached a shaky hand into his pocket to get his phone. "Ambulance," he whispered. Another spasm gripped him. He swallowed like he was about to vomit.

Rachel grabbed his phone. Was it 911 here? She didn't know. But poor old Edgar read her mind."999," he grunted and threw up on the carpet by his chair. "So sorry, child," he moaned.

Rachel didn't know whether to hold onto Edgar or dial the phone. "Hang on, Edgar," she said and punched in the numbers.

She had to ask him the address of his building and how to reach Duncan to tell him the emergency squad was coming, but finally she felt confident that an ambulance was on the way. She ran to the bathroom to get him a wet cloth and a towel to throw over the puddle of vomit. "Just a little longer, Edgar," she murmured as she wiped his face. "They're coming." He lay back but immediately sat up again. The pain must've been twisting his guts. She hated seeing him hurt so bad.

Rachel held his hand for a moment but had a hard time staying still. She paced the room, going from Edgar to open the apartment door and then back to his chair. He pointed at his phone and managed to say that she should call his mother, Margo. God, he thought he was dying. Rachel assured him she would, but not until help arrived. It seemed like hours, but soon she heard the elevator stop, and Duncan stepped into the room ahead of the British equivalent of EMTs. One of them gave her a reassuring smile and said, "Step out of the way, luv. We'll take care of him." The other two set a stretcher down by Edgar's chair.

Rachel stood clutching the wet washcloth and watching them take Edgar's vitals and loosen his tie. Her own heart was hammering like crazy. Duncan patted her arm, murmuring, "It'll all come right, Miss, I'm sure it will."

She couldn't make out much of what the EMTs were saying, but they must've come to a decision to take Edgar to the hospital. She certainly hoped so. In one quick motion they had Edgar on the stretcher, and before she knew it, they were easing him out the door. "I'm coming," she called to the one carrying the equipment bag, and she darted over to the chair where her purse lay.

"No, Miss. We can't allow you in the ambulance. We're taking him to Chelsea. You can follow along there."

Panicked, Rachel stood motionless as she heard them load Edgar onto the elevator and leave. Duncan said, "You'll want to go."

Still holding her bag and Edgar's cell phone, she nodded. She had no idea how she'd do it. "What's Chelsea?" she whispered.

"A hospital. I'll call you a taxi, Miss Bowman." How had Duncan remembered her name? "It's a raw night. Rather rainy. You'll want your jacket."

Rachel nodded and picked up her coat.

"Come along. I need to lock up Mr. Tremaine's flat." The porter guided her into the hall. "The cooker wasn't on, was it?" he asked.

Rachel shook her head.

Once they were in the lobby, Duncan made a quick phone call and then helped her into her jacket. "Here." He handed her a key. "I go off duty at ten, so if you come in late you'll need this."

Rachel felt stiff and stupid. "Where exactly am I going?"

"Chelsea and Westminster Hospital. It's in the Fulham Road. They'll take fine care of Mr. Tremaine."

"And where am I here?" Edgar had told her when she'd phoned for the ambulance, but she'd already forgotten.

Duncan turned to his desk and scribbled the address on a piece of paper. "My home number's on there too. Call if you need me, Miss Bowman."

"Thank you," she whispered. "Is there anyone I should call besides his mother?" At the time, she didn't think it was at all strange that the building's porter would know whom she should contact. He seemed to know everything.

"I'd say his nephew Jeremy. I'm sure his number is in Mr. Tremaine's mobile." Duncan paused and gestured toward the door. "I believe I see your taxi, Miss." He opened the front door for her and walked down the steps to open the cab's door. "Do you think Mr. Fel would want to know? There was a time. . ." His voice was lost in the shushing of rain and slamming of car doors.

It was raining enough to shine the streets and make halos around streetlights. Rachel took a deep breath and then glanced at her bag. Damn, she had only euros. Would the cabbie take them? She realized she was gritting her teeth. Poor Edgar. She didn't think he was having a heart attack, but he was desperately sick. She started to dig

Edgar's phone out of her bag to make her calls but decided to wait. Maybe she'd know more once she got to the hospital.

It was a short trip. The cabbie reached behind the seat and opened her door. "Hope all's well, luv," he said in English that was almost harder to decipher than French.

"The fare," she stammered. "All I have are euros."

"No problem." He gave her a wide smile. "It's on the tick."

She had no idea what he meant but tried to smile back at him. "Thank you," she said.

Once inside, signs directed Rachel down corridors to the Emergency area. They called it Accident and Emergency, she noted, and arrows pointed to A and E, which was fine after she figured it out. She went up to the nurse's station. "I'm here for Mr. Edgar Tremaine," she said softly, not knowing whether Edgar's writing qualified him as a celebrity or not. They were probably used to celebrities. In a city as large as London, J. K. Rowling could be a patient here. Hell, the Queen herself would have to go to some hospital if she got appendicitis. Rachel wondered if Edgar's problem could be appendicitis.

"Family?" a stony-faced nurse asked.

"Um, no. Friend. But he doesn't have family in town." She held up Edgar's phone. "I wanted to see how he's doing before I call them."

The nurse looked down at a book. "He was just brought in. No information yet." And that was all she was willing to say. She did point, however, to a waiting room where several people sat on lined-up chairs and raised their heads every time a hospital worker walked by. It was going to be a long night.

A large sign stated that mobile use was not permitted in that area, so Rachel retraced her steps until she reached the front door and stepped into the damp night. Later she'd ask where she could use her phone, but just then she'd rather be outside the intimidating hospital. She checked Edgar's contacts and found Margo's number. Edgar's mother was probably ancient and would have no idea who Rachel was. She hated the thought of upsetting her.

The phone rang several times but didn't go to voice mail. Rachel pictured a frail old lady with a walker taking laborious steps to the telephone. "Tremaine," boomed a fruity British voice.

"Mrs. Tremaine?" Rachel felt awkward as hell. "Margo?"

"Yes, who is this?" The woman certainly didn't sound feeble.

Rachel told her, and Margo seemed to know all about her. "What has that boy done now?" she asked.

Rachel had a moment of confusion until she realized that Edgar was the boy in question. "He's sick, ma'am. I called an ambulance, and they've taken him to the hospital. I'm here with him, but they won't tell me anything or let me see him yet."

There was an unladylike snort from the other end. "Which hospital?" Margo sounded more like a drill sergeant than an old lady.

"Chelsea Westminster, ma'am. Do you want me to call you back when I find out something? Even if it's late?"

"Of course I do." The voice was imperious. "What's ailing him?"

"Oh, severe pain. I thought maybe it was a heart attack, but he didn't seem to be pointing at his heart. I don't know, but he's very sick." Rachel felt miserable. She wished she knew more.

"Probably ate something that had gone off. He'll be fine. Strong as an ox, Edgar. All the Tremaines are," Margo replied. "My side of the family as well."

"Maybe." Rachel doubted it. "I thought I should call his nephew too. Jeremy?"

"No need. He's right here. I'll tell him. Ring me back, right?"

"Yes, ma'am." Rachel took a deep breath.

That had been easier than she'd feared, and Jeremy was notified now too. She started to go back into the hospital. Although she was standing under an overhang, her feet were getting soaked. And then she remembered that Duncan had said she should call Sébastien. Well, that wouldn't be nearly as awkward as Edgar's mother.

As she knew from experience, Sébastien wasn't very good about answering his phone. Rachel couldn't decide whether he'd respond more readily to her number or Edgar's. They both had him in their contacts. She chose Edgar's, and Sébastien actually answered it. "It's Rachel," she said. "Edgar got sick and I called an ambulance and he's in the hospital right now but they won't let me see him and I don't know what's wrong with him." She did it all in one breath and felt like she was nine years old and about to cry. And truly, tears were welling up in her eyes.

"Slow down, Raquel," Sébastien said. He must be at home. The only background noise she heard was soft music. "When did this happen?"

"Just a little bit ago. He had this terrible pain."

"His heart?"

"Maybe. I don't know. I called his mother, and she said he'd probably eaten something bad, but we ate the same things."

"Ah, Margo," he said with a little chuckle. But then his voice became very serious. "Is it bad, Raquel? Tell me."

"I don't know. They won't say."

He was silent for a moment. "Give it an hour. Call me back if you hear anything before, but certainly in an hour."

"Okay."

"I can come," he said. "Somehow."

She knew it would be difficult to arrange a flight or train on a Saturday night. She was surprised he even suggested it. "No, not yet. I'll call in an hour."

Trudging back to the waiting area, Rachel noted the time: seven-thirty. Sébastien would expect precision. In the waiting room, the same people were sitting in the same uncomfortable chairs. A few old magazines were stacked on a table. She wasn't interested. Some of the people in the room were waiting to hear about patients, she figured, but others were patients waiting to be called back. They looked as if they'd sat there for hours. A little girl with bright red cheeks was whimpering into her well-dressed mother's neck. One older man had an elastic bandage wrapped around his wrist. Another man in an ancient tweed suit kept coughing. Finally a woman came to the area and said, "Bradford." The little girl and her mother left.

Rachel had visited an emergency room exactly once in her life, when she'd been fourteen and happened upon a yellow jacket's nest with the lawn mower. She remembered waiting forever. She supposed emergency rooms were similar no matter where they were. Fifteen minutes passed. Two people went back; three came in. Thirty minutes passed. She was worried to death about Edgar, but her stomach was growling something fierce. It seemed rude and unsympathetic to be hungry. At eight-twenty, a nurse called for Mr. Tremaine's family, and Rachel figured she was it. Her heart started pounding again.

The nurse pointed down a hallway. "He's comfortable now," she said. "But a little woozy. We're sending him up to radiology in a few minutes but thought you might want to peep in on him before he goes."

The nurse's shoes squeaked on the shiny floor. "Is he going to be all right?" Rachel asked.

"He's stable."

The nurse entered a tiny room and pulled a curtain back so Rachel could see Edgar, lying in a bed. He wore a hospital gown and had tubes in his arm. "Five minutes," the nurse said.

Edgar's eyes were closed, which was sort of scary, but his color was rosy again. "Edgar?" Rachel whispered.

His eyes opened and he gave her a goofy smile. "Dear girl," he murmured.

"Do you still hurt?" She squeezed his hand. It was warm.

"No, I'm quite comfortable, child." He frowned. "I wonder what that was."

"The pain? I think they'll find out. You're going for tests in a minute."

He patted her hand. "You go home now, Rachel. I'm sorry to have ruined your evening."

"No sir," Rachel replied. "I'm seeing this through."

He waved an airy hand. "Melodrama, dear, it's all melodrama."

With great rumbles and creaks, a young man rolled a wheelchair into Edgar's cubicle. "We're taking a ride," he announced. His lilting accent was different from the others she'd heard. He looked like he was from India.

"Radiology?" she asked.

"Ah, yes." The young man smiled at her, at Edgar, at the ceiling.

As he maneuvered Edgar into the chair, she said, "I'll be here, Edgar."

Rachel didn't know what to do or where to wait. The nurse who'd brought her to Edgar's bed was nowhere in sight. Finally Rachel asked a clerk who was busy typing data into a computer. "They won't bring him back here," she said. "They'll keep him in Radiology until they know something, and then he'll either be released or assigned a room."

"How will I know?"

The woman smiled. "Yank, aren't you? My great-aunt married one during the war. They moved to Minnesota. Are you from Minnesota?"

"No." Impatience was burbling up in her gut, but she fought it. "Sorry. I've never been there."

The woman nodded. "I've never been to Scotland. Isn't that something?"

Rachel tried not to sigh.

"Well, ducks, you can wait in the Radiology area and try to flag someone down. Reception will know too, but if they're releasing him you'll be more on the spot upstairs."

"Okay. How do I get there?"

The woman gave her directions. "But there's no sense in hurrying. They'll do their films or scans, and then someone has to read them." She shuffled some papers and read one. "And Mr. Tremaine had a blood draw too." She rolled her eyes. "Hours," she said. "Don't you just love Mr. Tremaine's books? I've read them all. Inspector Hannaford is dreamy, isn't he? I can't wait to tell my sister that he was here. It's almost like having a film star, isn't it? Are you a relation?"

Rachel shook her head. "Is there food somewhere? I haven't had dinner or anything. And I need to know where I can use my phone."

"Of course. I'll direct you."

Two hours later, with a sausage roll, Coke, and Cadbury Flake lying heavy in her stomach, Rachel finally got word that Edgar would be admitted. She'd called Sébastien at 8:32 to hear him give her hell about being two minutes late and not having anything to report. At 11:50, after talking once again to Margo, she called him again. "It's his gall bladder," she said.

"Really," drawled Sébastien. He wouldn't have been drawling if he hadn't been relieved. "That's nothing serious, is it? Why are they keeping him?"

"They say it's infected, so they're putting him on antibiotics until Monday when they're doing surgery to remove it."

There was a mumble in French.

"I think I should stay through his surgery, don't you? He doesn't have family here. Of course I know that would mean missing my class. . . ." Her voice trailed off. There'd be an explosion about that. But she was almost too tired to care.

"Absolutely. I want updates, Raquel. Frequent ones."

"Okay."

"Maybe I'll come over tomorrow," he said.

"Okay." It surprised her, but Rachel didn't know what else to say.

"But I'm not sure."

She could picture him biting his nails. "I'm going back to Edgar's flat as soon as he's settled, but I've given the hospital my number. I'll let you know if anything changes or if there are problems in the night."

He didn't say anything for a few seconds. "You're very good to us, Raquel," he murmured and clicked off.

A

Edgar's building was locked, but the key Duncan had given her worked, and she walked through the shadowy lobby to the elevator. Lift. Whatever. She was cold and tired. Inside the apartment, she spent the next half hour putting back furniture the ambulance crew had rearranged and cleaning up poor Edgar's vomit . She thought about fixing herself a drink or a cup of tea. She'd never been much of a tea drinker, but it seemed like the right thing to do in London. Halfway to the kitchen, she changed her mind. Instead, she went to her room, undressed, and cleaned her face and teeth. She felt as though she could sleep for days. But she did leave both Edgar's and her phones on and within easy reach on the bedside table. With a giant yawn, she turned off the light and gave Paddington a squeeze. She was asleep before Kurt's face could materialize in her brain.

At first she paid no attention to the heavy thump that awakened her. She was used to Sébastien clomping around his apartment at all hours, but then Rachel remembered that she was in London, at Edgar's flat. And she was supposed to be alone.

There was light coming from under the door, but she couldn't remember if she'd turned off the hall light or not. Heart racing, she glanced at the clock. Three-forty-five. Surely they wouldn't have released Edgar in the middle of the night without calling her. Her heart was jumping around like crazy, just as it had when Edgar got sick. But she didn't move. She'd always heard that you should fake sleep when burglars invaded a house. They'd take things, but they wouldn't hurt you. She squinched her eyes shut and lay tense as a spring under the comforter. Then her door was opened with a flourish and someone flipped the switch to flood the room with light. Rachel sat straight up and screeched, "Get the hell out of here!" at the same time a man muttered, "Bloody hell."

Rachel blinked against the bright light and clutched at the covers, pulling them up to her chin. Her nightgown was one of those

96

wispy, almost-clothing pieces from Gisèle's shop. The man was young, his hair was wet, and he had a duffel bag. And he was scowling at her.

"Who are you and what are you doing here?" she yelled.

"Jeremy Hastings. And who the hell are you?"

Edgar's nephew. Edgar's *rude* nephew. "I'm Rachel Bowman," she said, gathering up her dignity a little more with each word. "I'm Mr. Tremaine's guest, and I've been with him at the hospital."

He blew a disgusted bit of air through his nose.

"I called your grandmother," she went on. "I said I was staying here until Edgar's surgery." The jerk might not know it, but he was getting the iciest Rachel possible. She clenched her fists, wadding the covers into pleats.

He looked totally put out. "I left Cornwall as soon as you called. Drove for hours only to find out they won't let me in hospital at this hour, and now I don't have a bed."

"I called Cornwall twice more," Rachel said. "I told Margo I was staying here."

He slumped against the doorframe. "I left before you called those other times. Margo doesn't believe in mobiles."

"Well." Rachel stared at him. His light brown hair was waving from the damp, and his cheeks were very pink. He didn't look very threatening. Edgar had said he was some kind of landscaper. She couldn't think of any horror movies featuring landscapers, just maniacs with chain saws. "I suppose you could bunk down in your uncle's room, couldn't you? I don't guess I care."

He rubbed his face and mumbled, "I think not." He switched off the light and closed the door.

"Lock the door on your way out," she yelled.

Chapter Ten

"*Oklahoma*, of course. If I didn't know better, Gumby, I'd think you were trying to coddle the invalid."

Sébastien gave me a look that could've frozen a rain forest. "All right," he said. "If you think I'm being soft, 'Somewhere That's Green'"

I was amazed that he'd made the trip over to see me. Thrilled, actually, but I'd never let on."'Somewhere That's Green'? I don't know," I said, and I didn't.

He paused before he told me the answer. A little shake of the head, a little arrogant posturing. "*Little Shop of Horrors.* That's fourteen for you, twelve for me," he announced, glancing at the tally he'd been marking in the back of the hospital's Bible. God knows, I'd tried to stop him from doing that. At least I hope God knows.

"'Soon It's Gonna Rain,'" I countered.

"*Fantasticks.*" He made a mark under his name. "Where's Raquel?"

"Does she like the way you mispronounce her name?"

"Never asked." Sébastien raised his legs to rest his boots at the bottom of my bed. "You're stalling. And I must leave in an hour to make my train."

"No, I'm not. She said she'd be back at three. What time is it?"

"Three." He squinted at me. "Well? Ask me one."

"'Feed the Birds,'" I said.

He did have to think on that one. I rarely won. For that matter I rarely came as close to winning as I was today, and we'd played "Musicals" nearly the whole time we'd lived together.

He snapped his fingers. "*Mary Poppins.* Silly show." Another mark. "We're tied."

I thought hard. Maybe the drugs they'd given me the night before were befuddling me. I couldn't think of anything difficult. As a last resort, I said, "'I Hate Men. '"

Sébastien grinned. "No, you don't."

I raised an eyebrow.

Lifting his feet off the bed, he squirmed. "Hmm."

"Now who's stalling?"

Before he could reply, Rachel breezed into the room carrying a lumpy carrier bag. She'd come to the hospital just after breakfast but left at midday when Jeremy had arrived. "How are you doing?" she said to me. She nodded at Sébastien. "I figured you'd come." She pulled a packet of ginger biscuits, a bunch of grapes, and an apple from the bag and piled them on the bedside cabinet. "You said they weren't planning on giving you supper tonight, so I thought if you ate something now, it might hold you until after the surgery." She took off her jacket and perched at the end of the bed. Sébastien sat in the only chair.

"Very considerate of you, Rachel," I said and gave Sébastien a pointed look. "Well? 'I Hate Men. '" Rachel looked confused. "We're playing Musicals." She shrugged.

Sébastien looked down his magnificent nose. "I don't know. Probably some obscure show that played for six nights."

I smiled and plucked off a couple of grapes. "*Kiss Me Kate*. Not exactly obscure." I could do *smug* as well as Sébastien.

Paying no attention to us, Rachel gestured toward the window and said, "Look at the gorgeous flowers. Calla lilies. Nice."

"From Jeremy," I said and popped a grape in my mouth.

She went to the window to touch the flowers. "You ought to do a calla lily dress, Sébastien. Look at the lines of them."

At first he frowned, but then he narrowed his eyes, focusing on the white blossoms. I could almost hear the machinery in his head cranking away. He picked up his pencil and reached for the Bible. "Absolutely not," I warned him.

Rachel sighed and came back to the bed where she'd laid the empty bag. "Here." She handed him the grocer's receipt. "Sketch away."

I opened the ginger biscuits. "I'd love to have a cup of tea with these," I said.

"Are you allowed?" asked Rachel.

When I nodded, she mumbled something about seeing what she could do and left the room. "Isn't she wonderful?" I said to Sébastien, who was intent upon his drawing. "She's taking the very best care of me.

"Mmm, hmm." He sketched another few seconds and looked up. "Such an ordinary girl to have affected us so much," he said, shaking his head. "This book you're writing with her in it, is it good?"

I nodded. "Very good."

"What is it about her that inspires us?"

"Youth? Innocence? I don't know." I chuckled. "But Jeremy thinks Rachel's a witch."

Sébastien tucked the sketch into his pocket. "Why?"

"It seems that he arrived at my flat in the middle of the night, charged right into the guest room, and found Rachel sleeping in what he considers his bed."

Sébastien raised an eyebrow. "Did he try to join her?"

"Dear heavens! Of course he didn't. Rachel didn't know who he was and screamed at him. That was enough for Jeremy to turn tail and run. He was still angry and embarrassed this morning."

"He's always been a backward child."

"Jeremy's thirty, and he's not backward," I said with asperity. "He's a bit shy but very well-mannered, especially around women. I'm sure Rachel's presence was as much of a shock to him as his was to her."

Sébastien held out his hand for some grapes. "Are they both staying there tonight? This could get amusing."

"Evil man." I broke off a branch of grapes for him. "No, Jeremy checked into a hotel as soon as he left our outraged Rachel."

"No guts," Sébastien mumbled around a grape. "No glory."

"I'm feeling rather like a parent, Gumby. What a peculiar sensation."

A

Sitting in yet another waiting room, Rachel figured she could play the silent game as well as Jeremy, maybe better after all those years of watching her mother do it. It was eight-fifteen, Monday morning, and they'd wheeled Edgar up to surgery thirty minutes ago. For all of those thirty minutes, Jeremy had sat across the waiting room from her, as far away as he could get, and buried his nose in an ancient women's magazine. She doubted that he was absorbing much about knitting patterns for the holidays or hearty soups for autumn . She, however, had snagged a book off Edgar's bookshelf and was already deep into the story. When she wasn't looking over the top of the pages at Jeremy. It was fine with her if he never spoke.

Sébastien had already called once, and she'd told him that Edgar was fine when he left for surgery. They'd given him something that made him sleepy and silly, but he'd smiled at both her and Jeremy as two orderlies rolled him down the hall. "Be good, children," he'd said.

The book was a mystery by P. D. James, whom Edgar praised every time he talked to Rachel about what he called his *genre*. He said he only wished he could write mysteries as well as Phyllis. Rachel figured that must be the P part of the author's name. And the writing was engaging, or would've been if Rachel had possessed an ounce of patience. Uh oh. Just then Jeremy looked up from his magazine about the time Rachel was glancing at him. Their eyes met. "The doctor said it would be quite a while before we heard anything," she said, like she'd intended to catch his eye. "I'm going to find some coffee. Want to come with me or would you like me to get you some?" This was so silly. So she'd screamed at him. He needed to get over it.

"No, thank you," he mumbled and looked back down at the magazine in his lap. A lock of light brown hair fell over his forehead. So many of these European men had longer hair than she was used to. Except Edgar, of course, and he had very little hair at all. She tried to picture Jeremy as bald.

"Suit yourself." She stood, stretched, and went off to what the woman two nights ago had called the canteen. She might do better if she left the hospital, but she was afraid to be gone too long.

She found coffee, she took yet another call from Sébastien, she wandered outside for a minute. The sun was shining at last, and she looked up at the clear sky, the same sky that hovered over Paris and Morton, Ohio, U. S. A. Six months ago she would never have imagined being in London or Paris, let alone dealing with a sick author or a cranky fashion designer. Life was beyond weird, she thought. But she couldn't complain about it being boring. For a moment she thought about slogging through the days at Hollister County High School. Lesson plans and grading. Faculty meetings and pep rallies. As lost as she sometimes felt in Europe, she had no real desire to go home. Finally she returned to the waiting room. Jeremy had his laptop out and was staring at the screen like he'd found the hiding place of the Holy Grail. Geez, but he was unfriendly. Rachel looked at her watch for the gazillionth time and picked up her book. Time crawled. Much later, the doctor, sort of scary-looking in his scrubs, came to tell them that Edgar had done fine. He was in recovery, would probably be there another hour or so, and then they could see him. Rachel nodded, but Jeremy stopped the doctor before he could leave." I talked to you before," he said. "I'm Mr. Tremaine's nephew, and, as you recall, I plan to take him to Cornwall for his recuperation as soon as he's able. In an ambulance if you prefer. We've hired a day nurse to care for him." He looked very earnest." How soon do you think he could travel?"

The doctor mumbled about it being too soon to tell; he couldn't recommend travel just yet. But if there were an ambulance and a trained nurse. . . he'd just have to let him know later. Jeremy whipped a card from his pocket." I want to see him, of course, but I'd like to set up arrangements to move my uncle as soon as possible. Here's my number."

As the doctor left, Jeremy glanced at her. His face had a triumphant look, like he'd gone one up on her. "Oh, good," she said. "I'm glad there will be someone to take care of Edgar." She placed a bookmark between the pages. "I'm afraid I can't." She would have, if he'd needed her, and she was fairly sure Sébastien wouldn't have cared. She could make up all the nonsense she'd miss in her modeling class, but she wasn't about to let this Jeremy guy think he'd beaten her.

"I didn't expect you to," he replied in a voice that made her want to rake her fingernails down his handsome face. Like he was sure she was way too full of herself to alter her schedule for Edgar. But he'd actually spoken to her. That was a change.

It didn't last. They sat in silence another hour before a nurse came and said they could see Mr. Tremaine, one at a time. Jeremy motioned to Rachel. "You, first," he said. "I'm sure you're in a hurry to leave."

What a jerk, she thought as she gritted her teeth into something resembling a smile and followed the nurse. How could nice old Edgar have such a loser for a nephew? Edgar was pale and drowsy, but he gave Rachel a wan smile. "There's my girl," he mumbled.

"Here I am," Rachel agreed. "But I'll be going back to Paris this evening. Jeremy says he plans to take you to Cornwall to recuperate as soon as you're able."

Edgar nodded. "He told me that yesterday. Wish you could come," he said.

"Me too. Maybe someday." She patted his arm. "Get well."

He smiled. "I will. Must finish the book."

"Not today."

"No, not today. Give Sébastien my love."

Rachel blinked. "Okay," she said and leaned over to kiss his pale cheek.

She slept on the train and didn't get back to Sébastien's apartment until after nine o'clock. He wasn't there. After calling her every hour the entire day, she'd thought he'd be anxious to talk to her about Edgar, but the most predictable thing about Sébastien was his unpredictability. At least that's what Edgar had said to her. When she went into the kitchen to see what was in the refrigerator, she noticed a box on the kitchen table. Beside it, in Sébastien's eccentric scrawl, a note said that she should try these and see if she liked them. Opening the box she found four miniature vials with glass stoppers. Each contained maybe a quarter of an ounce of fluid. She unstoppered one and sniffed. Yep, perfume. Okay, but not great. She daubed some on her wrists and opened the fridge. It suddenly occurred to her that she had eaten nothing but a muffin all day. And she hadn't thought about Kurt even once.

Chapter Eleven

She must be homesick. That was Rachel's diagnosis anyway. All the next week she dragged around, going to modeling classes, visiting poor, broken Notre Dame for the third time, and finishing the mystery she'd borrowed from Edgar. She called him every day and was pleased to hear his voice strengthening. She didn't think of Kurt all that often, leading her to the conclusion that her feelings for him had been nearly as superficial as his. But she still felt sort of depressed. Blue, Granny would've called it.

In modeling class, they started addressing hair and makeup, which Rachel enjoyed. But no matter what else was on the agenda for the day, they always worked on movement, which she hated. Rachel felt as silly as when she'd performed her mock strut for Edgar. The instructor pursed her lips every time it was Rachel's turn. The other students, male and female, whispered about her. Maybe they thought she didn't understand French; maybe they didn't care if she did. She figured she carried at least forty pounds and eight years more than anybody in the class, and that included the men. Having done enough lying with Kurt to keep hellfire perpetually burning her britches, she refused to invent some stupid excuse for being in the class. She simply told those who asked that she was intrigued by modeling. Enough.

She was also very, very tired of being alone. All through September and October, except for what she called the Kurt Weeks, she'd explored the city, going back to her favorite spots again and again. She'd enjoyed it, but discovering wonderful places wasn't much fun without someone to share them with. It was mid-November. Back home, there'd be corn shocks and pumpkins, leftover from Halloween to decorate for Thanksgiving. Back home there'd be people to talk to. Her mother had finally choked out an email or two, wondering if Rachel could come home for the holiday. But it was a workday in France. Rachel had classes until nearly the end of November, and despite the nicely growing chunk of change in her French bank account, Rachel didn't want to spend that much money on a weekend visit when she'd be jet-lagged the entire time.

One gloomy Friday, she was leaving her class when her phone rang. The number wasn't familiar. "Hello," she said tentatively.

"Rachel! It's Jesse Kemper. We quit early today, and I thought maybe we could meet up for that coffee or a drink or something. Are you busy?"

She was rarely busy. "Sure. Where?"

They agreed on a café near Sylvestri and arrived at nearly the same time. Like Sébastien, Jesse's height made him easy to find. He drank a huge cup of latté and she nursed a strawberry smoothie. "So why do you love Maine?" he asked.

She was surprised he remembered but went on about rocky beaches, deep forests, and of course, her moose sighting. He was from the far north of the state and had a French-Canadian mother.

"I was brought up bilingual, but I never dreamed our French was nearly a different language in Paris." He grinned. "I found out in a hurry."

"And I was teaching French to high school kids. Didn't exactly expand my vocabulary." Rachel relaxed. He was easy to talk to. "So why are you here?"

He squirmed a bit, trying to fit his long legs under the tiny table." All I've ever wanted was to design clothes. Made me a first-class geek of questionable masculinity in high school and college." He played with an empty sugar packet. Big hands. She would've figured him for a basketball player. "Of course I had to come to Paris. I was sure my portfolio would open a dozen doors." He smiled. "It didn't. I spent the first two months and all my money visiting every atelier in town. Different from you, I hear. You sorta 'fell' into modeling, right?"

"Ha, ha." But she smiled. "I was a tourist. I never wanted to be a model, let alone someone's muse, as Sébastien calls me, and I still don't."

"I guess Himself is quite persuasive."

"No shit. But it will be over soon." She frowned. "So you took a job at Sylvestri, hoping for a break?"

Jesse nodded. "I envy you your experience. To learn about fashion from Fel would be amazing."

"I imagine you're learning bunches working in graphic design. Was that your degree?"

He nodded. "Oh, I am. And I sketch every chance I get. The things he's designing for you are fabulous. I'm trying to use those for inspiration without being derivative."

Here we go, Rachel thought. I'm another freaking inspiration.

"But you're really on the inside," he said. "I'd give anything for that."

She shrugged. "Why don't you just show Sébastien your designs?"

Jesse paled. "I couldn't do that. It would be presumptuous and might ruin any chances I'd have anywhere else."

"I doubt it."

Rachel took another sip of her smoothie. Jesse made her feel like she was back home. She frowned. "Do you ever feel homesick, but you know you don't really want to go home?"

His face broke into the friendliest of smiles. "I know what you mean. We're both from small towns, so this is grand and wonderful." He waved his long arms at Paris. "But we miss our people. And probably more, the ease of familiarity."

She grinned back. "That's it exactly. I didn't quite know how to say it. But you've been here longer. Does it get more familiar?"

"Sure. And I have a job not much different from one I'd have in the States, unfortunately."

She nodded.

They spent another hour talking about everything: music, Paris, movies, parents, and French food. They'd finished their drinks and still were talking when Jesse looked at his watch. "This has been super, but I need to be someplace in a half hour. We both love movies; do you want to meet up for a show on Sunday?"

She'd loved talking to him. He didn't attract her in any romantic way, but he felt like a good friend. "Sounds great," she said.

He stood. "It's a date. I'll call you."

She wondered if he would.

A

The next afternoon she decided to blow some of her cash and bought a laptop. She'd grown impatient with going to Internet cafés to return her mail when she chose not to write on her phone; besides, her ancient laptop had been alternately freezing up and running hot before she left. This was something practical she could take home when she left, she told herself. Or more practical than the heels she'd bought to go out with Kurt.

That evening she was setting up the computer in the kitchen when Sébastien came in. "*Bonsoir*," she said while adding names to her address book.

"Hello." He still refused to let her speak French.

"I talked to Edgar. They're taking his staples out on Monday."

Sébastien grimaced. He was squeamish about medical things.

"Have you had supper? Yvonne made a yummy quiche."

He shook his head. "How was class?"

"Fine. We're supposed to bring an ensemble to wear on Monday." She pronounced it *ensemble,* in French, just for meanness.

"Not the purple gown," he declared.

"Of course not." She got into her email and found a brief note from her brother asking to use her car again while theirs was in the shop. She replied with an even briefer "Yes."

Sébastien poured a glass of wine from the bottle that nearly always sat by the kitchen sink. He raised another glass. "You?"

"Sure," she said. "I thought I'd wear that black swing coat you hate."

He set wine next to her laptop. "With your coloring, you should never wear black." He made it sound like a pronouncement from Moses.

"You do. Besides, it's slimming." She sipped. That would be one thing she'd miss about Paris and Sébastien. She'd acquired a taste for good wine. She hardly ever drank Cokes any more.

He sat down. "What I am doing is not a, what do you call it? Fad? Fashion will change. With the Renaissance Collection, I will end this nonsense about skinny women. I am starting a revolution."

Rachel glanced at her address book. It looked right. "If you liked women, you'd want yours skinny too, just like all men." Except for Kurt, but she wasn't sure what attraction she'd held for him. Maybe she'd reminded him of his mother's cooking. Or maybe she was just another conquest. She should've looked to see if he made notches on his bed. And she didn't quite know what to make of Jesse.

Sébastien didn't deign to reply to this. He pointed at the little box of perfumes over by the refrigerator. "Did you try the scents?"

"Three of them. One smelled like toilet bowl cleaner, one reminded me of fruit salad, and one was pretty good. I'll try the last one soon. Why? Are you thinking about branching out into perfumes?" She closed the laptop.

"Probably not. People send me these things." He waved his arms around. "Sunglasses, scarves, bed linens, for God's sake."

"Sylvestri already does sunglasses and perfumes. And luggage too, right?"

He nodded.

"So why do they think you need more perfumes?"

"People send them to me, not Sylvestri. They want me to start my own lines."

Rachel frowned. "Are you allowed to do that?"

"But of course," he replied, like she'd said something stupid. "I design for Sylvestri, but I am still Sébastien Fel."

The one and only. "Well, it might be fun having your own products. And profitable. I'll give that last perfume a try."

Sébastien shrugged. "More work. More time away from the designs."

"Maybe you should have your own design house. Own the whole shebang."

He frowned at *shebang* but seemed to understand what she meant. "I have considered it," he said. "No Dumont to please with all the numbers."

"I've never seen him," Rachel said. She got up and poured a little more wine into her glass. "Is he scary?"

Sébastien said. "To some, but never to me. He allows me total creative freedom as long as the profits are good. I'd be a fool to leave and have to worry about numbers."

A

Early the next week Rachel had an inspiration. She would make Thanksgiving Dinner for Sébastien, maybe Madame Pauline and her husband as well. And Jesse. They'd seen a movie, and texted a few times. She bet he'd be feeling homesick at Thanksgiving too. It would have to be on Saturday; Sébastien worked late or had clients to woo nearly every weeknight, and she still had classes. She would have to find a pumpkin and turkey and all sorts of things at the market. And, she must email her mother for her pumpkin pie recipe, although she suspected that her mother used canned pumpkin, probably not available in Paris. Anyway, it was something to do, and Yvonne, who rarely said anything more than hello to Rachel, seemed amused by the plan and agreed to help.

The next Saturday morning, Rachel was fighting with a French pumpkin, not quite the same as the ones in the USA. The pumpkin guts were slimy and gooey, and she was wondering how she could ever turn the squash into a smooth, custardy pie. The turkey was basted with butter and white wine, fancier than Jean Bowman's recipe, and ready to go into the oven. Rachel had made cornbread last night, and it was already crumbled for Granny's stuffing. While she was wrestling with the pumpkin pulp and thinking she was alone, a strange man walked into the kitchen, making her nearly drop her knife. He wore only briefs, extremely brief briefs, and was very hairy. She hadn't heard the door, hadn't known anyone was in the apartment, but there he was. She didn't like it.

He mumbled a greeting, in French, and opened the refrigerator. "What the hell is that?" He pointed at the big bird that took up all of one shelf.

"*C'est la dinde*," she replied, frowning at him.

He pulled out a bottle of orange juice and drank straight from it. Rachel's mother had always hated it when Rob did that. "My name is Rachel," she said, continuing in French and hoping he'd identify himself. Where was Sébastien? Had this guy spent the night with him? Sébastien had never brought men home before, at least as far as she knew. And she probably would've known.

The strange man couldn't be bothered to quit gulping juice. Finally, he lowered the bottle and wiped his mouth on the back of his hand. "Max," he said." Are you the housekeeper?"

"No." She grabbed a handful of pumpkin fiber and seed and deposited it in a bowl. Some of the mess stuck to her hand.

Max looked at the goo and turned a little green. "Then who are you?" He wasn't much taller than she was but had broad enough shoulders to look tough. And insistent.

"I'm Rachel," she repeated. "Sébastien's friend. Where is he?"

The man shrugged. "He left very early this morning. He said I should go, but what's the hurry? I went back to sleep." He peered at the empty coffeemaker. "Make me some coffee, dear. I'm hungover." Or at least that's what she thought he said.

When she didn't move, he gave her a long look. "That accent. American, hmm?" He pointed and switched to English. "Coffee. Now." And left the kitchen.

Nervy son of a bitch, she thought, washing her hands. She made coffee and went back to her pumpkin. She needed to cook the shell now. While she was cutting it into chunks, she heard the front door. Sébastien, she hoped. "Tell your boyfriend his coffee's ready," she shouted. Two weeks ago, Sébastien had been concerned enough about Edgar to visit him in the hospital, and she'd hoped maybe they'd get back together. She felt sure that Edgar still cared about Sébastien. But it didn't look promising. Sébastien obviously liked jerks, and Edgar was a good guy.

Sébastien came into the kitchen with a bundle of papers. They looked like some of Jesse's graphic work. He was perturbed. "He's still here?"

Rachel didn't look up from her work. The pumpkin skin was tough. "Mm, hmm." It was sort of fun seeing Sébastien irritated at someone other than her.

"He talked to you?"

"It felt more like he was ordering me around, but yes."

Sébastien made a disgusted noise and left the room. She heard muffled shouting from down the hall, and not long after that, both Sébastien and Max left. She yelled after them that dinner was at seven-thirty. She wasn't sure Sébastien heard her, but she'd been reminding him of her Thanksgiving meal for days. He'd better be there.

A

Rachel upended the final perfume vial and touched a bit onto her wrists and neck. This one smelled heavenly. She wished she had a whole big bottle of it. Slipping into Polly's creation, the asymmetrical dark green jacket that matched her skirt, she decided she'd done fairly well. The golden turkey was resting, waiting to be carved. The two pumpkin pies looked perfect. And she didn't look too bad herself. Sébastien and Madame Pauline had insisted that Rachel needed a skirt suit, but this was the first time she'd worn it. She wondered if Jesse would like the design. Lord, she was surrounded by fashion critics.

Crystal and silver gleamed on Sébastien's dining room table. Yvonne had ironed a heavy damask tablecloth into submission, and the autumn flowers Rachel had bought and arranged looked festive. She glanced at her watch. It was seven-thirty. Where was Sébastien? Within a minute, Madame Pauline and her husband arrived. Rachel almost giggled at the sight of Monsieur Robert, Charlie, he said to call him. He was short, bald, and a little dumpy. He had a very red nose and smiled continuously, especially when he stuttered the little bit of English he

110

knew. Madame Pauline beamed and helped him communicate. They were obviously crazy about each other. Well, Rachel thought, her granny had always said there was a lid for every pot.

In another minute, Jesse was there, holding a bottle of wine and grinning at everyone. He switched back and forth from English to French so quickly that Rachel's head spun, all the while telling little jokes to Charlie and complimenting Madame Pauline. "Where's Himself?" he whispered in Rachel's ear. She shrugged, but Jesse seemed relieved. He'd gladly accepted her invitation but was honest about his trepidation in meeting Sébastien.

She poured wine, chatted, did the best she could. Dinner would be ruined if she waited much longer to serve. Jesse was gracious and helped her bring dishes to the table. Madame Pauline admired Rachel's suit, which figured since she'd sewn it. When Rachel said they must begin, the Roberts shrugged and said but of course. Charlie carved the bird like a surgeon and lay slices on their plates with grace and precision. "We dig in now?" he asked with a thick accent and a giant grin.

Rachel said, in French, that yes, they should.

It was more fun than she would've expected, even without the Great Designer. Rachel told them about school pageants featuring Pilgrims and Indians. And how in first grade she'd had to portray a bowl of mashed potatoes in a Thanksgiving play. Jesse said he'd been a turkey. They laughed. And this led somehow to discussions of Benjamin Franklin in Paris and John Wayne cowboy movies. Rachel had fiddled with the food so long that she had little appetite, but Charlie exclaimed over every dish and went nearly orgasmic over the pumpkin pie. Jesse ate a phenomenal amount of mashed potatoes, in tribute to Rachel, he said. They all drank a lot of wine, and Madame Pauline got the giggles at least twice. But there was no sign of Sébastien.

After the Roberts left, insisting that Rachel must come dine with them soon, she changed into jeans and her Paris sweatshirt to clean up the mess with Jesse. The kitchen looked like a bomb had exploded, but Rachel plodded through it, filling the refrigerator with leftovers while Jesse loaded the dishwasher with plates.

"Wonder where Sébastien was?" Jesse looked uncomfortable at using the informal first name.

"I don't know." Rachel dumped the heavy silverware into the sink. "Probably out with his boyfriend." She told him about Max.

"Kinda rude though, with all the trouble you went to." He started drying spoons.

"He is rude. All the time, but every once in a while I see a softer side." Rachel shook her head. "Not often."

Jesse was silent. Then he spoke very fast. "I was wanting to ask you something."

"Yeah?" She passed him a handful of forks.

"Would you mind looking at my designs sometime and telling me what you think?" He paused. "No hurry."

Rachel looked up at him. Jesse's face was bony, not particularly attractive until he smiled, and then the lights came on. He wasn't smiling. "Of course. But you said you have a sister, right?"

He nodded.

"You might as well show them to her for all I know about design and fashion."

"I'm sure you've picked up all kinds of knowledge from Madame Robert and Monsieur Fel." He kept drying the same fork.

"And so have you. But I don't mind. I'll tell you what I think for what it's worth."

"Thanks," he said. You would've thought it was a life or death matter. "Maybe you could come over to my place sometime. It's a dump, but it's in a pretty little neighborhood." He waved his dish towel. "I wouldn't want to bring them here."

Jesse was flat out terrified of Sébastien; that was obvious. "Fine. We'll do it soon. And, by the way, your suit is terrific. Mr. Fel?"

"Sort of. Mostly Madame Pauline. Thanks. It's fun to wear."

When they'd finished the dishes, he left, giving her a big hug and saying she'd made a lonely holiday happy.

Rachel said she was glad, hugged him back, and actually kissed him on the neck, standing on tiptoes to reach that high. And then she was alone again. She didn't know why she'd been tempted to count on Sébastien. He'd never given her any indication that he was more than some kind of strange employer. She sat at the kitchen table with a Coke and looked at the dirty roasting pan sitting by the sink. Maybe it was her. Kurt had dumped her for who knows whom, and Sébastien must find hairy Max much more fascinating than dinner with Rachel. Hadn't Kurt told her that dining at home with her would be boring? Okay, they didn't really like her. But she had to endure it for only another few months. She could tough it out, she supposed.

She opened her laptop and re-read the most recent message from Shelley, two weeks old now. It was full of exclamation points, mostly about Shelley, her children, and school, but she'd written, "Oh, Rachel! Paris! Fashion! Lovers! Parties! Tell me all about it. What's new?" Rachel hadn't known how to reply to it.

She glanced at the sink, focusing on the violets rather than the pan and wrote:

Hey Shelley—good to hear from you. I hope both boys' ear infections are history by now and that they send that Halfhill kid to Juvie instead of back to your classroom. Sounds like everybody's about the same. Did you have a nice Thanksgiving? I wanted to make your apple-cranberry casserole, but I couldn't find any cranberries. I used dried cherries instead and it was great! You should try it sometime.

God, she was talking recipes. And she was supposed to be having the time of her life: partying, modeling, living like a rock star. Rachel rubbed her face. Truth or not?

I'm taking a class—can't tell you what—hush, hush! But it still leaves me with lots of time for Paris, fabulous Paris! The wine's great too. No parties since the photographer dumped me ☹. Thanks for the sympathy, but I'm over him now! He was just a diversion, not nearly as much fun as my new lingerie! This is all too exciting to believe☺. I should be home in February and we'll have a night out when I can tell you ALL the secrets.

Hug the boys---
Rachel

What a load of happy horseshit, she thought and went over to the sink to scrub the roasting pan.

Chapter Twelve

"Would you like lunch?" asked Madame Pauline. Rachel was at the *atelier* for a fitting of the incredible copper-brown outfit that she loved nearly as much as the purple dress. Several people started matching up shoes, jewelry and other accessories with her outfits, costumes, whatever, and it had taken forever. Even with all that, she'd been hanging out for an hour. She told herself that she wasn't really waiting to bump into Sébastien, although it would be nice. He hadn't been home in four days. She told herself that it didn't matter, that she just didn't have anything better to do.

"Sure." She was almost positive Madame Pauline had figured out how lonesome she was and felt sorry for her. At dinner the other night, Charlie and Madame Pauline had talked about their two daughters, away from home now and sorely missed. Maybe Polly was adopting her.

They exited the building into cool, bright sunlight. "Charlie says you are *très jolie*," Madame Pauline said with a smile. "He wonders if you can do American fried chicken."

Rachel grinned. "Sure. Better than the Colonel. I'll cook it for him sometime."

Madame Pauline nodded, then frowned." And you will eat much of it yourself, yes? They tell me your fitting was bad. They must take the seams in."

Rachel shrugged. "I haven't been trying to lose weight."

Madame Pauline ducked into a dark doorway. "Lovely food here," she said. "Edgar told me about this restaurant years ago."

Rachel blinked to adjust to the dim interior. "I miss him."

"I too, but he must get well before he comes to Paris again." Madame Pauline tapped her fingers on the tablecloth, and a waiter flew to the table. She ordered wine.

"How's Sébastien?" Rachel kept her voice level. It shouldn't matter. He was just her boss.

The woman shrugged. "Very busy. Dumont has him looking over some sketches to hire a new junior designer, and he's scheduling a conference call for you models next week." She took a deep breath. "Dozens of fittings this week and next." She shook her head as if this was beyond belief. "Why? Have you not seen Sébastien?"

"No." Rachel didn't want to say more. She did her own version of the Parisian shrug but didn't suppose it fooled Madame Pauline, who frowned for a moment and then seemed to think twice about discussing Sébastien.

The waiter materialized and, without bothering to ask Rachel what she wanted, Madame Pauline ordered in a flurry of French. Rachel thought she might be getting scallops.

"It is okay that you lost some weight." Madame Pauline unfolded her napkin and gave Rachel a little smile. She could almost imagine calling the woman Polly. "But you must stay exactly the same now. There isn't time for more adjustments." She sipped from the glass of white wine the waiter had just delivered. "We should have all five costumes done in another week or so. Sébastien has nearly finished the final one."

This sounded like good news, so Rachel wondered why Madame Pauline shook her head. "Why? What's wrong?"

"I do not see how you are going to do five costumes. It isn't done."

Rachel sipped her wine too, and thought how decadent it was to be drinking at lunch. "The models usually come down the runway zoom, zoom, zoom, don't they?"

Madame Pauline nodded. "Zoom," she said in a thin voice. "Although Sébastien has decided you will go out and back one at a time." She shook her head again. "Not what we usually do."

Rachel tried to look sympathetic, but all she could think was that the models would be too wide to pass each other.

Madame Pauline took a larger slug of wine. "You know Claude? Sylvestri's director of the shows?"

"Yes."

"Sébastien dismissed him. He argued with Sébastien about the show, the models, the clothes. He said they were all preposterous." She snapped her fingers. "Gone. I do not know who will be directing the show." She sighed. "Claude also said it was absurd to have five costumes for one model." She kept shaking her head.

The waiter set plates in front of them. Yep, those were scallops, covered in what looked like a white wine cream sauce. Rachel took a bite: the food was, of course, heavenly. She'd have no trouble maintaining her weight with dishes like this. Madame Pauline had a small green salad with a few shrimp decorating the edges. Of course. Rachel figured that there weren't but a few women in the world who could stand in front of a full-length mirror without finding fault with their bodies, size two or twenty. Did Sébastien really think he'd change the world's perception of beauty with one collection of gorgeous but oversized clothes? Rachel agreed with Claude, but it didn't matter. Like Madame Pauline, she felt compelled to make the best of Sébastien's ideas.

Rachel touched one of the little scallops with her fork. "Well," she drawled, an idea hatching as she talked. "It's unconventional, but everything about this show is different, right?"

Madame Pauline's eyebrows went up as she chewed.

"What about having little interludes between the models?" Rachel stopped and tried to envision it. "Not between every costume, but every five or six, say. Music, whatever. Nothing lengthy. Even two minutes would make a difference, wouldn't it?"

Madame Pauline nodded. "It would make a huge difference," she said. "What kinds of things could we use?"

Rachel popped another savory scallop into her mouth. "The collection's supposed to be based on the Renaissance, isn't it? Didn't they have minstrels, jugglers? I don't know that much about it. Fools?" She grinned. "Maybe that's me."

Madame Pauline patted her arm. "No, no. You are not a fool. But I like the idea. It needs thought and um. . ." She was searching for an English word.

"Research," Rachel supplied. "Edgar would know all about this. What if I call him this afternoon? He probably needs something to do while he's recuperating down in Cornwall."

"Perfect," Madame Pauline declared. Her eyes were shining. "And if we have two dressers for you, everything very organized, it might work."

"Some of the other models have two changes, right?" Rachel tried one of the cute roasted carrots. Yum. Butter.

"Yes. At least six of them will. But that is no problem. We have done that before." She set down her fork. "You realize that you will start and finish the show, Rachel?"

"Yeah. Sébastien told me." She looked at her lap. "Lucky me." Lifting her head, she said, "There might not be any audience left by the time I finish the first lap."

Madame Pauline said no, sixteen different ways, but Rachel could see it happening. Very easily.

A

I'd just emailed the completed manuscript to my editor when the phone rang. Forced inactivity had served me well; I'd completed over a hundred pages in ten days. Feeling as though such a weighty piece of business deserved a hefty bourbon, even if it was early afternoon, I considered letting it go to voice mail, but I didn't. "Tremaine," I said.

"Hi Edgar. It's Rachel. How are you feeling?"

"Splendid, my dear. I just sent my book to the dragon lady."

"Who's that?"

"My editor. She's a combination of Margo and every autocratic nanny I ever tortured. How are you? I wish you were here. The sun is shining in lovely Cornwall, and I feel like drinking bourbon in celebration of your book."

She giggled. "It's not my book, Edgar. I'm just glad I could help out." She paused. "I wish I could celebrate with you too, but are you supposed to be drinking yet?"

"Dear God, another bloody autocratic nanny."

Again I received the giggle I'd been hoping for. "Okay," she said. "I need your help."

I expected something dire, but she outlined the problem with costume changes and her idea for Renaissance entertainments between the acts, so to speak. "I can do some research," I said. "But you might have acrobats or jugglers or dancers. Certainly musicians," I went on. "Perhaps playing genuine Renaissance instruments like lutes and tambors, things of that sort."

"Lutes and what?"

It was a joy to hear her voice. She'd been emailing nearly every day since she bought her laptop, but I missed the child." A tambor is a drum. Citterns, of course. All kinds of instruments. I'm sure there are Renaissance musicians in Paris. You'll just need to find them. Put Sébastien's show manager on that. What's his name? Claude?"

"Claude got fired." She laughed again. "No, wait, I'm learning Brit. Another language, you know. Claude was sacked."

"Very good."

"But I'll find out who took his place and tell him. Could you find me an article or something on the instruments?"

"You bet," I said. "I'm learning Yank."

"There you go. Are you sure you're recovering well?"

"I am. I'm walking every day and saw my local physician. He declares that I'm on the mend, and I'm sure I'll get the same verdict when I see the surgeon in London. I even went to Margo's last night for dinner."

"Brave Edgar," she said. "Is Jeremy taking good care of you?" Her voice sounded carefully neutral on this question. I wished she and Jeremy had made friends, but I'd be satisfied with an armed truce. "Indeed he is, although I'm getting rather weary of being mothered. I'm looking forward to returning to London. How's Sébastien?"

There was a tiny pause I didn't care for." All right, I guess."

"What? Is he mistreating you?"

"No. He hasn't been home for a while. Busy, I guess."

I knew the signs. "A new man?"

Her voice was soft. "Yes."

"That happens to Sébastien with some regularity, my dear. It won't last over another week. He's a serial snogger."

"A what?"

"Oh, you and Jeremy told me the American term weeks ago. What was it? A player?"

Again, I got the laugh I'd wanted, and we spoke for another couple of minutes about nothing in particular. A bit later, I consulted Google and performed the research I'd promised, but celebrating the new book had lost its appeal. Damn Sébastien.

A

After lunch, Rachel took the long way home. Modeling class had been cancelled, and she didn't know what to do with herself. From a street vendor, she bought some carnations, an extravagance that she'd never be able to afford back in Morton. Then she popped into a drug store and bought dark red nail polish. They'd had a brief session on manicures at modeling school, so she wanted to try out what she'd learned. Sébastien hated nail polish, called it "varnish," which Rachel finally figured out was the British word for it. But she didn't care what he thought in any language. She wandered through the store, eyeing the displays of cheap makeup and toiletries. Right now she could afford expensive, department store makeup and nail polish, but there was no sense in getting used to it. Poverty loomed. The clerk saw Rachel's flowers and grinned at her. "From your lover?" she asked.

Rachel said no and left, walking for another hour with no destination, like she'd done for weeks now. When she finally neared Sébastien's apartment she decided to go into the cookery shop across the street. She'd been intrigued by the place for weeks.

It smelled wonderful. Someone was demonstrating a recipe to a half-dozen enthusiastic cooks, and if Rachel hadn't been so full of scallops, she'd have been salivating. Gleaming pots of copper, steel, and enamel hung from ceiling hooks. Colorful linens lay stacked on tables. Marble rolling pins, wicked-looking knives, gadgets and googaws, as Granny would've said. It was probably because of the Thanksgiving dinner she'd prepared, or maybe she was having a fit of domesticity, but she wanted all of it. She picked up a luminous plate, pristine white, and thought how much she'd like a set of dishes. Back home she used her mother's castoffs, oatmeal beige and scratched. When she bothered with a plate. At least half her meals were eaten off the lovely black plastic of Lean Cuisine. A woman came up and offered to help Rachel, but she said she just wanted to browse, and she did, all through the stacks of aprons and the shelves of containers.

Then Rachel had a moment of inspiration. It was almost Christmas; tomorrow was December first. Her mother would love a piece or two of the copper cookware, and one of the bright tablecloths would be just right for Rob and Heather. Their stuff was all so practical and boring. She'd buy napkins too and maybe something more masculine later for Rob. So she spent a glorious half hour assembling Christmas gifts for her family, throwing in a couple of knives for her dad who considered himself the carving expert of the county, sort of like Madame Pauline's Charlie. The clerk said that certainly they could wrap the items in holiday paper and ship them. Rachel wrote out cards identifying which gift was for each person, gave the clerk all the addresses, and left the shop considerably poorer, but happy for the moment.

As she let herself into the echoing, empty apartment she remembered what Madame Pauline had said about her weight. She wasn't hungry, but she opened a Coke and a box of chocolates. Taking these to the living room, she sprawled on Sébastien's white leather sofa and decided she'd read and eat bonbons. Every woman's dream. As Shelley had said, Rachel was living it, wasn't she?

She'd been re-reading Edgar's mysteries, in order, and was on the third one. Sébastien had all of them and didn't care if she chose titles from the massive bookcase in the living room. Edgar's Inspector

Hannaford was wonderful. So quiet, so wise, so absolutely sexy in a tortured, lonesome way. Rachel felt proud that her character, Chloe, would be the one to break through the detective's protective reserve. Although she'd already read most of the books, knowing Chloe was down the road made the stories more meaningful. Gulping more chapters than chocolates, she read until she had to turn on lamps. About seven, she changed into one of Gisèle's lovely nightgowns and her on-loan robe from Sébastien. She remembered that it was one of the things she'd taken to Kurt's. Rachel waited for that particular bruise to start aching, but it barely twinged. Maybe, like she'd written to Shelley, she was getting over him.

If Sébastien were coming home at all, he'd be there by now. Wandering into the kitchen, Rachel buttered some bread, sliced some cheese, and washed an apple. Good old Yvonne. The pantry was full, and there was a bowl of some kind of chicken stew in the fridge, but Rachel didn't bother to heat it up. She took her plate into the living room, which would probably appall Sébastien, not that he'd ever know, and started reading again. She'd licked the last of the butter off her fingers when a key rattled in the door.

Damn, had Sébastien finally come home? Besides Yvonne, she didn't know of anyone else who had a key. The door opened and she heard heavy steps, just out of sight from where she sat. "Sébastien?" asked a male voice. God. It was Max again.

"He's not here," she said in French. Weird. Why had Max come here? She'd pretty much figured that Sébastien had been staying with him these last few days.

He walked into the room and slid his eyes around it as if he thought Sébastien might be hiding somewhere. Looking dejected, he asked, "Where is he?"

Rachel shrugged. She supposed Max was attractive if you liked the swarthy, dark type. He did have nice eyes, she supposed, and his body screamed tons of hours spent at the gym. She'd seen a lot more of it than she would've liked, but it was okay.

He unzipped his leather jacket, took it off, and sat in the black armchair like he was planning to stay. Uh, uh, thought Rachel. She wasn't going to entertain Sébastien's lover, especially if he was Sébastien's dumped lover. She was getting the feeling that this might be the case. "You live here?" he asked.

She looked down at her book and nodded. Maybe if she ignored him, he'd go away. Her eyes locked on the word 'Hannaford.' Where was the dashing inspector when a girl needed him?

Then Max laughed as if he'd made a big discovery, kind of like the old-fashioned cartoon characters who had light bulbs go on over their heads. "But of course," he said in rapid French. "So, Sébastien likes women too. I didn't know." He lifted his hand and turned it one way, then the other. "Sometimes this, sometimes that. I see."

Rachel shook her head. "No."

Max grinned. "We can play little games together, the three of us. Very nice." Shrugging, he said, "I don't mind women."

Decent of you, Rachel thought. She was feeling a little whiff of anxiety and wishing Sébastien or somebody would come through the door about then. "No," she said again, forcefully this time.

Max lifted his chin and appraised her. "Big woman," he said. "But fine bosoms." Or at least that's what she thought he said. She pulled the robe tight over her chest.

She pointed at the entryway. "Go." Then she stood, giving him what she hoped was an authoritative look.

He didn't budge. "Sébastien is so artistic, so creative. He likes variety, yes? Something new all the time. That's why he didn't come to me tonight. I understand. He will be here soon." He nodded. "Yes, and we will play little games, all three of us. Is there wine?"

"Leave now," Rachel insisted. She glanced around the room to find a weapon but the only possibility she could see was a heavy crystal ashtray. Sébastien would probably kill her if she broke it. "I mean it," she said, switching to English. "Get out of here, slimeball."

He rose but didn't leave. "I will get the wine," he said on his way to the kitchen. She thought she heard him mumble, "I'll need a lot of wine to do the cow."

Her phone was in her purse, back in her bedroom, but that was the last place she wanted to be just then. Besides, who would she call? The police? Jesse? She thought of escaping out the front door, screaming for the concierge, but she wasn't supposed to call attention to herself and either solution would result in that. Mind racing, she followed him into the kitchen where he was pouring two glasses of wine. He smiled when she came in.

"You have this all wrong," she said, speaking slowly so she would get the French right. "I am Sébastien's cousin. We are not lovers."

Max's eyes narrowed. "Cousins?"

Rachel nodded. "His mother and my mother are sisters. I am just staying here for a while."

"Why?"

None of your business, you hairy ape, Rachel thought, but she said, "I'm taking classes."

He took a huge gulp from one of the wineglasses and then got that cunning look back in his eyes. "Are you rich like Sébastien?"

At first, she wasn't sure which would be the better answer and started to say yes, thinking that money might equal power to Max and make him think twice about bothering with her. But before she could decide what to answer, he started unbuttoning his shirt, revealing gobs and gobs of dark, curly hair, and an evil light came up in his dark eyes. "Of course you are a rich girl; you are Sébastien Fel's cousin, and you are American. I told you I like women too. I will make you very happy," he crooned, stepping closer and closer to Rachel. "Forget him. I'm done with Sébastien anyway." He snapped his fingers. "You and I can travel. Cruises. Beaches. I have always wanted to go to the Caribbean. Have you? We will have a wonderful time. Here." He held out the other glass of wine. "Oh, yes." He touched her cheek.

She jerked away from him. "You piece of shit," she shouted in English. "You're in this for the money, aren't you?" She narrowed her eyes. "You're nothing but a hairy little whore." She started screaming, ranting that he'd taken advantage of Sébastien, that he was a snake, a worm, a son of a bitch. She stopped, breathless, only when she saw Max look past her, a flicker of concern in his eyes.

"Thank you, Raquel, but I can take over from here." Sébastien's slow, almost British drawl came from behind her. She had been yelling so loud she hadn't heard him come in. He gave Max a long, cold look. "My key?" he asked, now in French. "When did you copy that? While I slept?" Sébastien glanced at Rachel and switched back to English. "I would never have given it to him. I told him not to come here. Ever."

Max tried to act cool. He shrugged, chugged down the rest of his wine, and fished in his pocket for the key. He didn't bother buttoning his shirt, but Rachel wished he would. "You were angry when you left this morning," Max said. "I was very sad, and I wanted to apologize. I wanted to see you tonight to make everything better."

"I did leave. I was angry. And I also told you it was over." Sébastien took the key. "But I doubt that I broke your mercenary little heart. Good-bye."

Max tried for swagger as he sauntered across the kitchen. He paused at the doorway and sneered at the two of them. "You're old, Sébastien. Very, very old. And she's fat. You deserve each other." And he turned his back.

Rachel started to spit a retort, but Sébastien pressed a finger to his lips. "He's not worth the air," he said.

"No, he's not. He's more like something I'd scrape off the bottom of my shoe," she muttered and grabbed the wine Max had poured for her. She drank off about half of it and glared at Sébastien. "Are you stupid?"

He scratched his nose, looked out the window, and mumbled, "Probably." He set the key on the tiled counter. "I think we both have very bad taste in men."

A

Late on Saturday, I returned to my London flat. I hadn't been there since the night they carried me out on a stretcher. Although I'd alerted the housekeeper that I'd be arriving in the afternoon and she'd tidied the place, the rooms felt unused, muffled up. I sniffed and thought I could smell Rachel's perfume. Hannaford's Chloe must smell the same, so I tried to identify the subtle scent of it. Citrus, I thought. Maybe a hint of lily.

On Monday I lunched with my editor. Even though she tried for professional insouciance, I could tell she was pleased with me. After her second glass of wine, she became quite chatty and gushed about how much the publishers liked the manuscript. "They're wondering if you could do something Lord Peter Wimsey and Harriet Vane-ish with Hannaford and Chloe. A detective couple. A spot of romance. A bit of bedroom. And collaboration on solving murders, of course," she said. There was a light in her eyes that looked dangerously like enthusiasm. Or greed.

"Not my cup of tea," I replied, amused because I'd had the same ideas. It would be tremendous fun to write something of that ilk. I already had notes for the next book, to include Chloe's perfume and some serious kissing.

She scooped a lavish dollop of cream into her spoon and smiled. "Oh, I know you've had little experience with heterosexual romance, Edgar. But good authors should have imaginations broad enough to envision the possibilities."

I'd scraped the cream off the top of my apple tart and set it aside. The doctors had warned me that fatty foods might trouble me after the loss of my gall bladder, and I'd become very interested in a healthy diet over the last few weeks. "I'm insulted," I replied mildly. Actually, I'd had a brief affair with a nice, but not too nice, young woman when I was in my twenties, just to ascertain that I could do so, and to attempt a balance between my inclinations and Margo's stubborn insistence upon what she viewed as normalcy. Despite my lack of enthusiasm and my ultimate decision to pursue single-gendered romances in the future, the fling had been successful enough. "Of course I could write it," I said. "I simply might not choose to do so."

My editor stuffed more apple tart in her mouth and grinned, knowing that I was salivating much more over the creative possibilities than the pudding. "Get busy," she urged. "People will be clamoring for it. There's nothing so titillating as the seduction of an old bachelor. You've put new life into your series, Edgar." I left her, no doubt envisioning monumental sales.

Once I arrived back at the flat, I fired up my laptop and noodled around with my notes and other ideas for the new novel. The gray afternoon slid into evening without making much difference in the light, so I was surprised when my phone rang and I noticed it was after six. "Tremaine," I said.

It was Jeremy. "How are you? Did the trip wear you out?"

"I'm fine, Jeremy, and no, the trip didn't tire me at all. I'm fully recovered, you know. And already working on the next book." I appreciated the boy's concerns, but his mothering had turned into a psychological blister on my heel.

"Good." He paused. "Margo wanted to know."

Likely story. Margo was about as nurturing as Cinderella's step-mother. "Tell her I'm good."

"Okay. Are you staying in London until Christmas?"

Did the boy miss me? Once again I thought about how much my nephew needed a wife and kiddies, or at the very least a sexy young woman for recreational activities. Goodness, he had Penmore all to himself most of the time. He could have affairs without the nuisance of hotels or, God forbid, the backseats of cars. Of course, as reticent and mysterious as Jeremy was, he might be hosting weekly marathons of licentiousness at Penmore, for all I knew. "Yes, I'll probably return on the eighteenth or twentieth. A bit before Christmas. Are you getting us a tree?" He sold them at his greenhouse, along with mistletoe, holly, and ivy. And poinsettias. He grew hundreds of those during the holidays. Last year he'd produced a few blue ones. Bizarre.

"Yes. I'll get the decorating done before you arrive."

"Oh, let's wait and trim the old house together. A bit jollier, wouldn't you say?" For at least the thousandth time, I wished my sister and her husband had lived. Jeremy needed more in the way of family than an eccentric grandmother and a queer old uncle, but there you have it. We were all each other had.

"All right. I'll get in some of the usual things too."

By this he meant liquor, wine, oranges, sprouts, and a free-range turkey. I always cooked Christmas dinner for Margo and Jeremy.

We talked a bit longer, but I felt rather despondent when we hung up. All this discussion of Christmas reminded me of the years in Paris when I'd kept the holiday with Sébastien. I'd cooked even back then, and we'd always had a merry party on Christmas Eve: Polly, Charlie, and their daughters, now married and living far away. And usually there'd been another half dozen *couture* people stranded in the city. Paris is very lonesome at Christmas if one hasn't any family. Everything is closed. Even the cats disappear. Every Christmas Sébastien insisted that we go to midnight mass at some church or the other. Once we'd even trekked all the way to Notre Dame. He wasn't religious, not in the least, but he'd said that there was little in life more dramatic than midnight mass at Christmas. Maybe it was the memory of all those lovely Parisian Christmases that compelled me to provide at least a pale replica for Margo and Jeremy. And myself, I thought.

After making myself a ham sandwich, I took it and a bottle of ale into the study and tried to write the opening scene for the new book. There was no hurry, but I wanted to see Chloe and Hannaford fall in love. The process of writing produces a sort of innocent voyeurism that I adore. Maybe I'd have them marry by the end of this new one, but I doubted it. Best to give it a bit more suspense: maybe the one after this. I typed. I sipped. I typed, but it was no use. I kept running into roadblocks with my lovely Chloe. There must be so much more of her in this book if she were to be Hannaford's partner and lover. She needed to be effervescently American, and I simply didn't know how to write it. I needed Rachel.

Our earlier weekend had been so cruelly curtailed by my beastly gall bladder that I'd hardly had time for extensive observations before she, and the doctors, were observing me. Despite my illness, it had worked out satisfactorily since I hadn't needed as much Rachel for the first book. I did now, however, and I fervently wished she were here, in London.

December, at least until Christmas, was an exhaustingly busy month for Parisian fashion, as I recalled. But the workload was crushing for Sébastien and his staff, not as much for models, and the inspirational portion of Rachel's job description was long done. For Sébastien. It was, however, nowhere near complete for me. Maybe, I thought. He wouldn't let her go until a day or two before Christmas, and he'd demand her back before the New Year, but I would invite Rachel for Christmas. I'd keep her for myself down in Cornwall where distractions were decidedly less thick on the ground than in London. I could hear her speak and ask her questions, and Chloe would bloom. I smiled at the computer screen. It would be best not to ask Sébastien too soon. He'd have excuses. No, I'd wait until the middle of the month and request, no, demand to have Rachel for Christmas. The poor girl would be languishing in loneliness during the holidays anyway.

Chapter Thirteen

Jesse threw the door open and grabbed her hands. "Thank you so much for this," he said.

She wasn't so excited. What if the designs were terrible even to her uneducated eye? But she smiled and entered his basement apartment, a grim little space with muted light and harsh gold walls. It smelled of sour wine and cabbage from the café upstairs.

Jesse gestured toward a threadbare velvet chair that tried to separate a bed-sitting room from the kitchenette. The ceiling was so low that his head barely cleared it. He pulled a floor lamp over to the chair and handed her his portfolio. Then he snatched it back. "Do you want coffee or tea or something?"

She shook her head and took the portfolio again. "Calm down, Jesse. It's not like I'm an expert to make or break your dreams."

He nodded and sat on the daybed, covered with an old chenille bedspread. He must fold up like a grasshopper to sleep on it. Or else half his legs stuck out the end. She opened his work and scanned the first page. Interesting stuff. "Where do you work?"

He pointed to a tiny table in the kitchen. Neatly stacked under a small desk light were pens, colored pencils, erasers. "Pretty primitive workspace there, Jesse. Does Sébastien pay you nothing?"

"Not a whole lot, but do you have any clue how expensive apartments are in Paris? And I can't have a roommate. I must work."

Rachel knew who that sounded like. She turned the page. Really nice stuff. "These are fantastic, Jesse." Rachel turned the next page and pointed at a slim dress with what she thought they called a tulip skirt. "I mean it. The way the pieces flow and drape. What fabric would you use for this?" She pointed at a jacket.

He stood, bouncing on his toes, about to lose his cool completely while he watched her scrutinize his drawings. "Silk, preferably, but maybe a thin wool crepe."

Edging over to her, he asked, "You really think so? They're good?"

She turned back to the pages she'd already seen. Consistently good, at least in her opinion. She liked the colors he'd used and the way they varied.

"I do. You know I'm no expert, but these look super good to me."

He grinned. "I could kiss you."

"Feel free."

He stooped and planted a noisy kiss on her lips. Just a tiny bit more than a brother. And he blushed. "If I were going to fall in love with anyone, it would be you, Rachel."

She hadn't heard that one before.

"But I'm too ambitious to get involved with a girl. I know I'm obsessed. It wouldn't be fair."

She waved her hand. "We're good friends, Jesse, and just now for both of us that's more important than love." She actually meant it. "But here's what friends do." She closed his portfolio. "I'm taking this home. Don't worry. I'll guard it with my life. And I'm going to show it to Sébastien."

A look of sheer terror came into Jesse's eyes.

"I won't tell him who drew these until he says he loves them. I know he will. Then maybe he can write you an introduction letter to some house or maybe even hire you himself, and you can get started on your dream." She stood and hugged him. "What do you think of that?"

"I think you're even more wonderful than I imagined." He squeezed her until she was out of breath." And I think we need champagne."

A

"It looks like a freaking Weight Watcher's meeting in here." The big, cocoa-skinned woman surveyed the other models in the Sylvestri conference room, shook her gorgeous head, and spoke in an accent that traced its origins way south of the Ohio River. Rachel grinned at her. Six feet tall with long legs and incredible curves, the giant-sized model was also heavy, about the same as Rachel, but so much taller that it didn't seem as bad.

The tall woman smiled back at Rachel, stuck out her hand, and said, "Crystal, honey. Crystal Carter. What the hell is Fel thinking? Couture's for broomstick chicks."

"He's crazy," Rachel said as she shook Crystal's large hand. Nearly every café au lait finger wore a diamond, or three. "But also a genius. Rachel Bowman."

The other four models, as formal and uncommunicative as the furniture, were already sitting at the conference table. They smiled, friendly enough, but Rachel knew the girls were German and had only enough French and English for polite phrases. No wonder they hadn't laughed at Crystal's wit. They, too, were large girls. Three blondes and a brunette with beautiful faces and bodies built for power sports. And they were so young, probably no more than twenty. Rachel had learned that many models were retired by the time they were her age. She planned to retire in a month.

Crystal arranged herself at the table and patted the chair next to her for Rachel. "You sure are short for a model, plus or otherwise," she said. "I don't remember seeing you around."

Rachel supposed the high fashion modeling community was fairly small, and the plus sized one might even be smaller. She grinned. Or larger, however you wanted to look at it. "I'm not really a model," she said. "Oh, Sébastien made me take lessons, and I'll be doing Fashion Week, but I've never modeled before. I'm a French teacher."

Crystal tilted her head and gave Rachel a long look. "You're sure pretty enough," she decided. "So how'd you end up with this gig?" She waved her hand to include the German girls. "This is the real stuff. Career-making. Plus girls don't get this kind of opportunity ever. You sleeping with the big man?" She grinned, her teeth impossibly white against her crimson lipstick.

"Uh, no." Rachel didn't know how to explain it without sounding stuck on herself, and she didn't think Crystal would have much patience with arrogance. Rachel scrunched up her face. "Well," she said. "He says I was his inspiration. Sort of."

Crystal hooted loud enough for the German models to quit talking and look at her. "You're shitting me. This big French designer has a schoolteacher, a plus schoolteacher, inspiring his collection? You are joking, aren't you?"

Rachel shook her head and shrugged, making Crystal laugh again. This time the German girls looked at the doorway, not at the Americans, and all of them, even Crystal, sat up a little straighter. Jean-Pierre and Suzanne, in charge of models and dressers, walked into the room. Behind them was Chris, who'd replaced Claude as director of the show, and then, aloof and thin, impossible and brilliant, was Sébastien who wore a black suit for the occasion. With a black tee shirt.

Jean-Pierre started speaking in French. The German girls asked him to repeat phrases, and Suzanne, who evidently had a bit of German, tried to help. Rachel kept an English version running next to Crystal's ear. Diamonds there too.

Jean-Pierre welcomed them and said they were part of one of the greatest revolutions and innovations in fashion history. "Or one of the biggest fuck-ups," Crystal whispered. Rachel got the giggles, church giggles, the ones you couldn't stifle for anything. Sébastien glared at her, but she couldn't stop.

Jean-Pierre explained that in a minute they would be holding a conference call with all the other models for the Sylvestri show and that they should feel free to ask questions or voice their concerns. He worked his phone and then turned it on speaker. Rachel counted names as Jean-Pierre called roll. There should've been twenty-four, but he listed only twenty. Rachel whispered, "We're missing four."

"Quit," Crystal murmured. "I know a couple of them. Some girls think this show will make them, but others said they weren't going to risk their careers for such a damned-fool show even if it is Paris."

Jean-Pierre was repeating everything he'd already said to the models in the room. Rachel glanced at Sébastien. He hadn't told her that models were quitting. She wondered if he could possibly replace them this late; he'd had a hard enough time coming up with the ones he had. More of them were going to have to wear two costumes. It was a good thing he'd liked her idea about Renaissance entertainment during the show. She looked at Chris, a slight, nervous man who didn't seem capable of shooing a cat, let alone bucking Sébastien. At dinner the last couple of evenings Sébastien had complained about Chris, saying he was timid, gutless, that Sébastien himself was doing his job. She felt a twinge of sympathy for Sébastien. And Chris.

Over the phone, an American model was asking about her fitting schedule. Barely moving his mouth, Sébastien translated a phrase or two for Suzanne and told her to refer the model to Madame Pauline. Jean-Pierre asked if everyone had received travel documents, and all the models said they had. Several had already come. The rest, Madame Pauline had told Rachel, would be squeezed in over the next three weeks. Another girl on the phone, this one with what Rachel thought was a Dutch accent, asked about her changes. She said she had two costumes and was worried about it. Jean-Pierre assured her that it would be no problem at all. Crystal was shaking her head. "You got two exits too?" she hissed.

She held up her hand, fingers splayed.

"Five?" Crystal shouted, forgetting to whisper. "You really are shitting me this time. It can't be done."

Suzanne's head popped up. "Mademoiselle Carter? You have a question?"

"Yeah, I do. I'd like to know how in the hell we're going to do all these exits. Rachel here tells me she's got five."

Via telephone, there were gasps from all over the world. Everybody had enough English to understand what Crystal was saying. The German girls muttered among themselves. Rachel didn't know whether it was horror or jealousy. If it was the latter, she'd gladly give them some of her outfits. Hell, she'd give them all away, except maybe the purple dress that she still loved despite everything.

Jean-Pierre and Suzanne both looked at Chris who pinched his nose and cleared his throat. He didn't seem capable of coughing up any words, so finally Sébastien lifted his chin and spoke in English. "This is a grand collection," he said. Rachel noticed that he wore his glasses, which he hated and usually avoided wearing. "It is historic. Groundbreaking. This show marks a Renaissance of the true woman. A rebirth." He paused long enough that Rachel worried that he wasn't going to say anything more.

When he finally continued, his voice was so soft that she knew twenty pairs of ears from all over the world were straining to get every syllable. "This show is so new, so innovative that we will not only revolutionize the concept of beauty, we will change the way fashion is presented." He went on to talk about the interludes and the way the models' changes would be managed. "It will be beautiful," he assured them. "Everything about our Fashion Week will be beautiful, so you need not worry. If you haven't done so already, come for your fittings and see the lovely costumes. Prepare for the most exhilarating moment in your career. This is the epitome, the very pinnacle of couture."

Crystal turned her head to whisper in Rachel's ear. "When all this flops deader than a door nail, maybe he should go into politics. Or preaching. Smooth talker."

Rachel nodded and smiled, but she was more anxious than ever. All of them had gone forward with Sébastien's concept: Madame Pauline, Jean-Pierre and Suzanne, dozens of seamstresses, tailors, *vendeuses*, clerks, all of them trusting that Sébastien was the genius, that he knew what he was doing. Most of them had suffered doubts all along but ignored them. It was Sébastien Fel. He never made mistakes. After all these weeks she'd started believing in Sébastien too, even liking him, and she figured that everybody else involved in the collection had done the same thing. A lot of people would suffer if he failed.

The meeting wasn't quite over. First Suzanne and then Sébastien reminded all of them about the confidentiality agreement they had signed. Suzanne reiterated that it meant not saying a word about the clothes, the concept, or the show. When Sébastien spoke, he looked grave, like a stern professor in those glasses. "The concept is fresh. The clothes are unique. Do not endanger this with a momentary lapse in judgment. You may be begged and bribed, but I implore you not to reveal anything about this stunning collection. You must not admit that you are modeling for our show. To anyone." He said it first in French, then in English. Suzanne repeated his words to the German girls who nodded, and even Crystal, whom Rachel would never have taken for an easy believer, was whispering, "No, sir. Not me."

Sébastien left first. Jean-Pierre and Suzanne were still talking to a couple of models on the phone, but it was clear the meeting was over. "Well," said Crystal. "It's gonna be earth-shattering all right. A media feeding frenzy." She grinned. "I don't know whether it's a good thing or bad that I'm getting out of the business as soon as this show's over. I might double my income over this."

She and Rachel walked into the hallway. "So, why are you quitting?" asked Rachel.

Crystal smiled her American Dental Association smile. "I'm twenty-seven, a little old for modeling, and I'm getting married right after I finish up with Sylvestri. It doesn't get any better than this, according to most people in the business, and I never dreamed a plus girl like me would get this kind of opportunity. Leave 'em when you're on top, I figure. And my boyfriend is tired of waiting on me to get married."

Standing near the front door was a man so tall he made Sébastien look short. The guy was also broad enough to block a double doorway but wasn't one bit sloppy or fat. He lit up with his own fluorescent smile when he saw the two women. "Sugar," he said. Rachel couldn't believe such a soft, caressing voice could live in a neck the size of a Greek pillar.

Crystal smiled, almost simpered. "There he is. Rachel, this is my husband-to-be, my one and only Shawn, and that's spelled S-H-A-W-N. Shawn Anderson. Hey, honey." Tall as she was, Crystal looked almost petite when Shawn put his arm around her and squeezed.

"Proud to meet you, Rachel," he said, using his other hand to completely envelop Rachel's. He gave it a gentle squeeze. "You girls been having fun?"

Rachel smiled. "Not so much. Just information."

"Like a team meeting, working out the plays, hmm, baby," Shawn said. He squeezed Crystal again and then focused on Rachel. "Hey, you're American."

"From Ohio," Rachel said.

His smile grew even wider. "I played ball at Ohio State." Sylvestri's magnificent chandelier glowed on his shaved head.

It had to be the foot kind of ball. "We're a long way from home," Rachel said.

Shawn shook his head. "Ohio wasn't home for me, although I liked it just fine. I'm from Georgia and proud of it. Awful pretty down there, but I have to admit Paris is pretty too, what little I've seen of it."

Even if Shawn wasn't hinting, Rachel decided to take it that way. "What are you two doing this afternoon?" she asked. "You've already had your fitting, haven't you, Crystal? Would you like to see some of the sights?"

Crystal clapped her hands like a little girl. "Oh, I'd love that! Wouldn't you, Shawn? And Rachel lives in Paris right now and speaks French. It'd be like having our own personal tour guide."

"That'd be mighty nice of you, ma'am."

Rachel laughed. "I'm Rachel, not 'ma'am. ' Well, do you want to start from here? The Metro isn't far."

Crystal looked down. Her feet were snuggled into skyscraper heels. Red. "That's the subway, isn't it? I don't believe I want to do that much walking."

Shawn lifted his massive shoulders. "No problem. We'll just hire us a taxi for the afternoon. Evening too, if we want to."

Rachel felt her eyes widen. "Fine, but that'll cost a fortune."

Crystal giggled. "Honey, I don't model for the money. Shawn here played in the NFL for eight years and saved his salaries like his sweet mama told him to. We can afford a taxi."

"Okay," said Rachel. Yeah, that was a gigantic diamond in Shawn's ear, and he'd probably bought all those carats on Crystal's fingers. Well, then.

By this time the German models had congregated near the front door too. They smiled and tried to get by Shawn and Crystal. Rachel felt like Jack, flanked by all kinds of giants crowding around the beanstalk. "You girls need a taxi too?" she asked slowly. They all nodded.

Rachel opened the front door. There was often a taxi or two cruising down the street in front of Sylvestri. She'd just hail one cabbie who would discover that it was his lucky day financially and another who'd die from beauty shock from the big, beautiful German girls. Telling Shawn, Crystal, and the girls to wait, Rachel stepped through the doorway and glanced in both directions. No taxis, but just across the street, hiding behind his camera, was Kurt Mann. She would've recognized him anywhere. Her heart started thudding like a drum.

She ducked inside and shut the door. "Damn," she murmured.

"What's wrong?" asked Crystal. Shawn was helping her into what Rachel thought was a Burberry raincoat. Six months ago she wouldn't have known Burberry from L. L. Bean.

"A man, a photographer. He's right across the street." Rachel bit her lip. "I used to date him."

"And you don't want to see him." Crystal settled into her coat. "Is he a jerk?"

Rachel nodded.

"Want me to hit him?" Shawn offered.

"No." She frowned. "But thanks."

Crystal turned to Rachel. "Can't you just ignore him? There's a bunch of us all leaving at the same time. He wouldn't do anything weird, would he?"

Rachel said, "That's not what I'm worried about. If all of us go out there, he might figure out what's going on with Sébastien's collection." And it wouldn't take a genius to add up Rachel's lies, the purple dress, and the bevy of bountiful beauties into a correct equation. Kurt wasn't stupid.

One of the German girls worked very hard to say, "But I am sure models leave here day by day."

"Not models our size," said Rachel. She thought for a minute. "You all wait here while I go distract him. Then hail a cab. Where are you staying, Shawn?"

"The Ritz." He frowned. "I could distract him better than you, Rachel. I caught a glimpse, and he's not much bigger than a banty rooster. Want me to sit on him?"

Crystal puffed up like a toad. "And mess up those fine new Dior britches? I don't think so."

Rachel shook her head. "Thanks, but I can handle him. Okay, you two give me a minute, hail a cab, and go to the hotel. I'll meet you in the lobby in about an hour."

Crystal was grinning big time. "Sure. I love this spy stuff. Almost like the movies, isn't it, honey?"

"Where are you going now?" Rachel asked the others.

"We want the Louvre," said one of the blondes.

"Okay, see the hallway down there? There's a back door to the left." Rachel pointed and two of the models nodded. "Walk through to the next block and just to your right there's a taxi stand."

They looked confused.

Shawn stepped forward. "Ladies, my name is Shawn Baker, and I'm going to escort you all to your taxi." He looked back at Rachel and Crystal and grinned. "Do you want to go with us and get a taxi out back, Sugar?"

"No, I'll wait for you here and beat up that pissant photographer if Rachel has trouble," Crystal said. Rachel didn't doubt for a minute that she could.

The others left and Rachel took a deep breath. She had no idea what she'd say to Kurt, but Crystal did. "Smile a whole bunch and tell him life is good. Say you have a new lover. Don't matter if it's true or not."

"It's not," Rachel said. "Okay, I'm going. As soon as Shawn gets back, hail a cab. I'll see you at the Ritz."

Crystal giggled. "Tell him your new lover's thingie is twice as big as his."

"Oh, that's a good idea." Rachel grinned and opened the door. Kurt's camera was pointed directly at her. She shut the door and told herself to slow down. There was no need to hurry.

As soon as Kurt saw who it was, he lowered the camera and pasted a gigantic smile on his face. Rachel crossed the street, half hoping a car would hit her. That would be a diversion, and she wouldn't have to talk to him. It didn't happen. "Hey, Kurt," she called as she approached the sidewalk. "What's up?"

He kept smiling and put his arm around her like he was happy to see her. "Strudel," he said. "I have missed you."

I bet, she thought. He aimed a kiss at her, and she managed to give him her cheek. "When did you get back? I couldn't remember how long you said you'd be gone." Because he hadn't told her.

"Yesterday," he said.

She doubted it was true, but it didn't matter. Yeah, he looked good to her. It was taking a fair amount of self-control not to enjoy his smile, his dimples, even if he was a bastard. Or a banty rooster, whatever on earth that was. "Let's get a coffee," she suggested. Maybe she could get him to leave the premises entirely.

He hesitated.

Rachel pointed at his camera. "Taking pictures of people outside Sylvestri isn't your usual line of work, Kurt. Is there a movie star inside? Have you turned paparazzi?"

He shook his head, glanced back at the House of Sylvestri door, which stayed firmly closed, and then said, "Yes, a coffee. That would be nice. You look very good, my strudel. Good enough to eat."

Right. She gave him a huge smile. "Well, then, you won't have to buy a pastry with your coffee. So how was Egypt? I've never been."

They'd walked nearly a half block when Rachel saw a taxi heading toward the *atelier*. Good, Shawn should be back by now, and the giant couple could be on their way to the Ritz. Of course they were staying at the Ritz. Kurt was chattering about the photo shoot, about the Pyramids, about Greece. She let him talk until he asked, "So, what were you doing at Sylvestri?" His eyebrows stretched toward his hairline. He knew.

She could please him. She could give him all the secrets and be his strudel for another night or two, she supposed. It was only vaguely tempting. "I have a new lover," she said. He blinked at her. "A very large man."

🗼

It wasn't a good day to view Paris from the Eiffel Tower, but Shawn and Crystal didn't seem to mind. Mists shrouded the view and they couldn't even see Sacre-Coeur. Damp breezes fluttered Crystal's hair. Her skin looked dewy, but then it had looked that way during Sébastien's meeting. "So why was your ex waiting outside Sylvestri?" Crystal asked.

"I don't know for sure. He's a big fashion photographer, not paparazzi. Kurt Mann. Have you heard of him?"

Crystal brushed back a lock of hair. "Of course I have."

Rachel nodded. "The only thing I can think of is that word's gotten out about Sébastien's collection. I can't imagine Kurt wasting

136

his time snapping pictures of Sylvestri's customers, even if they are big names."

Crystal shook her head. "It would be very bad if he spills the beans."

"Why?" Shawn asked. "Seems like it would drum up business if people knew the show was going to be different."

"No, it would be devastating," said Rachel. "I don't mean any disrespect, but we're fat girls."

"I don't use that word," Crystal said.

"Okay, we're *plus* girls. When has a Parisian couturier ever considered us, let alone made us the theme of a collection? Sébastien can talk all he wants to about a Renaissance in fashion, but the world's not going to buy it." Rachel looked at the heavy clouds. "If the press, the fashion world, if anybody knows about it ahead of time, the show could be a circus, and nobody would take what Sébastien's doing seriously at all."

Shawn gave her a gentle smile. "And you care, don't you, Rachel? Sugar here is just high on being in a Paris fashion show, but you care about the team."

Rachel let out a breath. "I guess I do."

Crystal smiled, patted Rachel's hand, and murmured, "I like you, Rachel. You can call me Cryssie like my friends do. Now, where are we going next? And was Kurt Mann really your boyfriend? Lord, girl, you do get around."

They drove all over the city, stopping wherever Crystal took a notion to get out. Their driver, wearing a perpetual grin at his good luck, told stories that Rachel translated, and she thought everybody was having a good time. She was. It was an absolute joy to be able to talk to a young woman her age, American even, and be honest about all the Sébastien stuff. Shawn grinned at the two of them chattering and laughing over everything. Hours later, after shopping at the Galeries Lafayette, they were back in their personal taxi when Shawn said he was ready for dinner. Crystal nodded but was more intent upon her shopping bag.

"I told you they wouldn't have anything in our size," Rachel said after giving the cabbie the next destination.

"I know, but when all else fails you buy shoes. And handbags." Crystal pulled a fabulous red purse from the bag. "I wish you'd let me buy that turquoise one for you. Especially after all you're doing for us."

Rachel shook her head. "Shawn promised me dinner. That's enough."

"You better let me buy the best champagne too," Shawn said. "To celebrate Paris and making a new friend."

"Where are we going?" asked Crystal. She was changing purses, right then and there, pulling out a cosmetic bag, a toothbrush, and a passport.

"The Royale," said Rachel. "It was where Sébastien took me when he decided I was his inspiration."

Crystal touched Rachel's cheek. "Well, that's almost romantic, isn't it, Shawn? You sure Sébastien's not your lover?"

Rachel gave her a wry look. "I don't have the right equipment for that."

Shawn's eyebrows went up, but Crystal burst into her exuberant, hooting laugh. "I shoulda figured," she said.

Over dinner Rachel told them about meeting Sébastien on the bridge, about Edgar, about posing in her underwear while Sébastien sketched. It was a slow, sensuous meal, very Parisian. With Rachel translating, Shawn ordered all kinds of dishes for them to try as well as several wines and champagne."What's this?" asked Crystal.

"Well, it has truffles in it." Rachel wasn't sure what the dish was. Of course with all those wines sloshing around in her stomach, she wasn't sure about much at all except that she was having the best time ever. "Good?"

Crystal tried a mouthful. "Wonderful, but I don't taste any chocolate."

Rachel's giggles started fizzing as much as the champagne. "Truffles, the real ones, are kind of like mushrooms."

"Oh." Crystal looked down her glorious nose, which, along with her remarkable cheekbones, must've come from either an African or a Native American princess.

"Are you part Native American?" Rachel asked. It was way too personal, but she felt like she'd known these people for months, not hours. Come to think of it, she'd sort of lost her dignity the last time she'd eaten at the Royale too.

Crystal wasn't offended. As a matter of fact, she preened. "You noticed," she said. "My daddy is from East Tennessee, and his grandmother was full-blooded Cherokee." She flashed her eyes at Shawn. "That's where I get my looks, isn't it, honey?"

The more his Crystal carried on, the quieter Shawn got. He gave her a lazy smile. Hell, they were all feeling pretty relaxed at that point. "Don't care where you got them, Sugar. You're just beautiful."

Rachel supposed it was talking about family that made her think of her brother, the most rabid, passionate Ohio State Buckeye fan in the state. He'd swoon over her meeting Shawn Baker. But when she wrote Rob she needed to sound like she knew what she was talking about. "So what position did you play at Ohio State, Shawn?"

"Same as in the pros: tight end."

This brought a chuckle from Crystal who was slathering butter on yet another roll. "And it's still a mighty tight end, let me tell you."

Rachel didn't figure Rob would appreciate this bit of inside information. But it had her laughing so hard she nearly choked.

Suddenly Crystal put down the bread, turned serious, and widened her eyes. "I just had the most wonderful idea."

"What, Sugar?"

"Let's get married here, in Paris, right after Fashion Week. We could fly our families over, along with your preacher cousin to do the ceremony. And we could honeymoon at the Ritz, and Rachel could come to our wedding, be my bridesmaid."

Rachel started making negative noises, but neither Crystal nor Shawn paid her any attention.

"That sounds fine, but I thought you wanted to go to Tahiti for our honeymoon," he said.

"Well, I do. We could have our first honeymoon here and then another one in Tahiti. Kinda like an appetizer and then the main course."

Shawn laughed. "Whatever you want, Sugar. Actually, getting married here would be perfect," he said. "Not so much fuss and bother as having it with your family in Memphis and inviting all those people." He absolutely glowed, and Rachel didn't think it was the wine. "I'll talk to the manager at the Ritz in the morning. I bet they have a nice little parlor we can use."

Rachel thought they probably did, or they'd add one on to the back of the building for the kind of money Shawn was willing to pay. She tried to tell them she was leaving right after Fashion Week, and besides, didn't Crystal have a friend or relative she'd already invited to be her bridesmaid?

Well, yes. Her sister. But she was allowed to have more than one bridesmaid, wasn't she? Shawn said she could have a dozen if she wanted them. She was insistent. Rachel was her sister now too, and since this whole show was probably going to blow up into a huge disaster, said Crystal, they'd need to stick together. She grinned and Shawn glowed and Rachel finally said yes to staying for the wedding, but no to being a bridesmaid. "I'm honored," she said, "but I'll have more fun just watching. Really."

A

When she got home that evening, Rachel knew she needed to tell Sébastien about Kurt Mann, but even though it wasn't that late, she hoped Sébastien was in bed. She was a little drunk and a lot happy and she didn't want to think about Kurt or what his presence outside Sylvestri might mean. She tiptoed into the apartment and down the hallway, but she was out of luck. Sébastien, with his glasses on again, was sitting on the white sofa, reading a newspaper. A thick stack of them lay on the coffee table.

He looked at her over the top of his glasses. "A pleasant evening?"

Rachel nodded. Sébastien had a look on his face that made her give up on the idea of heading off to her room with nothing more than a "good night." She sat. "Really nice people," she said and slipped out of her black heels. They weren't as flashy or as tall as Crystal's, but they still pinched her toes. When had she stopped wearing gym shoes?

"Crystal Carter?"

Rachel nodded.

"She's quite well-regarded in America. And Polly says she looks sublime in the white suit. The calla lily concept you suggested."

She'd nearly forgotten about that.

"I understand that you saw Kurt Mann today." His voice was neutral, but he tossed his glasses on the sofa and gave her a piercing stare. "What was he doing?"

How Sébastien discovered things, she didn't know. Maybe he'd been watching from Madame Pauline's office, a floor above the front door. Or maybe Madame Pauline had done the spying. Rachel explained the situation and what she'd done.

Sébastien nodded. "Clever. I do think he, or somebody, is on to us."

"I don't see how these things can be kept secret anyway."

He bit at his thumbnail. "They can't; little things get out. But this is far more newsworthy than hemlines or stripes, and, I'm sure, has been most profitable for Mann."

Rachel stretched out her big toe to fiddle with her shoe. "Money? I couldn't get why a major photographer like Kurt would stand around like he was waiting for Angelina Jolie."

"If he reports what he's learned to the press, it's career suicide. No one in fashion will ever trust him again. But someone would pay him very well." He pointed at the stack of newsprint. "I've been scouring all the papers and fashion rags for hints that he's told someone." He kept frowning. "But there's nothing about me or the collection."

Rachel slipped back into her shoes, hoping to escape. "Then there's nothing to worry about."

"Yet." Sébastien's frown deepened. "Was Kurt decent to you?"

"Pretty much. I did what Crystal suggested and told him that I had a new boyfriend."

A smile flickered across Sébastien's face. "You enjoyed that?"

"I did." She turned to go.

"Oh, Edgar called."

She stopped. "Is he okay?"

"Apparently." Sébastien's voice turned neutral again." He wants you to come to Cornwall for Christmas."

She loved the idea but didn't like his tone. "And am I allowed, Father?"

He didn't care whether she liked his tone or not. "I cannot possibly let you go until the twenty-third. Far, far too much to do." He lifted his chin. "Then you can, I suppose."

Rachel started to ask a lot of things, all focused around wondering who Sébastien Fel thought he was, her guardian? But she just nodded. It would be fun to see Edgar, and she'd been dreading Christmas alone in Paris.

Chapter Fourteen

There were more things to do before Christmas than she'd realized. She'd already had her final fittings on the purple dress, the coppery pants outfit, and the blue suit, which she thought looked a lot like Crystal's. But less than a week before Christmas, Polly called Rachel in for a fitting of the short yellow tunic, dress, whatever. Rachel didn't know what to call it.

Sébastien dubbed it a surcoat or tabard, but she wasn't familiar with those terms, if they were even English. It looked more like a sleeveless shift to her, one with a wide boat neck. Bright yellow linen, it had green vines embroidered down one side seam and across the bottom of the front. Rachel posed in front of the mirror while the fitter fiddled with it. "What do you think?" she asked Madame Pauline.

The woman frowned. "Your straps are showing. You must buy a strapless bra. Other models, I'd say no bra at all, but . . ." She left this hanging, just like Rachel's boobs would be if she didn't wear the appropriate foundation garment.

"Okay. Gisèle, I suppose?" Rachel didn't mind. She'd wanted to visit the woman before Christmas anyway. "But other than that?"

"I like it. It's unique." Madame Pauline lightly touched the embroidery. "There are tights to match."

"Tights?"

"Like a pageboy or knight." Madame Pauline sighed. "And they will be the very bitch to get on you in a hurry."

Rachel had never heard good old Polly say a swear word in French or English. But everybody was stressed to death.

Sébastien rarely appeared at the apartment before eight or nine in the evening. He was still working on the final costume, hers, of course, and he'd gone back to draping her in sheets every now and then. There was the after-show party to plan, which should have been entirely Dumont's responsibility, but the big boss was in Switzerland until the New Year and kept laying more and more of his duties on Sébastien, who seemed, strangely enough, reluctant to say no. Chris was no help whatsoever, said Sébastien. Yvonne provided food every evening, and Rachel heated it up, urging him to eat. But all he wanted to put in his mouth were his fingernails, which were bitten deep and bloody. This was not the right time to show him Jesse's designs. Bless him, he hadn't said a word about the delay.

Emails flew between Ohio and Paris. Jean Bowman all but ordered her daughter to come home for Christmas. Why had Rachel mailed her gifts? She could've brought them when she came home. Wayne Bowman wanted the same thing, but he was wistful rather than ticked off. He wished Rachel could see him carve the Christmas turkey with those fine new knives. He missed his little girl. It wouldn't be Christmas without her.

In an unusually long email, Rob had oozed appreciation for the gifts she'd sent. Rachel couldn't figure out why the message was so cheerful and brotherly until Jean broke the news a day or two later. Rachel was sure her mother had insisted on being the one to announce it: Rob was going to be a daddy next year. And Jean a grandmother. Couldn't Rachel sneak home for a short visit and help them celebrate the news? Rachel was happy for all of them, but she didn't see how it was important for her to be there. She'd certainly be home long before the child was born. Once again, Rob had managed to please their mother, while Rachel couldn't make the woman happy to save her life. Rachel grimaced at the computer screen as she tried to write gracious replies to her family. Didn't every family have a maiden aunt? The one who gave the child inappropriate gifts every Christmas and birthday? She supposed that was her new role.

That evening, Rachel was trying to coax Sébastien into eating more of Yvonne's roasted chicken when she told him about the baby, leaving out her mother's plea for Rachel to come home. She knew better than to bring it up; besides, she was looking forward to seeing Edgar. As she'd hoped, the baby news distracted Sébastien enough that he swallowed a few bites. He was so thin his jeans looked like they might float off his hipbones. "So you will be an aunt," he said. The line between his eyes relaxed.

"*Tante* Rachel," she said. "Try the potatoes. They're very good."

He ate a bite. "No French," he muttered.

She wondered if he'd ever let her speak French. She was doing very well, she thought, conversing easily with Yvonne and Madame Pauline and Gisèle.

Sébastien sipped some wine. "You must go to a shop I know. They have the most exquisite baby things." He tore off a bit of chicken with his poor, mutilated fingers. "I suppose you will learn the baby's gender before it's born. Most people do that now, right? Then you can choose something appropriate."

"Yes, but they won't do the ultrasound to learn whether it's a boy or girl for months." She'd learned all kinds of pregnancy stuff from Shelley. "I'll be back in Ohio long before then."

He stopped before the bite of chicken reached his mouth. "I keep forgetting that you're leaving," he said and set the shred back on his plate.

A

Even if Sylvestri wasn't claiming that much of her time, Rachel had bunches of holiday things to do. She went to a candy store and bought a box of *mendients* and *rochers,* whatever they were, for Gisèle. The confections were beautiful, almost too pretty to eat, and Rachel thought Gisèle would appreciate them. As Rachel entered the lingerie shop, she called out, "*Joyeux Noel!*"

Gisèle was at the counter folding silky chemises. She clapped her hands. "And a Merry Christmas to you too, my dear!"

Rachel handed her the candies. "I need a strapless bra." She'd had to look up the French word for strapless. "Beige," she said.

Gisèle nodded. "One of the ensembles requires it?"

"Yes, the yellow one." Gisèle had made her describe every outfit in detail.

The woman opened a drawer and pawed through it. "Does that imbecile still have you modeling five costumes?"

Heading for a dressing room, Rachel nodded.

"Even with those intervals you told me about, it will be almost impossible." Gisèle handed her two bras. "Try these." She paused. "You will have to wear this bra for all of them. There won't be time to change."

Rachel hadn't thought of that. She wriggled out of the brown velvet jacket. "Yeah, and one of the outfits has um, stockings, to go with it." She didn't know the word for tights.

From behind the rose pink curtain, she could hear Gisèle swear.

Ten minutes later, a beige strapless bra tucked in a bag by her purse, Rachel sat with Gisèle at the table in the back room. The candy box was open, and Gisèle was pouring tea. "I used to help with the dressing at Valenciana," she said. "I did a little of everything while I was there."

Gisèle pointed at the candy box, and Rachel took a *rocher*, which turned out to be a sugared almond. "Madame Pauline says I'll need two dressers." The candy was delicious. "She's so worried that she's threatening to be one of them herself."

Gisèle's eyebrows rose. "That would be an honor indeed."

Shrugging, Rachel replied, "We're all trying to make this succeed for Sébastien. We're worried about him."

"I too." Gisèle shook her head. "He defies the world, our Sébastien."

"And I guess the world usually likes it." Rachel sipped her tea. It was strong and sweet. "I'm not sure he'll get away with it this time."

"He has a certain charm," Gisèle said. "I remember. So eager, so sure. It's easy to believe in him no matter how crazy he gets." Her eyes got a faraway look. "Ah, those days! Before he went to Sylvestri, even before Valenciana. We had such fun with his early designs. Most of them were *pret à porter* then, but he'd try things out on me, on Pauline. Wonderful clothes. Take off your jacket."

Rachel blinked. She'd worn Gisèle's brown velvet jacket to show her how much she appreciated it. Maybe the woman wanted it back. She unbuttoned it and sat in a chilly camisole while Gisèle handled the fabric. "Here," she said, putting her finger on a small label in the side seam. The front of the label had a rounded design, printed in dark blue. Rachel had noticed it many times, but it had no meaning for her. Gisèle lifted the tiny flap of fabric. Underneath, embroidered in black thread was one word: FEL. She handed the jacket back to Rachel. "You are wearing an original Fel: not Sylvestri, not Valenciana, but Fel." She nodded like an old fortune teller. "I predict that there will be more, even if this collection fails. Perhaps it will not be bad for him to fail."

Rachel shivered at the thought more than the chilly kitchen. "Can't imagine what that would do to him," she murmured in English. She put the jacket back on.

"I think," said Gisèle, "that I will call Pauline. Maybe she will trust me to be your other dresser. She knows I care about Sébastien as much as she does." She smiled and tapped her plump hand against Rachel's." And you."

Rachel didn't know what to get Sébastien for Christmas. She didn't expect anything from him. After all, he'd already given her lovely clothes, perfume, and sunglasses, not to mention room, board, and a fabulous salary. And, as busy as he was, he'd probably forget the holiday just like he'd forgotten her Thanksgiving meal. But she wanted to give him something. She'd found gorgeous purple kid gloves for Madame Pauline and a basket of yummy bath things for Yvonne. She'd put together another basket for Jesse, filled with luscious and expensive food items. Sometimes she wondered if he truly had enough to eat. And, although he probably had something like it, she'd purchased a thick picture book of Paris to take to Edgar. But nothing for Sébastien. The man either had it or didn't like it.

On the day before she left, Rachel rummaged through his collection of dvds, desperate to think of something. Movie musicals took up two shelves. She scanned the titles and ordered *White Christmas*, which seemed appropriate, *The King and I*, and three others he didn't own. She hoped this wasn't because he hated them. Then she ran to the pricey kitchen store across the street. Remembering her earlier big purchases, the clerks couldn't do enough for her, and one actually ran to a market to buy popcorn for the expensive popper she bought. There, she thought while she waited for the gifts to be wrapped. Sébastien would have a night, or five, at the movies: perfect since she was going to be gone for a few days. Madame Pauline had assured her that Sébastien would come to her apartment for Christmas dinner, but Rachel still felt guilty about leaving him, especially now when things were so tense.

That evening he came home with luggage for Rachel and a hint of a smile on his face. "For your voyage," he said. "I do not want to see that disreputable duffel bag ever again."

The pieces were leather and unbelievably luxurious. And they'd cost him a bundle because they were not Sylvestri. "You're spoiling me, Sébastien," she said and hugged him for the first time ever. He didn't hug back but seemed pleased. "Take off your coat. I have a surprise for you too," she said.

She had to wait until he changed, opened wine, sifted through the mail, and then peered into the refrigerator to see what Yvonne had left.

"Now?" Rachel asked when she'd put Yvonne's cassoulet in the oven and Sébastien had poured more wine.

"You are such a child," he murmured.

"Yep. And you love it." She ran back to her room and brought the gifts, shiny and impressive in their silver paper.

"Good Lord," he said, sounding like Edgar. But he exclaimed over the movies and seemed fascinated by the popcorn popper, reading its instructions before he would sit down to eat.

He said, "Have you your tickets and reservations?"

Rachel nodded.

"You will get to Gare du Nord early tomorrow morning."

"Yes."

"And you will come back on the twenty-sixth."

"I will not." She grinned." As we agreed, I'll be back late on the twenty-seventh, and you better not say another word."

He shrugged then and said she'd better start packing her things into the new bags. He wanted to watch a movie with her.

"In a minute. I have something to show you," she said.

As she ran from the room, he said, "What now? More Christmas?"

Out of breath when she came back, she said, "No. And please don't get mad at me. I wanted you to look at these." She handed him Jesse's portfolio.

Sébastien frowned. "Whose are these?" He opened the first page.

"An American friend who lives here." She paused as Sébastien studied the drawings. "I volunteered to show them to you. He never asked."

"You have a friend?" He turned the page. "Or another lover?"

"No, a friend. Imagine that." She glared at him, but he was too intent on the portfolio to notice.

He turned a page. "These are quite good. Not professional quality, but there's a genuine talent here."

Rachel hugged herself.

"How did he learn this?' Sébastien asked.

"No real training except graphic design," she replied. "I think he just immersed himself in fashion. That's why he works in Paris and at Sylvestri."

"At Sylvestri? Where?" Sébastien frowned. "The designs are fresh, nothing derivative." He shut the portfolio. "You may tell him that I think he's talented. Does he want more from me? I cannot hire him. He's not quite ready for Sylvestri."

"He works in the graphic arts department, and his name is Jesse Kemper. And I don't think he wants anything more than your evaluation. But I want more." She touched Sébastien's hand. "He's a really good guy. Could you maybe give him a contact, or even a recommendation?"

Again, a glimmer of a smile turned his lips. "For you, Raquel, I will do that. Now, pack. I want popcorn and a movie. And remember, Eddie's house is frigid."

She grinned as she flew down the hall. Opening the medium-sized suitcase, she inhaled the leather, luxurious as gold, and started thinking about what she would pack. And then she stopped and picked up her phone to text.

Merry Christmas, Jesse!

Sébastien LOVED YOUR WORK and is going to help you find a spot somewhere!!!!!!! I'm so happy for you. Talk when I get back from England. xxx

She spent the whole day on trains, or at least it felt that way. Early in the morning she'd boarded the Eurostar for London, arriving there an hour and a half before her train left for Truro. Plenty of time except that she had to get from St. Pancras to a different station, and the irony was that the other station was Paddington. She thought of Edgar's bear.

It was a dreary day, but most of the train's passengers were heading toward Christmas celebrations and were, as Edgar would have put it, "very jolly." Two college boys kept asking if she'd like some of the brandy they'd brought to pass the time. One wore a Santa Claus hat and flirted with her. He kept telling her she needed to come sit on his knee and tell him what she wanted for Christmas. A couple of elderly ladies offered her candies from boxes they held in their laps. Rachel read for a while, dozed for a few minutes, but mostly watched the scenery. Once the train left the London suburbs, she saw lovely views of wintry countryside speed past her window. She didn't know what to expect from Christmas with Edgar but had some vague expectation of a Victorian celebration, right out of Dickens. Or maybe something even older, like Sébastien's Renaissance, complete with boar's heads and gobs of holly. It was easy enough to picture it that way. The church towers and spires, the rolling, barren hills, and the misty gray afternoon made her feel as if she were in an ancient fairy tale, one full of magic and mystery.

But the trip was long, five hours, and it grew dark very early, leaving Rachel with nothing to see but her own reflection in the glass. The college boys and friendly grannies were long gone, and she was tired and hungry by the time she reached Truro. Just as the train was slowing, she brushed on a bit of blush and put on lipstick, bright red for the holidays. She gathered up her new suitcase and carry on, both full because she hadn't known what to wear to an English Christmas, and stood on the platform. Only a few people had left the train in Truro, and within minutes they were gone and she was alone with no sign of Edgar. She was just searching for her phone when she heard, "Rachel?"

It wasn't Edgar. It was that unfriendly nephew of his.

Jeremy picked up her beautiful suitcases and walked toward the parking lot without saying another word. A damp breeze tousled her hair and pulled at his corduroy jacket. Heaving the cases into the back of an ancient van, he did at least mumble something about how nice they were and took care to set them flat on blankets rather than the rutted, and rusted, floor. Rachel nearly went to the wrong side of the vehicle but remembered and climbed into the seat on the left. The van smelled of soil and plants, and evergreen needles littered the floorboard.

He drove through town slowly enough that Rachel could've seen a bit of Truro if it hadn't been so dark. She saw what she supposed was a pub, a welcoming place decorated with bright multicolored Christmas lights. She was very hungry, but surely Edgar would have supper waiting. That was probably why he hadn't come to get her.

The van rattled at every bump. She watched Jeremy's dark profile as he drove, and wondered why he seemed to dislike her so much. Aside from the fact that she'd screamed at him. Good Lord, that had been weeks ago and hadn't been that important anyway. Finally he spoke. "Did you have a good trip?"

Rachel could just imagine Edgar schooling his nephew on manners. "Be cordial," Edgar would've said. "She's our guest."

"Long," Rachel replied. "I left Paris at eight-thirty this morning, but it was fine. I enjoyed seeing the countryside until it got dark."

He didn't reply. As he prepared to turn down a narrow road about the size of driveways back in Ohio, she caught a glimpse of his face. It was a nice face, or would've been if he smiled. A strong chin, stubborn, she thought, and eyelashes long enough to make her jealous. Thick, light-brown hair fell onto his forehead and crept a bit over the collar of his jacket. He wore rough, working clothes. She bet his fingernails were dirty.

"Is it far to Edgar's?" she asked. It didn't matter whether it was or not. She was trapped in a truck with a charm school dropout.

"About twenty-nine kilometers. But the roads are so narrow it takes over a half hour to get there."

She had no idea how far that was. Although she'd done pages and pages of math homework converting U. S. units of measurement to metric, she didn't remember a thing. But a half-hour with this guy would seem like forever.

"Eighteen miles or so." He didn't say it all snotty, like she would've expected, and she supposed it was nice of him to remember that Americans didn't think in metric, but as the minutes and miles crept by, he didn't say another word. She couldn't see much of anything out the window. A light or two here and there and hedges crowding the road.

Her stomach growled, and Jeremy must've heard it because a smile passed across his face as quick as a puff of wind. "Uncle Edgar will have tea waiting for us."

"Tea?" Rachel liked it well enough, and when she'd been here before, the Brits tended to serve it with cookies, which they called biscuits. It was all so confusing. But she needed much more than a couple of cookies.

"Supper," he said. "He said he was making soup."

"Ah," said Rachel. "Sounds good."

But then she realized that he'd said "us." And she remembered that Edgar had said his nephew lived with him in Cornwall. Somehow or the other she'd thought that she'd be spending Christmas with Edgar, just Edgar, like the weekend in London when he'd been sick. But she was having Christmas with Joy Boy here too, and, dear God, Granny Margo too, she guessed. Hell. Not only was the prospect daunting, she'd need to buy Christmas presents for them too. Tomorrow.

Jeremy turned twice more, each time onto even narrower lanes. She started to ask what they'd do if they met another car. There was no shoulder, but that was Jeremy's problem, not hers. She kept her head turned toward the window and away from him until she felt a pinch in her neck. She almost wished she'd stayed in Paris.

He made another turn and said, "We're on Tremaine property now."

They traveled down a long driveway with trees on either side. Up ahead she could see a faint glow of lights. Then the driveway curved into a circle fronting the house. Umm, not a house, Rachel thought, a mansion. It was built of light-colored stone, ghostly in the dark, and had a large front door. Windows to either side of the door sent light into the gloom, and the one at the far right end of the house showed a Christmas tree lit with white bulbs. "Wow," she mumbled. Jeremy didn't reply. "Amazing."

They'd no more than opened their doors when Edgar burst out. "Rachel! Was the trip tedious? Are you well? I'm so glad you're here. Happy Christmas."

There was no question of a hug this time. She threw her arms around him and kissed him on the cheek. "I'm fine. Are you? You look good."

He did. Maybe a few pounds thinner, but in the faint light he looked healthy and fit. All but pulling her into the house, Edgar chattered as she took off her coat, set down her purse, and took a deep breath. Jeremy went straight upstairs with her bags. "Do you want a drink? Or to freshen up? I've put you in the Ivy Room at the back. It's the warmest, and I thought you'd like the half-tester bed."

Whatever that was. "Sure. Both." She pointed upstairs. "Do I just follow the hallway?"

"Jeremy will show you. I'll have a drink waiting."

She climbed stairs that turned at a landing and led into a narrow hall lit by occasional sconces. It was deliciously spooky and ancient, and once again she felt like she was living in a story. Jeremy was coming toward her and simply pointed over his shoulder. Rude, she thought, but Edgar's welcome had cheered her up. Back home she would've searched for a lump of coal to give Jeremy for Christmas. She didn't know what the British equivalent was.

The room was, well, charming. Not a word she normally used, but Rachel was in Wonderland. A half-tester bed evidently was one with a sort of partial canopy and curtains, dark green velvet ones. Ivy-patterned paper covered the walls. The Ivy Room, she thought, of course. Rich wood gleamed. The white curtains and bedspread glowed. And on her bed was Paddington Bear. In all the confusion of Edgar's surgery, she'd left him in London, but Edgar had remembered. She squeezed the bear and smiled, giving a quick thought to what Old Jeremy might have thought of a toy perched on her bed.

Her suitcases sat next to a huge armoire with curlicues on top. Next to it was a door with a porcelain knob, and inside she found a bathroom with a gigantic tub on feet and snowy towels stacked on a stool. Wow, she thought again and reminded herself that she should show a little more sophistication. It wasn't like Sébastien's apartment was a shack, but this place was a movie set.

She'd unpack later, but she did scrounge around in her cases until she found her makeup bag. After slapping on a little powder, combing her hair, and spritzing on some Sylvestri Silver, Rachel went downstairs. Edgar stood in the hall, a wide area floored with bumpy stones and paneled in dark wood. "Here, my dear," he said, handing her a tall bourbon and Coke. "Cheers. I'm delighted you're here."

He led her into the room with the Christmas tree, a huge one that nearly touched the elaborate ceiling. The room was big enough to hold a formal dance, Rachel figured, but although there was furniture everywhere, an oversized sofa and two deep chairs were positioned near the fireplace where a cheerful fire cracked and popped. Jeremy slouched in one of the chairs. Rachel chose the sofa.

A

I thought she looked tired, but her cheeks were quite pink and she smiled as she took in the tree, the evergreen roping on the mantel, and the candles I'd lit while she was upstairs. I asked about Sébastien, the collection, Madame Pauline, and all the furor going on in Paris. But, being as selfish as I undoubtedly am, I didn't pay too much attention to Sébastien's woes. I was eager to ask Rachel the questions I'd written in my notebook. Of course she was here to celebrate Christmas, and I'd planned to do everything I could to make it wonderful for her, but I also wanted to pick her brain for material. I let her have a couple of sips of her drink and then opened my notebook.

"I hope you don't mind, but I've been dying to ask you some questions," I said. She nodded. "Tell me about American schools. When do children start, what are the schools called, how is the school year arranged?"

Bless her, she smiled at me, both with her mouth and those lovely deep green eyes. "Is Chloe a teacher now? Did you change her for this next book?"

"No, she's still a historian, but I need to know her background." I glanced at Jeremy who sipped on a pint of ale. He was watching Rachel with a carefully bland expression on his face. "I'll use little of this, but I need to know it to sound credible." I shrugged. "I've been doing some research, of course, but your impressions are more valuable."

Rachel talked, and I scribbled, pausing to ask frequent questions. She sipped nearly as frequently.

"Good, good," I said. "Now I need some vocabulary, American but also young. Slang."

She nodded.

"What slang adjective would you use for someone who backbites, slanders, says unkind things?"

Rachel had nearly finished her drink, and there was something a touch unfocused about her eyes. She giggled. "A troll? Snarky?"

"What?" I frowned. "I believe we've been using that one for a while."

153

Jeremy chuckled but said nothing. I admit I was monopolizing Rachel, not including him in the slightest, but he'd made no attempt to join in. Or did he consider Rachel snarky? Heavens! I wasn't surprised when Rachel glowered at him. She shrugged. "Maybe we borrowed it from you Brits." Ice clinked as she finished her drink. She looked around the room again and shut her eyes for a second. She seemed to be sinking deeper into the sofa.

"All right." I consulted my list. "Now, I was wondering what you call sponge bags in America. You know, the ones that hold your toothbrush and shampoo and . . ."

Jeremy interrupted me. "She's hungry, Uncle Edgar, and tired. Feed the girl before you grill her to death."

She demurred, but I was appalled both at my bad manners and that Jeremy had needed to remind me of my duties as host. "I'm so very sorry, Rachel. Come along and we'll eat."

I served up huge bowls of potato and leek soup, crusty rolls, and salad. She gobbled. I asked about her family and how they would be spending Christmas. Between bites, she told me and said that she was going to be an aunt. She didn't seem particularly excited about it. Throughout dinner, Jeremy kept glancing at Rachel but said nothing, the clod. I'd spoken to him about his behavior before she arrived, but my lecture had not improved his attitude. When Rachel finished, I said, "I have fresh apple cake for pudding."

I do believe she was a bit fuzzy from her cocktail. She shook her head like she didn't understand. She asked, "You have cake and pudding?"

There was another stifled chuckle from Jeremy, and Rachel glared at him again. I felt some sort of removed pity for her students back in Ohio.

"Oh, right," I said, understanding her confusion. "We call dessert pudding. And we call American pudding custard."

"Oh," she murmured. "Sure, I'd love some cake."

I left to fetch it and wondered if Jeremy would deign to make conversation while I was gone. I doubted it. When I returned all was silent, and she was peering around the dining room, a rather chilly chamber that Jeremy and I rarely used, preferring the coziness of the kitchen. I could see why Rachel found it daunting. Although the three of us had gathered at one end, the table was capable of seating eighteen. It was immense, as were the sideboard and chandelier above us. The room would look better Christmas Day when I'd set and filled the table with dishes. And Jeremy had promised to bring a centerpiece of roses and holly. Perhaps he could arrange a bit of ivy or juniper across the top of the sideboard as well: anything to give the room a bit of cheer.

Rachel praised my cake, and, as usual, Jeremy cleared and disappeared into the kitchen to do the washing up. Rachel followed him with her eyes and seemed surprised when she heard water running and plates rattling. I suppose she'd judged him useless as well as boorish as well she might, considering the way he'd been acting. I asked if she'd mind answering more questions for me, and she was quite gracious, saying she could do anything with a full stomach.

It was probably two hours later when I finished my list and made tea for both of us. The kitchen was tidy, as was always the case when Jeremy washed up, so I asked Rachel if she'd like to sit there to drink her tea. "What a huge room," she said as she took in the immense AGA, the Welsh dresser, the scoured table in the center of the room. "But then they all are," she murmured.

"It's the very dickens to heat and tidy, but impressive."

She nodded. "I like this room best."

"I do too. Most of the time when I'm here I live in the kitchen and my study." I pointed to the door by the pantry. "Jeremy does the same. His rooms are at the end of the front hall, behind the lounge." I remembered to translate into Yank. "The living room."

"I guess he went to his room after he finished the dishes," she said.

It didn't appear to have bothered her, but I said, "I do apologize for his manners. He's rather private."

Rachel shrugged and stirred her tea. "I need to go into Truro tomorrow," she said. "Is there a bus or something?"

"Yes, but it takes forever. What do you need?" I asked, thinking she'd forgotten her toothbrush or some other toiletry I could supply.

"I need to shop," she said with an apologetic smile. "I didn't think to bring gifts for Jeremy or Mrs. Tremaine."

"Margo," I corrected automatically. "My dear, you needn't buy anything for them. You're our guest."

She shook her head. "I absolutely do need to buy for them. I'd be embarrassed not to. What would your mother like?"

I couldn't help but smile. "Nothing. She never likes anything. Every year I buy her slippers, a bottle of brandy, and a box of glacé fruit because that's always what she says she wants. Then she tells me she doesn't like them. You'll never please her."

Rachel scrunched up her face. "That sounds like a challenge. Anyway, how can I get to town? I bet you have bunches of cooking to do tomorrow."

If she only knew. "I do," I admitted. "But Jeremy is working half-day. He can take you."

She tried to control it, but her expression deflated drastically. I'd have to speak to the boy. Brave girl that she was, she declared, "That's fine. What time does he leave? I certainly wouldn't want to make him late."

A

Sweet, old Edgar had offered her an alarm clock, but Rachel used her phone. It was still dark when it rang her awake. Taking a shower with an old-fashioned, hand-held sprayer was peculiar, but she managed to get dressed in jeans and a sweater and head downstairs, hair fixed but with only a touch of make-up, by seven-forty. Edgar had said that Jeremy left for work at eight. She hoped to get at least a cup of coffee before riding into town with Jolly Jeremy.

Both he and Edgar were sitting at the kitchen table, and she managed to get not only coffee but some scrambled eggs and toast. Outside it was as gray as the day before, but it wasn't raining. She was glad for that. And while Jeremy drove, she was also glad that she could see the countryside. She pointed to a broken brick ruin on a hillside. "What's that?"

Chatty as ever, Jeremy said, "An engine house."

She was determined to get him to talk. "What kind of engine house?"

"Tin mines," he said. "There weren't so many near here, but Cornwall had dozens of tin and sometimes copper mines a century or two ago." He pointed to the ruin. "Engine houses ran the pumps that cleared the mines of water. Truro was where they brought the tin for stamping. You can learn about it at a museum there if you want."

What was that: nearly five sentences? Jeremy must be out of breath from talking so much. He wore a nicer jacket today, brown again but suede, and when she glanced at his hands on the steering wheel, she saw that his nails were pink and clean. Maybe she'd misjudged him a little.

They were just entering Truro when he pulled off the main road at a sign that read "Hastings Garden Centre." She supposed this was his

156

place of business. There was a small building, probably the office, two large greenhouses, and a gravel lot containing trees and shrubs with their roots wrapped in burlap. Jeremy parked the van near a half dozen cut Christmas trees, standing separate from everything else. Rachel stepped close to sniff one. "I've always thought that unsold Christmas trees are very sad," she said. She expected one of his sneering chuckles.

He was unlocking the office, so she couldn't see his face. "I'll probably sell another two or three this morning. Some traditionalists still wait until Christmas Eve to trim their trees." He turned, but she couldn't see any scorn on his face. "It's a while yet until the shops open. Would you like a cup of tea?"

She couldn't believe how much tea these people drank. "No, thanks. But I would love to see your greenhouses."

His eyebrows raised a bit at that, and the morning light brightened his eyes. An interesting shade of brown. Pretty much the color of whiskey. "All right," he said.

The office was one large room divided by a long bar with a scratched and stained formica top. The front of the office had all the usual stuff: desk, computer, filing cabinet. Behind the bar there was a deep sink, cabinets and more countertop, and a tall, odd-looking refrigerator. Jeremy pointed at the microwave sitting at the far end of the counter. "You sure? I could make you a cuppa in a flash."

She supposed he was trying to be nice. "No, thanks." He led the way from the office to the first greenhouse where she saw pots of bright poinsettias clustered together. There were about a dozen of them, mostly red but a few of the marbled pinks her mother liked. "Will you sell those today too?" she asked.

"Some. I'll bring whatever's left home."

He'd taken off his jacket and wore an old, dark green sweater. He wore forest colors, she thought. She walked down the narrow aisle of the greenhouse and spotted two blue poinsettias. She laughed. "I've seen these at home. Paint, isn't it?"

He chuckled, surprised that she knew this. "Yes, vegetable dye, but don't tell Uncle Edgar. I've been saying there's a new variety that's blue, and he believes they grow that way." Jeremy touched one of the plants. "These are definitely coming home with me."

She wandered to the back corner where there were a few pots of bright cyclamen. She murmured, "These are gorgeous, but fragile as all get out, aren't they? My grandmother loved them, so we gave her one most Christmases. They were always dead by February."

"They require cool temperatures," he said. "That's why I have them back here away from the heaters."

"That's probably why they died. Granny kept her house at eighty." She smiled at him, and he smiled back, a smile so brilliant it made the gaudy flowers fade. She blinked and looked away. "So do you do mostly flowers or trees and shrubs?" For some strange reason her voice was unsteady.

"Mostly trees and shrubs, although I do bedding plants in the spring and rose bushes, hydrangeas, some other flowering ones too. And, of course, Christmas things." He pointed to the far table where there were a few fresh wreaths, some sprigs of holly, and long, snaky ropes of greenery.

Walking over to these, Rachel twitched her nose. "I love the smell," she said.

"Me too." He smiled. Again.

"Where do you get the holly and evergreens? These aren't pine, are they?"

"No. Juniper, yew, some balsam and hemlock. Holly, of course. It wouldn't be Christmas in Britain without holly." He broke a brown sprig off a wreath. "I cut most of it from the woodlands behind the house."

"I'd love to see your woods."

He went on talking like she hadn't said anything. "I have boys who collect mistletoe and sell it to me. For kissing balls, you know." His face turned as pink as the poinsettias. "I've sold all of them."

Rachel grinned. "That's good, isn't it? Lots of Christmas cheer in those houses." She touched the sharp edge of a holly sprig. "Do you make these? The wreaths and ropes?"

"Sure. I have wire frames for the wreaths. Tony, he's my bloke for planting trees and site landscaping, his wife makes the bows for me. All thumbs at that," he said.

"A green thumb's better than a ribbon thumb," she replied. And he laughed. Big time, much bigger than the quip deserved. "Do you do house plants?"

"A few. Mostly as pets. They're in the other greenhouse."

He tilted his head toward it, and she nodded.

The smell of earth and damp and green was stronger in the second house, mostly because there was no evergreen perfume to mask it. This greenhouse was mostly empty, but on the far side was a row of clay pots of all sizes.

"Oh, African violets. My favorite," she said.

"Really? I'd give you one, but I don't think you're allowed to take it across international borders. Don't know how well it would travel anyway."

"And no way I could take it back to the U. S. ," she said. "I'll be going home soon." She walked slowly down the row of plants. "Orchids," she said. "Very picky, aren't they? And jade plants. I have one at home that my dad is taking care of for me. He and I both love plants."

Jeremy had his hands in the pockets of his worn khakis. He kept smiling and nodding. "No one in my family is into plants," he said. "Oh, Uncle Edgar likes flowers around the outside of the house. But nothing much inside."

Rachel turned toward the empty greenhouse. "What will you have in here later?"

"I'll be starting bedding plants soon after the New Year. Annuals and a few perennials. Do you do much gardening? Besides the jade plant?" He asked it very seriously.

"Not much. When I lived at home, Dad and I would plant flowers every spring. You know, easy stuff like impatiens and begonias and zinnias. I like zinnias; they're so showy and tough. Do people here like them?"

He nodded.

"What I love most are peonies and lilacs," she said, almost babbling. "Peonies remind me of little girls in Easter dresses. And I'm fascinated by lupines except that I've tried and killed them three times and decided to quit."

He chuckled. "They grow well here."

"Cooler temperatures and lots of humidity. I saw them thriving in Maine when I traveled there. But Ohio can get very hot and dry in the summer." She paused and looked at her watch. Maybe she was boring him, but he didn't act like it. "Should you get to work on that centerpiece? I can go exploring if you need me to leave."

"I don't need you to leave," he said, and she thought he meant it. "But the shops are open by now." He went to the door. "Just walk up this road about a quarter of a mile, and you'll be in the center of town."

Rachel faltered a second. She didn't want to irritate him, especially now that he'd become friendly. "Should I get a bus back to the house or what?"

He shook his head. "No, no. I'll be closing up here about noon. Come back and we'll get lunch. If you finish your shopping earlier, come back. I'll be here." He didn't quite meet her eyes.

"Okay. Thanks."

Rachel started up the road at a good clip. This was going to be fine. If talking about plants made Jeremy happy, she'd talk about plants until she left. She loved them too. And she also loved Christmas Eve. It was her favorite day of the year. She passed doorway after doorway decorated with wreaths, mostly artificial but some fresh. She wondered if they were Jeremy's creations. As she neared the cathedral, she looked up and up. Just like a gawking tourist, she thought. Truro's was small compared to churches in Paris but had its own charm. She smiled at herself. When did 'charm' and 'charming' become part of her vocabulary? She imagined clever Inspector Hannaford going into the cathedral to speak to the vicar, like he had in Edgar's first book, and she peered down at the river from the bridge where Hannaford had gone over the details of the case until he realized who the murderer was. She glanced around but couldn't identify Hannaford's favorite pub. Maybe that had come entirely from Edgar's imagination.

It was early, but there were lots of people on the street, dipping into shops and carrying bags. Other last minute shoppers like her, she thought. What on earth was she going to buy Margo? If the woman criticized what Edgar bought her, what she'd even *asked* for, how could Rachel please her? She thought of books, candy, gloves, but none of those seemed right. Hoping for inspiration, she walked into a bookstore and sniffed. *L'eau de bookstore* must be the same everywhere in the world. She wandered among the shelves, not knowing if picky Mrs. Tremaine would prefer fiction or biography, cookbooks or poetry. She was about to give up and leave when she saw a small selection of stationery, writing papers and note cards. This might do. Picking up the most innocuous and most expensive box of heavy, creamy paper, she went to the clerk and asked if she could have it gift-wrapped. Certainly, the woman replied, and Rachel browsed among the books while she waited. Maybe she'd see something for Jeremy. Of course there were dozens of books on gardening, flowers, bulbs, trees, and everything else horticultural, but he probably had all of those he needed, plus he seemed like more of a hands-on kind of guy than a researcher.

The clerk wished her a happy Christmas when Rachel took her package and went back outside. It was hard enough to figure out gifts for people you knew, let alone near strangers. She window-shopped and then stopped at a clothing store that had things for men and women. Maybe there'd be something here.

She saw beautiful woolen sweaters, but that seemed too personal and she had no clue what size he wore. Besides, like the French ones, British sizes were foreign to her. The same went for shirts, and she almost giggled when she thought about buying him pants. She wasn't having any luck at all. Then she saw a table with stacks of yummy cashmere scarves in all kinds of beautiful colors. The price was, well, a little high, but at least she wouldn't appear cheap, and they were so soft. Her eyes went to a deep burgundy but immediately shifted to a brown scarf, sort of a rusty shade. It reminded her of gingerbread. Once again the clerk boxed and wrapped the gift for Rachel and smiled at her American accent.

Going back out into the chilly morning, Rachel felt good. She was done. It was Christmas Eve. And she was happy again. She didn't want to press her luck by going back to the garden center too early, so Rachel prowled around Truro, enjoying the holiday decorations and the delightful *foreignness* of a European country that spoke English. Sort of. She passed a bakery, for once not tempted since Jeremy had promised lunch. The holiday cakes and treats in the window amused her, and she suddenly had an idea. She still had the afternoon; she'd bake Christmas cookies. Back home, that had been her traditional Christmas job. But she didn't want to use up Edgar's ingredients. He probably had everything carefully planned out for his cooking. It wasn't like he could run down to the nearby Kroger's. She needed to find a grocery.

An hour later, laden down with gifts and a bag containing flour, sugar, butter, and little containers of red and green sugar, Rachel blew into Jeremy's office. The wind had picked up. "How are you doing?" she asked as she set down her bags.

"Splendid," he replied. She liked that word. "I finished the centerpiece." He pointed to the counter where a large vase held bright red roses, trailing ivy, twigs sugared with snow glitter, and bits of holly tucked here and there.

"Talk about splendid," Rachel exclaimed. "You could do florist work too."

His cheeks pinked up. "No, not my thing, but thanks. I buy any flowers I need from a florist in town. It's nearly noon, shall we leave?"

"Sounds good to me. Did you sell any more of those orphan trees?"

"Two," he said. "Wait here while I load up everything."

A few minutes later Rachel sat in Jeremy's van, a blue poinsettia in her lap and a red one tucked between her feet. He'd balanced the centerpiece between them, and a rose or two trembled about two inches from her nose. She sneezed. Jeremy fretted. "Are you all right? I hate to load you down like this."

She sniffed. "I'm fine. Besides, where else could you put them? They'd fall over in the back."

She was surprised when he drove out of town and took a turn away from the road to Edgar's. He said, "It's not very elegant, but I want to take you to a real Cornish pub. The building is over three hundred years old."

Rachel said that sounded good, that she wasn't into elegant. His damned eyebrow went up again. She wondered what Edgar had told him about her. Oh well, she'd start in again with irises and pansies if she had to thaw him out. Of course she wanted to see a three hundred year old building. She didn't know enough geology or whatever to guess at the history of the land itself, but a building that ancient in Ohio would be a museum with souvenir shops and guides in long dresses. Last night Edgar had shrugged when she asked how old his house was. "It was built just over a hundred years ago," he'd said, acting like that was nothing.

A bit farther down the road Jeremy stopped in a village so tiny she wondered if it had a name, but then it probably did. Everything had a name, including Edgar's house, "Penmore." She liked it. The pub was "The Fox and Hounds." She liked that too. "Here," said Jeremy, "let me unload you so you can get out." He carefully set the blue poinsettia in his seat and reached between her feet for the red one. It felt odd when his arm brushed her jeans.

The pub was noisy and cozy and smelled of beer and wood smoke. Jeremy was known here; several people called out his name. Tacky tinsel festooned the bar area, and a small pink tree blinked frantically. People had started their Christmas celebrations early, and the barman was busy filling glasses. Jeremy found them a tiny round table with a sticky top and paper coasters advertising beers and ales. "What do you want to eat and drink?" he asked.

"No menus?"

He shook his head and pointed at a chalkboard. Scrawled on it were fish and chips, jacket potatoes, and bangers and mash, among other things. "What on earth are bangers and mash?" she asked.

He grinned. "Sausages and mashed potatoes. You usually get some peas on the side. They're wonderful and about as British as you can get."

"They sound sort of, hmm, rude."

He laughed, and it lit up his face like sunlight forcing its way through the pub's grimy windows. "If you think that's bad, you should get spotted dick for pudding." His face had gone a deep pink.

Then she laughed, loud enough that a couple of nearby drinkers, both middle-aged, male, and paunchy, looked around and smiled at her. One winked. "Is it a disease?" she managed to gasp.

"Sponge cake with sauce. And currants."

She smiled. "We'll see. Sure, I'll try the bangers and mash."

"What to drink?"

"Well, I don't much like beer, and it seems too early for whiskey."

"It's Christmas Eve."

She frowned. "I don't know."

The winking man was eavesdropping. "Get her a scrumpy, mate. That'll make her laugh again." And he grinned at Rachel from behind a heavy, gray moustache.

Jeremy nodded and headed to the bar. It didn't surprise Rachel one bit when Moustache got up and stood by her table. "You're a Yank, aren't you?"

What a marvelous grasp of the obvious. She nodded.

"What are you doing in Cornwall?" His eyes were scrutinizing everything visible above the table. They stayed at breast level.

"I'm spending Christmas with Edgar Tremaine." She wished Jeremy would hurry back.

"Oh, our Edgar. Well, that's fine. Are you a writer too?"

"No."

"Now, that's a shame. I could tell you some very fine stories. And we might conjure up a few of our own, love. Spicy ones." His moustache made him look like a walrus. Where *was* Jeremy?

"I don't write." Dense, wasn't he?

He shifted his weight like he was getting ready to pull out a chair, and she just knew he intended to sit and then push his leg firmly against hers. She hadn't been in this sort of situation since college when some of the less attractive frat boys drank enough to forget she was fat. "What do you do then?" he asked and was halfway to sitting down when Jeremy appeared holding two glasses of golden liquid. One had a foamy head; the other didn't.

"Pardon me, mate," Jeremy said, setting down the glasses. "But she's mine."

Moustache moved away, smiling and winking, and Rachel felt much better. Except that she couldn't quite get her head around Jeremy's words. Was she his? What did he mean? She pointed to her glass. "What is this?"

"Scrumpy," he replied, taking a long drink from his beer. "Cider."

"Oh, I love apple cider," she said and lifted her glass.

"It's fermented apple cider, so watch yourself," he said and then grinned. "Or not. Around here they say that scrumpy leaves you legless but happy."

Then she made him explain what legless meant.

It seemed like she laughed through the entire lunch. As soon as their food came, Moustache Man stood to leave and handed Rachel a card, telling her to call him when she was finished with the "lawn and garden bloke." A few minutes later an ancient man came to their table and sang an off-key, wobbly version of "Hark the Herald Angels Sing" and then demanded a pint. Jeremy bought him one and wished him a happy holiday. He was laughing too. Everything was funny.

When they left the pub, Jeremy once again used Rachel as a carrier for the poinsettias. "I believe I am a little legless," she said, scrunching up her nose at a rose.

"From a half pint of cider?" He started the engine.

"I drank it awfully fast."

"Yes." Jeremy smiled at her. "I expect you do everything in life in great gulps."

Rachel searched his expression for criticism. Was he referring to her weight? She took a moment to reply. "I guess I do."

"I admire it," he said, still smiling. "I tend to take cautious little sips."

Okay, she got what he meant. And he was right. "You're probably smarter."

He shook his head. "I miss a lot." Jeremy squeezed her hand. It felt so friendly that she almost wanted to kiss him. Lord, she must be tipsy.

"Whether it's gulping or not, I haven't had this much fun in forever," she said.

This time his eyebrow rose over a twinkle. "But you didn't try the spotted dick."

This sent her off into new peals of laughter. "I will sometime. I promise. Will Edgar have that on the menu for Christmas Dinner?"

"I doubt it."

She took a deep breath and felt weeks of tension drain out of her. No Kurt, no Sébastien. And Jeremy was turning out to be fun. She asked, "I don't suppose you'd like to help me bake cookies, would you?"

"I'd love it, but I have some Christmas things to do. Sorry."

He actually did sound sorry. "That's okay. Last minute shopping?"

"Something like that." He turned his head toward her, and his eyes glowed as warm as a cozy fire. The scarf she'd bought him wasn't just the color of gingerbread; it was the color of his eyes. "But I'll certainly participate in eating those cookies," he said and grinned. And she felt more tipsy than ever.

⩜

I'd started slaving away in the kitchen the minute Jeremy and Rachel took off for Truro. The last of the mince pies were baking. I'd peeled sprouts and mixed up stuffing for tomorrow. And I'd fetched the plum pudding from the pantry and set it out for tomorrow's steaming. I was exhausted, although I'd never admit it to the children. They hovered too much as it was.

After making a cup of tea, I sat at the kitchen table and called Sébastien. What Rachel had said last night about his situation concerned me, and I'd time to fret about it through all the kitchen chores. As far back as I could remember, he'd always landed on his feet no matter how precarious the situation, but this was worrisome. I knew it was bothering Rachel. He actually answered his phone.

"Happy Christmas, Gumby," I said.

There was a grunt.

"How are you? Rachel arrived safe and sound, but she's worrying about you."

This brought a response. "Is she?"

"Yes. And I am too. What's going on?"

I heard him sigh. "Word's gotten out about the collection. Nothing published, but some of the models and staff are quitting. Rats leaving a sinking ship."

"Do you think you're sinking?"

He didn't answer for a minute. "I believe in the collection. These are the most beautiful garments I've ever designed."

"Then ignore them."

"They have no imagination, Eddie. No appreciation for art. These costumes are beautiful. The women are beautiful."

"Rachel certainly is."

"Are you done using her?" His tone was as sour as lemons.

"It's merely research, getting the American slant for my character. I'm not making her sit around in her underwear or holding her hostage as some people have done. And yes, I've finished my research, but I've certainly not finished enjoying her company."

A low throaty noise. Then, "I wish she were here."

"She'll be back soon. Are you going to Polly's tonight?"

"Yes. Oysters, of course. All the traditions." He paused. "Dumont called me yesterday from Switzerland."

"And?"

"He asked if the rumors were true. I questioned him about what he'd heard and told him that yes, they were true but blown out of proportion."

I was alarmed, but I made soothing noises.

"He swore at me. Can you believe that? I, I have been Sylvestri for years now. Then, he actually threatened to sack me."

"You cannot be serious." My heart was pounding. Dear God. Sébastien Fel sacked?

"He said that it was too late to cancel. He'd rather have a disaster than no show at all. But all the expenses, all the blame rests on my head. He is canceling the after-show party. Can you imagine? And if the collection is as poorly received as he fears, he says that right after the show, he will formally announce that Sébastien Fel is no longer affiliated with Sylvestri."

I wasn't sure, but I thought I heard an emotional wavering in Sébastien's voice. For all his drama, for all those years, this time it was justified. Of course Dumont would sack him. Only Sébastien's potent glamour had prevented all of us from realizing this. "I'm horrified, truly horrified. And yet you must see it through."

"He will change his mind once he sees the clothes. I'm certain of it."

I wasn't, but I couldn't think of a thing to say to Sébastien.

"Don't tell Raquel. I must act as if everything is normal. She must shine or there is no hope at all."

I promised him.

"The world will disagree with Dumont," he declared, his voice stronger now.

"Absolutely." But I knew this wasn't true. What would Sébastien do? High fashion was an incestuous world. Would he have to resort to designing wallpaper or towels for discount stores? I was appalled but managed to conceal it until we hung up.

As I gazed at the holiday tin full of mince pies, the polished silver, the sparkling wine glasses, I made every attempt to put this terrible news out of my head. It was Christmas, and I must make it the best ever for Rachel, especially with what she would be facing soon in Paris. It was bad enough that Jeremy was being an ass, and one never knew what Margo's mood might be. She might grill Rachel to the point of tears, although I had to smile at this notion. After months of living with Sébastien, Rachel tended to hold her own.

I ate a bite of lunch and took my notes to the study. Nothing relieved my mind of the horrors of reality better than writing. I'd been working for over an hour when I heard Rachel and Jeremy come in. When I went into the hall, he was placing a blue poinsettia in the lounge. "That is a truly eccentric plant," I observed. "What kind of horticultural magic did they do to come up with blue?"

Rachel had very pink cheeks. "Oh, it's a hybrid."

Jeremy started coughing like a consumptive, and Rachel giggled. Something was brewing, and I suspected it was distinctly alcoholic. "May I use the kitchen to bake Christmas cookies, Edgar? Do you mind? It's sort of a tradition for me, and I promise to clean up afterwards."

"Not at all," I said. "I've finished my culinary work for today." Jeremy disappeared, but she and I went to the kitchen where I could explain the mysteries of the AGA. Rachel did seem a little tipsy, so I said everything twice.

Chapter Sixteen

She found a radio in the kitchen and listened to Christmas music while she baked her butter cookies. Her mother had given over cookie baking to Rachel years ago, so she had the recipe memorized. It made nearly a hundred small cookies, but they kept forever and people could rarely eat just one or two. After showing her how to operate the stove, Edgar disappeared. To rest, she hoped; the kitchen and refrigerator looked as though he'd cooked all morning. Rachel had been baking for nearly two hours, humming along with carols and thinking about Ohio and her family, when Jeremy came into the kitchen. "Nearly finished?" he asked. His eyes immediately dropped from her face to her breasts, and she was beginning to wonder if he was no better than the Moustache Guy. Or maybe he was wondering why a fat girl was baking cookies. Then she looked down. A wide swath of flour covered the front of her sweater. She brushed at it with a towel.

"Yes. Maybe another fifteen minutes to clean up. Why?"

"At the greenhouse you said you'd like to see the woods where I get the holly and greenery for my wreaths. I thought you might want to walk back there before it gets dark." His eyes were wary again, like he expected her to say no.

Rachel glanced at the wide kitchen window. The sky was already a moody gray. "Sure," she said, "I'll hurry. Want a cookie? I mean, a biscuit?"

The minute they left the house, a chilly, damp wind cut through her jacket. She shivered. "Do you think it will snow?"

Walking over the lawn, Jeremy led her to a path far behind the house. "It never snows in Cornwall. In Scotland, yes, and the north of England. It even snows a flake or two in London sometimes, but never here. Are you too cold?"

A huge oak tree near the back of the yard creaked in the wind. "No." She put her hands in her pockets. "How far away from the sea are we?"

He pointed east. "Three miles, as a bird would fly. But that's just an inlet, not truly the sea."

"Is it rocky or beachy?" The path was rough, littered with tufts of tough grass. She walked carefully. "You have both in Cornwall, don't you?" She'd done a little research back when she first met Edgar and learned that he, like Inspector Hannaford, was from Cornwall.

"It's a small harbor. No rocks, but not much of a beach either."

Up ahead there were trees, close and clustered. She couldn't see very far into the woods, but it looked cold and dark. "I told you I went to Maine once, didn't I? Where they grow all those lupines? I loved the wild, rocky beaches there."

"We do have those. Maybe you can see them while you're here."

She gave him a little nod. There'd be little time for that.

"Watch your step here." He slowed as they neared the crowded, winter-bare trees and evergreens. Some of the larger trees were wrapped in ivy. "I take ivy cuttings here." He pointed. "Farther back I have a nursery for young trees. Do you want to see those?"

She nodded and stumbled on a gnarled root. He grabbed her cold hand. She'd forgotten gloves, but he wore leather ones that felt warm and strong.

"Look at this holly." They stood beside a tall tree, huge and bearing no resemblance to the holly shrubs she'd seen sometimes in Ohio. Rachel touched a spiny leaf with her free hand. This one had clusters and clusters of fiery berries. He said, "Enough here to keep all of Truro festive at Christmas, isn't there?"

"It's fantastic."

They moved on, and she let him keep hold of her hand. The ground was uneven, her fingers were icy, but the truth was that she liked the feel of his gloved hand around hers. Coming to a cleared area, she saw spindly saplings lined up like soldiers. "Baby trees," she said.

He smiled. "When someone wants a certain kind, Tony comes out here, digs it up, balls the roots, and takes it into town. If they like the look of it, he plants it for them." He shrugged into his suede jacket. "So, I'm constantly planting more out here."

The saplings were leafless and indistinguishable, just rows of spiny limbs whipped by the breeze. "What do you have here?" she asked. "And how can you tell what's what?"

"Maples, flowering crab apples, a few ash and oak. They're all tagged."

Jeremy's body shielded her from the wind. His shoulders truly were nice and wide, and she had a sudden urge to move closer to him. But she didn't. "And the flowering shrubs and bushes?"

He pointed. "Over there? See them?"

She nodded. "And up ahead?"

"More woodlands. Our property goes back quite a ways."

The woods ahead looked even darker and more enticing than what they'd passed through. Even though she was cold, Rachel wanted to walk on and on. She heard gulls calling, a sad, lonely sound, and the dark patch ahead looked almost spooky, like the fairy tale Christmas she'd fantasized about on the train. "I want to see," she said.

It was nearly dark, but Jeremy knew his woods. She wasn't afraid. Here there were more shrubs, wild ones, some with thorns that snagged at her jeans. The path had disappeared, and their feet sank into damp leaves that smelled old and earthy. She imagined bits and pieces from stories she barely remembered. Woodcutter's cottages. Enchanted forests. She halfway expected to see a gingerbread house and Gretel's blonde braids. Really. "It's a magic place," she whispered.

"I think so," he said, his voice nearly as quiet as hers. "There's magic in trees and plants."

She looked up at his face. He was taller than Kurt Mann, maybe six feet or so. "Druid," she said with a smile.

He chuckled. "Maybe." He stopped and touched the bark of a bare tree. "For luck," he said, and then pulling, just barely pulling her hand toward him, he shifted Rachel until they were facing each other. "Maybe there's this kind of magic here too." He kissed her, lips warm and cheeks cold. Then everything cold vanished, and she pressed against his jacket, her breath coming quick and warm.

His hand was in her hair, then against her back, and then she felt his glove on her face. They pulled apart. The sky was about one inch from being dark, and his eyes were hard to see. "Do you mind?" he asked. His voice had gone funny.

She smiled. "Do I act like I mind?"

Almost as if it were part of the wind's tune, the sound of bells drifted into the woods. She looked up at the inky sky. "From the village where we ate lunch," Jeremy explained. "It's Christmas Eve."

She kissed him this time. She shut her eyes, and in her mind she was a fairy princess, a lonesome heroine, an ancient legend. She didn't want the story to end.

A

I'd taken a hefty whiskey to sip in the bath and ended up dozing until the water chilled me awake. This would never do. I dressed in a hurry and sped downstairs to put a lasagna, made three days ago and frozen, in the oven. The kitchen was clean but empty, scented with spices from my pies and butter from Rachel's biscuits. Where were the children? Going into the lounge, I plugged in the lights on the tree, lit candles, and regretted that unless I could find Jeremy in a hurry I would have to make the fire. I called for both of them, but there was no answer. Vaguely worried, I peered out front and saw Jeremy's van. He would never take the BMW without asking me. Were they walking? In the dark? Or had Rachel found a convenient rock and bashed in Jeremy's head? They appeared to have thawed a bit when they'd come home from luncheon, but Rachel wouldn't put up with discourteous behavior for long. Jeremy was asking for a fine dressing down if he didn't change his behavior.

I'd started laying the fire when I heard them in the kitchen, Rachel laughing long and loud, and Jeremy talking and chuckling in his baritone. He seemed to be telling a story, but I couldn't make out the words. The two of them came into the lounge smelling of cold and trees. "Here, I'll do that, Uncle Edgar," Jeremy said, taking off his jacket and laying it on the arm of the sofa.

"I was concerned about you," I said with more petulance than I usually allow myself.

"I'm sorry," Rachel said. Her cheeks glowed and her curls were bewitchingly tangled. How lovely she was. "We went for a walk in the woods." She smiled at Jeremy. "The hundred acre wood."

He was squatting down, positioning the logs. "Actually I think it's more like sixty-seven acres, isn't it?" He looked at me, and I caught a strange light in his eyes.

Rachel scolded. "Don't you remember your Winnie the Pooh? And you a British boy." She gave Jeremy a dazzling smile.

When she draped her jacket over Jeremy's and unconsciously patted the two of them, I figured out the situation. Well, well, well. Once upon a time I'd hoped, but I'd given it up when they'd behaved so acrimoniously during my illness. I said, "Drinks anyone? It's Christmas Eve."

A

Although she'd not come upstairs until nearly one, Rachel woke early, way before daylight. Her first thought was: it's Christmas. She stretched and yawned. She'd always been the first one up on Christmas mornings, rousing her parents, punching her brother awake. They'd never really minded, she thought, but sometimes it had been as early as

171

five or five-thirty. Glancing at her phone she saw that it was, sure enough, five-thirty, but she had no desire to go back to sleep.

Another day with Jeremy, she thought, and smiled through a yawn. Was she, as he put it, gulping again? Rushing into something like a fool? It felt more than right, and this time she wasn't ignoring advice from wise people like Gisèle and Edgar. Actually, Edgar was cheering them on.

Last night he'd been in a particularly good mood and had made friends with the whiskey bottle. He'd swayed a little when he declared he was off to bed. Pausing at the doorway he'd smiled, raised his hand like the Pope, and said, "Bless you, my children." She and Jeremy had laughed.

"He knows," Jeremy had said.

Rachel had teased him. "Knows what?"

"That I'm falling for you."

They'd talked for hours, intoxicated with each other rather than liquor.

"I lived in the U. S. for a while," he'd said. "When I was twelve or so."

"Where?"

"Texas. Very peculiar for a Brit."

This had amused her. "Did you have lots of little American friends when you lived in Texas?"

He'd arranged his arm across her shoulders, very cozy, and replied, "I didn't have any. They thought I talked funny. I mostly rode my bicycle, watched the telly, and developed an addiction for Big Macs." He'd grinned, which made her smile every time he did it. "I did learn how to say, 'hi, ya'll. '" He'd sounded nearly as southern as Crystal.

Rachel had laughed. "No little Texas girlfriends? Lots of cute cheerleaders down there."

Still smiling, Jeremy had touched her hair. "There was one girl, and she was a cheerleader, middle school, you know. So pretty, and her name was Devon. I was certain that gave us some kind of special connection." He'd paused to let Rachel recall that the next English county over was Devon. "Umm, Devon didn't see it that way."

"Stupid girl," Rachel had murmured, leaning against him and kissing his neck at that soft spot just under the jawbone. "Where did you go to college?"

"Near here. In Exeter, actually. I studied business, which is a bit of a joke. Not good at that sort of thing at all."

"But you run a business," Rachel had said.

"It was supposed to be a very different sort of business. My schooling was intended to set me up as a banker. Margo's idea. And I did work at a Barclay's for two miserable years. When Uncle Edgar came back to live in England he saw how unhappy I was and encouraged me to do what I wanted. He helped me buy the greenhouses." Jeremy'd smiled. "And took all sorts of hell from Margo about it."

"And you lived happily ever after."

He'd traced the line of her jaw. "It could happen." And he'd kissed her again, sending fizzy sensations all over her body.

A bit later she'd asked, "You love this house, don't you?"

"I do. And the land and the trees and even the spots of damp on the kitchen walls."

"Why do you love it so much?"

"These are the only roots I have. When I was a kid we never lived anywhere long enough to call it home. Then my parents died. I have Uncle Edgar, Margo, and this land. That's it. And I'm the kind of bloke that needs roots."

"Like ivy?"

"No. Ivy clings. Roots just need a place to stay and grow and be happy."

After a really pleasant pause that involved lips and tongues and some fairly heavy breathing, she'd said, "I'm sorry I screeched at you in London, but it was a shock when you burst into Edgar's guest room. Why were you so mean to me afterwards?" She'd rested her head against his shoulder, smelling the green scent of him, loving the soft wool against her cheek.

"I was afraid of you."

"Oh, come on."

"Still am, to tell the truth. You're so beautiful. The image of you sitting up in bed was so brilliant that I carried it around in my head like a photo. I couldn't imagine someone as lovely as you, a model for God's sake, even having the time of day for me."

"I don't believe you."

"It's true. I swear."

"On what?"

"Penmore. Margo and Uncle Edgar. I swear it on everything I have or know."

She'd kissed him that time, cradling his skull with her hands to feel his silky hair between her fingers. "I'm not beautiful," she murmured. "I'm fat."

"You're perfect." He'd sat up and stared at the waning fire. "I told you; I'm wary. I wait to be sure."

She'd pulled at her sweater where it'd bunched up around her belly. "Well, if it's other girls you're talking about, I'm glad you waited." He'd looked hard at her, the fire dancing in his eyes. "I swear too," she'd said.

A

Rachel got out of bed. The floor was icy. If this was the warmest bedroom in the house, she hated to think what the others were like. But after she got the hot water going in the bathroom, she felt better. On the bed, she set out the Sylvestri green suit. It seemed formal compared to what she, Edgar, and Jeremy had been wearing yesterday, but it was Christmas and Margo was coming.

The house was as silent as an old mansion could be with all its creaks and groans. She tried to creep down the hall and stairway as quietly as possible, but she was wearing those damned black pumps that were about as quiet as double jackhammers. She turned her ankle on the front hall's stone floor and had to stifle her swearing. She was simply not a stiletto girl. The lounge was dark, but she eased her way to the Christmas tree and plugged it in. At least two dozen packages, including hers, shimmered under the tree. She lit candles and then went to the kitchen to make coffee. Surely Edgar would be up soon. He'd said he had to stuff the turkey and get it into the oven very early.

Rachel waited and thought about the difficulties of long-distance relationships. Really long distance relationships. She drank coffee and wondered how she could persuade Jeremy to come to Paris. And then to Ohio. She ate three cookies and remembered how he had said she was perfect, not fat. Finally she heard Edgar come down the steps. "Merry Christmas," she said.

He groaned. "Coffee. Please. How can whiskey be so good in the evening and so vile the next day?"

Two cups of coffee seemed to revive him. He quickly threw together some breakfast and attacked the turkey. It was another hour before Jeremy was up, helping himself to the eggs and bacon warming on the stove. The first faint scents of turkey were filling the kitchen. He took in her suit, her shoes, her eyeliner and lipstick, and then kissed her cheek. "You look very intimidating again. But gorgeous. Merry Christmas."

Then he had to go fetch his grandmother, in Edgar's BMW, because Margo wouldn't consider riding in Jeremy's van. Rachel wondered if he'd ask her to go with him but hoped he wouldn't. She didn't quite understand why Jeremy had said she was scary, but she sure as hell was afraid of Margo, and with good reason, she thought. But Jeremy never suggested it. He put on his jacket, kissed her cheek again, and left. Rachel let out a long breath.

Edgar went from one cooking chore to another: peeling potatoes, steaming the pudding, and roasting chestnuts. Although he didn't say as much, he seemed to want Rachel out of his kitchen. She wandered upstairs, opening bedroom doors and admiring the furniture and colors. Edgar's was at the front of the house and huge, filled with antiques and some paintings Rachel figured were worth a bundle.

Downstairs she sat and read for a while by the tree and then continued to snoop, opening the door to Jeremy's room before she suffered a fit of conscience about what she was doing. She quickly shut the door, seeing only that the room was neat and his double bed was covered in a dark green comforter nearly the same color as her suit. She went back to the kitchen to ask Edgar once again if she could help. Waiting this long for Christmas presents, and Jeremy, was torture.

Edgar allowed her to set the table and place paper tubes that looked like huge twists of taffy by each plate. He called them crackers. She'd just finished when she heard the car pull up to the front door. Margo. Rachel would've preferred dealing with six Sébastien Fels, all in foul moods.

"They're here," Rachel called back to the kitchen.

She heard a stifled "damn," and Edgar emerged from the kitchen patting his hair and shrugging into a tweed blazer. "She will expect to be entertained," he mumbled. "And I have dozens of things left to do."

"I'll help," Rachel said, but she hoped it was with the cooking, not with Margo.

Before Edgar could reply, Jeremy threw open the front door, and a tiny, gray-haired woman in a dark blue coat entered the hall like the Queen sweeping into Buckingham Palace. "A raw day," she observed in the same firm voice Rachel remembered from the telephone. "My coat, Jeremy," she said, impatient for him to set down a large shopping bag and a folded afghan.

Edgar sprang forward to kiss his mother on both well-rouged cheeks. "Margo," he declared. "Happy Christmas."

"I suppose," she said. "Put that rug near the fire, Jeremy. You know I always freeze in this house." She gave Rachel a piercing stare from eyes that looked much younger than the rest of her face. "So this is the American girl." She pronounced it more like "gel."

Edgar sputtered at not having the chance to introduce her, but Rachel smiled and held out her hand. God help her, she felt like she should curtsey. "I'm Rachel Bowman, ma'am. Pleased to meet you."

Margo wrapped her clawed little paw around Rachel's hand and gave it a firm pump. "Margo Tremaine. A well-fed little specimen, aren't you?"

Edgar coughed, and out of the corner of her eye she saw Jeremy narrow his eyes and start to speak. Rachel hurried to say, "I'm from Ohio, ma'am. We grow a lot of corn in Ohio."

Margo's nose twitched, and then she laughed, a dignified snort of a laugh, and said, "Happy Christmas, Rachel, and please call me Margo. I'm not the queen to be ma'amed."

Could've fooled her, Rachel thought, but she smiled, nodded, and returned the Christmas greetings. Edgar excused himself to go to the kitchen, and Margo sat in the chair nearest the fire, draping the crocheted afghan over her lap. "Sherry," she barked at Jeremy.

It wasn't even noon yet, but what the hell, Rachel thought as she accepted a tiny glass of sherry from Jeremy, who smiled at her and winked. That helped because she certainly didn't like the sherry when she tasted it, and Margo had decided that interrogating Rachel was an interesting pre-dinner activity. "What does your father do?" she asked. And it went on from there. For over an hour.

Jeremy was no help. He slouched in the chair opposite his grandmother until she told him to sit up. He was silent and seemed amused by all the questions. Rachel had little luck distracting the woman from her nosiness. When Rachel asked if Margo crocheted and if she'd made her afghan, Margo said, "My what? Whatever is an afghan, other than a resident of Afghanistan? No, I do not crochet, no patience for that sort of fiddly thing. I bought this at the church jumble sale."

Margo asked about Rachel's brother, her education, and finally about her career. "So you are a model?" She said the word like most people would say "hooker."

"Not really. This is just a fluke." Rachel's vocabulary deserted her. "And temporary."

Margo frowned. "Then what are you?"

Rachel considered a philosophical treatise on existentialism but knew she wasn't up to it. "Like I said before, I'm a French teacher."

She must've been looking flustered because Jeremy, no longer finding humor in the situation, stood, offered to get Margo more sherry, and suggested that Edgar might need Rachel's help. "She's brilliant in the kitchen," he told his grandmother. "You must sample one of the Christmas biscuits she made."

Rachel was gone before she could hear Margo's reply. She dashed into the kitchen and told Edgar, "I'll help or I'll hide in a corner, but please let me stay in here!"

A

Thank God she hadn't spilled gravy down her front or broken the fragile stem of her wineglass. They'd nearly made it to the end of Christmas dinner. Margo, a touch mellowed by, Jeremy had whispered, four glasses of sherry, had pronounced the turkey dry, the sprouts bitter, and the wine indifferent, but she'd generally left Rachel alone during the meal. Edgar came back into the dining room brandishing a flaming plum pudding, which he set on the table in front of Rachel. It looked like fiery fruitcake to her. "I told you about stir-up Sunday," he said, "when we start the pudding and let it steam."

"And then you keep it for a month," she said, peering at the dark mound to see if there was mold anywhere.

He must've noticed her hard look. "Of course it is well-preserved with brandy."

Jeremy, sitting beside her and squeezing her hand as he'd done frequently through the meal, whispered, "Like some old women I know."

Rachel stifled a giggle. "And now, here it is."

Edgar was smiling like the kindly uncle he was, and even Margo looked benign. Or tiddly, as Edgar called it. "Your first English Christmas," he said.

177

But not her last, she hoped. She loved the feel of Jeremy's rough hand, a man's hand with calluses from hard work, and the warmth of it seemed to rise up to her cheeks. She lifted her glass and declared, "To Christmas. To England and especially to Cornwall."

A

We taught Rachel how to do crackers, and she exclaimed over the cheap little mirror that was in hers. After reading the jokes and admiring each other's paper crowns, I suggested that we adjourn to the lounge for gifts. Margo was nodding, about to go face-first onto the damask, but I knew she'd liven up over the prospect of presents. She always pretended not to like her plunder, but I'd figured out long ago that she loved it.

"You can take off your crown now," I said to Rachel who looked more fetching than usual today. Perhaps it was the suit, obviously Sébastien's creation, but I thought it might be my newly attentive nephew contributing to her glow. "Sit, sit," I said. "Jeremy, will you do the honors?"

He piled gifts beside each of us, and, as was our custom, we took turns opening them. I was more interested in what I'd given Rachel than any of the others, although Jeremy seemed genuinely pleased with the antique clock I'd bought him, and I admired the shirt he'd chosen for me. "There are two from me," I said to Rachel. "In the green paper."

She ripped into the paper, greedy as a child, which made me love her even more. The watch pleased her very much and she quickly fastened it around her wrist, but her eyes turned shiny when she opened the galley copy of *Foreign Affairs*. "Is this it? The book with Chloe?" She held the volume with her fingertips.

"It's only the galley. The published ones will be much finer, but yes, it's your book, my dear. Utterly and completely yours. Look at the dedication." I'd made it "To My Dearest Rachel." The publishers customarily give me only one galley copy, but I had raised holy hell to get another for my girl.

She flipped to the front and jumped up to wade through wrapping paper to my chair where she gave me a hug and a smacking, big kiss on the cheek. "I love you, Edgar," she declared.

Well, even though Margo harrumphed at this show of emotion, of course that made me feel fine, and I praised the Paris book she'd

178

bought me. She couldn't know that thoughts of Paris always made me feel melancholy. "Who's next? Jeremy?"

He shook his head. "Margo."

So Rachel opened her gift from Margo. As Rachel fought with the paper and ribbons, she wore a pleasant expression as if she were planning to be delighted even if it was a dead frog, but when she uncovered a box of stationery and note cards, Rachel's face revealed more alarm than the gift could possibly warrant. I thought it a perfectly fitting purchase for a stranger, and a second later Rachel voiced the same thought. "How nice, Margo. I'll enjoy these," she said. The girl had been reared properly, even if it was in Ohio.

I'm sure Margo hadn't noticed the earlier expression. She did her best Lady Bountiful nod and started opening her present from Rachel, but I caught mischief in Jeremy's eyes; he seemed to know, or guess, what was going on. Margo pulled the last of the paper off and held up the very same box of stationery and note cards. Rachel looked like she had a toothache. Margo blinked once, twice, and then dissolved into laughter. "My, but you have splendid taste, Rachel," she said dryly, once she'd quit snorting.

As usual, Margo responded to my gifts with disdain and to Jeremy's with indifference, but every few minutes she glanced at Rachel and offered up what almost sounded like a giggle.

I was curious to see what Rachel had bought for Jeremy, surely before this little crush had begun. He opened the box and took out a fine brown scarf, which he immediately hung around his neck. Kissing her cheek, which was fiery at this point, he whispered something in her ear that made her go even redder. "Now mine," he said.

It was a small box, and I had no idea when or what he'd bought. A week ago he'd scowled at me when I reminded him that he should purchase some small gift for our guest. If I knew my boy, he was quite excited about what was inside. Rachel picked at the paper slowly, not ripping it away as she'd done with mine and Margo's. She lifted the lid and gasped. Good Lord, it wasn't a ring, was it? Surely not.

It wasn't. She lifted a small pendant on a fine chain. "It's beautiful," she whispered.

It was a violet, purple enameled on gold, and it looked familiar.

"That was your mother's." Margo's voice was harsh. "So that's what you were doing yesterday in my attic."

Rachel's fingers, holding the chain, hovered in the air, as if she didn't know whether she should put the necklace back in the box or around her neck.

"Yes, it's Mum's," Jeremy replied and took the necklace from Rachel to fasten it around her neck. He looked at Rachel and then at the necklace. "Since I couldn't give you real plants, I decided on a violet that will never fade or die."

It wasn't one of Vivian's finer pieces. As I recalled, she'd favored rather expensive rubies, along with an exceptional set of pearls. The violet necklace was hardly more than costume stuff, but it was Vivian's, and that made it significant. Rachel seemed to realize this. Her eyes were green as emeralds as she touched the posy at her neck. Margo was watching her, and I could see realization flooding through her now too. "Hmm," she said. "I do prefer that things are used rather than collecting dust. Let me see you, girl." Rachel leaned forward on the couch and raised her chin to let Margo peer at the necklace. "It suits you," she said, and I feared Rachel was going to hug Margo, which would have been the wrong approach entirely.

But she didn't. After this finale, Margo declared she wished to go home, probably to telephone her cronies and talk about the American girl and how she'd captivated her strong, silent nephew who'd always cared more about soil than sex. Normally Jeremy would've taken her home, but he and Rachel were eating each other up with their eyes, and I took pity on them. I told Jeremy I'd drive Margo to Truro if they washed up the mountains of dishes I'd dirtied.

A

Jeremy rolled up his sleeves and looked at the total devastation of Edgar's kitchen. "A long journey," he muttered.

"Begins with a single step," Rachel finished. She grimaced. "I have to go upstairs and put on some other shoes. These are killing me."

"Wait." Jeremy grabbed her hand and walked her back through the dining room and front hall to his room. Turning on a light, he went to a chest of drawers and pulled out thick green socks. "They even match your suit," he said with a grin.

She sat on the bedspread, green as she'd noticed this morning, and wondered if he truly was a druid. All this green and brown. He still wore her scarf around his neck. Slipping out of the merciless shoes, she drew a sock over one foot and sighed. "Heaven," she murmured. For

180

the briefest moment she remembered her moose socks and Kurt, and then the memory vanished like it had never happened.

Jeremy was next to her on the bed in no more than a second, his arms around her, his mouth on hers. "No. This is heaven," he said against her lips.

She felt a giggle rising up from her stomach. "We're supposed to be cleaning the kitchen."

"Time enough. He'll be gone over an hour." Jeremy eased her down onto the bed, one hand behind her head and one skimming across the wool crepe covering her breast.

She thought he meant they had time enough to make love and waited for him to unbutton her jacket. She'd halfway planned for it; there was nothing underneath the jacket but one of Gisèle's prettiest bras. But he didn't go any farther, and she was afraid of being pushy or looking like what her Granny had always called a brazen hussy. So she kissed him, and when he raised up to look at her, she grabbed both ends of the scarf to pull him back to her lips. This made him laugh, and then he did sit up. "You're amazing," he said.

She sat up too and put on the other sock. "Is this real?" she asked. "Is it real or am I living in a fairy tale?"

His fingers brushed her cheek. "It's real unless you want to pretend it isn't."

She touched the violet lying against her skin. "No, I'd want to keep pretending."

Chapter Seventeen

When she entered the kitchen the next morning, Jeremy called out, "A fine Boxing Day to you, young miss." Bacon was sizzling on the stove.

She put up her fists like she was in the ring. "Same to ya, buddy."

He poured two cups of coffee. "Actually, it has nothing to do with pugilistic sports. The history of Boxing Day goes back . . ."

She took one of the cups and interrupted him. Sometimes he did remind her of his uncle. "I know. Boxes. I looked it up." She sipped. "Where's Edgar?"

"Packing." Jeremy added milk and sugar to his cup.

"Why?"

He shrugged. "Uncle Edgar takes these notions. He said he called Tony last night and asked if he could take him to London this morning. I expect Tony leapt at the chance to get away from his three kids and make a nice packet at the same time. Uncle Edgar pays him well for these jaunts."

Rachel frowned. Was Edgar tired of her company? Had she committed some breach of etiquette? She sank down into one of the kitchen chairs. "Is it my fault?"

Jeremy turned a slice of bacon. "Of course not. He told me he wanted to get back to his warm flat and work on all the information you gave him, but I suspect something else." He turned to grin at Rachel. "He sees what's going on. I think he wants to give us some time alone."

She plucked at the cuff of her sweater. "And just what *is* going on?" Yesterday afternoon they'd cleaned up the kitchen and finished it before Edgar returned from Truro. Then she'd gone to her room to make a lengthy phone call to her family, they'd picked at turkey sandwiches, and all three of them had watched the telly until ten-thirty when they'd gone to their individual bedrooms. After all the hot kissing and touching, she'd expected a discreet knock at her door and had gone to bed naked, laying there frozen and expectant until she finally got so cold she put on her flannel gown. Honestly, she was more glad than disappointed about it. He wasn't Kurt.

The tip of Jeremy's nose turned pink. "What's going on? Weel, I be tryin' to woo you, lass," he said in what she figured was a pretty good Scottish accent.

"Oh," she faltered.

They'd nearly finished breakfast when Edgar bustled into the kitchen, refusing food but sitting next to Rachel and taking her hand. "Forgive me for being rude, my dear, but I'm eager to get back to London where I can write without my fingers freezing."

"That's okay."

He looked at Jeremy and pointed at the window. "Do you really intend to take Rachel out in this?"

She hadn't noticed, but it was as if a cloud was perching on the kitchen window. Thick, soggy fog.

"It'll lift," Jeremy said.

Edgar cocked an eyebrow. "Well, I hope it does for Tony's sake too. He should be here any minute. Now, Rachel," he said, turning to her, "if Sébastien turns loose of you for even a minute, come to London. We never finished our sight-seeing did we? Blasted gall bladder. And do email and call. I'm so delighted and proud that you chose to come to Cornwall for Christmas."

Rachel thanked him, lifted her sleeve to show him she was wearing his watch, gave him a big hug, and promised to stay in touch. And then he was gone, and it was just the two of them. She was falling for Jeremy too. Actually, when she looked at his deep eyes and floppy hair and when she felt his sweet smile focused on her, she knew she was already a goner, but being alone with him felt awkward. If Edgar had intended this as another Christmas gift, she needed the instruction manual.

Jeremy said, "We'll be fine without him, you know. I can make eggs and turkey sandwiches."

He was so sweet.

"Are you dressed warmly enough? Sensible shoes?" He looked at her feet and nodded at her gym shoes.

"Yes sir," she replied. It was kind of him to offer to drive her around Cornwall today, but since the cat was away, wouldn't the mice be warm and cozy staying at home? She didn't get the impression that Jeremy would find that boring like Kurt had. But Jeremy seemed to be excited about showing her Cornwall, and that was a good thing too. She was so confused. "Ready when you are," she said.

He had to tell her that they were again heading toward Truro. She couldn't see a thing and wondered how Jeremy could maneuver the van in the thick haze. Once in town, she knew where she was, but in no time they'd crossed to the other side and continued on. "It's a shame you can't see more," he said. "But on the way back you'll be able to."

"You're sure?"

"Yep. I know Cornish fogs."

She laid her hand on his leg, dark green corduroys today, and he covered it with his gloved one. "Damn, I was going to see if there were any gloves in the house small enough for you," he said.

She liked that. Rarely had "small enough for you" been said about her. "I'll be fine."

He was right about the weather. Another half-hour down the road and the fog lightened to where she could see hedgerows and a tree here and there. It probably would be clear enough to see the dramatic rocky shore he'd promised her. It would blow her away, he'd said. Maybe literally, as she watched tree limbs sway in the wind. She was looking forward to it, but what she really wanted was to inch her finger up the little corduroy ridges of his pants. Maybe she was a brazen hussy. Rachel felt like she had to keep touching him just to make sure he was real.

"If I turned off that way, we'd end up in a mining area," he said after many more miles. "Maybe we'll zip through there later." He took his eyes off the road long enough to smile at her. "You are so beautiful."

There, she felt better again. For a minute. "Did you put Margo's sherry in your coffee this morning?" she quipped.

He shook his head. "You just won't believe it, will you?"

"I believe it when you say it," she said. "But that's because you like me."

"What marrrr-velous perception you have, me lass." He did his Scots imitation again, hiding behind it, she figured. They were making a wonderful, glorious mess of this romance thing, weren't they?

He drove down a tiny lane and then another that was little more than gravel ending in a deserted parking lot. An abandoned trailer crouched at the far side, and there was a sign warning visitors about the cliffs. "Ready?" he asked.

She nodded and got out, wind whipping at her clothing the second she left the van. Jeremy put on one of those flat newsboy hats that made him look old-fashioned and strangely dashing. "Here, give me your hand," he said.

They walked toward the edge where the sea had cut, chewed, and swallowed the rocks for centuries. "What do you think?" he asked, raising his voice to be heard over the roar of the surf.

Scattered far beneath them, mammoth chunks of stone lay on a bit of beach, lashings of white foam licking at them. She had to shout. "Amazing. Why are they called the Bedruthan Steps?"

With his other hand he pointed down. "Legends. Don't they look a bit like steps? Steps for a giant? And the local giant was named Bedruthan."

Rachel edged closer, the loose rocks crumbling under her feet. The wind rocked her, nearly throwing her off-balance, and when she glanced up at the roiling clouds, she did waver. "Careful," Jeremy said, pulling her close.

"It's wild," she shouted. "I've never seen anything like it."

The twin roars of wind and surf drowned the cries of gulls gliding over the waves. Relentlessly the water rushed at the rocks, broke, and came again. Rachel felt as if she could fly, soar like the gulls. But menace and danger were here too. "Have there been shipwrecks?" she asked.

Jeremy nodded. "Several." He still had her arm clutched tight against his side. "Today's weather isn't calm, but it's certainly not a storm either. Imagine a full-blown gale hitting these rocks."

She did and shivered at the image.

"You're cold," he said.

She pulled her arm from his and put her hands on either side of her head. "Just my ears," she said with a smile. "You were smart to bring a hat."

"Here." From around his neck he unwound the brown scarf she'd given him and draped it over her head. His face sweetly serious, he tied the scarf under her chin. It felt good against her ears.

"I must look awfully silly," she said.

"I care a great deal more about how you feel than how you look," he said, raising his eyes from the knot to her face. He pointed to the right. "There's a rough path that gets you down to the beach. Are you game?"

Rachel nodded, still taking in what he'd said about feeling and looking. Inside her head she repeated his words. I need to memorize them for later, she thought, when he's no longer here.

Later, back in the van, she untied his scarf. It smelled of him, some kind of herbed soap and *l'eau d'un homme*, she thought. "Thanks, this really helped," she said.

He was pouring tea from a thermos. "This will help too." He let her drink first from the single cup. "We'll motor into St. Mawgan and see if there are any pubs open for lunch. It's fairly deserted in the winter but still something to see. Does that suit you?"

The tea was warm rather than hot, but it felt good in her throat. She nodded and handed him back the cup. Whether he meant to or not, his lips found the same place she'd drunk, and this made her smile.

They drove. St. Mawgan was a pretty place with a harbor and colorful cottages. At the only open pub, they ate sitting hip to hip, and she could almost imagine eating, drinking, and driving around with him the rest of her life. But she'd made that mistake before. She remembered fantasizing about a future with John Shumate, the guy back in college, except that he'd done most of the dreaming. "See," he'd said, "I'm thinking that your teaching salary can support us while I'm in law school, and then when I'm set up in a practice, you can stay home with the kids and have a beer waiting when I get home." John had grinned, squeezed her, and she'd wanted to die. The next week she'd broken up with him.

And then only, what, a couple of months ago she'd indulged in dreams about Kurt Mann. What a joke that had been. But she remembered playing with the idea of living in his apartment, traveling with him when he had foreign shoots. She was doing it again, and she was a fool.

And she was an insecure fool too. What she needed was affirmation, even if it was far too early for him to say he loved her. Or wanted her, which wasn't the same thing, she knew, but it would make her feel better. As they left the cozy pub, Rachel was full of cider courage, and at that very moment she wished Jeremy would get a room, or, at worst, pull off the road and do some serious planting in the back of the van. She giggled.

He smiled at her as he shut his door. "Something amusing you?"

"I'm just happy."

"Good." He squeezed her knee, and heat flooded her veins.

By the time they arrived back at Penmore, the cider had faded, but her cheeks were still hot. Maybe it was windburn. The house felt empty without Edgar. She felt pretty damned empty herself when she thought about leaving the next day. Mumbling something to Jeremy about freshening up, she went upstairs. Somehow or the other she had to know where this was going. If anywhere.

Twenty minutes later she came downstairs in fresh makeup and the brown velvet jacket. Maybe making herself as pretty as she could would dazzle Jeremy into some kind of commitment. Jeremy had started a fire and turned on the Christmas tree. "You look lovely," he said.

She smiled at him.

"Would you like a drink?" he asked.

"Yes, please. Just a Coke." No more alcohol for her.

When he handed her a glass, he said, "Cheers" and tipped his pint. She stared at the fire, and he put his arm around her shoulders. The kissing would begin again soon.

"It's a shame we had such dreadful weather. You should see St. Mawgan in the summer." His voice was relaxed, easy. He had no idea Rachel was seething like a kettle. "Flowers everywhere, all kinds of color. You should come back and see it."

She'd be back in Morton by then. Taking a shuddery breath, she gulped down half the Coke, making the ice cubes rattle when she set it on the table. Jeremy looked puzzled, maybe even concerned, but she charged ahead, grabbing his free hand and guiding it to her chest.

His eyes widened. Slowly, cautiously setting his drink beside her empty glass, he murmured, "Lovely." He shut his eyes and pulled her close, his hand staying where she'd placed it. He kissed her neck.

She waited. She had to leave in the morning, and she'd be damned if she'd leave with nothing, no assurances, no confirmation, no nothing. She clutched his back, smelling the wind on him, the sea. His lips were against her ear, murmuring her name, and then he kissed her. That was all. Not that his kisses weren't very nice. Exciting even, but she was starting to feel like a teenager forever making out on the living room couch. She dropped her head to break off the kiss. "I don't understand," she said. "I can't read you. Does my body turn you off?" The thought of another loss so soon after Kurt was beyond horrible.

Jeremy's eyes were glazed, then surprised, then hurt. She almost quit. But she didn't. "Why won't you make love to me?"

Very quietly he said, "I thought that was what I was doing, Rachel." He pulled away. She'd pushed too hard. She'd blown it. "I know about your life in Paris. The high fashion. The photographer," he said, his voice steely. "I can't compete with a man who's had every gorgeous model in the world, including you."

She'd never expected this. Her mouth opened, but she didn't know what to say.

"I'm just an ordinary Cornish landscaper, not an international playboy."

Edgar must have told Jeremy everything. She didn't know whether to be glad or appalled. She shook her head. "But I don't want him."

He ignored her. "This isn't just toys and games for the holidays for me. No. I don't do that." His jaw was set and firm. It was very attractive.

"I don't want that either," she protested.

"Tomorrow you'll go back to Paris, and that will be the end of it for you. I'm not going to let you hurt me more than it already does. I'm not casual about all this like your photographer."

She reached for his hand, but he kept it clenched. "I don't want him," she repeated. "I don't love him."

His eyes bore into hers. Nothing gentle about that brown now.

"I love you." As soon as she said it, she knew she meant it.

His hand loosened until she could grasp his fingers. His face relaxed into a smile. "Really? Well, then," he said. "Why didn't you say so sooner? That changes everything." He stood, pulling her up with him, and held her close against him. Yeah, he wanted her all right. There was another kiss, oh, what a kiss. "You're sure?" he murmured. "This soon?"

"Yes." She grinned. "I gulp, remember? But this time I won't regret it."

He touched her face. "I've loved you since you screamed at me."

This made her laugh, but her smile faded. "This isn't fair at all. I have to leave tomorrow."

"Then we have to make the most of the time we have," he said. He clutched her hand and started walking back toward his bedroom, but hesitated once more. "If this is what you want?" His eyes searched her face.

"Yes." Yes, yes, yes, she thought.

In his room, he turned on a lamp and threw back the green bedspread. With sure fingers, he undid her jacket buttons and kissed the tops of her breasts. For about two seconds, Rachel thought about asking him to turn off the light. In the dark he wouldn't be able to see the rolls at her waist or the pudge at her belly. But she decided it didn't matter; besides, she wanted to see him. Off came his sweater, then his shirt. She helped with his belt and unfastened his pants, and he mumbled something having to do with God or Jesus. It made her laugh. She wasn't in the enchanted woods any more. This was real. He hesitated one more time, his hands on her face and his eyes asking permission. "I love you," she said again. And he smiled.

A

"Hungry?" he asked, curving against her. His bed felt like the safest place on earth.

She laughed. "I am. It seems terribly unromantic to admit it."

"I believe there's turkey."

They both laughed. There was turkey enough to feed them for days. Except she wouldn't be here for days. She glanced at the lovely gold watch from Edgar. Five-thirty. She had tonight, and then she'd leave. "Did you really think that?" she asked. "That me going back to Paris would be the end of it?"

He tucked a soft blanket around her. "I hoped not."

She struggled against him to see his face. "Believe me."

He wasn't smiling any more. "I want to, but there are so many complications: Paris, Sébastien, modeling, Ohio. You have a lot of choices."

"None of those is as important as you. Us."

He shrugged. "Time will tell, but I know what you want more than anything."

"What?"

"A turkey sandwich."

A

They'd eaten, and then Jeremy brewed tea in a dark brown pot that sat between them, along with the tin of Rachel's Christmas cookies. "These are addictive," he said as he grabbed another green-sprinkled disc.

She nodded, still chewing on one.

"You should take them back to Paris with you. I'll never eat all of them."

Rachel shook her head. "No, I'll leave them, and yes, you could eat all of them."

"And become as rotund as your Santa Claus."

She raised an eyebrow. "Then we'd match."

189

"Nonsense." He touched her cheek. "When am I ever going to convince you that you're gorgeous the way you are?"

She scrunched her nose. "Never." Putting the lid on the tin, she said, "Give them to Tony and his kids. They'll eat them up in a hurry."

The kitchen was warm, and golden light spilled onto the table. Above the sink, the window was black, and it seemed very cozy, very comfortable sitting next to Jeremy in his house. Rachel considered calling Sébastien and begging for another day, but even if he granted her one, and she was sure it would be only one, she still would have to leave. With every passing hour she became more convinced that she belonged in Cornwall with Jeremy. She wished she could persuade Jeremy of that.

"Say." His face had turned soft, shy. He looked about twelve. "What if I told you something I haven't revealed to anybody?"

Rachel chuckled. "I love secrets. Sure."

He went over to what he and Edgar called a Welsh dresser and opened a drawer. Pulling out a folder, he said, "I've probably lost my mind, but I'm thinking about submitting a garden design to the RHS for one of their shows." He opened the folder and smoothed an oversized piece of graph paper onto the table in front of her.

Rachel had to squint at the squiggles and lines on the paper before she realized they represented plants and shrubs. "What's the RHS?"

"Royal Horticultural Society." He leaned over the table, arm warm against her, and pointed. "I drew two. This one is for a seaside garden."

She could see tiny words by the squiggles: lavender, thrift, rosemary.

"And this one's an edible garden with nasturtiums, roses, herbs, and such."

He said no more, but there was an eagerness in his eyes that begged her to approve. "They're lovely," she said and meant it. "Creative." She studied the drawings "You can eat violets?"

He put a finger on the enameled one at her neck and smiled. "Yes. Sugared violets are considered a great delicacy." He straightened. "They'd probably reject me. No one's heard of Hastings Garden Centre, let alone Jeremy Hastings." He sat again. "Of course I wouldn't apply for Chelsea, just one of the smaller shows."

"Chelsea?"

"That's the grand one. In London. The royals come and all the posh folk. I'm not nearly good enough for it."

Rachel frowned. "Of course you are. But I guess it's smart to get your feet wet somewhere else first." She looked back at the drawings. "Edgar doesn't know you're thinking about this?"

Jeremy shook his head.

"Well, he'd approve, and I'm proud that you shared it with me. Is it a contest? Can you win a prize?"

"Yes. But, of course that's too much to hope for my first time." He lowered his eyes. "I'm just concerned about being laughed out of the place."

She reached over to touch his arm. "You won't be. But it isn't the end of the world to be laughed at." She tilted her head and pointed to herself. "Living proof, especially in another few weeks."

Using both hands to pull her head close, he said, "Never."

She moved forward until their mouths met. Against his lips she murmured, "Oh, they'll laugh. But now I don't care."

A

They made love again in his forest green bedroom, and although it started with laughter, this time the ending was tinged with melancholy. They both knew he was taking her to her train at eight-thirty in the morning. All the clocks were moving too quickly. "I have to pack," she said, her cheek against his chest.

"I wish I were selfish enough to beg you to stay, but I can't ask you to neglect your obligations." His voice was a soothing rumble in her ear.

"I wish I were the kind of person who could."

"Then you wouldn't be Rachel."

She shook her head at this. "I'm not as good as that. I ignored my teaching obligations to work for Sébastien, and I still feel guilty about it. But I won't let Sébastien down. Especially now." She sighed and sat up. "Come to Paris with me?" She knew he wouldn't.

"No. I have obligations too." He ran a finger down her spine.

"The garden show?"

"No. The business. The house. Margo."

"It's just six weeks," she said. "We could plan for what we'll do after Fashion Week."

He shook his head. "Let's see what happens."

Neither of them slept much. They talked, dozed, kissed. Rachel figured she could sleep on the train. He made breakfast, but neither of them was hungry. All the way to Truro their smiles kept fading, and when he stopped his van at the station, Rachel was doing everything she could to keep from crying. "I have your email and cell," she said, clearing her throat. "And you have mine."

He nodded.

"You'll call?"

He nodded again and opened his door. From the back of the van, he unloaded her new luggage. Funny how she didn't care about that now. "Kiss me one more time?"

He did but didn't offer to pick up her bags or wait with her. "I have to leave now." He stuck his hands in his pockets. "I love you, Rachel." And he got back into the van and drove off. She picked up the bags and made her way to the platform. A brisk Cornish breeze whipped at her face. It was, of course, the wind that brought tears to her eyes.

Chapter Eighteen

I waited as long as I could stand it, nearly noon, before I called Jeremy. "Well?" I asked.

"Well what? She's gone. We didn't elope, and we didn't scream at each other. You'll forgive me if I don't discuss what we did do." Jeremy's voice sounded desolate.

I lined up pens on my desk. "Do you love her?"

"Of course I do."

"Does she love you?"

"She says she does."

I frowned. "What's that supposed to mean?"

"That she promises she'll love me forever, but promises can be so much air in the wind when fame, fortune, and Paris beckon."

Where had this cynicism come from? We Tremaines are dreamers, optimists. I am. Vivian was. Every glass our father raised was half-full. Even Margo is the hopeful type, if one digs below her ever-thickening crust. "Do you think Rachel is a liar?" I couldn't help punching iron into my words.

"No. But everything happened so fast; she may change her mind. Perhaps it was simply a holiday fling for her. And even if it wasn't, I'm not about to stand in the way of her career or whatever she wants to do with her life. I have to give her the freedom to choose."

His words were sensible, but I didn't like them. "You can believe in Rachel Bowman," I said with some spirit.

He didn't reply at once, and when he did, his voice was low. "I do, Uncle Edgar. No matter what she chooses, I do believe in her."

Interminable hours later I rang Rachel. Her voice wasn't particularly cheery either. I questioned her. "I'm fine, Edgar. Just tired," she said.

Of course I couldn't let her know I'd spoken with Jeremy. Damn, but matchmaking is a deceitful web. "Did Jeremy descend into rudeness again?"

"Oh, no. I just miss him already." Did I hear a bit of a choke in her voice? "I'd give anything to be back in Cornwall with him rather than here."

"I know, my pet, but it's only for a bit."

"That's what I kept telling Jeremy, but he acts like he'll never see me again." She took a long shuddery breath. "I'm just afraid he'll convince himself of that and never give me a chance."

My fear exactly, but I made all the right soothing noises. I knew better than to attempt to convince Sébastien to let Rachel come to London, let alone Cornwall, for another quick trip. He needed her, and, at this point, I thought perhaps his need was greater than Jeremy's. Ah, if I could only orchestrate peoples' lives the way I managed my characters.

A

At first she'd called Jeremy two or three times a day, but he rarely took her calls until evening, so she waited until then. Once she skipped two days, hoping he'd call her, but he didn't. She didn't understand. He was sweet and cheerful when she called, always picking up with a warm "hello" like her voice made him happy. He refused to talk about the future, though, and she always felt worse after they'd spoken. She figured she probably should be making reservations for her flight back to Ohio right after Crystal's wedding, but she kept waiting, hoping that something concrete, something *real* would come from Jeremy. More than ever, Cornwall felt like a dream.

She walked every day, watching for Paris to come back to life after the holidays. Window-shopping at Printemps and Galeries Lafayette, she thought of Crystal and Shawn and how much she wished Jeremy and she were a couple like them. She strolled past the boutiques on Rue Bonaparte, all closed, their holiday finery mocking her loneliness. Rachel thought about visiting Gisèle but remembered that she'd traveled to her son's house for Christmas. Sébastien and Polly were frantically busy, as was Jesse, although he had met her for coffee a few times. Yvonne had a few days off around New Year's, so Rachel cooked, not that Sébastien came home to eat what she'd prepared. And she did a little cleaning, just to pass the time.

New Year's Eve was particularly bad. Sébastien was out; she had no clue where, and, still clinging to secrecy, he hadn't invited her along. She bought herself a bottle of champagne and dipped strawberries in a glass of bubbly as she read Edgar's book. It was fun to find herself in Chloe, although she was pretty sure she'd never been as attractive or intelligent or engaging as Edgar's creation. Still, it was a good book, and at this point, Inspector Hannaford was about as real a lover as Jeremy. Frowning at the strawberry seeds in the bottom, she polished off her second glass of champagne and decided she wouldn't call him, even if it killed her. And then her phone rang.

It was her father, saying they wanted to wish her a happy New Year, and then, fifteen minutes into that call, she got one from Shelley, who wondered if she was partying with celebrities. Not bloody likely, Rachel thought in Hannaford's voice. And then her phone beeped again. Finally. It was Jeremy.

"Happy New Year," he said.

"Same to you." He couldn't miss the smile in her voice. He simply couldn't.

"What are you doing?" This sounded hearty, too hearty, like he was afraid she had a date or was doing something exciting.

"I'm sitting in Sébastien's living room by myself, drinking champagne by myself, and reading Edgar's book by myself. How about you?"

He laughed, and she heard relief in it. "Even worse, I fear. No champagne. I've taken down the Christmas tree, hoovered the lounge, and felt thoroughly sorry for myself."

"Poor baby." But she couldn't help but say, "You could be here. With me."

"Perhaps. Although I always spend New Year's Day with Margo."

"Really."

He didn't speak for a bit. "My parents died on New Year's Day. Margo and I eat and play cards. We don't stage a memorial or anything, but we're always together."

"Oh, Jeremy. I'm so sorry."

"It's all right. I didn't tell you for sympathy."

"But it is sad."

"Not if I manage to get enough sherry down Margo."

So she told him about getting a call from Crystal about ordering the flowers for the wedding.

"What is she choosing?"

"She's leaving it all up to me." Rachel told him what she'd thought about, and he made some suggestions. It felt as though they were partners, and she liked it. Then she said she had to go the day after New Year's for the first fitting on her last dress.

"Sébastien's cutting it a bit fine, isn't he?" Jeremy asked.

"That's what I think. But I don't say anything. It's like living with the walking dead around here."

"Is he home?"

"No."

"Then he's not completely dead."

They chatted another ten minutes, Rachel wracking her brain to think of anything light and newsy to keep him on the phone. But she had to bring up their relationship. She couldn't help it. After another long pause she said, "Think what a happy new year it will be, Jeremy. You and me."

His voice was very low. "I hope so, Rachel."

"I know so. I love you."

"I love you too. Enjoy your lonesome champagne."

𝐀

Two weeks later she received a call from Madame Pauline. "You must come back this afternoon, Rachel. Sébastien has changed the dress again." Even over the telephone, Polly sounded both weary and exasperated.

"Okay. What's the problem with this dress anyway?"

"What's the problem with everything, *cherie?* Be here at three?"

Leaving an hour early for her fitting, Rachel trudged through a cold rain to the flower shop Sébastien had recommended as being the best in Paris. Rachel figured that the people at the Ritz were perfectly capable of handling flowers along with every other detail of Crystal and Shawn's wedding, but Cryssie had wanted to include her in some way. It was sweet. She'd said, "Honey, I love flowers, but I don't know a thing about them. I trust you to make sure they're perfect. I'll email you pictures of our dresses and hats."

Weddings. Here she was handling details for someone else's ceremony. And the extra fitting was for the last dress of the show, traditionally the wedding dress, according to Madame Pauline. Rachel wiped raindrops from her cheek. She'd been a bridesmaid for Shelley and another college friend. She could've been a bridesmaid for Crystal. Never a bride though, Rachel thought. Her boyfriend wouldn't even commit to a quick trip to London. She just knew that she could convince Sébastien to let her meet Jeremy in London for a night or two.

But Jeremy never considered it. He kept saying there was no point in getting together until after the show.

She didn't know the French words for calla lilies or orange blossoms, but she didn't have trouble ordering a fortune in blooms for Crystal's wedding. On a whim, she bought a bouquet of cheerful snapdragons for Madame Pauline. She'd sounded like she needed cheering up.

"How very sweet," Madame Pauline said. She looked as though she was about to burst into tears.

"Is he driving you crazy?" Rachel asked.

Madame Pauline took a deep breath. "I must remember the genius, the creativity."

"Or else you'd kill him?" Rachel pointed across the hall. "Is the lion in his den? Do I have a minute before I need to be downstairs?"

Madame Pauline nodded yes to both questions. "He may not see you," she warned.

Rachel shrugged, nodded her way past Sébastien's guard—she was new, and Rachel thought her name was Nicole—and knocked on his door. "What?" he growled, *en Francais*.

"It's Rachel, you old grump. I'm coming in."

He was at his desk, glasses perched on his nose, and he looked seventy. "When's the last time you ate?" asked Rachel. "You look like hell."

He mimicked her voice. "And you look like a drowned cat."

"Hmm." Rachel sat on the sofa where Edgar had napped the night she'd posed in her underwear. "Want me to go out for soup or something?"

"I do not." He took off the glasses, and she noticed his poor fingernails. "Don't you have a fitting?"

"In a little bit. But I wanted to talk to you first. I think Madame Pauline's about to have a nervous breakdown. We're all trying the best we can. Why don't you ease up, Sébastien?"

He shook his head. "It is always like this before a show. Polly will survive."

Rachel lowered her voice. "So will you. It's not *that* important."

Raising his chin, he countered, "Have you become Edgar, Raquel? Telling me that it's nothing?" He snapped his fingers. "That all this is just *clothes*?"

"No. But it is just work, and people are more important than work." His stare was probably meant to intimidate her, but he should know by now that it didn't. "People including you, Sébastien. Come home early. We'll eat whatever Yvonne has left us and watch one of your dreadful musicals."

There was a hint of a smile at this, but he immediately looked down and shooed her away with his long fingers. "Okay, okay. I'll be home by seven. Go to your fitting."

A

January had to be the longest, dullest, dreariest month of the year, Rachel thought. She sent dozens of emails, phoned her parents and Crystal and, of course, Jeremy. She babysat Sébastien as much as he would let her. Nobody said anything, but everyone at Sylvestri acted as if a disaster of cataclysmic proportions was due the evening of February 11. There were a few exceptions to the gloom. Although Crystal thought the show would bomb, "The world ain't ready to recognize true womanly beauty," she was in a joyful tizz about marrying her Shawn. And Gisèle was ecstatic that Madame Pauline was allowing her to serve as Rachel's second dresser. But mostly things were stressful as hell and stayed that way. Edgar fretted over Sébastien. Sébastien fretted over Rachel's final dress. And Madame Pauline fretted over everything. Jeremy listened to all this and made sympathetic comments, but he wouldn't let her say a word about any kind of future after the show. So Rachel was fretting too, although it had little to do with fashion. At this point she regarded the show as something to be endured, sort of like a root canal.

Saturday afternoon, Jesse texted her and begged her to meet him at a bistro near his apartment. She hadn't heard from him much since New Year's and was glad to see him. Wrapped in an ancient parka, he sat near the door, vibrating with enthusiasm. "Sit. What do you want to drink? How are you? I've missed you."

"Fine, thanks. I'll have tea. I've missed you too."

He summoned a waiter. "I had to go to Chartres for a photo shoot and then was swamped with all the posters and publicity for the show. But guess what I got today?"

She unbuttoned her coat. "What?"

He shoved his phone in her hand and she read an email from Z. Forester, a company that designed high-class ready to wear in New York. They wanted to hire him.

"Oh, Jesse! That's wonderful." She clapped her hands, and the waiter glared at her. "You do want it, don't you?"

"Want it? It's a dream come true." He even put his hand on his heart. "And it's all thanks to you."

"Actually, it's Sébastien Fel you should thank."

"And I will. I will."

Her tea and his coffee arrived, and Jesse kept smiling. "I was wondering something," he said. She poured two packets of sugar in her tea. "You've talked about how you don't love modeling and you miss home, but that home is incredibly boring. Why don't you come with me to New York? We could share an apartment so it wouldn't be so expensive, and I bet you could find a great job in fashion other than modeling with your Fel connections. What do you think?"

What did she think? "Wow, Jesse. This is out of the blue." New York to explore. A roommate to share expenses. Intriguing. "It sounds exciting."

"But?" His eyes were lit up like candles, begging her to say yes. "Before you say anything, I want you to know that I won't leave Sylvestri until after the show. I owe Himself that and more. Z. Forester knows that. And after this show, well, I figured you wouldn't want to stay in Paris."

"No, I won't."

He ducked his head. "It might be sort of humiliating."

"You think it'll be as bad as that?"

Jesse nodded. "I'm even a little worried that Mr. Fel's recommendation might pale after this show bombs. I'm hoping for a contract before then."

It sounded sort of mercenary, but she couldn't blame him. She rubbed her face, took a sip of tea. "You're probably right, although I hope you aren't."

He nodded, serious for a moment, and then smiled again. "Think how much fun we'll have exploring New York: restaurants, shops, galleries, and, for you, tons of bookstores." He lowered his voice. "I love doing things with you. I want to have time enough to really get to know you." He put his long fingers around her hand. It was sweet.

She'd never told him about Jeremy. She'd hardly seen Jesse since Christmas, and then all they'd talked about was the show. Was it unkind to lead him on even if he saw her as no more than a roommate?

His plan was tempting especially if Mr. Will We or Won't We wouldn't commit. "It's a great idea, Jesse, and I might just do it."

He beamed and squeezed her hand.

"But I can't give you an answer yet. I just can't." She touched his arm with her other hand. "Is that okay?"

"Absolutely." And he started babbling about Z. Forester.

That evening Rachel was reading when Sébastien limped through the door. "Have you hurt yourself?" she asked.

He grimaced. "Twisted my ankle. It will be fine."

She had him sit on the sofa, propped his foot, and made him an icebag. "Food, beverage, painkiller?" she asked.

His face was grey. "Nothing."

Sitting beside him, she said, "I have some good news."

"That would be welcome."

"Jesse Kemper got a job offer from Z. Forester. He's so excited and grateful."

Sébastien waved his hand. "A good start for him."

"He's giving notice and leaving a couple of weeks after the show." She shifted the icebag a bit. "He wants me to go with him to New York."

Sébastien frowned. "I thought you said you had good news."

"It is, for Jesse."

"What about Edgar's nephew? Are you fickle, Raquel?" A tiny smile glimmered across his lips.

"Oh, Jesse is just a friend. I think he mostly wants me as a roommate. New York is nearly as expensive as Paris. He thinks I can get a job in fashion even though I've told him I don't want to model."

"You will have fabulous modeling offers, but you will have them here too." He shifted. "And I can get you all kinds of positions at Sylvestri." He locked eyes with her. "Not Ohio? Not the nephew? I think Paris is a better choice."

She squirmed. "I don't know. Jeremy doesn't seem to think I want him, even though I do." She whispered, "But definitely not Ohio. Not unless I have to."

"You have time. Wait until after the show before you make up your mind. Oh, and I do think I'd like one of Edgar's milky, sweet teas. With a biscuit, mind you."

A

On the afternoon of the Sylvestri dress rehearsal, Rachel slogged through wet streets and spitting snow to the Ritz. Crystal had arrived the day before and said Rachel must come meet her sister and mother. They'd leave for rehearsal from the hotel. Rachel felt like a naïve tourist again when she walked through the lobby. Such splendor. And Crystal's suite was nearly as grand. She was grinning as she let Rachel in. "Isn't this place a sight?" she said. "C'mon in and meet my mama and baby sis."

Mrs. Carter was about Rachel's height, a beautiful woman whose smooth skin and fine eyes had been passed down to her daughters. Ava was as gorgeous and tall and friendly as her sister. "We're so glad to meet you," said Ava, clutching Rachel's hand. "Crystal got her a true friend when she met you."

They offered Rachel tea, coffee, wine, sandwiches, cake, and real homemade Memphis barbecue Mrs. Carter had managed to smuggle onto the plane. "Do they fix barbecue in Ohio? I had Mama bring some of hers from home." Crystal mopped at a drip of sauce on her silk shirt. "I've ruined it, Mama."

"Let me work on it," Mrs. Carter said, and Crystal unbuttoned her shirt.

Rachel took a bite. "Yes, but not as good as this. Where's Shawn?"

Crystal grinned. She didn't have a problem in the world sitting around and eating in her bra even though her umm, *plus-ness*, showed. "He and his cousin will be here tomorrow morning," she said. "Had some kind of a meeting today, but he'll be here for the show."

Rachel gobbled down the last of the fantastic barbecue. She'd missed American food. Turning to Ava she asked, "Are you a model too?"

The woman gave her one of those laughs that made everybody in the room want to join in. "Lord, no. I'm a nurse just like our mama. Couldn't pay me enough to strut around under those hot lights and put on makeup every day."

"Well, I'm not doing it after tomorrow," Crystal declared. "Shawn and I are getting married and then we're flying off to Tahiti for two weeks." She shut her eyes as if she were imagining tropical bliss. "And then I'm gonna spend my time having babies and keeping my man happy." She pushed another Coke can at Rachel. "How about you? Has this experience given you a taste for modeling?"

Rachel shook her head.

"'Cause if you do, I have all kinds of contacts in the States. You could have more work than you wanted."

Rachel shook her head again. "Thanks, but this is more than enough modeling for me. Besides, we all think the show's going to be a disaster. Who'd want me then?"

Crystal crossed her mile-long legs. "It won't matter. It might be one of those three-day disasters in the news, but then Sébastien and everybody else will do just fine and profit from the publicity. I'm serious; just say the word and you got an agent and contracts waiting for you." She raised a perfect eyebrow. "Or maybe you're thinking about settling down with that English dude you were telling me about. Hmm?"

Ava laughed. "Does he talk like Prince Harry? I could get into hearing that across a pillow."

A flush flared on Rachel's cheeks. "Maybe a little. I don't know. It's early yet."

"He'd better hurry," said Crystal. "Forty-eight hours from now you're gonna be having men all over the world saving your pictures on Instagram."

Ava gave Rachel's arm a little punch. "You'll be famous, Rachel, even if the show is a bust."

A

They took a taxi to the Louvre; Sébastien had said it was the perfect venue for a Renaissance collection and had booked an empty gallery back in September. A catwalk extended into the cavernous room. Dainty chairs were clustered around the runway. Hung on the walls were replicas of fine tapestries and giant-sized reproductions of Renaissance art. Jesse had said that Sébastien was really proud of this idea. It was noisy. Workmen were adjusting lights. A half-dozen entertainers, all dressed in black satin, practiced juggling and playing instruments. The tiny DJ from *Le Club Clic*, Emma, was setting up her turntables. She was one of the few good things that had come from Kurt Mann. Rachel had persuaded Sébastien to hire her for the runway music.

Acting as though the rehearsal was after-school detention, Suzanne stood by the backstage entrance, ticking models' names off a list. She pointed to a large room that was semi-divided into nearly two dozen cubicles by clothes racks and chairs. The first section was Rachel's since she had so many changes. Crystal was dressing across the clothes rack in the next area because she now had three exits. "If you can do five, I can surely to God do three," she'd said when she heard the news.

Inside the makeshift room, Gisèle and Madame Pauline had organized each ensemble, taken pictures of the clothes and accessories and clipped them to the appropriate hangers, and stood guard so that not a shoe, not a hairbrush, not even an earring went astray. They acted like generals planning a battle. Setting her bag of makeup and hair supplies on a rickety card table, Rachel stripped out of her clothes and wrapped what looked like an artist's smock around her body. Gisèle made sure she had on the correct lingerie while Rachel did her own makeup and hair. The professionals who were supposed to do these had quit yesterday. Jean-Pierre, totally oblivious to all the big, nearly naked women, checked to make sure each model's hair and makeup were what had been proscribed earlier. It was crazy. More than ever Rachel realized that she'd told Crystal the truth; she'd never want this as a career. Of course, she never wanted to teach French to Ohio teenagers again either. She thought about Jeremy and Penmore and then put them firmly out of her mind. She hadn't been able to talk to him for two days.

Gisèle and Polly waited and fussed, chatting a hundred miles an hour, and Rachel realized that she understood every word they spoke. Her French had really improved. Recently she'd decided that Madame Pauline had seen her in her underwear so many times that she could call her Polly now. She jumped into the rapid conversation, in French, and Polly smiled when Rachel used her nickname. The dressers consulted their watches. Time was very important, they said. And they commanded Rachel to stand on an X marked on the floor in tape. "Always there," said Polly. "Every change."

Gisèle slipped the purple dress over Rachel's head while Polly knelt to ease Rachel's feet into slippers a shade or two darker than the dress. "What's this?" Gisèle asked, fingering the violet pendant around Rachel's neck. "It isn't on the list."

"It stays or I go."

Polly frowned. "The color does coordinate with the dress."

"But not with the other pieces," said Gisèle.

Rachel stood her ground. "Then we'll hide it. But I'm not taking it off."

Both women did perfect Parisian shrugs and pushed Rachel to the catwalk's starting spot where she hesitated, waiting for Jean-Pierre's cue and trying to breathe. Here she was, an overweight teacher from Ohio, about to prance down a Parisian runway in fabulous couture clothes. Tomorrow there would be celebrities and photographers, reporters and the top fashionistas in the world watching her model Sébastien's creations. Holy shit.

Jean-Pierre pinched her arm and mouthed, "Go." And before Rachel could think any more, she was on the catwalk. Sébastien and Suzanne stood at the end appraising everything. Emma's electronic music pulsed nearly as fast as Rachel's drumming heart. Sébastien shouted, "Head up, Raquel. Pout, no smile. You're bored, bored with all this. You are a Renaissance princess." She tried for the expression her sophomore girls took on when she talked to them about their grades. When she'd turned and arrived back at the doorway, she gave a twisted smile to Crystal who was up next.

The change into the coppery pants outfit was quick and easy, although she hated the monstrously high platform shoes she had to wear. She'd practiced, but damn, it was different on the catwalk. "Faster," Sébastien called to her when she started down it. "These people have the attention spans of squirrels." Rachel pushed on.

Then came the deep blue suit, somewhat like the white one Crystal was modeling at the end, although Rachel's had a collar that resembled a ruff and a much shorter skirt. Gisèle and Polly were feeling good about their teamwork. "Lovely," Polly breathed as Gisèle pushed her out the door. Rachel heard the "minstrels" finishing an ancient ballad, and then Emma cued her with a heavy bass beat.

It was the yellow outfit that gave them trouble. Scraping a chair onto the X, Gisèle ordered Rachel to sit as soon as they'd stripped off the suit. Each of them took a leg and tried to force the tights up Rachel's legs. All she could think of was packing ten pounds of potatoes in a five-pound bag. "I might be able to do it quicker," she said as they struggled with the gossamer silk. They ignored her.

"Stand," barked Polly.

"The vines are crooked," moaned Gisèle. "Sit."

"Two minutes," someone called from the door. Rachel had been ready at the two minute warning the other times.

Polly's eyes were wild. "She's sweating."

"Well, I'm sorry," retorted Rachel.

"Powder," shouted Gisèle.

Polly picked up the box of face powder from the card table, but Gisèle shook her head. "It'll stain." Her eyes scoured the room, finally landing on the foot powder Rachel had tossed in her bag. She'd thought it might come in handy forcing herself into shoes without stockings. "There," she screeched and lunged for the tin.

"One minute." The voice was ominous.

"Coat her legs."

"Will it show?"

"Here, start again."

The tights reached her waist at the same moment Gisèle threw the yellow dress over her head and hissed, "Hide the necklace."

Calm. You are a princess, Rachel told herself as she walked out, about ten seconds late. "That will not do," Suzanne shrieked from the end of the catwalk.

"Chill," Rachel said, even though she was never, ever, ever to speak from the runway. "We'll have it tomorrow." She hoped.

Her final dress ended the show, and it truly was a masterpiece. Rachel hadn't seen it completed until that minute. After the yellow dress, the last one was easy. It slipped over her head, a shimmering fall of tissue silk the color of old parchment. It had a square neck, a shirred bosom, and an empire waist marked with bronze braid. Hanging from this were ropes of the braid, twisted into coils that hung in various lengths. The hem was raised a bit in the front but fell to a train in the back. Talk about princess-wear, Rachel thought. Catching a glimpse in the mirror, she considered the word 'beautiful' for the first time in her life. Standing on her mark, she waited while Polly and Gisèle attached a cone-shaped headdress with swathes of gold, bronze, and cream veil, like the ones girls in fairy tales wore. Well, the hat, or whatever Sébastien called it, was pretty awful, she thought as she glanced in the mirror. Made her look like a cone-head. But the dress was kick-ass.

"The necklace," Gisèle moaned. "It shows."

"Not under this." Polly fastened a heavy necklace of bronze discs around Rachel's neck.

"Am I supposed to wear that?" Rachel thought the necklace was hideous.

"One minute," came from the door.

Polly nodded. "It's on the list."

Rachel swished down the catwalk. Sébastien had nothing bad to say, and Suzanne was moved enough to whisper, "Magnificent."

Rachel turned, winked at Emma, and cut a little dance move. But rehearsal wasn't over. Sébastien called all of them out, including the dressers, the entertainers, and Emma. "It's running too long," he announced in French. Crystal scooted over to Rachel for translation.

"We must cut half of the *entré acts*."

Polly hushed Gisèle's protests immediately. She was right; if the remaining acts were timed properly Rachel could still do it. "And Raquel," he said, switching to English, "we cut your suit. It's much like the other one," he nodded at Crystal, "and it will save a minute." This was fine by Rachel and a relief to Polly and Gisèle.

He conferred with Suzanne. "Oh, yes. A bit more lipstick, ladies. And Emma? Don't forget to adjust your music to allow for losing the Renaissance acts. Suzanne will show you where." He nodded at the jugglers and musicians "You will all be paid in full, of course." Rachel wondered if it was coming out of Sébastien's pocket.

Crystal looked worried. "You upset about the suit?" she asked Rachel.

"No. Why should I be? It's one less change."

Crystal sniffed. "Some models would be tearing somebody's hair out over losing an exit."

Rachel grinned. "I gotta keep telling you, Cryssie. I'm not a model."

A

The Carter women invited Rachel back to the Ritz for room service supper and pedicures. . Rachel loved Cryssie and her family, but she was too jumpy about the next day to get into the fun. "I'm going to have a quiet evening," she said. "Good for my complexion, right?"

As usual, she had the apartment to herself. She was sitting at the kitchen table, reading a good-luck text from Jesse, and staring at the violets perched in front of the black window when her phone rang. "I wanted to wish you luck for tomorrow," Jeremy said.

She felt color come up in her cheeks. Talk about good for the complexion. "Thanks. I wish you could be here."

"Oh, I'd just be in the way."

Rachel shook her head like he could see her. "No, you wouldn't." She paused. "I'm scared."

"You'll be beautiful. You are beautiful. It will be fine." His voice was warm.

"If you say so." She changed the subject. "What are you doing right now?"

She heard him chuckle. "I believe I'm talking to you."

Rachel made a growling noise. "You know what I mean."

"I've finished washing up my dishes, and I'm getting ready to read through some seed catalogs. How's that for exciting?"

She laughed. "Sounds wonderful. I'm drinking wine and staring into space."

"Ah," he said. "Dreaming?"

"Yeah."

"About what?" There was that little edge his voice sometimes got.

"About you."

He gave her his little happy laugh. "How flattering."

"True, though. When can we see each other?"

A tiny pause. "Sometime. We'll talk about it after all the excitement is over."

It's what he always said. "Twenty-four hours?" She hated sounding needy, but she couldn't help it.

"No, Rachel, but soon."

Chapter Nineteen

It was still dark the next morning when Rachel was awakened by loud voices. Actually it was only one loud voice. She wrapped Sébastien's robe around her and glanced at the spider web clock that she'd grown to like. Six-fifteen. Damn, it was early, and show nerves had kept her awake until late.

There were lights on in the living room. She crept down the hall expecting to see Mad Max again, but the man yelling at Sébastien was middle-aged and elegant. His back was to Rachel, and he was waggling his finger at Sébastien who sat, fully dressed, on the sofa. She wondered if he'd been to bed. Sébastien saw her and frowned, but she didn't move.

The man's French was fast, but she was good now. He was accusing Sébastien of lying, of ruining Sylvestri, and of disgracing French couture. Sébastien simply looked at him. The television was on, and Rachel eased far enough into the room to see one of the cheerful morning shows. The female commentator was raving away about Fashion Week and its surprises when a photo flashed onto the screen. It was Rachel. In the purple dress. At first she was confused; there'd been no press at last night's rehearsal. Those were sealed up tighter than champagne, according to Polly. And then she realized that the photograph was one of the many Kurt Mann had taken. She tried not to groan.

Sébastien looked as though he'd been groaning for hours. Over the last few weeks, he'd gradually turned into a zombie, but this morning he was even worse, Rachel thought: thin, gray, stooped. The angry man was still at it, and she finally figured out he must be Dumont, Sébastien's boss. He kept raging on, saying that not only was Sébastien finished at the House of Sylvestri, he was finished in Paris. In France. He would make sure of it. Sébastien didn't say a word.

Rachel whispered, "*Merde,*" rushed back to her room, and shut the door. As soon as she turned her phone on, it rang, a journalist asking for an interview. She hung up on her. Then another call, this one from a television reporter, followed by someone who wanted her to model hair products. She turned off the ringer and checked her messages: thirty of them, all within the last hour. Ignoring these, she clicked on Edgar's name and prayed he'd pick up.

208

I was proofing the last pages of *Foreign Affairs* when my phone rang. Beastly hour, but excitement about the book had kept me from sleeping later. Rachel didn't even bother with a hello.

"Edgar, it's all over the news. Kurt Mann must've told the press about the collection and sent along those pictures he took of me, and right now in the living room, Dumont's firing Sébastien. I don't know what to do." Before I could say anything, she wailed, "They have pictures of me on the TV news."

"Child, child. Do calm down. You say Dumont's there?"

"Yes."

"Make Sébastien ring me the minute he leaves. Don't go anywhere. There are probably hordes of reporters outside the building." I heard clicks on her phone.

"Oh, God. They keep calling me."

"Don't answer. Jesus." I thought for a second. "How did they get your number?"

She moaned, "Kurt, I guess. This is all my fault."

"It most definitely is not. Will the show go on as scheduled?"

"I don't know."

"Hang up now. But have Sébastien ring me."

I used my mouse to make two or three clicks to the Internet, and there she was, gorgeous but far from the slender norm for models. A headline said, "FEL FALLS." I glanced through the copy: "Paris in an uproar," "No comment yet from Sylvestri," "Fashion journalists say they'll give Fel's fat ladies a pass." I swore mightily. And then I dialed Jeremy's number.

I didn't wait for a hello. "We have to get to Paris," I said.

"What? What's going on, Uncle Edgar?"

"Fire up your laptop. There's an absolute uproar in Paris about Sébastien's collection. And they're focusing on Rachel."

"What?" he repeated. I could hear him clicking, and then he said, "Bloody hell. Have you talked to her?"

I told him about Rachel's call.

"Why didn't she ring me?" he asked.

"Perhaps she doesn't think you care about this part of her life." I heard him sputtering but didn't wait for an answer. "Look, I need to make calls. The show, if they have it, is at four. We have to get to Paris before then." I looked at my watch. "It's no problem for me, but you're a bit farther afield."

I could hear him muttering, reading the copy accompanying Rachel's photos. "Where did these pictures come from? I thought this fashion stuff was supposed to be secret."

"It is. That bastard of a photographer leaked all this to the press. For an astronomical fee, I would imagine. He also gave out her phone number. Probably for even more money."

"Did he romance her just for this?" His voice had risen about an octave.

"I suspect so."

"How can I get to Paris in time?"

That was my boy. "Give me a few minutes. I think I can charter a plane."

"Wicked expensive."

"Hang the cost. This is Rachel." And Sébastien, I thought as I hung up.

A

She made coffee and led Sébastien by the hand to the kitchen table. "Drink," she ordered. The only response he'd made to Dumont was to say that the clothes were exquisite, that he shouldn't judge until he'd seen the ensembles. Dumont had slammed the door on his way out. Fingers trembling, Rachel poured herself a cup and burned her tongue. In a minute she'd get Sébastien to call Edgar, but he didn't look as if he could even speak at this point.

She'd turned her phone to vibrate, and it felt like she had a sex toy in her pocket. She glanced at the messages and texts. Three were from Crystal. She called her.

"What in the everlovin' hell is going on, Rachel? Shawn called me from the airport and said you're all over the TV, and they're showing a mob of reporters waiting outside your building. The big man, Dupont or Dumont or whatever, told them he'd fired Sébastien. What's the deal?"

Rachel ducked into the living room and spoke softly. "The world's not ready for fat girls, Cryssie. That's what."

"But the clothes," Crystal moaned. "They're freakin' gorgeous. I've never worn clothes like that."

"Obviously it's not just about the clothes." She shifted so she could glance at Sébastien. He was staring at the kitchen wall. She'd expected a tantrum, but he was deadly silent. Frightening.

"Well, do we have a show or not?"

"I don't know, but as soon as I do I'll call you."

"Okay. And Shawn says if you need him to bust some reporter asses, he'll be there."

"I appreciate it. There's just one ass I'd like busted right now."

"That shit of a photographer? Is he at the bottom of all this?"

"Yeah, the very bottom."

"Jeremy?"

"Here."

"Can you get to Exeter by noon?"

"Easy."

"I'll be landing about then to pick you up and fly on to Paris. We'll make it, I think."

"I'll be there."

I had just enough time to put water on for tea and wish I still smoked when the phone rang. Sébastien said, "Eddie."

"Dear Gumby. This is a colossal cock-up, isn't it?"

"If they could have seen the show, they wouldn't be crucifying me like this."

I doubted it. The reviews would've been horrendous, but there was no point in telling him. "I know, old boy. I'm so sorry."

"And Raquel. They're smearing those pictures of her all over the Web and television. Poor girl." His voice was weak, but he wasn't playing the diva.

"She'll survive. She's young." And in love, I might have added, but I didn't want to confuse things just then. "And she does look sensational."

A crack of light came into his voice. "She does, doesn't she?"

"So, you'll cancel the show?"

He sighed. "I must. Only the ghouls will come. I don't even know if the models will show up."

"Oh, they'll be there. How many fat models get a chance to do haute couture?"

"They are not fat," he insisted. Sébastien, Queen of Denial.

"I say you go on. Flaunt them. But you better get some extra security."

"Do you really think so?"

"As you say, if you've any chance at redemption, the world needs to see those clothes." I took a sip of scalding tea and looked at the kitchen clock. I'd need to leave soon.

"That's true. You are very wise, Eddie." His voice became stronger with every word. "I must call everyone."

"Let Polly do some of it. You know she'll stick with you, and I'm sure she's wondering what's going on."

He was quiet for a moment. "Do you think Dumont will sack her too? I worry about that. And all the other people." He paused again. "He said I'll never work in France again. Me, Eddie. Me."

I did want to sympathize with him, but he needed courage more than pity. "We'll cross that one tomorrow. Call Polly. And I'll be at the Louvre by four."

"You're coming?" He was incredulous.

"Of course I'm coming, as long as you inform security that I'm allowed in without an invitation. Make sure of that."

A

"Raquel!" Sébastien sounded like his old, bossy self.

"Ring Yvonne and tell her to buy all the papers on her way here. She knows which ones. Then see if that model's gigantic boyfriend can smuggle you to the Ritz to hide. We both must leave here soon. Oh, and Eddie's coming to the show."

"We're doing the show?"

"Yes. Get busy."

By nine o'clock things had calmed down considerably, although Yvonne said the mob of journalists outside showed no sign of diminishing. She spread the papers on the coffee table, and Rachel's spirits sank with each one. Several of the celebrities and fashionistas on their guest list had been interviewed and said they wouldn't dream of attending. There were photos of Rachel in the purple dress of course, but also ones of her leaving Sébastien's apartment and the *atelier,* usually looking sloppy and fat. She'd had no idea she was being watched. It made her feel dirty and exposed and violated to realize that someone, probably Kurt Mann, had been stalking her. She kept deleting messages without listening to them, waiting for Shawn or Crystal to call. They'd said they needed a little time to figure out how to sneak Sébastien and Rachel past the hordes. She glanced at Sébastien and worried as he picked up the dreadful papers, his hands trembling so much the pages waved.

Yvonne made breakfast, started soup. Nothing was going to ruffle her feathers. Sébastien was glued to his phone. Rachel knew he'd called Polly, Suzanne, and Jean-Pierre. But he'd made dozens more calls to make sure the show went off as planned. She shuddered. She'd be the first one down the runway. In the infamous purple dress.

A

"Where the fuck have you been?" Jeremy shouted over the plane's engine. "It's one-thirty."

Language, language; Margo would've had a fit, but I myself had been thinking in expletives all day. "A delay at the airport. A delay at take-off. We'll still make it. We have to."

Jeremy wore a suit, to my recollection the only suit he owned, had a small bag over one shoulder, and carried a bouquet of red roses covered in cello wrap. "Nice touch," I commented.

He shrugged. "Roses. Cliché, but they were the only decent flowers in the shop." We sat, and I held the flowers while he buckled himself in. "Does she know I'm coming?"

"Not from me. Haven't you called her?"

He took the flowers. "I tried twice but didn't leave a message. Maybe it's better as a surprise."

She'd be surprised all right. "I hate small planes," I muttered.

A

Shawn had a plan. "Okay, here's the deal. In football you want to split the defense, right?" he asked.

Rachel said she guessed so.

"If we can have someone tell them that you're, say, already at the Louvre, and Sébastien's been at Sylvestri the last several hours, most of them are gonna scram."

Shawn was a sweetheart, an absolute sweetheart. And his tender, loving care made Jeremy look an awful lot like a loser. Surely

213

Edgar had told him what was going on. Why hadn't he called? "Makes sense," she said. "How can we make this happen?"

"That's the problem. A phone call's gonna get real complicated. Who do we call? The newspapers? It'll take forever to circulate to the journalists." He'd truly given this some thought. "Is there anybody there but you and Sébastien?"

She started to say no, but that was a lie. Yvonne was in the living room dusting away like it was any other day. "There's the housekeeper," Rachel said.

"Perfect. Have her leave and tell the media there's nobody in the apartment. She should give them specific but bogus locations like the ones I suggested. Wait about twenty minutes before you send her out, and I'll get a taxi close to the back entrance. I've already done a quick surveillance of your building. That's what took me so long to get back to you. Be waiting at the back door, and I'll get out of the cab and escort you two in case any of them are watching the back. Oh, how do I say 'wait' in French? I'll need to say it to the driver."

She told him and he repeated it five times like he was memorizing one of his old play books. "Is this going to work?" Rachel asked.

Shawn hesitated. "It's the best plan I can come up with."

The only protest Yvonne made was that she hadn't finished her work or the soup. Sébastien was very pale but dressed immaculately in what he would wear to the show. Rachel asked him, "Where are you really going?"

"To Polly's. She's contacting everyone." He frowned like he was trying to remember something. "Oh, yes," he said. "Don't forget to take everything you need for hair and makeup. We won't come back here until after the show."

She'd figured this but nodded at him. His hands were still shaking. Yvonne had on her jacket and was waiting for Rachel's cue. "The soup is in the refrigerator." Yvonne pursed her lips. "It should simmer another hour."

Sébastien patted Yvonne's arm. "I thank you for this."

She left, and Rachel and Sébastien stood at the window where they could see the crowd below. After a bit, Rachel located Yvonne's spiky black hair and watched while the woman stopped and spoke to reporters. Two thirds of them scattered immediately. "I hope the ones out back left too," Rachel said.

"Shall we go?" Sébastien was grim and silent as he trudged down the steps, and Rachel was wired so tight she was nearly hyperventilating. They glanced out the back door window and saw a taxi and three photojournalists. "He's here," Sébastien said, but before opening the door he murmured, "I'm sorry, Raquel. I never wanted you ridiculed like this."

She wouldn't have considered it two days ago, but she stretched up to kiss his cheek. "I'm more worried about you."

He flapped his hand at this and opened the door. The reporters started flashing photos and pushing microphones in their faces, but Shawn broke through and scattered them. In no time, the cab took off for the Ritz, and Shawn grinned. "Lousy defense," he muttered.

A

Rachel was playing gin rummy with Crystal, Ava, and Mrs. Carter and trying to concentrate on her cards. Crystal had ordered sandwiches and soft drinks, but Rachel couldn't eat, and neither could Shawn who prowled the suite, phone to his ear. He had more family arriving for the wedding so he was waiting for them to contact him, and Sébastien had taken Shawn's number, figuring that Rachel's phone was so jammed it would be useless. He'd talked to Shawn twice already, figuring out how they'd get the women to the Louvre.

"Have you heard from that Brit of yours? Crystal asked.

Rachel shook her head. "But his uncle is flying over for the show."

"That's the writer guy who used to be tight with Sébastien, right?"

"Yes."

"Well, you'd think he'd tell his nephew what's going on." Crystal's eyes went to Shawn, standing over by the window. Rachel knew she was comparing and also knew who the winner was. Maybe Jeremy had tried to call, though. She touched the phone in her pocket and wondered if it was worth sifting through all the media messages to see if he had.

Phone to his ear, Shawn called over to Crystal. "Honey, Sébastien says your dresser isn't coming. Several of them quit."

"No problem," said Ava. "Mama and I can dress our girl." Mrs. Carter nodded.

Shawn relayed this to Sébastien. Then he said, "You're gonna just have one, Rachel. The other one has to help another model."

"Fine." She didn't care much at this point whether she hit her marks on time or not, but she could imagine Gisèle and Polly fighting over her. "Which one?" she asked.

Shawn asked and broke into a smile. There'd been few enough of those today. "Polly. They flipped a coin." She smiled back at him.

The afternoon dragged. Shawn was still pacing, talking to his family and directing them to the hotel; the women were still playing cards, or trying to. Finally he said they should gather up their stuff. They had no problem leaving the Ritz, but a mass of reporters stood outside the Louvre entrance the models were supposed to use. Shawn paid the cabbie and told the women, "Don't look left or right. Don't speak. Don't hesitate. I'm blocking."

The Carter women surrounded Rachel: one Amazonian sister on either side of her and Mrs. Carter in the rear, nearly walking on Rachel's heels. In front of Rachel, Shawn looked big and mean enough to split the crowd like a double-decker sandwich. But Rachel couldn't help but look at the crush of media. She felt her face go hot as the reporters shouted her name and aimed cameras at her. She didn't see Kurt, but as they neared the door, she caught a glimpse of Lucy, the belligerent ex-Sylvestri model. She didn't look pissed off now. Catching Rachel's eye, she gave her a smile triumphant enough for the cover of *Vogue* and made a rude gesture. It took all of Rachel's restraint not to return it. Lucy and Kurt had plotted this, she realized. She'd been set up months ago.

Shawn soon herded his women inside, and although getting into the building and seeing Lucy had unnerved Rachel, it was nothing compared to the jitters that started when she went to her tiny cubicle and saw the purple dress. She'd asked Sébastien if they should cut the dress that everyone had already seen. But he'd been adamant about Rachel wearing it. Polly was setting baby powder for those infernal yellow tights on the card table. "I don't know if I can do this," Rachel said to her.

"But of course you can." Polly waved her graceful hands, but Rachel doubted if she was as calm as she looked. "Out. Walk. In. Change. Nothing to it. You ignore everything else."

It sounded easy.

Chapter Twenty

"What time is it now?" Jeremy asked.

He wore a watch, his father's actually. I don't know why he kept asking me. I was having trouble enough keeping my equilibrium as our toy-sized plane circled the Paris airport for the fourth time. "We'll get there. Soldier on."

But even I was having doubts when it took us forever to clear the airport, and our cab drove into massive traffic. The cabbie muttered something about Fashion Week, accompanied by a few choice words in what I thought was Arabic. I kept mumbling, "Please hurry," in the best French I could muster.

"The minute she walks out, they're going to murder her," said Jeremy. "Why didn't he cancel the damned thing?"

"I persuaded him not to," I said.

He gave me a vile look.

"Security won't let them get anywhere near the runway," I said. I hoped.

Jeremy's vile look did not disappear. "But they'll boo and hiss and yell ugly things at her. And they'll be flashing cameras like they're at a crime scene." He looked out the window at gray Parisian skies and dozens of cars honking their horns. "It is a crime scene," he muttered. "And Rachel's the victim."

A

Rachel stood by Suzanne and waited for Emma's cue. Bless her heart; the spunky DJ had not even considered bailing on them. "It is a job, no?" she'd said.

"Is there anybody out there?" Rachel asked. She was afraid to look.

She hadn't heard Sébastien come up behind her. "Full, actually," he said. "Although some of the celebrities seem to have given their invitations to the vultures. The head of security said he had press handing them cards with Hollywood actresses' names on them."

"Great," Rachel muttered. She took a shuddery breath. In one hour it would be over. In one hour she could go back to Sébastien's apartment and hide. Going to New York with Jesse was sounding better and better.

Emma started, right on time, and Rachel's stomach clutched. "You are a beautiful princess, Raquel," Sébastien murmured. In French. "Head up."

She started walking, trying to set her face into a haughty pout. But before she'd taken two steps onto the runway, flashes blinded her, and the roar of the crowd all but drowned out Emma's rumbling bass. All of them knew that purple dress. For a second, she was back in the locker room, and Jennifer and her buddies were mocking her about candy bars. Butter butt. Her stomach kept churning, and she knew her face was bright red under the pale makeup. This was hell.

She made her turn, but the noise and flashes didn't fade. She glimpsed Jesse giving her a double thumbs-up, but she focused on Sébastien's pale, drawn face at the end of the catwalk. She didn't matter. The crowd didn't matter. Maybe the next exit wouldn't be so bad. Maybe they'd calm down after seeing more outfits. Crystal suddenly appeared next to Sébastien, waiting to go on. She flashed a huge grin. "Screw 'em," she whispered to Rachel. "You're fine, girl. Real fine." And she swished past Rachel to take the runway.

Rachel was trembling all over, and when she touched Sébastien's arm, she realized that he was too.

A

"She didn't see us." Jeremy was blatantly disappointed.

"No, but she was lovely, wasn't she?" I poked his arm. "Did you see the necklace?"

"Yeah. She had on the necklace." He glared at the jeering crowd like he wanted to murder them. So did I. "Would this have happened anyway? Even if the news hadn't gotten out?" he asked.

"I think so, but they wouldn't have been lying in wait for her." Our brave girl, I thought.

Rachel's friend Crystal was next. "She's incredible," Jeremy whispered.

I realized that the crowd had settled down a bit after the purple dress. More than a few had left. I admired Crystal's suit. One couldn't live with a designer all those years and not pick up a few nuances. The cut was superb, and the idea was fresh. Crystal looked magnificent, and every strutting step said that she knew it. Despite the catcalls.

"Go," urged Polly. "You look lovely." It was the copper outfit.

Rachel could hear one of the models crying. She wouldn't. She absolutely wouldn't allow herself to fall apart.

As she stood next to Sébastien, Rachel clutched her toes against those damned platform shoes. "They are not so noisy now," he said, again in French. Had he lost his concentration or had she passed a test?

"They'll rev it up when they see me," she muttered. One of the German girls, who looked like she too could cry at any minute, was nearly to them, and Rachel took a deep breath and then a step.

There were still some boos and shouts, but at least she could hear Emma's mixes now. To Rachel's right were several empty chairs. Then, just as she was nearing the end of the runway, she saw Jeremy, his lap full of roses, and she took a clumsy step. Her ankle swayed, and she heard a collective, sympathetic sigh from the crowd who'd booed her seconds before. She could imagine the headline: "Fat Frump Falls on Ass." She looked right into Jeremy's concerned eyes, straightened her foot, and winked. Models never smiled. She turned and those damned shoes seemed to float her back to the doorway. Sébastien beamed, truly smiled at her. "I wondered when you'd see them," he said.

"He came, Polly! He's out there," she squealed, once she was in her cubicle.

"That's nice. Jacket," Polly ordered. "We have the damned tights next."

Rachel wriggled out of the copper jacket. "Crystal," she shouted over the garment rack, "Jeremy came."

"Wow, honey. From zero to hero in sixty seconds, right?"

Polly squeezed out a cloud of baby powder and patted it onto Rachel's legs. She sneezed. None of this mattered if Jeremy was there. Polly helped her shimmy into the tights and slipped the yellow dress over her head. "Two minutes," Suzanne called.

Polly brushed powder out of Rachel's hair. "Hide the necklace."

The violet pendant didn't match in any possible way with the wild yellow dress. It actually looked pretty stupid with it, but Rachel shook her head and straightened the gold chain. "This is more important," she said.

Polly smiled, squeezed her arm, and said, "You are beautiful, Rachel."

Rachel grinned back at her. "You know, Polly, I think maybe I am."

By the time she wore the ecru wedding dress down the catwalk, there was actually some applause. Of course Jeremy and Edgar were doing most of the clapping, along with Shawn and Jesse. Sébastien went out, a sour little smile on his face, and took his bows to loud boos. Backstage, Rachel lifted off the outrageous veiled headdress and handed it to Polly who wrapped it in tissue and left. She'd want to see Sébastien, of course. All Rachel could think was that Jeremy would be there any minute now. She heard Crystal and Ava laughing. But many of the other models, already dressed in street clothes, escaped silently down the hallway. They didn't pause to say good-bye or anything. Still wearing the lovely gown, Rachel sat on the only chair and waited, thinking how strange it was that life could be so awful and wonderful at the same time.

His face was nearly as flushed as the roses he held. Tossing the flowers onto the card table, he reached for her shoulders and pulled her up into a kiss. "You're brilliant," he breathed against her lips. "So brave. So beautiful." Then he lifted his hands from her dress like it was hot. "My hands are snagging the gown."

She laughed. "Does it matter? When would I ever wear this?"

Hardly taking his eyes off her, he touched her cheek, her hair. "I was afraid we wouldn't get here in time," he said.

She reached behind her neck to unfasten the ugly bronze necklace. Her fingers were shaking too much to manage it. "Help me?" she asked.

He handed her the necklace and straightened the violet underneath. "I saw," he said. "But you didn't know I was coming."

"I never take it off."

Just then Edgar and Sébastien came into the cubicle, followed by Polly, Gisèle, and Jesse. Rachel wasn't surprised by the hugs from the women or Edgar or Jesse, but when Sébastien grasped her in a quick, hard embrace, she felt more like crying than she had on the runway. "*Ma cherié* Raquel," he whispered, kissing her forehead. She was stunned.

Someone pulled in chairs, and Edgar opened a bottle of champagne. Trust Edgar to try to make a celebration out of a disaster. "To the indomitable, impossible, incredible Sébastien Fel," he shouted as he lifted his glass. "And to our lovely and much-loved Rachel. Well done, both of you."

She smiled. She smiled more than she had since she'd left Cornwall. The show was over, thank God. She felt like she could breathe again. Even Sébastien had a weak smile of relief on his face. Rachel drank, Jeremy holding her hand and beaming at her. She wasn't sure, but she thought Edgar might be holding Sébastien's hand too.

Jesse, not stupid by any means, looked at her and Jeremy and saw how things were. His smile was sad, and Rachel felt like a giant jerk, but, as he left, Jesse kissed his fingers at her and mouthed, "Keep in touch."

Polly, ever-practical Polly, drank half her glass and said, "And now what?" She raised her eyebrows at Sébastien.

He shook his head. "I don't know. No more Sylvestri, obviously."

Gisèle said, "I think you should design lingerie. Women love beautiful undergarments, and you could have great fun working with them."

Edgar grinned. "I say, Sébastien, lingerie would be an intriguing challenge: engineering and art at the same time."

Shawn and the Carter women paused in the hallway just outside. Crystal had overheard Edgar. "And some of us need real engineering when it comes to our underwear, Mr. Fel. Good idea."

Rachel laughed. "Join us."

Shawn shook his head. "No, I gotta get my women home." He gave Jeremy a long glance. "You got Rachel covered?"

"Absolutely." Jeremy grinned, but his face went bright red.

Shawn winked, but Crystal rolled her eyes and pointed her finger at them. "Wedding. Tomorrow. Four o'clock. All of you." She looked around to include everybody. She blew a kiss at Rachel. "Bye, honey."

They left and everything went quiet. She no longer heard workmen taking down the tapestries and prints or Emma packing up her gear. "Lingerie," mused Sébastien. "I'd never considered it."

"I think you should do perfume too," said Rachel. "Remember that wonderful scent you gave me to try?"

"I do," he said. A tiny fire started crackling behind his eyes. "I still have the perfumier's number. Dumont says I'll never work again in France, but how can he stop me from selling perfume?" He smiled, straightened his back, and looked once more like arrogant old Sébastien. "And lingerie."

"Sunglasses," offered Edgar. "Suitcases, bed linens, makeup, and china."

Sébastien looked down his long nose. "You are embarrassing yourself again, Eddie."

Edgar shrugged, a perfect imitation of the ones Polly and Sébastien did so well. "Let it be said that I am, if nothing else, consistent."

A

Sometime after they'd all finished another bottle of champagne, Rachel overheard Sébastien murmur, "Come home with me, Eddie." Then they left with Gisèle. Rachel changed into jeans behind the clothing rack, and Polly packed up all of Rachel's outfits into boxes and garment bags. Then Polly left too, and the room that had been so charged with frenetic energy, and fear, died down to silence. They'd be turning the lights out soon.

"What now?" asked Jeremy. He looked serious and responsible in his suit.

Rachel giggled. "I'm hungry. I haven't eaten much all day, and that dab of champagne went straight to my head."

"Legless but happy," he said, winking at her like the old lecher at the pub. "You'll have to help me find a restaurant. I don't know Paris at all."

She hitched her bag over her shoulder and cradled the roses in her arm. "No problem. I wonder if there are still reporters outside."

"I doubt it. They're on to the next show by now, I'd think."

They walked out onto the plaza where the Louvre's pyramid glowed. There were hardly any people at all. "Are you going back tonight?" she asked, afraid it was true.

"No. Uncle Edgar and I booked the plane for a one-way trip."

"Then where will you stay?" The early evening sky had cleared, and the air was chilly. A few clouds bearded the moon.

"Hadn't thought about it."

"Most of the better hotels are full for Fashion Week."

His hand rested on her shoulder as they walked. She liked that. "I don't know where Uncle Edgar plans to stay," he said.

"Oh, I do. That's why I'm a little uncomfortable asking you back to Sébastien's."

He stopped walking and stared at her. "Do you think? Sébastien again?"

She grinned. "Or still, at least as far as Edgar's concerned. I'm pretty sure."

"Well." He seemed surprised but pleased. "Uncle Edgar would like that very much." They started moving again.

She thought for a minute. "I know a hotel."

"But you said most of them are booked."

"Not the one I'm thinking of. Fashionistas wouldn't dream of such a common place." She leaned her head against his hand. "It's where I stayed back in August, before I met Sébastien and was a poor little tourist. Austere, I think the guidebooks call it."

"Sounds fine," he said. "Although it's hard to envision you as a poor little tourist."

This time she stopped, making him do the same. "I was, Jeremy. I was a nobody from Ohio." Shrugging, she added, "I still am."

She saw a taxi a half-block down and held up her roses to hail it. She told the cabbie the name of the hotel but then had to give him the address. He'd never heard of it.

"I thought you were hungry," Jeremy said. His hip was tight against hers. Warm.

"Ravenous," she said, trying not to crush the roses when she kissed him. "But I can wait."

The same gloomy clerk manned the desk, but her sour look disappeared the minute she recognized Rachel. "Mademoiselle Bowman," she exclaimed. "Rachel."

"Yep," she said. "I'd like Room 315 again if it's available." It seemed like some kind of an omen to return to it.

"But of course," the clerk said. "I just want you to know that you are an inspiration to all of us."

Rachel's head jerked up.

The clerk went on, her plain face turning pink. "An ordinary girl, a beautiful girl, but ordinary. To be elevated to such heights!" She raised her eyes to the dingy ceiling.

"Well, um, thank you," Rachel said. "By the way, do you have a vase I could borrow for my flowers?"

The clerk frowned. "No, I'm sorry, but we do not." Not *that* much of an inspiration, Rachel thought.

Jeremy set his credit card on the desk and went to a credenza that held a vase of dusty silk flowers. He dumped them out. "This'll do," he said, holding up the vase. "We'll return it in the morning."

Rachel was still giggling when they got on the noisy elevator.

"It worked, didn't it?" Jeremy touched his lips to hers. "This elevator sounds like the Tardis."

"The what?"

"More like the *who*." He shook his head. "The Tardis is a spaceship from a British television show called *Dr. Who*."

"Oh, my brother used to watch that," Rachel exclaimed. "All these different doctors and aliens that look like they've been constructed at the junkyard." The elevator opened.

"That's it," he said. "Nice to know your brother and I are fellow geeks."

"You're no geek."

He opened the door to their room. "Yes, I am, but you don't seem to mind. You're ordinary, or so you say, and I'm a geek. A perfect pair. What's this?" He pointed at the twin beds. "An ancient French method of contraception?"

"We'll push them together," she said, dropping her bag and taking the flowers and vase off to the bathroom. She heard him moving furniture. And then it felt awkward. After fiddling with blossoms that looked remarkably fresh despite the day they'd had, Rachel walked back into the bedroom and felt a rush of panic. They'd had one night together in his house, but that had seemed domestic. Rachel remembered how her friend Shelley used to love to dump her kids on their grandparents and take off with her husband for a weekend. "Hotel sex," she'd said. "It's the best."

Rachel nodded at his suit, crisp tie, and shiny shoes. "I feel awfully informal in my jeans," she murmured. He was so handsome, so, well, intimidating if she forgot about the greenhouse and the corduroys and the blue poinsettias.

"Then let's even the playing field." He took off his jacket and loosened his tie.

"Okay," she said slowly, setting down the vase and reaching to unbutton his shirt. He slid out of it and tugged at her sweater until she held up her arms. "How many times have you dressed and undressed today?" He unbuttoned her jeans.

"I couldn't begin to count," she murmured. "But this time's the best."

The rest of their clothes came off, with kisses interrupting one sock from another, one shoe from the next. Then they were skin to skin, lying on cheap sheets that smelled of bleach. "If the lady does permit?" he asked. Still cautious. Would he always be?

"Oui, Madame le permettrait." She touched his cheek and felt the stubble on it. It had been hours since he'd shaved. "What time did you start your adventure this morning anyway?" She raised herself over him, offering her breasts.

His reply was muffled. "Six-thirty."

"You must be dead on your feet," she murmured. Her voice was already breathless.

"Mmm. Dead on my feet and flat on my back."

He moved under her, and she shifted to meet him. To hell with foreplay, she thought. She wanted him now. She heard him catch his breath.

"Rachel," he said.

"Hmm?" She bent her head to kiss him.

"I love you."

"And I love you, Jeremy."

They were both exhausted, but it didn't matter. Eyes shut, she was breathing hard, harder, when he said again, "Rachel."

"Yes." She was almost there, too close for talking, really. Too close for thinking.

"The beds are coming apart."

She pushed once more before she could make herself stop.

"I'm, um, falling into the crack."

When she opened her eyes she could see Jeremy sagging in the middle, arms outstretched to keep himself from falling through, and she had to laugh. She laughed so hard she almost pushed him to the floor. "Oh, God," she cried, sliding to the side and wiping tears from her cheeks. "You have fallen for me, haven't you?"

He struggled to extricate himself from the crevice. "You might say that." Then he was laughing too, and still giggling, they rolled together onto one narrow bed. Rachel heard her laughter replaced by ragged breathing, and then she gave way to a little snort of humor that buried itself in his chest. "We do have the best fun, don't we?" she asked, kissing his shoulder.

"Actually, we do." He twined his fingers in her curls.

A

"So do you want to come to Crystal's wedding with me?" He'd never said. She didn't know when he was going back to England. She still didn't know when she was going back to Ohio, or even if she was. They'd finally made themselves get out of bed to eat dinner, and right this minute all she did know was that she couldn't wait for the food to arrive.

He poured a little more wine in Rachel's glass. "Sure. I wore my suit." He grinned at her. "And I did bring a change of underwear and shirt."

"Socks too?" She couldn't take her eyes off him: the way his soft hair dipped over his forehead, his plump lower lip.

"Socks too." He gazed around the small dining room. "Nice place. Quiet."

"I came here once with the photographer jerk." She didn't like to say Kurt's name. "But that's no reason to hate the restaurant."

Jeremy cocked his head to the side. "Were you in love with him?"

She didn't avoid his eyes. "No. Infatuated maybe." She looked down at a tiny stain on the tablecloth. "Mostly I was flattered that he wanted me, and that wasn't even true. He just wanted money."

Jeremy's voice was off-hand, blank. "But he must've been charming, sophisticated." He lifted a shoulder. "Much more than I am." This was a test. Over material she thought they'd already covered.

She looked him squarely in the eye and said, "Love's honest. It's not about being charming or measuring up."

His face softened. "Uncle Edgar's right. You are the most wonderful girl."

She felt her cheeks go pink. "Well, I don't know," she started.

"I do."

She felt breathless but squirmy. Changing the subject, she asked, "Did you send your plans to the garden show people?"

"I did. Right after you left."

"Good. You'll get in."

"Maybe. I decided gulping was better than sipping," he said.

They ate, drank more wine, and then walked along the chilly Parisian streets to their dumpy little hotel. Along the way, she pointed to some of her favorite spots: one of the bridges, a café, the dark hulk of the Opera. He said, "You'll miss Paris, won't you?" She was snuggled against him, his topcoat warm and sturdy against her side.

"I love Paris," she said. "And I'll come back, but I don't want to stay here with nothing to do."

"I bet you could get all kinds of modeling jobs."

"I doubt it." She grinned up at him. "Besides, I think Sébastien has a new roommate now. A new *old* roommate."

"You really do believe they're getting back together?"

"I really do."

Jeremy shook his head. "Uncle Edgar never said a word to me, of course, but I think he's grieved for Sébastien for years. Actually, I've always disliked the man for hurting my uncle."

"Sébastien's okay, once you get past all the posing. And I think he's figured out what's important." She swung around in front of Jeremy and threw her arms around his neck. The brown scarf was knotted there. She'd noticed. "Like us."

He kissed her and, with an evil little glint in his eyes, said he thought they should be heading back to the hotel, like now.

Chapter Twenty One

It had, I thought, turned out to be quite simple. Sébastien and I had hugged the children, Polly had told him that she'd follow him anywhere, and we'd left the dressing area with Gisèle. She'd gone on, but Sébastien paused at the exit, acting oddly uncertain. I hadn't replied to his invitation, nor would I until I knew for sure. "Have you a place to stay the night?" he'd asked. He hadn't quite met my eyes.

I'd said no, but if I couldn't find a hotel I could always impose upon Polly.

He'd glanced at my face and then away again. "As I said in there," he gestured back toward the dressing room, "you could stay with me." He'd spoken very quietly.

"If I were to do that," I'd said, "it wouldn't be for one night."

He'd nodded, but I wasn't sure he understood. "I wouldn't leave again, Gumby."

"I wouldn't want you to leave," he'd said as he opened the door. Fresh, damp, Parisian air blew over us. "Ever."

So, I suppose Sébastien and I presented a pretty picture of domesticity when Rachel and Jeremy arrived the next day. I was wearing Sébastien's cashmere robe; I could smell Rachel's perfume on it. Sébastien was dressed in his Chinese pajamas and bizarre Arabian slippers, the curly-toed oddities propped up on the coffee table alongside our coffee cups while we read the dire and abysmal reviews of Sylvestri's show in the papers. Yvonne was hoovering the bedrooms. Sébastien had turned on the television but muted it while cheery newspeople interviewed fashion vampires bent on ravishing him.

The children came in looking wind-blown and happy, Jeremy in his suit and topcoat, Rachel in her jeans. She said she'd come to change for the wedding and asked if we were going. I waited to see what Sébastien would say.

"I don't think so," he said. "But I've sent Miss Carter the costumes she wore yesterday as a wedding gift." His mouth slipped into a distant smile. "I like her."

Jeremy stared at his shoe resting on his knee. "Are you going back to London today, Uncle Edgar?"

Ah, I'd embarrassed him. What fun. I delight in being eccentric enough to cause young people discomfort. "No. Actually I'm moving to Paris. As of now."

Jeremy's eyes flew to my face. Sébastien cleared his throat, and Rachel choked out a little cough. Must have been some allergens floating about in the air. "For good?" Jeremy managed to squeak.

"It seems that way." I do nonchalance rather well, if I do say so myself. "I plan to keep the London flat for quick trips to confer with my editor, and for you, of course. Margo still comes to the city two or three times a year too. It will see some use."

Jeremy nodded and glanced at Rachel. She had that delightfully mischievous glint in her eyes that I love, the dear. "I'm going to have some of my things shipped over," I said. "And I called this morning to have them express my laptop and the galleys. Must finish those." I smiled at Rachel.

Sébastien cleared his throat again. "You are, of course, welcome to stay as long as you like, Raquel." Jeremy picked up one of the papers and stared at the picture of Rachel, not in that damned purple dress this time, but in the glorious final gown. The headline, however, was far from complimentary. Jeremy glared at it.

An odd little cloud passed over her face. "Thanks, Sébastien, but I'll be leaving soon."

"There's no rush," said Sébastien, "and I've learned of some fabulous opportunities for you here and elsewhere in Europe." He put his glasses back on, vain man, and read: "'Bowman, who has no other modeling experience, is likely to be courted by many *prêt-à-porter* designers. Karl Dietrich and Tonio Landry who both design garments in a wide range of sizes have expressed interest. '"

"Who are they?" she asked.

"Ready to wear designers. German and British. They often copy my work. Now they want to steal my model." His chin went up. "Some people appreciate my taste."

"I'm glad for that," said Rachel, "but you know I have no interest in modeling."

Sébastien shook his head. "You'd be turning down a fortune, Raquel. Right this minute you are famous, so you must jump at every opportunity. A month from now no one will remember your name. And any loyalty you might feel for me is foolish. I cannot design haute couture anymore; Dumont will make sure of that." I knew how hard it was for him to say this.

Jeremy lowered his newspaper and watched Rachel. "It's not loyalty," she said, "although I'm really, really grateful for what you've done for me, Sébastien." She shook her head. "I just don't want to model again."

"A shame," Sébastien said. "So back to Ohio or are you going to New York with Jesse?"

Jeremy's mouth flew open. Mine did as well. Who was Jesse?

Yvonne had turned off the vacuum cleaner, and the room was silent, like we were waiting for a director, or author, to show us our next scene. Sébastien glanced at the television and saw that the illustrious Kristof Pauli was answering a perky blonde's questions. He clicked up the volume.

"I saw him at a party! I know who he is." Rachel pointed at the screen.

I gave her an indulgent smile. Sébastien's eyes were locked on Pauli, his hero.

"Have you had a chance to see photographs of Fel's designs?" the woman asked.

Pauli had a face carved of stone, no emotion at all registered on it. "I attended the show," he said. I had a bit of trouble understanding his Italian-accented French.

This disconcerted the blonde. "Did Fel know you were there?" Sébastien shook his head.

A cat's whisker of amusement flew across Pauli's face. "No. No one did."

"So, as a master couturier, were you as shocked as everyone else?" She looked greedy.

He faced the camera rather than the interviewer, his dark eyes hooded and cool. "I was shocked, yes. At the sheer genius of Sébastien Fel. This collection was magnificent, the work of an artist, a maestro."

Little Miss Blonde had twists in her knickers. She stammered. "But, but Dumont, the head of Sylvestri has fired Fel and swears he'll never work in France again."

Pauli glanced at the floor, at the camera, anywhere but at the blonde. He lifted a nonchalant hand. "Then he must come to Italy," he said.

I clapped my hands, and Rachel started cheering so loud, I couldn't make out how the woman concluded the interview. Pauli said nothing more. A remarkable grin transformed Sébastien's face. And Jeremy still looked as if he'd been shot.

Then the phone started ringing. Sébastien answered it and said, "I am not sure. Call Monday."

It rang again. "No comment," he said.

And again. He set down his phone and let voice mail handle the flood of calls. "Raquel?" he asked. "Are you sure? I would love to have your company on another adventure."

She was grinning but shook her head. "I'm sure. And I sure am happy for you."

I felt as though I should open champagne yet again. Sébastien turned off the television as if nothing had happened, and Yvonne clattered pots in the kitchen. I wondered how I might adjust to living in Italy. This reminded me that I was moving, an annoying process, and still had business to see to. "Jeremy," I started. "Will you be going back to England soon?"

This time Rachel's eyes were drilling into my nephew.

"Very soon," he said through tight lips. Ah, yes. Jesse.

"Then could I ask a favor? Could you stay over at the flat and pack up some of my clothes? Duncan will ship them off tomorrow, but I hate to ask him to root around in my cupboards." Yes, I was deflecting.

"Sure. I planned to stay there tonight. Anything else?"

"No, I don't think so." I frowned.

"Jeremy," she murmured.

He ignored her.

"Jesse is a friend from Sylvestri who just got a position in New York. He didn't know about you and me and asked if I wanted to go with him as his roommate. It's nothing. I never had any intention of going."

Still, he ignored her.

Saying she was going to have a bath, Rachel quietly disappeared down the hall. What little I could see of her face was pale. I turned back to Jeremy. "You're making a horrendous mistake."

Sébastien pointed his chin at Jeremy. "Fool."

A

She shut the bedroom door and opened the closet to get her green suit. There, in immaculate linen garment bags, were her Sylvestri outfits. And her suitcases. He was leaving tonight, not that he'd bothered to tell her that. And he wouldn't believe her about Jesse. She sat on the bed and let the tears come. She guessed she should call to get a flight back to the U. S., tomorrow if she was lucky. It was foolish to hold onto

231

hope at this point. Reaching for a tissue, she decided she'd have to impose on Sébastien and Edgar one more night. She couldn't bear the thought of going back to the old hotel. It would be like starting over again, like she'd never met Sébastien and Edgar. Or Jeremy.

She pulled off her sweater, smelling a hint of Jeremy's scent, green and woodsy. Fleeting, flimsy; sort of like the man himself. Nothing about these last few months had felt real, including him. Maybe she truly had been caught in some kind of strange enchanted world. Maybe.

A

It was a gorgeous room full of gorgeous people, Rachel thought. Shawn's two brothers, both as muscled, tall, and handsome as he, had arrived along with his mother, an elegant woman glittering with tasteful, expensive jewelry. Shawn took care of his women. He introduced her and Jeremy to all his family including his grinning, cherub-faced cousin who wore a black suit and carried a Bible. Rachel scrutinized the flower arrangements. Beautiful, even Jeremy had said so. "Creative," he added. "Nice work."

She was surprised he was talking to her. Hell, she was surprised he had come with her. But he'd been quietly pleasant ever since they left for the wedding. Maybe Sébastien and Edgar had urged him to be gentle in breaking up with her. She, however, was having a hard time. Knowing that he was leaving in a few hours was not only bitterly sad, she was getting downright angry.

They sat on ornate little chairs that screamed "The Ritz," although Rachel wondered if the spindly legs were up to the task of all the huge people in the room. Jeremy reached over to hold her hand, and she felt like crying again. Somebody else's wedding was a terrible place to end a romance. There was a steady murmuring from the guests, and then a soft strain of melody came from the violinist seated by a long window, hushing the group of maybe twenty-five people. Crystal's father, who was, of course, a very tall man, escorted Mrs. Carter into the room. They were divorced, Cryssie had said, but got along pretty well for about fifteen minutes at a time. Mrs. Carter wore a dark blue suit with a sky blue hat. It was easy to see where Crystal got her poise, Rachel thought.

Then Ava came in with one of Shawn's brothers. She wore a light blue suit with an indigo hat. Nice, Rachel thought. She'd chosen violets, yellow roses, and tons of baby's breath for Mrs. Carter's and Ava's bouquets. The contrast was good. "Wait'll you see Cryssie," she murmured to Jeremy.

The bride was, in every sense of the word, magnificent. Dressed in a long yellow sheath with an asymmetrical swath of deep blue cutting into the skirt, Crystal made the room her personal runway. Everyone stood, not because it was customary, but because they had to respect such beauty. The calla lilies, orange blossoms, and white roses worked perfectly, she thought. Rachel glanced at Shawn and saw absolute adoration on his face. A lethal pang of regret ran through Rachel's gut. Would she ever have that?

They watched while Shawn's cousin went through the old, traditional words. Jeremy's hand tightened on hers, and she didn't know whether to clutch it or slap it away. He bent his head to whisper in her ear, "We could do this, you know."

She turned to see his face. It was very serious, but his eyes were shining. She murmured, "What do you mean?"

Again, she felt his breath in her ear. It made her shiver. "I said, we could get married." He paused. "If you wanted to."

Crystal was saying, "I do" about the same time Rachel exclaimed, "Yes!"

Cryssie stopped, turned around to look at Rachel, and said to the preacher, "We might have another job for you, Daniel." Shawn raised his fist and everybody laughed and clapped.

The cake was beautiful, the champagne was excellent, and the hugs were warm. Best of all, though, was Jeremy's arm, sometimes draped around her or sometimes tucked under hers. "Well," Crystal said, "are you all gonna invite us to your wedding or are you gonna run off tonight?"

"You're invited," said Jeremy.

"Whenever it is," added Rachel. "Wherever it is."

Crystal laughed. "Guess you two got some planning to do, don't you? Honey," she called to Shawn, "How do you feel about going back to Ohio?"

🗼

Rachel was pretty sure *she* wouldn't be going back to Ohio any time soon, not even for her wedding. As soon as they could, the two of them left the reception and rushed back to Sébastien's apartment where they told Edgar and Sébastien the news. Rachel flew to her room to throw

233

clothes in her suitcases and returned to find the three men drinking wine and smiling at each other. "Would you mind shipping the costumes for me?" she asked Edgar and Sébastien. "I don't want them crushed into my bags."

Edgar couldn't quit smiling and hugging them. "Of course, my dear. We'll get Polly to smuggle out some of Sylvestri's special boxes for them. Right?" He looked at Sébastien while he patted Rachel's arm. "But where shall I send them?"

"Penmore," Jeremy and Rachel said at the same time.

"Perhaps you will marry in the wedding gown," said Sébastien. He wasn't one to grin and hug like Edgar, but he couldn't seem to lose a little, satisfied smile.

"That would be amazing," said Rachel. "But, sorry Sébastien, not that awful hat."

"Hennin," he corrected. "It is historically correct. But." He shrugged.

"When does your train leave?" asked Edgar.

Jeremy picked up Rachel's suitcases. "Soon. I've already called for a cab."

Edgar hugged Rachel again. "I'm so happy, my dear. Let us know all the plans."

Sébastien gave her a hard look. "By the way, I've been speaking English for the benefit of these two." He gestured at Edgar and Jeremy. "But you may have noticed that I now allow you to speak French, Raquel."

She grinned. "Then, *au revoir, Sébastien*," she said, giving his name its French pronounciation. "*Je te remercie mille fois, chéri.*"

As she was following Jeremy to the door, Sébastien called out, "I will want your assistance in naming the new perfume."

And Edgar said, "I may have more Chloe questions, my dear."

"That's what email is for, you two," growled Jeremy as they left.

A

Being half of a couple made it so much easier. Getting the tickets, handling the luggage, finding a seat. She didn't have to place a book or bag on the seat next to her to discourage company. She had company. Jeremy took off his overcoat and helped her remove her jacket. "Will you be warm enough?" he asked.

She smiled and nodded.

"So we'll go back to Cornwall in the morning," he said.

She nodded again.

"And then we'll get married."

"Can we get married in that little church near Penmore?"

"I believe so."

"Do you think they'll ring their bells for us?"

He squeezed her hand. "I'm sure they will."

Her mind spun with thoughts. "But we do have to wait a while, Jeremy."

"Oh?" It was a very dead, very serious 'oh.'

She scooted up in her seat so she could look at him directly. "I want my family there. And they don't have passports. It'll take a few weeks."

His face relaxed into a smile. "I didn't think of passports. Of course you'll want your family there, especially since you're going to be living in Cornwall."

She knew how he'd answer but asked because she wanted to hear it: "Will it be okay if I stay with you until the wedding?"

He shut his eyes and nodded. "I don't want you anywhere else."

She settled back into her seat. The train had started now, and this time she wasn't even thinking of the gazillion gallons of water that would soon be sitting over her head. "My dad will like you," she said.

"I hope so. Why?"

"Oh, you two can talk about plants forever."

"It worked for us."

She grinned again, or still. She couldn't quit grinning.

"What about your mother?"

Rachel scrunched up her nose. "She and my brother are a lot alike—hard to please, but hey, you could pretend you're a duke or something. She'd probably like that."

"I will not." He raised his eyebrows. Oh, those wonderful whiskey brown eyes. "But we could pretend Penmore is haunted by one. Would that impress her?"

She laughed. "It just might." Then she sobered. "What about Margo? Will she be upset that you're marrying me?"

He touched her lips with his finger. "Not at all. She likes you; she told me so New Year's Day. She even called you 'plucky.' That's high praise from Margo."

"Well, then." She kissed his rough finger. A gardener's hand.

"Will you want a honeymoon?" he asked.

She shook her head. "I've traveled enough. I just want to settle in at Penmore." Then she had a delicious thought. "I know what our honeymoon could be."

He smiled at her.

"We could make love in every room at Penmore, a different one every time. How's that for a honeymoon? With all those rooms, it could last for days and days."

He laughed and squeezed her hand. "Maybe not so many as you would think."

The train was quiet with only a few passengers besides them. They could probably make out if they wanted to. Or snog, she thought with a little giggle. She was grinning when she looked at him, but his face was serious. "What will you do?" he asked. "I can't see you rattling around Penmore all day with nothing to do. We will have a housekeeper. I don't expect you to be a scullery maid."

"I don't know. I hadn't thought that far." She pictured Penmore, all those rooms, all that land. "I could help you get ready for the garden show."

"That would be nice, but temporary."

"I wonder," she started.

"You wonder what? Would you want to teach?"

She shook her head. No. Absolutely not. "I wondered if you could sell herbs at the nursery. I'd love to try my hand at herb gardening, and there's certainly enough room for a patch at Penmore. If you and Margo and Edgar wouldn't mind me digging it up."

He grinned. "What a fabulous idea! And I bet some of the restaurants, especially the finer ones along the coast, would love to buy locally grown herbs."

She shrugged. "Maybe even some vegetables if I really got into it." She grabbed both his rough hands and thought how hers might soon feel the same. It was fine by her. "I love to dig in the dirt."

"Me too. Obviously." He kissed her hard then with a big smack. But then, damn it, he turned serious again. "I'm going to ask you one more time, and then I solemnly swear I will never bring it up again."

"What?"

"Are you absolutely sure you'll be satisfied with just Penmore, gardens, me?" He wouldn't let her answer. "You could lead a glamorous life with beautiful clothes and people paying fat fees to hire your gorgeous face. Really, Rachel. I have to know."

She couldn't help it. Despite his earnest, serious expression, she just had to burst out in giggles so loud that a lone passenger five rows ahead turned around to stare at them. "Fat fees! That's good, Jeremy, really good."

A hint of a smile touched his mouth but disappeared. He was serious. Rachel reached for his hand, put it on her heart, and covered it with hers. "I swear this is the truth. Are you listening, Jeremy? Because I want you to get this into your thick head once and for all. Here's the question: Do I want a glamorous life with people whispering about how fat I am and me feeling like a freak around all those skinny models? Do I want to deal with sleazy photographers and other people who'll use me and spit me out? Would I ever in a million years trade you, wonderful, amazing you for all that false fairy tale crap?"

She paused, thinking about years of looking at him, laughing with him, planting roots and dreams together with him. He was waiting. He had to hear it one more time. She grinned and said, "Fat chance!"

Acknowledgements

I am grateful for each and every reader who has spared the time and energy to read my words. Writing is like cooking a huge meal and hoping people will come eat it. Thank you for grabbing a plate.

As always, I thank those who have helped me along the way with this little book, giving me ideas, critiques, editing skills, and encouragement. Chief among these are my husband Jim and son Matthew who light my way. My wise women, including Cheryl Eschenbach, Joyce Hurst, Susan Johnson, Annabel Ihrig, and, always, Gwyn Hyman Rubio are jewels beyond compare. Thank you all.

Lastly, I want to thank Ellie Herring, a wizard of a designer herself, for the creative artistry of the cover. I do not speak French so I have long-time friend, super supporter, and French professor Kathy Kurk to thank for the phrases in the book. If there are errors, they are mine in not transcribing her impeccable work correctly.

J.T. Cooper grew up in Lexington, Kentucky and, as an only child spent much of her time reading and pretending. Pretty good apprenticeship for a writer. She lives now in Florence, Kentucky with her husband and a smiling Corgi.

www.jtcooperauthor.com

www.ingramcontent.com/pod-product-compliance
Lightning Source LLC
Chambersburg PA
CBHW021148110726
47900CB00002B/474